PRAISE FOR JACI BURTON'S NOVELS

"A wild ride."   —Lora Leigh, #1 *New York Times* bestselling author

"[Jaci Burton] delivers the passionate, inventive, sexually explicit love scenes that fans expect . . . However, [it] isn't just about hot sex. Burton offers plenty of emotion and conflict in a memorable, relationship-driven story."   —*USA Today*

"One of the strongest sports romance series available."
        —Dear Author

"Endearing characters, a strong romance, and an engaging plot all wrapped up in one sexy package."   —Romance Novel News

"Both sensual and raw . . . Plenty of romance, sexy men, hot steamy loving, and humor."   —Smexy Books

"Holy smokes! I am pretty sure I saw steam rising from every page."
        —Fresh Fiction

"Hot, hot, hot! . . . Romance at its best! Highly recommended! Very steamy."   —Coffee Table Reviews

"Burton knocks it out of the park . . . With snappy back-and-forth dialogue as well as hot, sweaty, and utterly engaging bedroom play, readers will not be able to race through this book fast enough!"
        —*RT Book Reviews*

MISTLETOE GAMES

Three eNovellas together in print for the first time
HOLIDAY GAMES · HOLIDAY ON ICE · HOT HOLIDAY NIGHTS

JACI BURTON

BERKLEY
New York

BERKLEY
An imprint of Penguin Random House LLC
375 Hudson Street, New York, New York 10014

Holiday Games copyright © 2013 by Jaci Burton
Holiday on Ice copyright © 2014 by Jaci Burton
Hot Holiday Nights copyright © 2015 by Jaci Burton
Excerpt from *Rules of Contact* copyright © 2016 by Jaci Burton

Holiday Games, *Holiday on Ice*, and *Hot Holiday Nights* were
previously published as eNovellas.

Library of Congress Cataloging-in-Publication Data

Names: Burton, Jaci, author.
Title: Mistletoe games / Jaci Burton.
Description: New York, NY : Berkley Books, [2016]
Identifiers: LCCN 2015050638| ISBN 9780451488138 (trade) |
ISBN 9780451488145 (ebook)
Subjects: | GSAFD: Erotic fiction.
Classification: LCC PS3602.U776 M57 2016 | DDC 813/.6—dc23
LC record available at http://lccn.loc.gov/2015050638

First Edition: October 2016

Printed in the United States of America
1   3   5   7   9   10   8   6   4   2

Cover photo by Claudio Marinesco
Cover design by Rita Frangie
Book design by Kristin del Rosario

CONTENTS

HOLIDAY GAMES

This one is for my readers.
Thank you for loving all the Rileys as much as I do.

ONE

NOT PREGNANT.

Liz Riley sat in her bathroom, crushing disappointment tightening her stomach as she stared at the pregnancy test.

Not pregnant. Again.

Her period was three days late. She'd been so certain this time.

Dammit. The word *failure* wasn't in her lexicon. She'd always succeeded, usually found a way to get what she wanted. Even when faced with a temporary roadblock, she wrangled her way around it and won. She was one of the best sports agents in the business, and always got what she wanted.

But that was business, and this was personal. For the past year, she'd tried—and failed—numerous times to get pregnant.

She tossed the stick into the trash and stared at herself in the mirror.

"This sucks."

"What sucks?"

She whirled to face her husband, Gavin, the love of her life and the only man who could have ever made her want to have a baby.

She twined her arms around him. "Nothing. Okay, it's something. I might have a pimple coming up on my chin."

He gasped. "Oh, God, no. Not a pimple. It's the end of the world."

She glared. "This is serious."

He tilted her chin up. "There's nothing on your chin. And even if there was, you'd still be the sexiest damn redhead I've ever laid my eyes on."

He pressed a kiss to her chin, then let his lips trail down over her neck. Her woes temporarily forgotten, she leaned against him, loving the feel of his body pressed along hers. He'd just gotten out of the shower, and the fresh, clean scent of him never failed to hit all of her hot buttons.

Then again, she liked him sweaty, too. After a practice or a game, with dirt and perspiration rolling down his face, he wore his work on his body, and she loved him that way.

As his former agent, she knew how hard he worked at baseball. He was the best first baseman she'd ever represented. Of course, as soon as they'd fallen in love, she'd had to bow out of representing him, but she never stopped appreciating what a fine specimen of an athlete he was.

Or what an amazing and giving lover he was.

Like now, as he set her on the bathroom counter, spread her legs, and dropped to his knees, burying his face between her thighs.

She shuddered as he slid his tongue along her sex. Gavin always knew exactly how to pleasure her.

"Oh, yes," she murmured, sliding her fingers through the softness of his hair, directing him to where she needed his mouth. And when he hummed against her clit, she arched against him, so close already she could come right now.

But not yet, not when the sensations he brought out of her with his tongue were so delicious. She wanted to wait just a little longer.

The distant sounds of knocking permeated her senses. But she was right on the edge, so close to coming that she blocked out everything else.

"I'm almost there, Gavin. Just like that."

And when he pressed his tongue against her clit and licked her, she came with a loud cry, holding his head there as she rode out an amazing orgasm that left her shuddering.

He rose up and kissed her with the same hard passion that always left her breathless.

She heard the rapping at the door again. Only this time, the doorbell accompanied the knock.

Gavin pulled back. "Was that the front door?"

Then realization slammed into her. "Oh, shit. I forgot Jenna and Tara were coming over."

"*Oh, shit* is right." He looked down, and she followed his gaze where his erection bobbed hard and tempting against her leg.

She let out a rueful sigh. "So much for the hot sex. I guess I'll get the door."

"Good idea. I'll be here thinking about what we could have been doing. No. Bad idea. I'll think about on-base averages, and then I'll get dressed."

She laughed, slid off the counter, and hurriedly threw on some clothes before running downstairs to get the door.

Jenna arched a brow. "What the hell? I was about to call you. Were you in the shower?"

"I'm sorry. I was upstairs getting dressed. I'm running late this morning."

"Are you sure this is a good time?" Tara asked, giving her a hug.

"It's a perfect time. Come on in."

Jenna brushed by. "You were probably having sex with my brother."

Liz followed them into the living room. "And if I was, you so wouldn't want the details about that."

"You're right. I wouldn't." Jenna laid a bag next to the sofa, then turned back to Liz. "Your face is all flushed. Oh, my God, you *were* having sex. Geez, Liz, you could have called us and told us to come back later."

"No way. It was an impromptu thing."

Tara crossed her arms, a serene smile on her face. "So, a quickie, huh?"

"More like half a quickie."

"Ouch," Tara said.

"You have lousy timing, Jenna," Gavin said as he sauntered downstairs and into the living room.

"Hey, Tara's here, too, you know."

"Yeah, but you're my sister, so I'll blame you."

He gave both Jenna and Tara hugs and asked, "Who wants coffee?"

"I definitely do," Jenna said.

Tara nodded. "I'd love some."

"Tea for me," Liz said.

"Since when do you not drink coffee?" Jenna's eyes widened. "Are you pregnant?"

"No. Just working on putting healthy stuff into my body just in case it happens someday. Which, so far, it hasn't."

Jenna squeezed her hand. "I'm sorry. I should stop asking you all the time about it. I'm as excited for you to have a baby as you are."

Liz looked into the kitchen, then returned her attention to her sisters-in-law. "I took a test this morning because I was a little late. It was negative."

Tara frowned. "I'm sorry. That has to be frustrating to want it so badly. But you just need to relax and give it time."

Liz gave her a look. "When have you ever known me to relax?"

"Good point. But maybe if you did try to relax a little, it might happen?"

"I don't know. We've been trying for a while. And I know I'm not in my twenties anymore, so maybe there's something wrong."

"Did you ask your doctor?"

Liz waved her hand. "She ran tests on both of us. Gavin's fine.

She said I'm fine, and that there's no reason I can't conceive. And she also said I should relax."

Jenna laughed. "Okay, so just enjoy the sex thing and let it happen."

"That's the problem. It's been a year. I'm not pregnant. Clearly I'm not trying hard enough."

Jenna gave her a look. "I can't imagine there's anything you try to accomplish that you don't give your all to. Even this."

"Maybe."

Gavin came in with drinks for all of them. "Thanks, babe," Liz said.

"My pleasure. What were you all whispering about in here?"

Jenna gave Gavin an innocent look. "My wedding stuff, of course. Do you want to take a seat and hear all the details?"

Gavin looked horrified. "God, no. It's bad enough you're putting me in a tux and making me take part in it. Do I have to hear details, too?"

Liz loved the terrified look on his face. Like Jenna would ask him to go over invitations or something. "No. You're dismissed."

"Thank God. I'm going to the gym."

He grabbed his gym bag and kissed Liz good-bye.

After he left, Liz motioned to the bag sitting next to the sofa. "So, what's going on with the wedding stuff?"

Jenna grinned. "Tara brought over the place cards the other day. I thought you might want to see them."

"You know I do. I can't believe the wedding is only a few weeks away."

"I can't, either. Ty and I put it off for so long. The whole wedding thing just wasn't important, because we love each other and are committed. I really wanted to just go to city hall or maybe to Vegas for a quickie wedding."

"But then there's your mother," Tara said. "Who would have never forgiven you."

Jenna nodded. "Exactly. Denying her a wedding, especially for her only daughter, just wasn't an option, especially after the two of you married Mick and Gavin in such elaborate ways."

"Uh, sorry?" Liz said with a grin. "I never thought I was the fancy-wedding type. Or even the marrying type. Until Gavin came along."

"I can relate, believe me. I never believed in the whole commitment thing until Ty. And marriage wasn't all that important to me, but I loved Ty and he wanted to get married, and then there's Mom. So I caved." Jenna took a deep breath. "And so here we are."

Tara dipped her hand into the bag and pulled a place card out, handing it over to Liz. "With these."

The place cards had a purple border, matching the color of the tips of Jenna's hair, and the ink was in Ty's hockey team color. The upper quadrant had a musical note and a hockey stick coming up through it, signifying parts of both Jenna and Tyler, with their initials woven through it.

"I love these. So much," Liz said.

"Me, too," Jenna said. "You don't think they're hokey or stupid?"

"Of course not. They're you. And Ty. And perfect."

Jenna grinned. "Thank you. I love them, too. Tara helped me with the design."

Liz slid her glance over to Tara. "It's what you do best."

"Thanks. I'm ridiculously excited about this wedding. At least this time I'm not pregnant."

"And how is our gorgeous nephew?"

"Pulling himself up to stand."

"Oh, my God. Already?"

"Yes. Mick thinks he'll be walking soon. He said when he was a baby, he walked at ten months, so he thinks Sam will walk early, too. I'm not ready yet. I want him to stay my cuddly baby as long as possible, though he can crawl through the house like a speed demon. I have to watch him every second, or he disappears. We've already got the gate up across the stairs."

"He's adorable, Tara. And where is he?" Jenna asked.

"With your parents. When I told your mom I was meeting with the two of you this morning, she asked if she could have him for a couple of hours."

"Figures. She's always grabbing Sam."

Tara leaned back on the sofa. "You know you can have him whenever you want. Or come over whenever you want."

"Sure. In my spare time, when I'm not overseeing the bar, or working at the club."

"Oh, cry me a river," Liz interjected. "I never get to see him, either."

"I never thought the two of you would be fighting over my baby. You are the two least likely women I'd ever have guessed would have motherly instincts."

"Hey," Jenna said. "I love your baby. Not that I want any of my own right now. Too busy. But your kids? Love them madly."

"That's because one is in college, and the other you can love and cuddle and spoil, but you don't have to keep him."

Jenna nodded. "Exactly."

Liz laughed. "Speaking of the one in college, how is Nathan doing?"

A streak of motherly pride crossed Tara's face. "He's doing so well. He's putting his studies first, which I insisted on. And of course as you know, Texas ended up winning the Big 12 Conference championship this season. I'd like to think Nathan leading the team at quarterback had a lot to do with that."

"He's an exceptional quarterback, like his father," Liz said. "I watched every game. He has a natural talent, very much like Mick's."

"Agree," Jenna said. "In some ways, he's better than Mick, because of the way he runs. He confuses the hell out of the defense."

Liz nodded. "I'm eager to get my hands on him and get him an NFL contract."

Tara looked horrified. "Oh, God, don't tell him that. He'll want to come out next year, and Mick and I want him to stay in school and finish up his degree."

Liz laughed. "My lips are sealed. And I tend to agree with you. Some of these boys leave school too soon, the lure of the big contract and big money too much to resist. The longer they stay in college, the more experience they gain. At least that's what I always advise them."

"Obviously, they don't always listen."

She shrugged. "Bottom line is the choice is theirs to make. Many of them go on to have highly successful careers, but it's my hope they all get their degrees. Or at least stay through their junior years, then finish up their degrees later."

Tara nodded. "We're going to push for Nathan to stay in school as long as possible, but you're right, it's his career and his choice. We just hope he makes the right one."

They went over wedding planning, then went out to lunch. Liz parted ways with Tara and Jenna, then headed home, hoping to find Gavin there. Instead, he'd left a message on her phone letting her know he was going for a tux fitting, and then lunch.

Which was fine with her. She had some work to do, anyway, so she opened her laptop and answered a few emails. When she was done, she reviewed her calendar.

It was going to be an extremely busy holiday season. Not only was Jenna getting married—with Liz taking a very active role in that, which she was very excited about—but in addition, she and Gavin would be hosting Christmas for the Riley family in their home this year. Since this was the first time they'd have the entire family over for Christmas, Liz felt the burden of doing everything just right.

Not that Gavin's family put high expectations on Christmas or anything. His parents were the kindest people she'd ever known. Kathleen and Jimmy Riley had been family to her—more parents to her than her own—since before she and Gavin had ever gotten together. She loved them so much, and they were genuinely warm people. So there was no pressure, other than the normal pressure she put on herself, which was always high.

But still, there'd be a lot of coordinating to do. The Riley family was formidable, and now that there were wives and kids and significant others in the picture, Christmas was going to be huge this year. And Liz intended for this to be the best holiday ever.

She made a few notes about food. Catering was out, unfortunately, because the Rileys just wouldn't go for that. Nothing but homemade at Christmas. Kathleen would help her, of course, and so would Tara, along with Kathleen's sister-in-law, Cara. They'd all have to get together and discuss options.

This would totally work.

She leaned back in her chair and stretched, then thought about Gavin and that wretched pregnancy test from earlier.

She pushed back and stood, heading into the kitchen to make a cup of tea. She'd be damned if she'd let her body defeat her. She poured tea into her cup and leaned against the kitchen counter.

If someone had told her two years ago that she would be married and trying to have a baby, she'd have laughed in their face. She'd been totally career driven, and there had been no man on her radar.

Except Gavin, of course. She'd always loved Gavin, but in secret. He'd been the man of her dreams, someone she'd been close to as a client only. Never in her wildest dreams had she ever thought she and Gavin would get together, let alone fall in love and end up married. That's when her desire for a child—someone who was part of both of them—had started to take hold. She was almost in her midthirties now. If she was ever going to have children, it was time to get going on that. A now-or-never kind of thing, because she wasn't getting any younger.

Which was why she wouldn't let her dream of having a child go up in smoke.

Giving up wasn't an option. They just needed to have more sex. Gavin was strong and virile, and she was still young enough. She worked out and ate right. There was no reason they couldn't get pregnant. Gavin was off season right now, which meant he was more available than usual, and that meant more time for sex. Granted, she'd be more than a little busy with the wedding and holiday planning, but if there was one thing Liz knew how to do, it was make time for sex.

She smiled against the rim of her teacup.

Operation Make a Baby was on.

TWO

GAVIN SMIRKED AT HIS SOON-TO-BE BROTHER-IN-LAW while they sat waiting in the tuxedo shop. "So, Tyler, what are your intentions toward my baby sister?"

"I plan to marry the hell out of her, if that's okay with you."

Gavin shrugged. "Are you sure you know what you're getting into? She's kind of a pain in the ass. Moody. Sometimes grouchy as hell."

"Sounds like that's how she treats you. She's great to me."

Gavin laughed. "You're probably right."

"I don't know," Mick said. "She's always liked me."

"Bullshit. She fought with you as much as she fought with me."

Mick arched a brow at Gavin. "That's not the way I remember it. She always ran to me when you were picking on her."

"No. It was me. She hated both of you and ran to her favorite cousin."

Gavin laughed at Cole.

"Anderson party?"

"Oooh, we're a party," Gavin said, nudging Ty when he stood.

"Not yet," Ty said. "But as soon as all this tuxedo crap is over with, we're heading to the bar."

"Sounds like a plan," Gavin said.

It took about an hour to pick out the tuxes, though Jenna had already made a couple suggestions, and Ty, not really caring, went with what Jenna wanted. They were all fitted, except for Ty's two teammates and friends Victor and Eddie, who couldn't make it. But now that the tuxes had been selected, they could stop in and get their measurements anytime. All Gavin cared about was that his part was done. They were out of there as fast as possible, so they could head to Riley's Bar.

"We're lucky we could all be together this week," Mick said. "Fortunately, we're playing Cole's team, so I'm actually in town in time for the tux fitting."

"Yeah, it worked out well," Ty said.

"We're going to kick your ass."

"In your fucking dreams, Cole," Mick said.

"We'll see, pretty boy. You're getting kind of old to play football. Shouldn't you think about moving into the broadcast booth or something? Maybe play stay-at-home dad while Tara makes the big bucks?"

Gavin snorted.

"Hey," Mick said. "You're my brother. Shouldn't you be on my side?"

"I'm on nobody's side when it comes to family playing family. I'm just going to enjoy the two of you trash-talking each other."

Cole smirked and leaned back in his chair. When Renee, their waitress, came over, she high-fived them all.

"I was wondering when the Riley crew would come in. Beers?"

"I'll definitely have one," Tyler said.

Gavin nodded. "Me, too."

"Soda for me," Mick said.

"Soda here, too," Cole said. "Though I could drink ten beers and still kick your ass come game time."

Gavin rolled his eyes at Ty. "Here we go again."

Ty laughed. "I wonder if we should take bets on whether they'll come to blows or not."

"They won't. But it's fun to watch them bullshit each other about whose team is better."

Ty nodded. "I can't wait for the game on Sunday. The bar should be packed. Are you gonna go to the game?"

"Wouldn't miss it. You?"

"Are you kidding? Jenna would kill me if I wasn't there for the game. It's a big family day for the Rileys."

"I think we're gonna have a lot of big Riley days coming up in the next few weeks," Mick said.

Ty grinned. "Yeah. Seems that way."

"Are you excited?" Cole asked.

"You know, I didn't think I'd be. I mean, Jenna and I wanted this to be low-key, but it didn't quite work out that way."

"I know how that is. Liz and I were the same way," Gavin said. "We were going to have a small thing, which turned into a big thing because . . . well, my mom wanted a big wedding, and then Liz decided maybe just having a small wedding wasn't going to work. Suddenly it was this huge affair. Can't blame that all on the parents, though. Weddings seem to take on a life of their own."

Ty laughed. "Yeah. It is becoming kind of an event, and I can't say I'm all that disappointed about it. Despite Jenna not wanting to make a big deal out of the wedding, I know secretly she's pretty excited about having the family all together to celebrate us getting married. I don't think she would have really been happy if we'd eloped or gotten married at city hall."

Gavin nodded and took a long pull of the beer Renee had set down in front of him. "I know what you mean. Liz was never about the big wedding. Until it came time to plan the big wedding. Then she became driven, like planning a wedding had been the one and only thing she'd dreamed about doing since she was a little girl."

"Women, right?"

"Yeah. Can't figure them out. Don't even try. Just go with it."

"That's what I do, man. I just try and keep her happy. If she's happy, then I'm happy."

Gavin tipped his beer against Ty's. "Amen to that."

The conversation reverted back to Cole and Mick's heavily testosterone-laden one-upmanship over who was going to beat whom. In the end, the two of them just ended up laughing and toasted each other, then they got down to the business of eating burgers, until they got on the topic of the wedding again, which put Ty on the hot seat for making them all wear tuxes.

Ty didn't take the bait. Instead, he chewed a mouthful of cheeseburger and swallowed. "Not my fault. Talk to Jenna. I would have been happy in jeans."

"You'd throw your fiancée—my sweet baby sister—under the bus like that?" Mick asked.

Ty reached for his beer. "Yup."

"Wait till I tell her," Gavin said.

"Go for it," Ty said with a shrug. "She'll back me up."

Cole slapped Ty on the back. "That's what I like about you. No fear."

Mick took off after lunch to do some football-related thing. And Cole had to leave for the airport to pick up Savannah.

"Has she been out of town again?" Gavin asked.

"Yeah. She's been doing a consulting thing for a client in Chicago for the past couple weeks."

"Rough on both of you with all the travel, isn't it?"

"We manage. At least the homecomings are hot." Cole waggled his brows.

Tyler laughed. "Speaking of hot fiancées, I need to go see mine.

We have . . . God forbid . . . wedding stuff that I promised to discuss with her. Thanks for meeting with me today, guys."

They all took off. Gavin headed home, figuring Liz would be out doing some of that wedding stuff, too.

So he was surprised to see her car in the garage when he pulled in.

"Liz?" he called when he walked through the door.

She didn't answer. He looked for her downstairs, but didn't find her, so he headed upstairs. It was already getting dark outside, and cloudy, as he looked out the window in the landing.

There was a light on in their bedroom, so he pushed the door open.

And his jaw dropped.

Liz was on the bed, the only light in the room from candles lit on the nightstands. She was dressed in some silky, flimsy thing that rode high on her thighs and barely covered her breasts.

He went hard in an instant.

"Did we have a date I didn't know about?" he asked as he entered the room.

She was reclining on her side, her head resting on her hand. "No, but we were interrupted this morning. I thought we could finish what we started."

She patted the bed.

"Hell, yes."

As he walked toward the bed, he kicked off his shoes and pulled his shirt over his head. Liz sat up and crawled toward the end of the bed, her breasts nearly visible as she bent over.

"I like whatever it is you're wearing. Or almost not wearing."

She tilted her head back and gave him one hell of a sexy smile. "I bought it to tease you with."

While she unzipped his pants, he drew one of her straps down. "You aren't going to be wearing it long."

She sat on her heels. "That's the idea."

He shucked his jeans and underwear, his cock springing right into her hands. "Now, this is about where we were this morning, weren't we?"

Her hands were warm, her mouth inches away from giving him exactly what he'd spent the day thinking about. "I've been aching for your mouth on me all day."

"Is that right?" She fell forward onto her stomach, that slinky little thing she wore creeping up over her shapely ass, revealing that she had . . . absolutely nothing on underneath it.

His cock twitched and he surged forward, thrusting it into her hands.

"A little eager, are you?"

He looked down at her. "You know it. Now suck me."

"I get all tingly when you give me orders." She put her beautiful lips around his cockhead, at the same time her tongue wound around him. Then she drew him into the sweet heat of her mouth, inch by slow, torturous inch, deliberately prolonging his pleasure.

"Aw, babe, that's so good." He bent forward and lifted the shift she wore, revealing the globes of her ass. He smoothed his hand over her flesh, parting it with his fingers so he could get to her pussy.

She was wet, and he slid his fingers into her at the same time she engulfed him, taking him deep.

"Fuck," he whispered, closing his eyes as she sucked him. "You're so good at that."

Her answering hum around his cock made his balls tighten. And when she withdrew, his cock wet from her mouth, it was all he could do not to shove back into the sweet warm cavern and come down her throat. But he wanted to explore her body. She'd gone to all the trouble of the candles and wearing that outfit that was driving him crazy. He wanted to be inside her, drawing her close, inhaling her scent and pumping into her. That's where he wanted to come.

So he pulled her up to her knees, drew her body against his, and kissed her, sweeping his hands over her curves and enjoying the feel of her breasts against his chest. Even after more than a year of marriage, Liz hit his hot buttons. She turned him on with an animal passion that still surprised him. He could never seem to get enough of her, and now that baseball season was over and he was home on a regular basis, he could indulge in his need for her.

He pushed her onto her back on the bed.

"Anxious?" she asked, her voice a husky, teasing caress.

"Yeah." He spread her legs and eased his cock into her, watching her face as he entered her. One thing he'd always loved about Liz was the way she enjoyed sex—no-holds-barred, always fully into it. She loved making love with him as much as he enjoyed being with her. And as she arched her hips and took him inside, he knew once again that he'd found the perfect woman for him.

He grasped her hips and pulled her down on his cock, listening to the sounds of her breathing, the moans and whimpers she made as he pumped into her. That silk riding over her hips drove him crazy, so he leaned over her, pulled the straps down, and took one of her nipples into his mouth, sucking it as he fucked her.

"Yes," she whispered against him. "Harder."

He gave her what she asked for, both with his mouth and with his cock. Her pussy squeezed his dick, making him fight for control.

"Kiss me," she said, and he moved up to take her mouth.

She sucked his tongue, making him groan and plunge his cock deeper. Liz moaned, writhing underneath him.

"That's going to make me come," she said.

He lifted up, met her gaze, and ground against her, giving her what she needed—a slow, hard, deep movement that made her eyes widen.

And when she came, she raked her nails down his arms and shuddered against him. Unable to hold back, he went with her, his orgasm rocking his world and stealing his breath, like it always did.

Liz wrapped her legs around him and held him there while they both settled from the aftermath. She smoothed her hands down his arms, pressing a kiss and a love bite to his shoulder.

"That was a great way to end the day," he said.

"I'm glad you enjoyed it. I sure did."

He rolled to his side, bringing Liz with him. She shivered, so he pulled up the blankets and they lay there. He hadn't been much of an after-sex cuddler before Liz came into his life, but now he enjoyed holding her in his arms, listening to her breathe.

"I took a pregnancy test this morning," she said.

He stilled. "And?"

"Negative."

He heard the flat tone of her voice. She tried to be nonchalant about it, but he knew how much it hurt her, how much she wanted to have a baby. He wanted to have one with her, so he kept the disappointment out of his voice. "It's okay, babe. We'll keep trying."

She sighed. "Yes, we will."

This was such a touchy subject, and Gavin never knew how to approach it. "It's going to happen."

She sat up in bed and leaned against the pillows. "I know it will. I'm determined."

He pushed up and sat next to her, giving her a grin. "If there's one thing I know about you, it's that you won't let anything stand in your way. But you have to relax about this. We'll get there."

"You're so sure. How can you be so sure?"

"Easy. I have insider information."

She tilted her head to the side and frowned. "Huh?"

"Let's check the magic cock of knowledge and see what it says."

She gave him a look of utter disbelief. "What the hell are you talking about?"

He pulled the sheet back, grabbed his shaft. "You know, like the Magic 8 Ball."

She studied his dick and balls. "I don't know, Gavin. I only see two balls down there. Not eight. Unless you've been hiding six more somewhere."

He laughed. "Trust me. My cock knows all."

She arched a brow, raised her knees, and wrapped her arms around them. "Okay, this is interesting. Do go on."

He shook his cock back and forth, like all the kids used to do with their Magic 8 Balls. He could tell Liz was trying hard not to laugh.

"Oh, magic cock, is there a baby in our future?" he asked.

Her lips curved. "And what does the magic cock of knowledge say?"

He grasped his balls in his hand. "It says I've got your baby right here."

She laughed, then rolled over on top of him. "You always know just the right thing to say."

He wrapped his arms around her and tugged her close. "Stick with me, babe. You'll never go wrong."

THREE

THE FAMILY HAD GOTTEN A SUITE AT THE STADIUM FOR the football game, all of them gathered together to share Mick and Cole's day.

Liz had stopped off at the owner's suite first thing to schmooze with Ted Miller, the owner of the St. Louis Traders, the home stadium. As an agent, it was her job to make sure her clients were well represented. Not that she represented Cole, but she had clients on the Traders as well as the San Francisco Sabers. She didn't take up too much of Ted's time, because she had a stopover to make at Irvin Stokes' suite as well. Touching base with the owner of the Sabers was equally as important. She wanted him to know she was there to support all of her clients. It was a perfect opportunity to mix in a little business with pleasure.

As soon as she finished with the work portion of her day, she went back to the family suite. Opening the door was like a burst of warmth and her heart swelled. Having no family of her own—at least, no family that loved and supported her—the Rileys belonged to her now.

"Liz. I was wondering where you'd wandered off to."

Gavin's mother had spotted her immediately, which wasn't at all a surprise. Kathleen Riley was great at taking care of her family, always making sure everyone felt welcome.

"I had some work to take care of."

Kathleen shook her head. "You're always working. When do you ever take a day off?"

Liz laid her hand over Kathleen's arm. "I take plenty of days off, Mom. Don't you worry about me. So what's to eat in here?"

"Well, not my lasagna for sure. But there's a lot of good stuff including some antipasto, chicken wings . . ."

Kathleen led her to the food, and Liz was hungry, so she filled a plate and grabbed something to drink. Kathleen chatted with her for a few more minutes and then wandered off to see to another family member. Liz spotted Savannah and Alicia huddled together at one of the tables and made her way over to them.

"Private conversation?" she asked, not wanting to intrude in case they were talking about something they'd rather she didn't hear.

Savannah offered up a smile. "Not at all, Liz. Please, come join us."

Liz took a seat and set down her plate and drink. "How are the boys looking out there?"

"Just warm-ups," Alicia said. "So nothing exciting yet."

"Good. Then I have time to eat while Savannah tells me about her trip to Chicago."

"It was good. And not sports-related for a change, so that was rather refreshing."

"As I recall, some CEO of a tech company, wasn't it?" Liz asked.

"Yes. A young techno-wizard, came out of nowhere. One of those kids that created something out of nothing and is now a multimillionaire. But now he's taking his company public and he needed an image makeover in the worst way. He's brilliant, but a bit socially awkward, and his style— Well, let's just say it was better suited to his parents' basement than to the cover of *Time* magazine."

Alicia smiled. "You're just the right person to give him the social and style makeover he needed."

"It was fun, actually. He's a great young man and he's definitely going places. I brought in a team to assist me with a fashion makeover and he and I spent a lot of time working on the social aspects of his persona. He's smart and very hip and I didn't want to change that about him. He just needed a few lessons in how to respond to the media so he didn't come across as . . ."

Savannah seemed at a loss for words. Then again, she was nicer and more politically correct than Liz.

"A douche?" Liz offered.

Savannah laughed. "Yes. That, exactly. He didn't need to go all *GQ* or turn into some stuffy exec. He just needed to become more comfortable in front of the camera. He's a very quick learner, so I believe he'll do just fine. Really, he's just a sweetheart. I also met his girlfriend, an Ivy League grad and law student who's going to be a wonderful asset to him, both professionally and personally."

"Sounds like a perfect combination. I'm glad it all worked out for you."

"Thanks, Liz. I'm just glad to be back home for a while. I missed Cole. And the timing couldn't be more perfect. I wouldn't have wanted to miss this game."

"None of us want to miss this game," Alicia said. "The cousins playing each other is always a big deal to the Rileys."

"And speaking of you and Cole, when are the two of you going to be planning your wedding?" Liz asked.

Savannah grinned. "I know, our schedules have been ridiculous, and I've been lucky to have so much work to do lately. But we've set a date for next May."

Alicia grinned. "That's fabulous. And it's about time."

"Hey, it's time for you and Garrett, too."

"I know. We're getting there. Talking about it. Taking things slowly. Finding a house and discussing all things marriage-related. We're considering a late fall wedding next year, maybe after baseball season."

Liz smiled. "I love that everyone's in love. Getting married. Talking about getting married. Shacking up."

Alicia laughed. "I guess we'll get through Jenna and Ty's wedding first."

"Yes."

"I heard my name mentioned. Are you saying bad things about me?"

Jenna sat with them.

"Awful things about you," Liz said. "Mainly about your hair, and your butt."

Jenna cracked a smile. "Yeah, well, speaking of my butt, you can kiss it."

"No, we were talking about who's married, who's engaged, and who's house shopping. And Savannah set a wedding date."

"I heard about that. So Savannah's next. And then Alicia."

"Apparently. And I'm the old married woman."

"No, that's Tara because she and Mick got married first."

"Where *is* Tara?" Alicia asked.

"She texted me a little while ago and said she had a brunch event to do this morning, but that she'd be here," Jenna said.

"Good. I know she wouldn't want to miss the game," Liz said. "Who has Sam?"

"The babysitter," Jenna said. "Since everyone in the family is here today, she figured Sam would get too tired to spend all day at the game. Not a good venue for a little one."

"That makes sense."

After Liz finished her plate, they all grabbed their seats and watched the pregame festivities, cheering loudly for both Mick and Cole as the teams were announced and took the field. Kathleen and Jimmy wore their Sabers jerseys, and of course since Cara and Jack were Cole's and Alicia's parents, they countered by wearing their Traders jerseys. The rest of the family interspersed, some wearing Traders colors, some Sabers.

It was quite the mix.

Tara showed up just as they were doing the coin toss.

"Sorry I'm late. Did I miss the kickoff?"

"No," Liz said. "Not yet."

"Ugh. The event went a little long and I couldn't leave. And I'm starving. I'm going to wolf down some food and settle in."

Liz rubbed her back. "Relax so you don't get indigestion."

Tara laughed. "I know. I know. It's just been that kind of week. Sam's had a cold, and Mick of course had his head in the game. Plus, I had this party to plan. It's always everything at once. And Nathan will be home next week and I'm so excited about that, too."

"You have a lot going on."

"I do. But right now I have these mozzarella cheese sticks calling my name."

Liz laughed. "I hear you. Priorities, honey."

Tara finally settled and relaxed, and then it was game time. Liz felt the electricity in the filled-to-capacity stadium. Both teams were doing well in the standings, so this game meant something to both the Traders and the Sabers. The Traders were in first place in their division, and the Sabers were one game behind in theirs. And as the Sabers kicked off to the Traders, Liz held her breath. Even though she had no loyalty to either team, she felt for both Mick and Cole, knew what it was like to have a game that meant so much.

Grant Cassidy, the quarterback, took the ball for the Traders and Cole lined up on the left side of the field. Liz took a glance at the row in front of her and saw Savannah leaning forward, her gaze glued to Cole. Liz knew what it was like to watch her man. When Gavin was playing, her heart was in her throat, willing him to play well. Next to her, Tara was just as intent on the game even though Mick wasn't out on the field.

It was a post pattern, and Cole made a perfect catch from Cassidy, gaining twenty-four yards, a big first play for the Traders that had everyone on their feet cheering.

In typical Riley fashion, everyone cheered, even Tara, though she muttered "dammit" under her breath.

Liz laughed. "Going to be a tough game, isn't it?"

"I love Cole. He's family. He's Savannah's fiancé. But right now he's my husband's opponent. So while I want him to do well . . . I don't want him to do well. It's a dilemma."

Savannah turned around in her seat. "You can go ahead and boo and curse, honey. It won't hurt my feelings because I'll likely do the same thing every time your husband hits a completion for the Sabers."

Tara laughed. "You're on."

And so it went, and by the end of the first half Mick's team was up by a touchdown. Everyone got up to stretch, mingle, and refill their drinks.

"That was intense," Tara said. "But Mick's doing well."

"He is. Damn him," Savannah said. "But Cole had that awesome touchdown catch."

"He did," Tara said with a smile. "Damn him."

"I might have to sit between the two of you during the second half," Jenna said. "If it's close, you might start emptying your purses and throwing your cell phones at each other."

Tara laughed. "I don't think we'll come to blows over a football game."

"Doubtful," Savannah said. "We just want our guys to win. But they've both lost before, so I think we can take it no matter what happens."

"What? There's not going to be a girl fight in the suite?" Gavin asked, coming over to put his arm around Liz's shoulders.

"I'm afraid not," Tara said.

"I'm so disappointed. And I have my camera phone ready to take pictures and video."

Savannah rolled her eyes and shot Tara a look. "Men."

"Agreed," Tara said, moving away with Savannah to get a drink.

Liz poked him in the ribs with her elbow.

"Ow. What did I say?"

She laughed and put her arms around him. "Enjoying the game and family time?"

"Yeah. It's a pretty good game, too. I honestly don't have any idea how it's going to turn out. The Traders have a tough defense, but Mick is strong in the pocket and the Sabers have got offensive weapons that just can't be beat. And then there's Grant Cassidy, who has a wicked accurate arm and lots of choices on who to throw it to. The Traders' receiver corps is stout this season, which makes it hard for the defense to cover."

"I think the key to this game is going to be who has the strongest defense, and which of the quarterbacks has the best arm."

Gavin squinted at her. "Care to lay some money on the outcome?"

She laughed. "Not on your life. I have players on both teams and I'm not betting on the outcome of this game."

"Wuss. I'm going to hit up the guys. I know they'll get in on the action."

"You do that."

After halftime, Liz settled in her seat for the game. The Traders got the ball to score the second half, and Cole took a pass from Cassidy on a key third-down play and ran it in for a touchdown.

The family went crazy celebrating. With the game tied, Liz felt the tension and excitement in the suite. And when the Sabers kicked a field goal near the end of the third quarter, it was crunch time. The game was so close, the teams so evenly matched, she had no idea how the fourth quarter was going to play out.

The first eight minutes of the fourth quarter was a nail biter, totally defensive on both sides. No points were scored, and neither team could make any headway.

On a critical third down, Mick had the ball and did a rollout, looking for receivers. The Sabers defenders pushed hard. Liz cringed when the defensive back came around past the offensive lineman, making a beeline for Mick.

Tara stood. "Oh, shit," she whispered.

Liz had heard her, though, and thought much the same thing. Mick was going to get sacked.

But Mick must have seen him, because he tucked the ball in and made a run for it, the offensive line turning to block for him. Since they hadn't expected the run, and especially not from Mick, he had an open field and ran for fifteen yards and a first down.

Tara jumped up and threw her arms in the air and roared out a warrior-worthy yell. The guys all clapped and Mick's dad, who sat next to Gavin, grinned broadly as he slapped Gavin on the back.

"Did ya see that?"

Gavin grinned back. "I did, Dad. Pretty damned good for an old guy like Mick."

"Old guy my butt. That kid still has a lot of years of football left in him."

"I agree with your dad," Liz said. "He might be a little over thirty, but Mick is still a champion."

And he proved it by throwing three completions on the next three plays, one to Kip Meecham, their hotshot young rookie tight end for a touchdown, which put the Sabers ahead with three minutes left to go.

But the Traders weren't the kind of team to give up. Cassidy took the ball after the kickoff and they drove down the field to the thirty-five-yard line. There were twenty-five seconds to go and the

Traders had one time-out left. The tension was so thick in the stadium it seemed as if no one was even breathing.

And when Cassidy handed it off to the running back, who ran for twelve yards, they called a time-out and brought in the kicker to try for a field goal.

"I can't even breathe," Savannah said, clutching Liz's hand tight.

The field goal was good. The game was tied.

They were going to overtime.

"This is intense," Tara said, heading to the bar. "I need a damn drink."

"I'm going with you," Savannah said.

They all took a few minutes to relax. Liz leaned back in her chair and took it all in, watching the family mingle and talk.

"Having fun?" Gavin asked as he hopped into the seat next to her.

"I'm having a great time, but I'm also a wreck. What a game."

"I know. We couldn't ask for a better game for Mick and Cole to play against each other." He took a sip of water and pressed a kiss to her lips. "Your guys are doing well on both sides, too."

She grinned, knowing he was talking about the players she represented. "They are, aren't they? Overall, a perfect day. But someone's going to have to win."

"Definitely."

Overtime was a whole different animal and that fifteen minutes seemed like the longest fifteen minutes of the entire family's life. Liz couldn't sit anymore. Most of the family was standing and pacing back and forth as the Traders won the toss and marched down the field. Cole took a slant pass and ran for eighteen yards, then another for twelve, setting up a field goal, putting the Traders ahead.

When the Sabers got the ball, Mick threw a long pass that just tipped off the hands of the receiver. The groans in the suite were loud. He missed another pass, then got sacked. It was looking like the Traders were going to win.

But on third down he threw a bullet to the wide receiver who swerved and missed the tackle and rocketed down the sidelines to the end zone.

Liz cheered for Mick and for the Sabers. It was a great comeback on what she had feared was going to be a bitter defeat. She felt awful for Savannah, though, and went over to her and hugged her.

"Such a tough loss."

Savannah nodded. "It was. But it was a great game and two amazing teams. I know Cole is going to be upset."

"He shouldn't be. I know he will be, but he played an amazing game."

Liz gave victory hugs to Kathleen and Jimmy, and commiseration ones to Jack and Cara. They were all going to meet up at Riley's Bar, so she and Gavin headed over there. She felt both pumped up and sad about the game. It was hard when you had family on both sides, but there was nothing you could do. Short of a tie, someone had to lose.

"How do you handle it?" she asked Gavin on the ride over.

"Handle what?"

"Losing."

He shrugged. "It's part of the game. You deal. It blows, especially in a close game like today's. Cole will hate it, because he's competitive and because of what it means for his team. Plus, he didn't want to lose, especially to his cousin. But he's a man and a decent one. He'll suck it up."

She understood about losing. She spoke with a lot of her clients about it, especially those going through rough patches. Fortunately, Cole's career was on an uptick right now and they were having a winning season. One game wouldn't matter all that much. She looked forward to seeing him at Riley's Bar and being able to congratulate him on the game today. He'd played well and his stats showed it.

Still, Gavin was right—it sucked to lose. As she sat back in the car and looked over at her husband, she was consumed with the thought of having a baby. His baby. A child who looked like him, with his dark hair and his drive and sense of honor. And maybe a child who had a touch of her ambition. She was going to make it happen, one way or the other.

If she was one thing, it was tenacious. She might not be a Riley by blood, but she was still part of the family, and she understood grit and determination. And, like every member of the Riley family, she didn't give up.

FOUR

CHRISTMAS DECORATIONS WERE UP, WHICH ALWAYS put Liz in the holiday spirit. She wasn't sure Gavin had been all that happy about having to drag a six-and-a-half-foot live tree into the house, especially since she'd insisted they go to one of those places where they could cut their own tree.

He'd told her they had plenty of trees on the property and she could wander around, pick one out, and he'd chop it down. Then they wouldn't have to drive the truck an hour outside the city to get one.

Clearly, the man had no Christmas spirit. Besides, she loved all the trees on the property and wasn't about to cut one of those down when there were places specifically set up for that very function. And those places would replant trees.

Since they'd be celebrating Christmas at their house this year, everything had to be perfect. She'd spent the past two weeks running nonstop. Between the holiday and Jenna and Ty's wedding, there was something to do every week. In between those two functions, she also had work to do with her clients.

Frankly, she was exhausted. But as Gavin climbed up on the ladder to put the star on the top of the Christmas tree, she was satisfied that at least the decorating part was finished.

"Does it look okay?" he asked.

She found herself staring at his butt, which looked mighty fine in his jeans. Then she realized she had to add more sex to her list of things to do. How else was she going to get pregnant if she didn't jump her husband—repeatedly.

"Perfect. Just . . . perfect."

He turned around. "You're staring at my ass, Liz."

"Oh . . . was I?" She leveled a smirk at him.

"We had sex this morning."

"And your point?"

He climbed down the ladder and folded it up. "No point at all." He brushed her lips as he walked by. "Except we're going to my parents' for dinner tonight, remember?"

"Oh, yeah."

"So your nefarious plans to take advantage of my body are going to have to wait."

"We'll see about that."

He paused, ladder in hand. "Planning to seduce me in my old childhood bedroom?"

She waggled her brows. "That's a distinct possibility."

"I'd like to see you try, considering the entire family will be there. Minus Mick, who's not in town."

"See? One person down. That should make it so much easier to grab some alone time for a quickie."

"Uh-huh. Good luck with that."

"Now you're challenging me. You know how much I love a challenge."

He walked away, shaking his head. As if he didn't believe she could find a way to get him alone in his parents' house for sex. Did he not know her at all? When she was determined to have something, nothing got in her way.

Not even a houseful of Rileys.

She went upstairs to change. Gavin came up to change, too, and they headed over to his parents' house. As soon as they walked in, the smell of baked bread assailed her. Her stomach growled. Gavin looked over at her.

"Hungry?"

"Ravenous." She gave him a direct look.

"I believe you're trying to seduce me."

She saw Gavin's mother coming toward them down the hall, so she gave him a quick smile. "I don't know what you're talking about."

She hugged Kathleen, then Jimmy, who'd entered the room behind Kathleen. The house was full, the women gathered in the kitchen and the guys in the living room. She made her way into the throng of females, all talking over each other in groups.

"And then he said he wanted a bigger house," Tara said with a roll of her eyes.

"Bigger than the five bedroom?" Kathleen asked. "For what?"

"I have no idea. Maybe he thinks we're going to have six more kids or something. If he does, he's going to need to practice polygamy, because this uterus is closed for business."

Liz laughed and poured a glass of iced tea. "What? You're not going to pop out two or three more?"

"I don't think so. I have an eighteen-year-old son and one that's just about ready to walk. That's more than enough children for me to handle."

"Maybe he doesn't like the house," Jenna suggested, popping a cherry tomato into her mouth.

"I saw that, Jenna. Those are for the salad."

"Sorry, Mom." Jenna winked at Liz, who smiled at her.

"He loves the house. It has plenty of room both inside and out. Plus there's the game room. So I don't know what he was thinking."

"Does he miss living in San Francisco? Do you?"

Liz caught the look of concern on Kathleen's face.

"Not at all, Mom. Mick's only there for home games with the Sabers, and the condo there is fine for him. St. Louis is home to us—to me and to Nathan and to Sam. This is where we're staying."

"Okay. I just wanted to be sure."

Tara slid off the barstool and went over to hug Kathleen. "Don't worry about us leaving. We're happy here. My guess is Mick thinks I want a bigger office space, or maybe a separate place to house an office."

"Do you?"

"No. I like working outside the house. I need my retail space where clients can see me. Plus, would we really want my staff traipsing in and out of our house?"

"Lord. I know I wouldn't," Savannah said.

"Neither would I," Liz agreed. She knew having people other than family in her house would drive her crazy. Of course, she sometimes answered emails or made phone calls from home at night or on the weekends, but primarily she worked nine to five. "I need my office. It's where the majority of my work gets done. I like to keep my office and home life separate."

"Amen," Tara said. "Plus I get walk-in traffic at the shop. I'd never want to lose that."

"Or have them show up at your house," Jenna said.

Tara nodded. "Exactly."

"So I understand where Mick is coming from. He knows I miss Sam when I'm at work, but I also love my job and want to continue to do it."

Kathleen rubbed her arm. "He just wants you to be happy."

Tara smiled. "I am happy. Happier than I ever thought I'd be."

"And speaking of all things happy," Jenna said, "I have a few wedding details. Well, actually they're not wedding details so much as they are the fun stuff before the wedding details. We have final dress fittings on Thursday night, and the bachelorette party trip is this weekend. Just in case any of you forgot, which I'm hoping you didn't."

"I definitely didn't forget," Liz said. "I've been looking forward to that trip for months."

"Me, too," Savannah said. "I can't wait."

"Everyone's coming, right?"

"I will not be coming to the bachelorette party," Jenna's mom said.

"Aww, Mom, you know you're welcome to come."

Kathleen gave Jenna a smile. "I'll be babysitting my adorable grandson this weekend so Tara can go. Besides, I've done my partying. You girls can go have some fun drinking and carousing. I'll be happy to have Sam all to myself."

Liz took out her phone. "By the way, I'm going to be out of town Monday through Thursday, but I'll be back Thursday afternoon."

Alicia nodded and grabbed her phone. "Are we doing the fitting at the bridal shop on Thursday? And what time?"

"Yes," Jenna said. "At six thirty."

"No problem."

"Six thirty works for me, too," Liz said. "My flight gets in at three."

"What are we synchronizing our phones for, ladies?" Gavin asked as he walked in to get a beer. "Planning epic world domination?"

Liz laughed. "Sort of. Wedding stuff."

"No, *pre*-wedding stuff," Jenna corrected. "Dress fittings and the bachelorette party."

Jenna turned to him. "Speaking of, care to share the details of the bachelor party with me?"

Gavin shot Jenna an enigmatic smile. "Nope."

"Damn you, Gavin."

He grinned at Jenna, screwed the top off his beer, then shot Liz a look. "You aren't going to get drunk and dance naked on the table at a bar, are you?"

"I don't know. Will you come rescue me if I do?"

"Sure. As soon as I get video."

She shook her head. "And all this time I thought you were my protective knight in shining armor."

He walked by and kissed her cheek. "How foolish of you, wife."

Good thing she knew he was joking.

It was also a good thing he wouldn't be at the bachelorette party. She intended to have a very good time.

GAVIN REENTERED THE LIVING ROOM, WHERE ALL THE guys were gathered around the television watching the game. Mick's team was playing Denver today in San Francisco. Cole would be playing the Monday night game, so he actually got to be at the house for Sunday dinner.

"Mick's arm looks strong," Jimmy said to Ty as Gavin took his seat on one of the chairs.

"It does," Ty said as they settled in to watch Mick take the offense after Denver scored a field goal.

There was a round of hysterical laughter coming from the kitchen.

"I can't believe you waded in there," Ty said. "What's going on?"

"Wedding stuff. Something about the dresses and the bachelorette party."

"Oh. Jenna's kind of excited."

Gavin took a long pull of his beer. "Yeah, I can tell. I hate to break it to you, but I think she's more excited about the bachelorette party."

Ty laughed. "I'm not surprised. There's a lot of stress with the wedding. She needs to get away and unwind."

"So you're not worried about her finding some hot male stripper and running off with him?"

Ty shot him a look. "Uh . . . no. After all, she has me to come home to."

Gavin snorted, then directed his attention back to the game.

After a while, the women came in to watch. Gavin made room on the oversize chair for Liz, who draped her legs over his.

At halftime, the Sabers were still ahead, and Gavin headed outside with the rest of the guys. It was a decent day, so they all shot some baskets, then grabbed more beer and lounged near the fire pit.

"We're set for the weekend," Ty said. "We have the trip to Vegas lined up."

"Cards and booze," Gavin said. "I'm ready."

Garrett grinned. "I'm giving Alicia a hard time and telling her we're club hopping at strip joints."

Cole shook his head. "Bet she's loving you for that."

"She didn't seem fazed by it. All she said was to remember she'd be doing the same thing."

Cole laughed. "Got you on that one, didn't she?"

"Hey, just remember, whatever my fiancée is doing will be the same thing your fiancée will be doing."

"Huh," Cole said, frowning. "Good point. Not sure I like the idea of hot, sweaty men rubbing all over my woman."

"I don't think there'll be any strippers," Gavin said. "That just doesn't seem like something Jenna would be interested in. But I'll check with Liz and see if I can find out what's actually going on."

"You really think Liz is going to tell you anything?"

Gavin nodded at Ty. "She will. With the right amount of persuasion."

They went inside and watched the rest of the game, which the Sabers won, fortunately. That made for a hot discussion about football at the dinner table. Of course coming off the recent loss to Mick, Cole nitpicked all of Mick's deficiencies, which meant Gavin's dad had to argue and defend Mick. Gavin just sat back silently and ate his lasagna, because there was no way he was going to defend his brother. Mick could defend himself just fine next time he and Cole met up.

"Gavin, could you help me upstairs for a minute?" Liz asked after the plates were cleared and everyone sat in the living room watching a movie.

"Sure." He got up and followed her upstairs.

She pulled him into his old bedroom, then shut and locked the door. When she pushed him onto one of the overstuffed chairs, he cocked a brow.

"Seriously?"

She unzipped her jeans and shimmied out of them, then removed her panties and climbed into the chair with him, straddling his lap. "You didn't think I'd forget about this, did you?"

He grasped her hips, his cock twitching to life as she rubbed against him. "I knew you wouldn't. When you get an idea into your head, it doesn't go away."

"No, it doesn't. You're not going to complain about it, are you?"

"Hell, no." He lifted her only long enough to free his cock, which had gone fully hard. "How much foreplay do you want?"

"None. I've been thinking about this all afternoon."

Sucking in a deep breath, he fit his cock to the entrance of her pussy and thrust into her, soaking in the sounds she made as she slid onto his dick.

Oh, yeah. He gripped her hips and began to lift her on and off of him, watching the way their bodies moved together. Being able to see her like this made him even harder.

"Faster," she said, holding tight to his arms as she leaned back, giving him a full-on view of her sex, of where they were connected.

"You make me want to come, Liz," he said, his jaw clenched tight as he fucked his cock deeper into her. She grasped her breasts through her top, squeezing them, inciting his desire even higher. He wanted to taste her, to touch her, to get her naked and lick her all over. None of which he had time for with his family downstairs. But seeing her like this, her body undulating against his, was a turn-on that made his dick go even harder.

He reached for her clit, wanting her to go off when he was inside her.

"Make me come, Gavin. Touch me there."

She let him have access to her, knowing he'd give her exactly what she needed.

It didn't take long. He knew her body, knew how responsive she was to his touch. And when she tightened around him, her pussy convulsing, he let go, driving into her as he came. She whimpered with her orgasm and fell forward, kissing him as her climax drove them both into long, shaking tremors that had them clutching tight to each other.

"God, you make me sweat," he murmured against her lips.

She pulled back and smiled at him. "It's good off-season exercise for you."

She climbed off and they dashed into the bathroom to clean up, then Liz got dressed.

As Gavin zipped his jeans, he looked at her in the mirror. "Now how are you going to explain this one to everyone?"

She grabbed a photo album from the bookshelf. "We were looking for old photos of you from your childhood and I needed your help to find a certain picture that I wanted to put up in the house." She rifled through the album and selected one of him when he was about eight years old.

"That one?" he asked.

"Yes. It's one of my favorites, when you switched to first base. I love this pose and that toothless grin on your face. I want to frame it."

He shook his head. "Okay."

His wife was one sexy mystery to him.

One of the many reasons he loved her so much.

FIVE

THERE WAS NOTHING LIKE A HOT WEEKEND IN JAMAICA to take Liz's mind off work, wedding, and holiday pressure. And the pressure of making a baby. Being with the girls this weekend was going to be amazing.

Jenna had originally thought about going to Las Vegas, but Ty had told her that was where he and the guys were going, and she didn't want to accidentally run into him. She truly wanted a girls-only experience, so Liz suggested they head toward Jamaica. Sure, it was out of the country, but Liz had connections and booked them into an all-inclusive resort. They were going to do the beach, and the spa, and then party away at the clubs until their feet were so sore they couldn't stand anymore.

Liz was going to make sure Jenna had the time of her life while she was still single. Not that they planned to get Jenna laid or anything, but she knew from experience that once you got married, you got wrapped up in each other, and less involved with all things related to the single life. Why not let Jenna cut loose and have a little fun?

Their rooms were beautiful and spacious, with a magnificent view of the ocean. She'd booked adjoining suites so they could all move back and forth and hang out together. She and Jenna were in one room, while Savannah, Tara, and Alicia were in the other.

Jenna got as far as opening her suitcase before she wandered out onto the terrace. "Get out here, Liz."

Liz followed.

"This is fucking fabulous. I'm never leaving. Ty's going to have to come down here for the wedding."

Liz grinned. "So you like it?"

Jenna looked at her. "What's not to like? It's warm, gorgeous, and there's no work to do. Put a drink in my hand and I'm telling you, you'll have to drag me kicking and screaming back on the plane."

"Let's get unpacked, hit the beach, and get started on those drinks, then."

Liz unpacked and changed into her swimsuit. She put on a cover-up and slipped on her sandals. By then, everyone else was unpacked. Jenna was nearly vibrating with excitement, so they all headed downstairs to the pool area.

Liz had called down to rent a cabana while everyone else was unpacking and changing.

"This is sweetly decadent," Savannah said as they were escorted to the sheltered, private space right on the beach. "I could definitely get used to this level of pampering."

Immediately, a waiter showed up to take their drink orders.

"I want something with rum in it," Jenna said. "I think just a rum and pineapple juice."

"Trying to keep it simple?" Alicia asked.

"Yes. Nothing too fruity. Those complicated recipes will sneak up on you and kick your ass."

"I'll have the same," Alicia said.

"I'll have rum and coconut juice," Savannah said.

Tara debated. "Actually, the pineapple juice does sound good. I'll have that one."

The waiter looked at Liz. "Just orange juice, plain, for me."

Jenna cocked a brow. "Designated driver?"

She laughed. "No. Just not in the mood for a cocktail yet."

The cabana was gorgeous, the sun warm, which made Liz glad for the shade since she'd burn to a crisp without it. Jenna and Tara made a beeline for the water and the waiter brought their drinks. Liz settled against the back of the chaise with her orange juice.

"I think I'm going to swim," Savannah said. "It looks so good."

"I'll join you," Alicia said, getting up from the chair. She looked over to Liz. "Are you coming?"

"No. I'm going to sit here and stare at the sea and bask for a while. You two go ahead."

Alicia grinned. "Okay."

After they left, Liz closed her eyes and soaked in the heat, suddenly aware of how much she missed Gavin already.

Ugh. Love was such an all-consuming thing. She'd never wanted to fall in love, had never thought she would. Unfortunately, she'd been in love with Gavin for what seemed like forever. She'd thought marrying him would settle her feelings, make them a little less . . . intense.

She'd been wrong. They'd only grown more, the yearnings she felt for him intensifying the more time they spent together. He was everything to her—kind and generous and fun and playful. He was a generous lover, and even when they argued, which was rarely, it was still with a fiery passion. And their arguments tended to fizzle out quickly, because they communicated so well.

She'd found the man of her dreams and she considered herself so lucky.

She should be wholly content. And she was. Except she wanted to have his baby, and Mother Nature or some cosmic force in the universe refused to grant her this one wish. Maybe it was because she was so exceptionally happy in all other facets of her relationship. Maybe this just wasn't meant to be, and she was going to have to learn to accept it.

They had already talked adoption, and she certainly wasn't opposed to that. She'd love a child they could raise together, no matter where that child came from. She was going to give it another six months to a year. If they weren't pregnant by then, they were going to start seriously pursuing adoption. By then she'd have figured for sure that pregnancy wasn't an option for her.

The women all came back, dripping wet.

"How was it?" she asked.

"Fantastic," Jenna said. "The water is warm and perfect. You should have joined us."

"I will the next go-round. My fair skin can only handle so much of that sun. Besides, I sat back and enjoyed the quiet, something I don't get a lot of with the fast pace of my job."

Savannah grabbed a towel and patted herself down. "I understand that. It's always run here, run there, grab a flight and run somewhere else." She took a seat in the chaise and let out a breath. "It's nice to just . . . sit and take a breath."

"Yes, it is."

Jenna stretched her legs out. "And here I am running you all ragged for my wedding."

Tara squeezed her hand. "Honey, this is paradise. It's hardly what I would call running us ragged."

"I just don't want to exhaust all of you. I know you live busy lives."

"And you don't?" Liz asked. "You have the club to run, and I know that despite the fact you turned over Riley's Bar to a new manager, you still have your thumbprint all over that place."

"I do not. Dave's doing a great job managing the bar. He doesn't need me meddling."

"But it's still a family-owned business, which means someone in the family has to watch over it, right?" Alicia asked.

Jenna shrugged. "I might look in every now and then. So does Dad."

Liz shot her a look. "Dad is happy being retired and stopping in the bar every now and then to visit with his old friends. Not check on liquor stock, personnel, and accounting."

Jenna sighed and cast a pleading gaze toward Savannah.

"Don't look at me," Savannah said. "I agree with them. I think you have your hands full and you take on too much."

"Well, someone has to do it. Dad has the health issues and he has to take it easy, so he can't deal with the stress. Mom can't deal with the financial issues because it's not her thing. I ran the bar for years before I started the music club. I know Dave is doing great as a manager and we all trust him completely . . ."

"But he's not a Riley," Liz finished for her.

Jenna sighed. "The family has to oversee the family business. That's just the way it is. The bottom line is, it's our business and we have to run it. I thought I could step away, but I just haven't been able to walk away completely yet."

Alicia turned around and sat sideways in the chaise so she faced Jenna. "I think you're just having trouble letting go. Do Uncle Jimmy and Aunt Kathleen believe there's any issue with trusting Dave to run Riley's Bar?"

Jenna looked at Alicia for a few seconds before shaking her head. "No. They have complete confidence in him."

"Okay. So do you have any issues with Dave?"

"No."

"Then maybe you're the one who has issues with letting go of something that was yours to manage for so many years," Liz suggested.

"You're probably right. I do have a problem with letting it go. I'm afraid something might happen. Something could get screwed up, and if it does, it'll be my fault."

"Why?" Savannah asked. "Because you wanted something for yourself? Because you had the nerve to chase your dream?"

Jenna looked down at her hands, then lifted her head, her gaze scanning all of them. "Yes. Part of me still feels like I don't deserve all of this."

"Okay," Liz said. "That's normal. You're happy. You have the career of your dreams, the man of your dreams, and I don't think there's any one of us who hasn't been in the same position and felt like it's too good to be true."

"Liz is right," Savannah said. "Once we get that happily ever after, where everything falls into place with career, and we're lucky enough to find someone who loves us for who we are, we can't help but have those self doubts creep in. Are we deserving enough? Surely something is wrong with this picture. When will something come along and screw everything up?"

"We're our own worst enemies when it comes to our happiness," Tara said.

"Why is that?" Jenna asked. "Why can't I just be happy about having everything I've ever wanted?"

Liz laughed. "The nature of women, I guess. As soon as we think we have everything we could ever want, something comes along to screw it up. Or at least we *think* something is screwing it up. Even if it's all in our heads and there's absolutely nothing wrong with our perfect lives."

Tara frowned. "Uh-oh. That sounds like a personal cry for help."

The waiter came and they ordered another round of drinks. Liz ordered a club soda this time.

"You're not drinking," Savannah said, giving her the once-over.

"I'm not pregnant, if that's what you're thinking," Liz said, taking a sip of her club soda. "And that's the problem. I want to be and I can't make it happen."

"I'm sorry," Savannah said. "I didn't know you'd been trying."

"For over a year. It's frustrating. I'm someone who gets what I want—at least in business. Even with Gavin. I secretly loved him for years. And he fell in love with me. It bowled me over that I got the man of my dreams. So why can't I have this, too?"

"This isn't exactly business, Liz," Alicia said. "And you ended up with Gavin because the two of you loved each other. But as far as fertility? That's something you have no control over."

Liz sighed. "Tell me about it."

"Is there a problem?" Savannah asked. "Have you talked to your gynecologist?"

"Yes. She's run tests on me and says all my girlie parts are fully functional, and Gavin's got champion sperm."

Savannah laughed. "Good to know."

"So it's really a matter of things just not . . . happening yet."

"Maybe you need to relax," Alicia said.

Tara nodded. "Same thing I told her. Just have sex and have fun with it."

"Again with the sex with my brother topic," Jenna said, wrinkling her nose. "Clearly, I'm never going to get away from it."

She'd have to remember to thank Jenna later for the subject change. She laughed. "Yes, enough of that topic. I think I'm ready for that dip in the water."

After lounging at the water all day, they headed up to their rooms to rest. Taking a nap in the afternoon was decadent, at least for Liz. And it made her feel refreshed.

They went out to dinner, then went for a walk along the beach. But they made it an early night and hung out in the room because everyone was tired from the trip. Plus, it was nice to just hang out. With their busy lives it was nice to just sit and talk with the girls. Tomorrow night they'd party.

The next morning they hit the pool early, staking out a couple of the best cabanas with water views. All the girls wanted to work on their tans, pre-wedding, while Liz was content to hide in the shade, limiting her sun exposure. A light tan worked fine for her.

"Again, I'm never leaving," Jenna said, sipping a cocktail in the cabana.

"I think Tyler might object to that."

Jenna grinned at Liz. "He can come live here with me. I'll open a bar."

"He might miss hockey," Savannah suggested.

"Are you suggesting I'm going to have to rethink my plan to relocate to Jamaica?"

"Possibly," Alicia said.

Jenna sighed. "Damn."

After spending the morning in the sun and the water, they changed and went shopping at some of the local markets. Jenna bought bracelets, Savannah bought a dress, Alicia bought earrings, and Liz found an exotic perfume she loved. Tara found something for Sam along with a watch for Mick.

They ate, then headed back to the resort. Alicia and Jenna went back to the pool for a couple of hours, but the rest of them took a nap.

Liz could definitely get used to this napping thing. It was decadent.

When it was time to leave for the evening, she took a shower and got dressed, choosing a short white dress and, of course, ridiculously high heels.

She came out to the living room where Tara was waiting with Savannah.

"You women are knockouts," she said. Tara wore a coral bandage dress, and Savannah a gold strapless. Jenna came out wearing a simple black cocktail dress and sexy matching heels, followed by Alicia in a slinky red number.

"We're going to kill tonight," Liz said with a grin.

"You look stunning," Jenna said. She put her hands on her hips and swiveled around in a circle. "Hell, we all look stunning. Men will be falling at our feet tonight. I'm going to want a lot of photos."

Tara pulled her phone out of her clutch. "I'll be the official photographer. At least until I get drunk."

Liz laughed. "I don't plan on drinking, so I'll take the photos."

"No drinking, again?" Alicia asked. "Are you sure you're okay?"

"Someone has to make sure all of you don't end up in Barbados by the end of the night, carried away by some smooth-talking hottie. I'm the designated babysitter, so the rest of you can party on."

"Sounds like a plan," Jenna said, "because I'm ready to have a cocktail."

After they had a most amazing dinner, they headed to a fantastic nightclub on the premises, with lights, perfect music, and some of the best drinks around. Liz had been here before and she loved this place, plus she knew the manager and the bouncers, so she knew her girls would be well taken care of tonight. And even more, they'd be safe.

They were escorted to their table in the VIP area and ordered drinks. Liz opted for a club soda with lime while the others ordered this and that with rum, of course. It wasn't long before she saw Sebastian, the manager, making his way toward their table. She got up and hugged him.

"Sebastian."

"Elizabeth. You look wonderful as usual. And this is your entourage?"

She smiled and introduced all of them one by one to Sebastian. "And this is our bride-to-be, Jenna."

"Ah, congratulations on your upcoming nuptials. It's been fifteen years for me and my lovely wife, Vita."

"How wonderful for you," Jenna said.

"Is Vita here tonight?" Liz asked.

Sebastian shook his head. "No, she's home with the children. She'll be sorry she missed you. And where is your husband?"

"He's in Las Vegas attending the bachelor party with Jenna's fiancé."

Sebastian laughed. "Gambling, yes?"

"Yes. And drinking."

"Then I'm glad you chose to come here. I'll make sure you have a good time tonight. Enjoy."

After their drinks came, Liz turned to them. "Well, what do you think of the place?"

"I think it's fantastic," Tara said. "Such a great choice."

Jenna took a couple deep swallows of her rum concoction, then grabbed Savannah's hand. "Come on, ladies. What I think is we should be on the dance floor."

"Oh, Jenna. Wait. You forgot your veil."

Jenna paused and narrowed her gaze at Tara. "You did not do this to me."

"Oh, we definitely did," Alicia said. "You can't be a bachelorette without having a little fun, and doing a little work. We have a sash for you, and a veil. And we have a bride-to-be to-do list for you tonight."

"I'm going to kill you. All of you."

"Yeah, you can do that later. After you check every item off the list," Alicia said, handing the list to Jenna.

Jenna perused the list, then looked up at them. "You all suck."

"And don't forget, I'll be here to take pictures. Lots of pictures."

Jenna glared at Liz. "You suck the most."

"That's what Gavin says."

"Oh, my God, Liz. Does it ever stop?"

Liz laughed. "No. I do enjoy torturing you."

This was going to be fun. Cheesy, but oh-so-much fun.

TWO HOURS LATER, JENNA HAD OBTAINED A CONDOM from a stranger, had gotten a guy's cell phone number, one guy had gleefully given up his boxers to her, one had bought her a drink, one had danced with her, another had let her take a pen and draw a tattoo on his hand, and one had offered up a photo of his girlfriend. A very charming man had even let her call his girlfriend—and the girlfriend had been a really good sport about it once Jenna had explained it was her bachelorette party and she was totally in love with her own fiancé.

Despite being reluctant about the list at first, after a few drinks and the number of shots these guys were buying her, Jenna was totally drunk and fully into completing the tasks.

Which meant Liz was glad she was stone-cold sober and staying glued to Jenna's side. Savannah and Alicia were off on the dance floor with Tara, who'd also decided to drink on the light side tonight, so at least she had some help, because Alicia and Savannah were feeling no pain. Jenna had warned them about those fruity, fancy rum drinks, but did they listen? No. They were currently swaying on the dance floor, holding on to each other, their once perfect hairstyles now droopy and flat.

They were adorable. Tara was snapping pictures and laughing as she danced around them, and doing a fine job of glaring at any men hoping to take advantage.

Good for her.

Sebastian had also stationed a couple of the bouncers nearby, so Liz knew her group was safe from anyone thinking to take advantage of her loopy friends tonight.

Jenna, meanwhile, blinked, frowned at her list, and bumped into Liz. "Whas thiz one say?"

She loved being sober when her friends were blitzed. "It says you have to kiss a bald man on the head."

"Oh, I can do that one easy sleazy, man." Jenna flipped around and lost her balance. Liz grabbed her.

"Okay, go find a bald guy."

"On my way." Jenna weaved her way in and out of the crowd, Liz right behind her. Then she turned around and bumped into her.

"Oh, there you are, Liz."

"Need something?"

"Yeah. What am I doing?"

"Looking for a bald guy so you can kiss his head."

"Oh, yeah. On it." This time, she wandered off in the opposite direction.

Shaking her head, Liz pivoted and followed. When Jenna stalled in the middle of the dance floor, Liz grabbed her arm.

"How about I help you out?"

Jenna frowned. "With what?"

She could tell this game was winding down. "Bald guy?"

"Oh, yeah. Nope, I'm totally in control here." She pushed her way out of the crowd of dancers and made her way to the bar, where there was a gorgeous and very bald dude leaning against it.

Jenna leaned against the bar. "Hey there, hot stuff. Can I kiss your head?"

"Excuse me?" The guy's girlfriend didn't seem too keen on the idea, for obvious reasons.

Liz said, "Bachelorette party to-do list. Totally harmless, I promise."

"Oh," the woman said with a grin. "I remember when I had to do all that shit. Hideous, but fun at the same time."

Liz nodded.

"Your friend looks shitfaced," the girl said.

Liz laughed. "Pretty much. I think we're going to wrap it up if your guy here gives the okay."

"Fine with me if my wife says yes."

The woman leaned forward and looked at Jenna. "Go for it, honey."

Liz got out her camera as Jenna kissed the top of his head. She got the shot and thanked the couple, then took Jenna by the hand.

"You about ready to call it a night?"

"Hell, no. I'm ready for another drink."

Liz rolled her eyes. Oh, Lord. This was going to be a long-ass night.

GAVIN GOT HIS SECOND CARD FROM THE DEALER.

A six, which gave him twelve.

What the fuck. A twelve? How could he keep getting such shitty hands?

"Dude," was all Ty said next to him. At least he commiserated.

Gavin flicked his fingers to take a card. He had to hit on the twelve. He had no choice.

He pulled a nine from the dealer and grinned.

Twenty-one.

The dealer ended up with eighteen and Gavin raked in winnings.

"You lucky sonofabitch," Mick said, setting down his bet for the next hand. "Who the fuck pulls a twenty-one out of a twelve?"

"I just did."

They played several rounds, and after that one winning hand, Gavin's luck changed. When the dealer reshuffled the deck, Gavin cashed out, figuring he wouldn't press his luck. He and Mick moved over to the craps tables. They both did well there, so Ty and Garrett joined them along with Ty's friends from his hockey team, Eddie Wolkowski and Victor Putinov.

"Too bad Cole can't be here," Gavin said. "He loves to gamble."

"Yeah, well, he has a game tomorrow and I have a bye this week, so he's shit out of luck," Mick said with a smile as he tossed the dice across the table.

Everyone surrounding the table cheered as the numbers came up a win.

"But I'm in the luck," Mick said with a wide grin.

It had been a good day. They'd gone to the shooting range earlier in the day. Nothing like firing off some machine gun rounds in a controlled environment to let off a little aggression. It turned out Victor was the most accurate. Ty had accused him of spending time in the Soviet military. Victor laughed and told them he used to hunt rabbits and that's why he was such a good shot, though he didn't need machine guns to take them down.

Then they'd headed over to the raceway and driven some very expensive cars. Gavin had chosen the Ferrari, which had been a once-in-a-lifetime experience. There was nothing like having all that power in his hands as he'd fired it up and taken it around the curves at the Las Vegas raceway. It had been a thrill not only to drive the car, but to watch the other guys drive the cars they'd chosen. Impressive machines, and a lot of fun.

Spending tonight gambling was more relaxing. It was nice to have an easy night just hanging with the guys and cutting loose. Guys didn't need glitz and glamour to have a good time. Gavin just wanted to make sure Ty was having fun, and from the pile of chips in front of him and the wide grin on his face, he seemed to be having a blast.

They hit the poker room later in the evening, drank several beers, and played well into the night. Gavin had given Ty a choice of gambling or hitting the clubs.

"I spend a lot of time in Riley's Club with Jenna," he said. "Lots of music and dancing and we always have a really good time. If I want to hit a club, I'll do it with my woman. Let's gamble."

It had been a good choice. This was quiet: just the guys, their beers, and their cards. Understated, and fucking perfect.

He sat in the sports book room and took a look at the betting, more or less to take a breather.

Mick joined him. The waitress came over and Mick ordered a soda while Gavin ordered another beer.

"Making bets on some of the games?" Mick asked.

"Nah. Just looking at the lines."

The waitress brought their drinks.

"How's Nathan doing?" Gavin asked.

"Good. He's finishing up finals and coming home next week. I can't wait to see him."

"Me, too. He's changed a lot since you and Tara first got together. He's a man now."

Mick laughed. "Yeah. He was just a kid when I first met Tara. A little unsure of himself, but still, he knew what he wanted. And now he's the damned quarterback at the University of Texas. His freshman year and they took the Big 12 Championship." Mick took a long swallow of soda with a smile on his face.

"Spoken like a proud father."

"I know. I can hardly believe it myself. But he's my kid. He might not have been born mine and he might not have my DNA, but he's still mine and has been since— Hell, since the first day I met him, I guess. I couldn't be more proud of everything he's accomplished."

"You've done some nudging along the way. There's no doubt you've had some influence on him."

"Yeah. A lot of don't-fuck-this-up-like-I-did influence. He knows what not to do. He's always gotten good grades, and he loves sports. He's focused. Though he said he wants to bring his girlfriend to be his date for Ty's wedding."

Gavin arched a brow. "Nathan has a girlfriend?"

"So he tells me. Some hottie who plays for the basketball team there."

"You said yes, right?"

"Of course I said yes. Though the poor girl will be subjected to all the Rileys. I'm not sure Nathan knows what he's dragging her into."

Gavin shrugged. "If she survives all of us at one time, she's a keeper."

Mick laughed. "You're right about that. Maybe he's smarter than I think. Trial by fire and all that."

"Hey, relax, Dad," Gavin teased. "He's doing good."

"I know. He's got it all together. I keep reminding myself that every day."

Gavin knew what Mick wasn't saying. "And he's not drinking."

"God, no. Not like I was in college, anyway. He knows I'll kick his ass from Texas back to Missouri if he does."

"I think he understands how important this is. And what you went through with your alcoholism and how it almost cost you your shot in the NFL. Like you said, he's a smart kid."

"Yeah, he is."

"So quit worrying and let's figure out who's going to kick Philadelphia's ass on Sunday."

Mick grinned and they stared at the board for a while. After that, they wandered out to find the others. Mick went back to playing blackjack with Garrett, while Gavin, Eddie, Victor, and Ty hit the poker tables.

Gavin wondered how Liz was doing with the women. Knowing her, she was probably showing them all a great time in Jamaica.

His woman knew how to party. He knew she had it well handled.

Still, she was on his mind, so when he took his next break he grabbed his phone and sent her a text, figuring she likely wouldn't see it until tomorrow.

I miss you. How's it going?

Surprisingly, she sent back a reply within a few minutes.

Everyone's drunk except me. And maybe Tara. And I miss you, too. I'm having fun with the girls, but Jamaica would be a lot more romantic if you were here.

He smiled and sent her another. *Yeah, fun here with the guys, but can't touch them like I can you.*

She replied back with, *God, I hope not. People will talk.*

He laughed and typed off one more text. *Have fun. Call me tomorrow. I love you.*

I love you, too, Gavin.

SIX

"NO ONE TOLD ME I'D HAVE TO FLY HOME WITH A HANG-over today. This is awful."

Jenna sat on the edge of the sofa, bent over with her hands covering her face.

Liz was curled up on the chair across from her, oh-so-happy not to have partaken in the debauchery of drink last night. She'd suffered many a hangover and she was glad to have escaped it this time.

Alicia came out of the bedroom and leaned against the doorway. "Can we stay another day? Because I feel like I'm going to die."

Liz fought the urge to laugh. Alicia's hair kind of resembled Einstein's at the moment.

"Did you sleep on your face last night?"

Alicia dragged her hair back. "I don't even remember getting back to the hotel last night."

Savannah pushed her way past Alicia and, if possible, looked even worse. She didn't make eye contact, just stared straight ahead. "I. Need. Coffee."

"It's over there." Liz hooked her thumb toward the cart. "There's also orange juice, tomato juice, and some pastries."

"Gag," Jenna said from her spot on the sofa.

"You should eat something," Liz said. "And tomato juice will help."

Jenna pulled a decorative pillow against her stomach. "Please stop mentioning food. Or drink."

"Hey, at least we had fun last night," Liz said.

"Did we?" Savannah asked as she walked by with a cup of coffee in hand. "I hope there's photographic evidence because I don't recall a thing." She laid the coffee down on the table and flopped into the chair. "Lord, who made me drink so much?"

Alicia had only made it as far as the sofa where Jenna was lying. She sat and pulled Jenna's legs on top of her lap. "I'm blaming Jenna for this."

"Me? How could this be my fault?"

"Good morning, everyone." Tara entered from the other side looking gorgeous, freshly showered, and obviously without a hangover.

"You bitch," Jenna said. "How can you look that good after last night?"

Tara poured herself a cup of coffee. "Easy. I only had two drinks. Someone had to help Liz corral you drunkards."

Alicia looked over at Savannah. "That explains how we got back to the hotel. Thank you both for taking care of us."

"It was our pleasure. The pictures of all of you are lovely, by the way," Liz said.

Jenna groaned. "Oh, God. What did I do?"

"You might have propositioned the bartender."

That shot her up straight on the sofa. "Shut the fuck up, Liz. I did not."

"You did. You told him you were madly in love with him and wanted him to come to St. Louis with you."

"Oh, shit. Tyler is going to kill me."

Tara laughed. "What she means is, you loved the way he mixed drinks and his interactions with the customers and you offered him a job at Riley's Club on the spot, even offering to pay his transportation to St. Louis."

"I did?"

"You did. He very kindly turned down your offer, saying he had a wife and a baby son and he was very happy living here."

"Fuck me. I must have been wasted. I don't remember any of that."

Liz held up her phone. "I have photos. And video."

"I hate you." Jenna sneered at her, then stood. "And it's obvious if I'm going to feel human again, I'm going to need some carbs, juice, and coffee, no matter how revolting the thought."

"I'll join you," Alicia said.

After they ate, everyone hit the pool for a little sweat session. When Liz suggested they go for a walk on the beach, Jenna groaned, saying she needed a nap.

"No, what you need is to sweat some of that alcohol out of your system."

"The logical part of me knows you're right. My stomach wants to tell you to fuck off."

Liz laughed and pulled Jenna out of the chaise.

They all took a long walk down the beach, the warm sun beating down on them. Liz had worn a hat and her cover-up and enough sunscreen to ward off a burn.

"This is nice," she said.

"What is?" Tara asked.

"Being here. With all of you."

Tara looped her arm in Liz's. "It has been fun. I had some reservations about coming. I thought I'd miss Sam too much."

"I sense a *but* in there."

"Actually, it's been good for me to get away. Between chasing after the baby and being back at work, things have been intense. I needed a break."

"I'm glad you had a chance to unwind. By the way, I have massages scheduled for all of us this afternoon before we have to pack."

Jenna sighed. "Have I mentioned how much I love you?"

"You might have said that about fifteen times last night."

Jenna laughed. "As long as I only said it to you, then I'm okay."

"Oh, you loved everyone last night. Me, the other girls . . ."

"The bartender," Tara added. "The cocktail waitress who kept bringing you drinks."

"Don't forget the bouncer at the club. You sang to him."

Jenna's face went blank. "I did not."

"Oh, you did. He liked it though. He sang with you."

Alicia laughed. "I do remember that part. Hysterical."

Jenna lifted her chin. "I'm not speaking to any of you ever again."

Savannah put her arm around Jenna. "Yes, you are, honey, because we're your bridesmaids. And we got stinking drunk with you and made fools of ourselves, too. Now if that isn't love, what is?"

Jenna smiled and laid her head on Savannah's shoulder. "I love you guys."

Liz rolled her eyes.

They had their massages later in the day, which to Liz felt like absolute heaven. By the time they all returned to the room to shower and pack, she was both reluctant and eager to get home. She'd loved having an all-women weekend, but she missed Gavin. And she wasn't going to get pregnant spending time away from her husband.

The trip home was long, and by the time everyone said their good-byes, she was counting the minutes until she walked in her front door. It was late, and she knew Gavin's flight got in well before hers.

He was probably asleep. The house was lit up, though, and

when she opened the garage door, she was surprised to see him still up.

"I thought you'd be sleeping," she said as she got out of the car.

He came over and enveloped her in his arms, pressing her against the car and kissing her deeply. She fell into his embrace, telling him without words just how much she'd missed him.

"Mmm," she said when he broke the kiss. "I missed that."

"Me, too. And I wanted to wait up for you and grab your luggage."

"Is that some kind of sexual euphemism?"

He laughed. "Well, no, but I can make it one if you want me to."

"That's all right. Carry on."

He pulled her bags out of the trunk of her car and carried them upstairs. She shrugged out of her jacket and hung it up, then followed him.

She'd been exhausted driving home, thinking of nothing more than throwing off her clothes and climbing in bed next to her sleeping husband. But since he wasn't asleep . . .

When he set her bags down, she came up behind him and pressed her body against his. "I missed you."

He grasped her hands. "I missed you, too, babe." He turned around. "Did you have fun in Jamaica?"

"We did."

He ran his finger across the tip of her nose. "It looks like you got a little sun."

She laughed. "Yeah, very little. You know my skin."

"I do. But I think I should inspect you fully to make sure you didn't get burned."

She kicked off her shoes. "Yes, you probably should."

He undid the buttons of her blouse one by one, his gaze burning into hers, making her hotter by the second. Her nipples tightened, achingly sensitive against her bra as he pushed her blouse off her shoulders.

Gavin traced the swell of her breasts. "I thought about you a lot while I was in Vegas," he said.

She shuddered as she inhaled. "Did you? I thought about you, too."

"Yeah." He walked around behind her and unhooked her bra, then leaned in to lift her hair and press a kiss against the side of her neck. "We're always apart when I'm playing ball, so I like being with you during the off-season. It sucked being separated."

"It did." Goose bumps prickled across her skin as he kissed his way across her neck toward her shoulder. He nipped at her shoulder and she tilted her head back. "Gavin."

"I like the way you say my name when you're turned on."

He came around and faced her, dragging her bra down her arms. Her pants were next, and she held on to his shoulders while he tugged them down, then looked up at her, pulled her by her hips toward his face.

He nuzzled her sex, making her draw in a deep breath. She'd missed this closeness, this passion they shared when it was just the two of them. And when he drew her panties down and put his mouth on her sex, her legs trembled. Gavin grasped her thighs and held her in place as his tongue and lips did magical things to her clit.

She threaded her fingers through his dark hair as she watched his tongue roll over her clit. "You make me want to come. I'm ready. So ready."

He put his lips flat against her and sucked, catapulting her into orgasm. She rocked against his face, crying out as her climax sent her reeling. When he stood, she cupped the back of his neck and brought him down for a deep, soulful kiss that only made her pussy quiver more.

Gavin pushed her onto the bed and dropped his jeans. He was inside her a heartbeat later, her pussy still spasming. She tightened around his cock, feeling every inch of him thicken inside her. And when he began to move within her, it was the sweetest pleasure, a reminder of why she loved being with him. He knew just how to touch her, the exact rhythm that would get her primed and ready to go again.

When he ground against her, she lifted up, making sure he was buried deep, loving the look of fierce passion that furrowed his brow, the dark, predatory need reflected in his eyes that told her he was right there with her.

She wrapped her legs around his hips and held him there, her body hovering on the brink of oblivion. He knew it, too, because he stopped moving, and it was as if the earth had stopped spinning, as if the two of them were suspended in space. All she could hear was their breathing, all she could feel was the hard pounding of their hearts against each other and his cock twitching inside her.

It was heaven, and pure, torturous hell at the same time.

Then he kissed her, drove hard within her, and she shattered like a broken lightbulb, every piece of her gloriously illuminated from the inside out as he shuddered and came with her. He groaned against her mouth, his tongue twining with hers as they rode out their orgasms together.

Out of breath, she held tight to him, so glad to be home and in his arms. Because nothing was more perfect than this.

"All is right in my world again," she said, pressing a kiss to his shoulder.

He disentangled and pulled her against him. "Mine, too. I had fun this weekend, but I'm happy to be back home. Happy to have you back, too."

She tilted her head back and he brushed his lips against hers.

She was glad to have this idyllic moment with him, because she knew the next few weeks were going to be anything but calm.

SEVEN

NATHAN HAD COME HOME, AND TARA AND MICK WERE having everyone over for dinner to welcome him. Plus, he'd brought his girlfriend with him, and he wanted to introduce her to the immediate family before the wedding so she wouldn't be too overwhelmed.

Which immediately made Liz curious because she'd known nothing about this girlfriend.

"Did Mick tell you anything about her?" Liz asked Gavin as they drove over to the house.

"Just that she's pretty and she plays for the basketball team at UT."

"Hmmm."

Gavin glanced over at her. "What does that mean?"

"Absolutely nothing. I wonder if this is a new thing, because Tara hasn't mentioned her to me."

"Imagine that. You, not in the know about something."

She laughed. "Shut up."

"I guess you'll just have to find out about her like the rest of us."

"I suppose so."

They pulled up in front of the house and parked, then headed to the front door. "Looks like everyone's already here."

He grabbed her hand. "We're not late, Liz. You're just worried you're going to miss some vital gossip about this hot mystery girlfriend of Nathan's."

She squeezed his hand. "I am not. I couldn't care less." Okay, maybe she did care. She'd kind of taken it upon herself to become Nathan's not-quite-related-except-by-marriage-but-cared-about-the-kid-deeply aunt. Plus, she was firmly convinced Nathan had a profound athletic future, so she was a little overprotective of him. The last thing he needed was some gorgeous groupie sticking her claws in him and riding his coattails all the way to the NFL.

Gavin paused. "Liz."

"Yes?"

"Mind your own business."

"What are you talking about?"

"Nathan. You don't want to step into that again. You know what kind of trouble you got yourself into before with Mick and Tara. You don't want to do it again."

"For God's sake, Gavin. I'm not even thinking about meddling in Nathan's personal life." Geez, her husband was annoyingly psychic at times.

And of course he was right. Which didn't mean she wouldn't ask this new girlfriend of Nathan's some probing questions. She wouldn't interfere, of course. It was more like . . . protecting him.

"Oh, you're here." Tara greeted them at the front door and led them inside. "The guys are in the game room."

"Later, gorgeous," Gavin said, giving her a swift kiss before heading toward the men.

Liz rolled her eyes. "I knew I'd lose him as soon as we walked in the door."

"I know, right? Mick loves the game room. So do his dad and his uncle. They're all like kids in there with the TV, pool table, and video games, and the rest of the stuff."

Tara led her into the kitchen. "Something to drink? I made this amazing nonalcoholic punch, plus there's wine, beer, and tea."

"I'd love some punch."

Tara poured her a glass. "Everyone else is in the family room."

"Is Nathan here?"

"I sent him and Sonja on an errand. They should be back soon."

"Sonja, huh? Nice name."

Tara smiled. "Nice girl. Wait till you meet her. You're going to fall madly in love with her."

"Is that right?"

"Yes. She's sweet. I can't believe he met someone like her. She's smart and so athletic. And funny, too."

Liz was going to reserve judgment about Sonja until she had a chance to grill—uh, talk to her.

She settled into the family room and visited with everyone, including Mick and Tara's little boy, Sam, who was pulling himself up on the furniture. His hair was dark and curly, and when he giggled, it shot straight to her heart. He had the sweetest smile and charmed everyone in the room as he made his way over to them, laughing every time he fell down.

When Sam came over to her and rested his cheek on her knee, every part of Liz ached. She picked him up and kissed his cheek, but after only a few seconds, he wriggled to get down.

"Okay, mobile man, I know you don't want to be cuddled right now. Off you go."

"I told you," Tara said. "I think my cuddling days are over."

"You might be surprised how much he still wants to cuddle his mama," Gavin's mom said to Tara. "He might want to be moving around right now, but wait until he falls and cries. Then he'll want you holding him."

"You're right, of course," Tara said.

After a few minutes, Liz heard the front door open.

"Mom, where do you want this stuff?"

"Excuse me," Tara said. "If I don't direct Nathan, he'll end up putting milk in the pantry."

Liz got up, too. "I'll help you."

She followed Tara into the kitchen.

Nathan was in there and she was struck by how much he'd matured in the past few years. He was taller, and had picked up a lot more muscle. He wore his hair shorter now, and it was a darker brown. Though still young, he was no longer a young boy. Now he was a young man.

"Hi, Nathan," she said.

He smiled at her. "Hey, Liz. How's it going?"

"It's going good. On errand duty?"

He grinned. "Always."

A tall, quite gorgeous young woman carried a bag in. "Where do you want this one, Mrs. Riley?"

"On the counter, Sonja. Thanks."

The girl had to be nearly five-eleven or maybe even six feet tall. Considering Nathan had shot up his senior year to six-four, he was still taller, but wow. She was beautiful, with café au lait skin, honey colored eyes, and sleek black hair.

Wow.

"Oh, Sonja, this is Nathan's Aunt Elizabeth, but we all call her Liz."

Liz stuck out her hand in greeting. "Nice to meet you, Sonja."

"Same here. And I'm probably never going to remember everyone's name so I'm going to apologize if I have to ask it again."

Liz laughed. "That's okay. Ask away."

"Hey, I warned you I had a big family," Nathan said, casting a grin at his girlfriend.

"You did."

"Where are you from, Sonja?"

"A small town in southwest Texas that no one's ever heard of. Nathan wanted to drag me here to see more big-city life."

"Well, St. Louis isn't exactly a huge city."

Sonja leaned against the counter. "Bigger than where I grew up, that's for sure."

"What's your major?"

"Marketing with a minor in communications. And I play for the UT basketball team."

"She's good at it, too. One hell of a guard," Nathan said. "You should keep your eye on her, Liz. She might go pro."

Sonja laughed. "I don't know about that. I'm just happy to have the scholarship so I can get my education."

"Yeah, and she's being modest. She really is good."

"Then I'll definitely keep my eye on you."

"Liz is a sports agent," Nathan said to Sonja. "She could get you a great deal."

"Nathan," Liz warned.

Sonja just looked at her. "I'm not even thinking that far ahead. I just want to get a degree." She elbowed Nathan. "Quit being so pushy. You're making your aunt uncomfortable."

He shoved back into her. "Hey, I believe in you."

She laughed. "Whatever."

He put his arm around her. "Come on. Let's go hang out."

"Dinner's in about thirty," Tara said.

"Okay."

After they left the room, Tara asked, "So? What do you think?"

"I think she's stunning."

"I know. Isn't she? Like fashion-model beautiful. And she's very smart. Nathan said she has a 4.0 GPA, plus she plays sports, too. She's outgoing and she really seems to be into Nathan and he's obviously very much into her."

And she very obviously wasn't at all how Liz had imagined her. So she relaxed on that count. "She's very sweet. Nothing like that first love, is there?"

"Well, I wouldn't know about that since my first love got me into a lot of trouble. But yeah, I like her. She seems grounded and reasonable and not flighty and all into Nathan just because he's the quarterback. She seems to have her own goals and ambitions. So that reassures me."

"I'm sure it does." Liz was a bit reassured, too. She wished Nathan didn't have a girlfriend at all, but she supposed that was a bit unrealistic. He was in college and out on his own now, and he needed to have some fun, to grow up some and become a man. He was going to likely have a lot of girlfriends in his lifetime.

She wasn't his mother, so she had no idea why she was so nervous about Nathan getting involved with Sonja. She should just let it go.

But she did watch them during dinner, when the family could really get noisy, talking over each other and often arguing over the most innocuous topic. Maybe they were on their best behavior tonight because Sonja was there and they didn't want to scare her off, but it was relatively calm. Plus, the baby was still awake and he captured a lot of attention. In fact, Nathan sat next to Sam and he and Sonja entertained him during dinner, feeding him and making him laugh.

Sonja seemed at ease with the family, which didn't happen often with strangers. After dinner she even helped Tara in the kitchen.

"You seem pretty comfortable around our crazy family," Liz remarked as she, Tara, Alicia, and Jenna, along with Gavin's mom and Alicia's mom, helped Tara with the after-dinner mess.

"Oh, I come from a big family. I have three sisters and two brothers."

Liz's eyes widened. "Really. Wow. So dinnertime is a lot like this."

Sonja laughed. "Yes. Exactly like this. Only maybe more yelling. My brothers are younger than me, so they're a little . . . boisterous."

"Boys do tend to be like that," Gavin's mother said from across the room.

Tara nodded. "Yes, they do. And I only had one. Well, one at a time, anyway."

"I imagine it takes parents ruling with an iron fist to keep a brood like that under control," Alicia said.

"My mother is pretty fierce. When she speaks, believe me, you listen."

"And your dad, too?"

"He died when my youngest brother was two years old. It's mostly been just my mom for a while."

Liz laid her hand on Sonja's arm. "I'm so sorry."

"I am, too." Tara pulled up a chair at the kitchen island. And suddenly the women surrounded Sonja.

"Oh. Wow. Well, I didn't mean to talk about it. But he got cancer and it took him pretty fast. It was hard on my mom having all us kids to deal with, but she had my aunts and uncles and my grandparents to help her. It's been okay, really."

Gavin's mom patted Sonja's hand. "It's nice that she had all the family to help support her."

"It was."

And Liz could tell Sonja was uncomfortable.

"Hey, how come the guys never help with the dishes?" Liz asked, sliding off the barstool. "Sonja, let's go track down Nathan and my husband and find out where they're lurking."

"Sure. If you all don't need me in here."

"We're fine. We're just about done anyway," Tara said.

As Liz led Sonja down the long hall toward the back of the house, Sonja turned to her. "Thanks for that."

"For what?"

"For pulling me out of that conversation. I miss my dad for sure. But I just don't like to talk about it."

"Understood. Especially with a bunch of people you don't really know."

She smiled. "Right. Not that I don't like all of you. You're all . . . great."

"Hey, you don't have to sell me. I get it. We're all pushy and nosy and overprotective, and we'll ask you a million questions if you let us. So don't let us and feel free to tell us to back off."

"Oh, I'd never do that. But I might have to ease my way in. Things with Nathan and I are just getting started. And we both have our priorities, which are school and career first."

The more she talked to Sonja, the more she liked her. "Those are good priorities to have."

"Yeah, I mean we're just eighteen. Plenty of time for all that romance later."

Liz laughed. "Yes. Much later."

GIVE A GUY A GAME ROOM, AND THE WORLD IS A HAPPY place. At least a guy's world is a happy place. There was pinball, pool, video games, and even a foosball table, which reminded Gavin of college and of old times in their family basement, when he and Mick would go at it for hours. Gavin, of course, was the Riley foosball champion.

Mick, on the other hand, remembered it differently, claiming he consistently kicked Gavin's butt. So they had to have a rematch.

Gavin won. Until Ty joined in and kicked his ass. And then Nathan took over and trounced all of them one by one.

Damned kids.

He sat back drinking a beer and watched Nathan and his girl-friend Sonja flipping the handles as they faced off against each other. She was pretty good at it, and Nathan didn't let up just because Sonja was a girl. It was a pretty fierce competition, but in the end, Nathan won again.

Garrett rubbed his hands together. "I'm going to take you down this time, kid."

"You'd like to think so, wouldn't you?" Nathan asked with a gleam in his eye.

Sonja sat at the bar with a soda and grinned as Nathan took Garrett down easily. And then the women came in and started their own tournament. Tara faced off with Liz, and then Sonja hopped in. It was clear that Sonja and Nathan were going to be the foosball champions tonight.

"She's cute," Gavin said to Mick as they watched.

"Who? Your wife? She's all right, but I'd have to say I prefer my own."

Gavin laughed. "I meant Sonja."

"Yeah, she is. Nathan really seems into her."

"I assume you've had a long conversation with him about sex and birth control and not screwing up his future in that way."

Mick shot him a look. "I've had lengthy conversations with that kid about everything that could screw up his life. Including that. He's tired of seeing me head his way. He knows what's what. He's not stupid."

"I figured, but just thought I'd throw it out there."

Mick took a swallow of water and laid his glass down on the table behind them. "Could you ever have imagined the day we'd be the old men talking to kids about not knocking up their girlfriends?"

"No. I never saw that one coming," Gavin said with a wry smile. "Time goes by fast and your kid has really grown up a lot in a few years. He's a man now."

"He is. And with that comes responsibility. The kind I blew off in college. So he'll just have to get used to my Dad lectures."

Gavin laughed. "I guess so. Hopefully someday I'll be able to give a few of those to my own kids."

"Any of those coming soon?"

"We're working on it." He shifted his gaze across the room to Liz, who caught his gaze and smiled at him, a hot, I-know-what-you're-thinking smile.

She made a motion with her head and went upstairs. As soon as Ty came over to talk to Mick, Gavin eased his way upstairs. She was in the kitchen.

"Do you want another beer?" she asked.

"No, I'm good right now."

"Okay. Then why don't you join me over here?" She pulled him into one of the downstairs bathrooms and shut the door, clicking the lock.

"Really, Liz? In my brother's house?"

She wound her arm around his neck and pushed him up against the wall. "I just want a kiss. It's been a long afternoon and evening of separation while you were hanging with the guys."

"You could have kissed me in the kitchen." He brushed his lips across hers, but lingered, enjoying the taste of her mouth, the way she leaned into him, pressing her body against his.

"It's more fun in here," she whispered against his lips.

He laid his hand on her butt and squeezed, his dick responding. "You make me hard."

She reached between them to palm his erection, rubbing back and forth. "Take me here. I'm wearing a dress. It'll be fast."

"What if I don't want fast? What if I want slow?"

"We'll do slow when we get home. I want you now."

Liz's sense of adventure never failed to get his motor running. She wasn't shy about having sex just about anywhere, including the bathroom of Mick and Tara's house. Plus, he knew she was eager to make a baby. They'd been doing it damn near every day, sometimes more than once a day.

He had to admit, he was on board for that. He lifted her dress and slipped his hand inside the sexy silken underwear to find her wet and ready for him. With his other hand, he reached for her breasts, sliding his hands over the full mounds to tease her nipples.

Her breath caught and she looked up at him with eyes that flashed with heat and desire.

He unzipped his jeans and turned her around and pushed her toward the sink, watching her face as he nestled behind her. He kicked her legs apart, then entered her, reaching around to rub her clit as he filled her with his shaft.

"Oh, yes," she whispered. "Just like that."

He bent and kissed her back and neck as he thrust into her, his cock and balls tight with need as he pulled out, then drove in harder. He felt her pussy surrounding him, pulsing as he continued to give her what she'd asked for. He strummed her clit, taking her right to the edge. He felt her body spasm as she hit the peak.

"Gavin." She met his gaze in the mirror, ecstasy etched on her face as she came.

With a low growl he poured into her, his legs shaking as he climaxed. He held tight to her hips, emptying and shuddering until he had nothing left.

Gavin breathed hard as he fought to recover from that mind-blowing experience. Not wanting to spend any more time in here than was necessary, he withdrew and they did a quick cleanup.

He pulled Liz against him, giving her a deep, passionate kiss.

"When we get home, it'll be slow and easy."

She grinned and brushed her lips against his. "I liked fast and hard."

"You make me crazy, you know that?"

"Good. Now let's head back downstairs before Mick and Tara think we've been fucking in their bathroom."

He laughed, shook his head, and followed his wife.

EIGHT

"I CAN'T BELIEVE JENNA AND TY ARE GETTING MAR-
ried tomorrow," Liz said. "It seems a little surreal to me that it's
here already."

Gavin turned the car off and pocketed the keys, then turned to
her. "Do you remember when we got married? How fast the time
crept up on us?"

Liz shot him a sexy smile. God, he looked good tonight dressed
in a suit. At the church earlier when they'd rehearsed for the wedding
they were coupled up. Walking down the aisle with him reminded
her of their wedding, which hadn't been so long ago. She still remembered each moment of it so vividly, of how nervous she had felt walking down the aisle, and how calm she became as soon as she'd seen
Gavin's face at the end of the aisle.

He'd looked gorgeous in his tux, so tall and sexy. Just like tonight in his suit. She wanted to crawl all over him in the car, but

she suppressed the urge since they were due inside the restaurant for dinner. And besides, the valet was standing right there to collect the keys from Gavin, so that might be slightly inappropriate. "Yes. It was a whirlwind. But I still remember every moment of it."

He crooked a grin at her. "Me, too. Especially our wedding night."

She laughed and pulled her coat tighter against the cold wind. Gavin came around and opened the door and they hurried inside.

It was beautiful inside the Hyatt. With Tara's help, Jenna and Ty had chosen a perfect location not only for their wedding reception, but also for the rehearsal dinner. They checked their coats and found Gavin's dad at the coat check.

"Your mom is already inside with Tara and Mick," Jimmy said.

"I think we're going to need to feed Jenna oxygen," Tara said, pulling Liz away from Gavin.

"Oh? Why's that?"

"No particular reason. And for every reason."

"Ah." Liz nodded. "Pre-wedding jitters."

"Exactly."

They found Jenna talking to the catering manager. "This is not the food I ordered."

Clyde looked confused. He opened a binder. "Ma'am, if you'd like to go over the forms you filled out, I can assure you it is."

"It can't be. I hate salmon. Who would order salmon?"

"Clyde. Let's go over a few things," Tara said, motioning him away from a near frantic Jenna, who then turned to Liz.

"The food isn't right. Look at this."

Liz blinked as Jenna fanned the paper in front of her.

Liz took the menu. "Jenna. Calm down. Tara will take care of everything. Remember, this is what she does for a living."

Jenna fell into a chair. "I'm not going to make it until tomorrow. Mick had a game on Thursday, so he just got back in the nick of time. Cole has a bye this weekend. Ty at least has a couple of days off, as do his two friends and teammates, who are ushers. And Gavin is off season. Do you have any idea what it was like trying to plan my wedding around the schedules of athletes in three sports, one that's off season, and two that are in season?"

"Actually, yes, I do."

"Oh, of course you do. Anyway, a fucking nightmare. And Christmas is next week. What the hell was I thinking getting married the week before Christmas? No one has time for this shit. No one's going to show up. I just know it."

Yeah, Jenna was on the first-class express to meltdown city. Direct flight, no stopovers.

Liz signaled for a waiter. "Bring me a shot of tequila. And make it a double."

The waiter nodded and Jenna lifted her head. "Oh, no. I'm not drinking tonight. I'm going to be calm and rational and not drunk and crazy."

"Okay." Liz leveled a direct look at her.

"I'm already crazy, aren't I?"

"No, you're stressed and nervous. It's normal. I was a spewing volcano the night before Gavin and I got married."

Jenna's lips curved. "I remember that. You suddenly decided the venue couldn't possibly be big enough for all the people who were invited, and we needed to move it somewhere else."

Liz laughed. "Yes. So trust me, I was a much bigger basket case than you could ever hope to be. This is just pre-wedding nervousness that all brides have. Tara calmed me down the day before mine, so now I'm going to do the same for you and tell you that your wedding is going to be perfect."

"We should have eloped. Or just had family at Riley's Bar."

"You are not having your wedding at Riley's. You are not working the bar on your wedding day." When the waiter came back, Liz handed Jenna the shot glass. "But you are going to take the edge off by taking a shot of tequila."

Jenna sighed. "You're right. I need this." Jenna downed the shot, grimaced, then blew out a breath. "Whew. That's better."

"Good. Now let's join the family, where you're going to be calm and happy and enjoy the night before your wedding."

"You're so bossy."

"I know. That's why you love me."

They joined the family in the private room that had been set up for them.

Jenna squeezed her arm. "You're right. This is lovely. And I'm not even going to think about tomorrow, because I know it's going to be perfect."

"Of course it's going to be perfect. Tara is in charge of event planning, and you know she's a genius."

"Did I hear my name?"

Tara moved in between them and Jenna hugged her.

"Sorry for the craziness earlier," Jenna said.

"You're entitled. We've been there and we know all about the stress. But trust me, everything is exactly as you wanted it for tomorrow. And for tonight."

"I know it is, and I haven't even thanked you for taking the time to arrange it all."

Tara smiled. "It's what I do."

"And you do it beautifully." Jenna gave Tara a tight squeeze and Liz sighed in relief.

Meltdown over.

The dinner was perfect, just as Liz knew it would be. And then the speeches started.

Ty's friend Eddie Wolkowski gave a great speech about love and hockey, friendship and relationships that made absolutely no sense at all but still brought everyone to their feet because Eddie was just that kind of guy you couldn't help but adore.

As matron of honor, Tara talked about friendship between two people who were there for each other. She talked about watching

Ty and Jenna fall in love, and how she couldn't imagine any two people who were more perfectly matched. It was a beautiful speech and she wished them well.

Ty's parents were there, so Ty's father, Sean, gave a short speech about how proud he was of his son and how he welcomed Jenna into the family. Ty's mother, Louise, also said she didn't think there'd ever be a woman good enough for her son, until she'd met Jenna. And that she wasn't losing her son, she was gaining the daughter she'd always wanted and she looked forward to the two of them visiting Chicago, hopefully soon. It was sweet and emotional and everyone clapped.

Jenna's dad was the last to toast by saying there was always room for another guy in the Riley family, and Ty had settled in just fine. He said he hadn't known about Jenna's dreams, but Ty had and he'd helped her achieve them. And then he'd gone on to say that he couldn't think of anyone who was better equipped to take care of his little girl than Tyler. He wished the two of them well, and said he knew his daughter was going to live her happily ever after with Ty.

Liz blinked back tears and Gavin squeezed her hand.

"Emotional, huh?"

Liz nodded and dabbed the corners of her eyes with her napkin. "Seems to be a lot of emotion where weddings are concerned. Especially this one. I'm so happy for Ty and Jenna and I can't wait for the wedding tomorrow."

"And here I thought you were so tough."

She laughed. "Yeah, well, don't tell anyone. It could affect my business."

After dinner, no one lingered. They'd be back here tomorrow night for the reception anyway, and tomorrow was going to be a big day.

Liz and Gavin headed home. She slipped off her heels, hung her dress in the closet, and went into the bathroom to get ready for bed.

"I'm shocked you didn't try to seduce me in the hotel," Gavin said as he came in to brush his teeth.

She smiled as she combed her hair. "I'm saving that one for tomorrow night when there are more people. Everyone will be relaxed, drinking, and not paying attention to us. Tonight, though, we're going to have to do it in the bed like a normal, boring married couple."

She walked out of the bathroom.

He followed, turning off the light. "How unfortunate."

She slipped under the covers. It was cold tonight, and snow was expected for tomorrow. "I hope it doesn't snow for Jenna and Ty's wedding. That could be a big mess."

He shrugged, crawled under the covers, and pulled her next to him. "It's a Saturday night, so it shouldn't be too bad traffic-wise."

"Unless we get a lot of snow."

He pulled her on top of him, his body already warming hers. "Quit worrying about the wedding. It's going to be fine."

"You're so sure about that."

"Positive."

Thoughts about the wedding fled as soon as Gavin put his hands on her ass. "Mmm, I like that."

"Which part? Your gorgeous breasts rubbing against my chest, or my hands on your ass?"

"Yes to both." She kissed him, and then he was the only thought in her head as his tongue slid over hers, expertly obliterating any thought but that of his cock hardening between her legs.

She rose up and rubbed a nipple between his lips. He grasped her breast and flicked the bud with his tongue, making her gasp. He knew what she wanted, that she needed him to take her nipple and suck, but still, he teased her by licking the areola and laying his tongue against it.

"Gavin."

He lifted his gaze to hers. "Yeah, babe."

"You know what I want."

He plumped her breast with his hand. "Not psychic here. You're going to have to tell me."

Such an obstinate man. "Suck my nipple into your mouth."

He brought her forward and took her nipple into his mouth, drawing it in deep.

"Yes, that's what I needed." She held on to his head while he sucked the bud, flattening it in between the roof of his mouth and his tongue. Her nipples were sensitive and the sensation shot straight to her core, making her swell with need for his cock.

She pulled her nipple out of his mouth, watched him stare at it.

"I wasn't finished with that."

She let out a low laugh. "You can come back to it. In the meantime, there's something I want to do."

She eased down his chest, stopping to lick and suck at his nipples, rewarded when he emitted a groan. She kissed her way down his abs, snaking her body over his, stopping to nip at his hip bone.

"I like where you're going," he said, tangling his fingers in her hair as she nuzzled the hairs on his lower belly.

She loved the way he smelled, so crisp and clean, and yet a musky scent that never failed to turn her on. His cock was hard and pointing toward his stomach. She wrapped her hand around the base of his shaft and stroked upward, slow and easy, then got up on her knees so she could put her lips around the crest.

"Elizabeth."

Hearing him say her full name in a deep whisper like that made her skin tingle. It spoke of need and desire, his voice on the edge of control.

Just where she wanted him as she swirled her tongue around the head of his cock and eased his shaft into her mouth. At this angle, with her above his cock, he could see it disappearing into her mouth inch by inch, could feel what he saw.

His hold on her hair tightened and he arched his hips, sliding his cock along her tongue. She closed her mouth around him and gave him pressure, hearing him groan as his cockhead hit the back of her throat. Giving Gavin this pleasure made her nipples tighten, her clit and pussy tingling with the need to have him pumping inside her just as he pumped his cock in her mouth.

And when he pulled out and dragged her up, kissing her until she was delirious, she knew he wanted the same thing.

He shifted her onto her back and slid inside her with one hard thrust. She moaned against his lips and arched into him, pulling him deeper inside her.

He rose up and looked at her. "I love the feel of you when I'm inside you, the way your pussy grips me and sucks me in."

The way he looked at her, his features tight with strain as he moved within her, never failed to make every nerve ending in her body come alive. She reached up and swept her hand across his face, rubbing her thumb along his bottom lip. He nipped at her thumb and she wrapped her hand around the nape of his neck to draw him down for a kiss. Kissing him while he made love to her was like dual pleasure, his tongue sliding along hers as his cock thrust within her, making her senseless as she climbed each peak toward the very pinnacle.

And when he ground his hips against her, brushing her clit again and again, she broke, crying out and raking her nails down his arms as she came. Gavin let go then, shuddering as he climaxed, his body lifting over hers as he emptied into her.

He dropped down on top of her and pressed kisses to her cheek and neck.

"You're killing me, Liz," he said.

She stroked his back and arms, smoothing the spots where she'd dug her nails into him. "I hope not. I need you around for at least a few more years."

He laughed and rolled to his side, pulling her against him. "All this sex. I'm not sure I'm up for it."

"Oh, you're up for it. I know your stamina level."

"Good thing you feed me vitamins."

She snuggled closer. "Good thing, huh?"

NINE

THE SKIES WERE GRAY AND OMINOUS ON JENNA AND Ty's wedding day for the entire day, the threat of snow hanging heavy in the air. Liz was certain that at any moment she'd see thick flakes come down from the sky. But so far they'd held off. Liz was going to keep her fingers crossed.

As they arrived at the church, all she could see were clouds. It was bad enough she was freezing to death in this sleeveless dress. She hoped the heat in the church was working well.

"I'll see you at the front of the church," Gavin said as he kissed her good-bye.

"Just like the last time." She smiled at him, patted his chest, and they walked in opposite directions.

She made her way to the bridal suite, where Jenna's mother and Tara were lacing up the back of Jenna's dress.

Jenna looked stunning in a cream taffeta halter dress with a dropped waist and tiers from her hips to the floor. A bow sat at her right hip. It was luscious and elegant and her tattoos made her look beautiful.

Liz stood in the doorway and took a moment to watch Jenna looking at herself in the mirror. The look of awe on Jenna's face was priceless.

"You look gorgeous, Jenna," Liz said as she came into the room.

Jenna gave her a serene smile. "It's kind of hard to believe this is happening. Me, in a wedding dress. Who'd have thought that day would ever come?"

"Me," Jenna's mom said, tears in her eyes.

"And me," Tara said, dabbing her eyes with a tissue.

"Don't you cry, Mom. I had to sit in a chair this afternoon for hours getting my makeup done. I don't want to do it again."

"All of you can stop with the blubbering. We all had to sit through makeup," Alicia said.

"Southern girls never cry," Savannah added, sniffling.

"We all look gorgeous," Liz said, smoothing down her dress. "And no one is allowed to cry. Except maybe Jenna and her mom, but not until the ceremony."

"You all look so beautiful," Ty's mother said. "And especially you, Jenna. My son is a very lucky man."

Jenna reached over to squeeze Louise's hand. "Thank you, Mom."

"We should be starting shortly." Savannah took her phone out of her clutch. "All we need now are the flowers."

"They're here," Tara said, checking her phone. "I need to get the florist to bring them in here. I'll be right back."

Tara ran to get the florist, who came in bearing the most beautiful flowers Liz had ever seen—short of her own wedding, of course. Cream roses and purple lilies highlighted Jenna's bouquet and were a perfect complement to her dress, and since the bridal party wore purple dresses, they had cream bouquets.

There was a knock on the door. Tara answered, then turned to them. "Five minutes. We should line up."

Jenna laid her hand on her stomach. "I've never been so nervous about anything in my entire life. Even singing for the first time didn't make my stomach flutter this much."

Her mom came to Jenna's side and put her arm around her. "You love Tyler. This is your moment. Be happy, and relaxed."

Jenna nodded. "You're right. I am happy. And excited."

They all stopped out in the foyer. Jenna's dad was there with a huge grin on his face. "You look beautiful, baby girl."

Jenna blinked away tears again. "Thank you, Dad. You look pretty handsome yourself."

"You sure you don't want to make a run for it? I've been working out. We can dash out the front door and into the limo. There's a game on. We can catch it at Riley's."

Jenna laughed. "As tempting as that sounds right now, I think I'm good here, Dad. But thanks for the offer."

He took her hand and tucked it into the crook of his arm. "Okay, then. Let's do this."

Liz could have kissed Jimmy for that bit of levity. It was just what Jenna needed to relax.

Everyone lined up in their positions. Gavin came and walked his mother down the aisle, then Ty's mother was escorted to her seat.

And as the music started to play, Liz was overcome with dizziness and nausea and leaned against Savannah.

"What's wrong?" Savannah asked, grasping her arm.

She took in a deep breath, then let it out. "Tight dress. No air. And probably too many flowers."

"Take deep breaths," Alicia said.

"Doing that."

"I can ask them to wait," Alicia said, a concerned look on her face.

Liz waved them on. "No, I'm good. Let's get this thing moving."

The bridesmaids moved down the aisle and Liz tried to quell the dizziness, holding the flowers as far away from her face as she could. The last thing Jenna needed was for Liz to face-plant walking down the aisle at her wedding. When it was Liz's turn, she breathed as normally as she could, smiled, and concentrated on Gavin's face. He smiled back at her, and she made it all the way to the altar, though she felt beads of sweat rolling down her back.

Great. Just great. It was probably the flu or something. Talk about bad luck.

But she focused on Jenna coming down the aisle with Gavin's father, and how beautiful she looked.

She'd get through this. And she was going to be fine.

Nothing was going to ruin Jenna and Ty's wedding day.

GAVIN COULDN'T BELIEVE THAT WAS HIS LITTLE SIS-ter coming down the aisle looking so beautiful, so grown up. His throat swelled with emotion as he watched their dad turning her over to Tyler, listened to the two of them making vows to watch over each other, to care for each other in hard times and in good times, and promise to love each other forever.

He wasn't an emotional sort, wasn't the kind to get choked up over things, but this was his sister, the one he'd teased mercilessly when they were kids. He'd pulled her hair and laughed when she ran to Mom about it. But he'd also picked her up and carried her into the house when she'd fallen off the swing and broke her arm.

She might have been his to tease, but she'd also been his responsibility to look after.

Now she wasn't his responsibility anymore. She was Tyler's. She was an adult and she was getting married. He'd had to pass the torch on to another man who'd take care of her when she was hurt, who'd calm her fears and tease her and laugh with her.

He realized he had tears in his eyes. He quickly swiped them away, then looked over at Mick, whose eyes were also filled with tears. Mick crooked a smile and nodded at him, and he knew Mick felt the same things he did.

And okay, maybe Jenna was getting married today, and he knew

Ty was a great guy and would always take care of her, but he and Mick would always be there for her, no matter what.

Because they were Rileys. And nothing would ever tear them apart.

"I now pronounce you husband and wife. You may kiss your bride."

As Jenna and Ty kissed, the church exploded in applause, music pealed, and the wedding party began to descend from the altar.

Gavin met up with Liz, who looked a little pale, but smiled as she slipped her arm in his. They did their part for the photographer, but when they reached the back of the church, he turned to her.

"Are you all right?"

She tipped her head to the side. "I'm fine. Why?"

"You look pale."

"Huh. Maybe I need more blush. And here I spent all that time getting my makeup done. I should ask for a refund."

He laughed. "Seriously, are you okay?"

"My dress is a little tight and I think they had the heat up a little high in the church. Wasn't it warm in there?"

"Not that I noticed. Why? Were you having hot flashes?"

"Kind of."

"Hard to believe considering how little you're wearing."

She tapped his arm. "I'm wearing plenty."

They were pulled apart then to greet guests on the way out. Then they had photos in the church. Gavin kept his eye on Liz, though, who smiled and seemed okay, but still looked pale. There was a winter flu going around, and the last thing she needed right now was to get sick. They had to host the holidays with the family next week, and he knew she was stressed about that, plus the whole trying-to-get-pregnant thing. She'd had a lot on her mind lately, and he hadn't been helping in trying to relax her.

He'd have to work on that.

After photos, they headed downtown to the Hyatt for the reception. Since they'd checked in to the hotel earlier in the afternoon, their car was parked there and they all got to take the limo to the hotel. Ty and Jenna still had photos with all the parents, then they'd come over in their limo. In the meantime, the bridal party was finished, so they were headed over to the reception.

"Glad to be done with all those photos. It was like being at a game. Only with fewer interviews." Cole cracked open a bottle of champagne.

"It wasn't that bad," Savannah said.

"That's because you're beautiful and you should have your photo taken every day." Cole kissed her cheek and handed her a glass.

He started pouring champagne into glasses and handing them around the limo. Mick handed Liz a glass, but she passed it on to Gavin.

"Not drinking?" he asked.

"I'm pacing myself. It's going to be a long night."

"And she doesn't want to end up naked table-dancing too early," Gavin said.

Mick laughed. "I'll keep my camera phone ready for that."

Tara nudged him. "You will not. And no one will be naked table-dancing."

"Are you sure about that?" Savannah asked. "You can't vet everyone on the guest list."

Tara sighed. "So true. Let's hope no one dances on the tables tonight."

"You're no fun," Mick said.

"My date is stripper," Ty's friend Victor said. "She could dance naked on tables."

Everyone looked at him. Victor laughed. "Just joking. She is kindergarten teacher."

"I'm telling Felicia you called her a stripper," Eddie said.

"You do that and I'll shove hockey stick up your ass. Also, will tell your date that you're seeing another waitress."

Victor and Eddie glared at each other.

Gavin snorted. "I really like these guys."

It was going to be an interesting night.

The Hyatt was decorated beautifully. The lighting had been set perfectly, the tables were elegant, and the views of the St. Louis Arch were stunning.

"Jenna's going to love this," Liz said to Tara. "You did such a wonderful job arranging everything."

Tara smiled. "Thank you. I hope she's happy with it."

They found their places at the head table and took their seats. Liz was happy to sit down. She blew out a breath and tried to quell the queasiness that hadn't quite gone away yet.

"Would you like something to drink?" Gavin asked.

Her savior. "How about a club soda?"

He frowned. "Still not feeling good?"

"There's a flu that's been going around. I'm hoping like hell I haven't caught it. This couldn't be a worse time."

He rubbed her back. "I'll go get that club soda for you."

She would not ruin Jenna's wedding day by being ill. Fortunately, her part was mostly done, photo-wise, but she didn't want to miss Jenna and Ty's special day.

Gavin brought her club soda and she took a sip. "Thanks. This will help."

"If you don't feel good I can take you up to the room."

She laid her hand over his. "I think I'll make it, but thank you. I'm sure the excitement of the night will overcome my stomach-ache. Besides, you have to dance with me."

"I can handle that."

The crowds were filling in, and the photographers had arrived. That meant Ty and Jenna weren't too far behind them. When she saw their parents arrive and take their seats, she stood, grasping Gavin's hand.

Soon the deejay announced the arrival of Mr. and Mrs. Tyler Anderson. A lump formed in Liz's throat at the thought of the two of them being married, and she blinked back tears as they entered the ballroom to loud applause from the guests.

They made such a beautiful couple. Liz couldn't be happier for her friend.

And as Jenna and Ty took the floor for their first dance, Gavin wrapped his arm around her waist while they watched Jenna and Ty sway to a beautiful love song. Just watching them look at each other, it was obvious they were so much in love.

Liz tilted her head back and smiled at Gavin. "I love you."

"I love you, too."

Her heart swelled and she felt like the luckiest woman in the world tonight. Even though it wasn't her wedding day, she felt reaffirmed in her love for Gavin.

Gavin grasped her hand when they asked the wedding party to take the floor for the next song. Now she was surrounded by family and friends, and she didn't even notice the photographer hovering close, because she only had eyes for her husband.

His fingers traveled down her back. "You look beautiful tonight."

"So do you. I have a weakness for a man in a tux."

"Just any man?"

"Oh, sure. Any random man in a tux that catches my eye will do. You know how easy I am."

He tugged her close and whispered in her ear. "I should spank you for that."

She laughed. "Promises, promises."

After the dance, everyone sat and had dinner, which gave Liz pause, but since her dizziness and nausea seemed to have disappeared, she decided to go ahead and eat.

Gavin looked over at her plate, then back at her. "You sure you're up for that?"

"Definitely. I really do think it was hot in the church, plus this dress is skintight. Add those two together, plus all the stress with the wedding and Christmas next week, and that's what got to me. I'm feeling a lot better now."

He leaned over and kissed her cheek. "Good. I hated the thought of you getting sick."

She was happy about that, too. She began to eat her meal, taking each bite slowly, gauging her body's reaction.

"You're certainly savoring each bite," Tara noticed after Gavin left to go get a beer.

Liz smiled. "It's fantastic food."

"I think so, too."

"Okay, so what do you think so far?" Jenna pulled up one of the empty chairs.

Liz squeezed her hand. "First, you made me cry during your ceremony today, you bitch. Second, you made a gorgeous bride. And third, this food is to die for."

"Everything Liz just said," Tara added with a nod.

Jenna grinned. "Thank you. Did you see my lip trembling when I was saying my vows to Ty? Oh, my God, I thought I was going to totally lose it and end up sobbing."

"I might have noticed that," Tara said.

"Why do you think *I* ended up crying? I don't think I teared up as much during my own wedding."

"Aww, Liz, you're becoming so sappy and sentimental," Jenna teased.

"Screw you. I am not. I'm a coldhearted bitch."

Tara patted her back. "Sure you are."

She glared at them. "I hate you both right now."

"It's no sin to be a marshmallow, you know. Especially around people you love."

Liz shot a look at Tara. "Fine. But in my professional life, I'll continue to be cold, calculating, and cutthroat."

"Of course you will," Jenna said with a firm nod. "We'd expect nothing less from you."

"Now that the wedding is over, I know you and Ty are looking forward to the honeymoon. Too bad it has to wait until after hockey season is over," Tara said.

Jenna shrugged. "We knew when we set the date that hockey season would be in full swing. We're fine with waiting. And this way we can enjoy two weeks in Tahiti after the Ice season is over."

"You're going to love it there," Liz said. "And it's a honeymoon worth waiting for."

Jenna smiled. "I think so."

Tara grasped Liz's arm. "Just look at that."

Liz followed Tara's gaze to the dance floor, where Nathan and Sonja were dancing. They looked gorgeous together, with Nathan looking much too grown-up in his suit and Sonja absolutely beautiful in a smoking-hot copper-colored cocktail dress.

And they only had eyes for each other.

"Awww, young love. It's so adorable," Jenna said.

Tara shot her a look. "Do you think they're in love?"

"I think they're hot for each other. One look at them and you can see that."

Tara worried her bottom lip. "On the one hand, I'm happy for him. I like Sonja. She's smart and levelheaded and I think she'll keep him on his toes."

"On the other hand, you don't want him to get hurt. Or lose his focus," Liz said.

Tara nodded.

"You do realize you can't protect him against everything." Jenna grasped Tara's hand. "He's going to grow up. He'll get hurt."

"I know. I'm not one of those clingy mothers who wants to hold on to her babies forever. He has to get out there and make his own way in the world."

"That's a good outlook," Jenna said. "But still, you want what's best for him."

"They do look good together, don't they?" Liz asked. "And maybe she's what's best for him right now. She seems to have all the right priorities."

"I hope so." Tara watched her son on the dance floor.

Liz turned to Tara. "I had a nice conversation with Sonja at your house. It seemed to me she had her head on straight. I think she really likes Nathan, but she's putting school first."

Tara took a deep breath. "That's what Nathan's told me. But you know how those hormones are."

"They won't screw it up, Tara. I know they won't."

Tara nodded at Liz. "I hope you're right about that. And in the end, he's an adult now. He has to make his choices—and live with them, right?"

Liz laughed. "So true. Just like we all did when we were that age."

"Lord, don't remind me," Tara said. "Hopefully he's listened to Mick and to me, and he won't repeat our mistakes."

"He's fine, Tara. He's awesome, in fact. Now let him get out there and become the amazing adult you know he's going to become," Jenna said with a big smile.

Tara's eyes brimmed with tears. "What would I do without you two?"

"You'd be lost, woman," Liz said. "Totally lost."

Tara laughed, then hugged them both.

The night passed in a whirlwind of photos and dancing and a lot of crowds. At least Liz's nausea had gone away, seemingly for good. She danced with her father-in-law and her brothers-in-law, as well as several of Ty's teammates. Her feet were sore, she was tired and sweating, and oh, dear God, if she didn't get out of this dress soon, she was certain it was going to compress some internal organs. She headed over to the table just to take a breather and sip from her glass of water.

This damn dress had fit only two weeks ago during the final fitting. She had to cut down on eating and maybe get a little more exercise.

Damn holidays. And dinners at her mother-in-law's house. She was enjoying delving into the pasta a little too much lately, and now she was paying the price.

She wanted to sit down and ease her shoes off under the table, and maybe just close her eyes for a second.

She wondered where Gavin was, but she couldn't find him through the sea of bodies on the dance floor. He was probably somewhere with the guys, no doubt talking sports.

They hadn't had sex today. They needed to have sex. If they had any chance at all of making a baby, it was important they keep up the daily sex routine. And yes, she was well aware she didn't ovulate thirty days out of the month, but her cycle was screwed up lately, and the best time to have sex was . . . all the time.

She smiled at the thought. Nothing wrong with practicing, was there? They'd certainly done plenty of that, and she had no complaints. She knew Gavin didn't.

Just the thought of touching him, kissing him, had her breasts swelling against her oh-my-God-this-dress-is-too-tight bodice.

Now all she had to do was find Gavin, and make a subtle suggestion . . .

GAVIN WAS GATHERED WITH THE GUYS AT THE BAR, knocking back another beer and listening to Cole and Mick talk about the games tomorrow. He was stuck in the middle of them grousing about linemen not covering plays and upcoming contract negotiations. But his gaze was on his wife, who leaned against the table and sipped water while she watched the dance floor.

Liz looked tired. He should take her upstairs. He knew she'd object, that she was determined to stay until every guest had left the ballroom. Though he didn't know why. This party could go on for a while.

He pushed off the bar and headed toward her, circumventing the dance floor and coming around the back of the tables. She hadn't seen him, though she was looking for him, her neck stretching as she lifted up on her toes to scan the room, which gave him a great view of her fantastic legs. She caught sight of him as he came up on her left and gave him a half smile.

"There you are. Were you at the bar?"

He laid his beer on the table and tugged her close. "I was. Listening to Mick and Cole talk football."

She rested her palm on his chest. "How . . . riveting."

"You can't imagine. How are you feeling?"

"Perfect. And you?"

"Restless. Want to dance?"

She shook her head. "I was actually thinking we could go someplace"—she looked around—"I was going to say private, but I don't think there's anyplace secluded in this ballroom."

"Doesn't look like it. Grab your purse and come with me." He took her hand and led her out of the ballroom and toward the elevators. They rode up to their floor.

"It's a little early to leave for the night."

He gave her a smile. "Just a short break."

He inserted the key and opened the door to their suite. Liz laid her bag on the table, went to the sofa, and sat. Gavin went to the bar and pulled out a bottle of sparkling water.

"You read my mind."

He opened the bottle and poured it into a glass he'd filled with ice and brought it over to her, kneeling in front of her as he handed her the glass.

"This looks promising," she said as she accepted the glass and took a sip.

Gavin lifted her foot and slipped off her shoes. "Again, I don't know why you torture yourself by wearing these heels."

Liz resisted the urge to groan. It felt so good to have those things off. "It was part of the uniform. All the women wore them today."

"You wear them every day."

"And you like my legs when I do."

He tucked the shoes aside and started massaging the balls of her feet. This time she did moan.

"I'd like your legs if you walked around in bunny slippers."

She laughed at that. "You would. But there's not a chance in hell that bunny slippers are in my future. Or my shoe closet."

"Some day you'll be huge and pregnant and then what'll you do? You'll topple over in those things." He motioned with his head toward her four-and-a-half-inch heels.

She couldn't help but lay her hand on her stomach and make a very fervent wish that that day would come. "I'll wear very stylish sandals. But not bunny slippers."

Gavin raised her leg up and pressed a kiss to her ankle. "This foot would be cute in slippers."

"Only if they're sexy kitten-heeled ones."

"You, my very delicious wife, have a fetish."

"So do you, my leg-obsessed husband."

He smoothed his hand over her calves. "You think so?"

"I know so."

"I have a fetish for you and your sexy body." He smoothed his hand over her dress, dragging it up and over her thighs. "And I have an obsession about your scent."

When he kissed her inner thigh, she gasped, unable to help the sounds that escaped her throat when he dragged her underwear down her legs. Her dress was oh-so-tight and she could barely breathe in it, so the fast, in-and-out pants Gavin's soft kisses along her inner thigh caused were only making it more difficult to catch a breath.

But she'd make any sacrifice if he'd only move his tongue closer. And when he scooted her butt to the edge of the sofa and put his mouth on her clit, she let out a whimper of sweet satisfaction.

"Oh, Gavin, yes. Right there." He was still fully dressed, and he looked so amazingly sexy in his tux with his head buried between her legs, his mouth doing delicious things to her pussy.

She gripped the edge of the sofa and lifted, giving him access, spreading her legs wider so he could slide his tongue along her folds. He captured the bud between his lips and sucked, and she was lost, shattering in a wild climax that left her shaking.

Then he was above her, kissing her with a deep, soulful kiss. He pulled her up and took her into the bedroom, his hand on the zipper of her dress as they made their way into the darkness of the room.

They didn't need lights on, just the touch of their hands on each other as Gavin pulled her zipper down. She breathed a sigh of relief as he pulled off her tight dress and laid it on the chair. She turned and undid his tie while he shrugged out of his jacket and went to work on the cuff links.

"Too many parts to this tux," she whispered, her body vibrating in anticipation of his touch.

Once his buttons were undone, she spread her hands over the warm expanse of his chest.

"I like you touching me," he said, reaching around to unclasp her bra and remove it.

She resisted the urge to moan in relief as her breasts spilled out. Being naked felt wonderful after feeling so restricted all day. She moved into Gavin and rubbed her breasts over his chest.

"I'm trying to get my pants off here, and you're distracting me," he grumbled.

She laughed. "Well hurry up."

He unzipped and dropped his pants, then lifted her into his arms. "You're impatient."

"Just a little."

He carried her to the bed and pulled back the cover, depositing her in the middle of the bed before coming down next to her. "Is that right?"

She rolled over to face him. "Yes. I've been wanting to get you alone all night."

He framed her face with his hands. "Now we're alone. And I'm all yours."

She reached down and grasped his cock in her hand, stroking him. "All of you, huh?"

She raised her leg over his hip and placed the tip of his cock at the entrance to her pussy. He pushed and entered her, but not fully.

"Gavin," she warned.

He gifted her with that wickedly devilish smile of his that never failed to make her shiver.

"Something you want?"

"Yeah. Your cock."

"I love when you get demanding. Take it."

She surged forward and slid onto his cock. Gavin gripped her hip and squeezed as she moved against him, but then he took over, thrusting ever so slowly, torturing her with his movements that never failed to make her wet, to make her pussy clench around his cock.

"Oh, babe . . . what you do to me," he said, spearing her again even as he swept her hair away from her face so he could kiss her.

Liz lost herself in Gavin's kiss, in the way he moved within her, his body grinding against hers and taking her right to the peak. And when he rolled her onto her back, deepening the pressure, she wrapped her legs tight around him to hold him where she needed him.

"Yes, there," she whispered, stroking her hands over his shoulders, tightening them on his arms when she felt her orgasm drawing near.

"That's it, babe," he said, deepening and quickening his strokes. He knew her so well, knew her body as well as she did, and recognized when she tightened around him that she was close to the edge. He knew just what to do to make her fall.

He slowed down, and rolled against her, rocking his body against her clit.

"Oh, yes, I'm coming." She arched against him and shattered.

Gavin slipped his hand under her butt, gripping her tightly as the waves of her climax electrified her. And when he shuddered against her and groaned, it only served to prolong her own orgasm.

When she could breathe again, she realized they were stuck together.

"I'm a mess," she said, sliding her fingers over his back. "I'll need a shower before we go back downstairs."

He rolled over and tugged her next to him. "Or . . . we could just stay here."

She pondered the thought. "You don't think we'd be missed?"

"I think they'll manage just fine without us."

It was a tempting thought. She was exhausted, and the thought of climbing back into that tight dress made her want to cry.

"Maybe we can just rest here for a few minutes. Then we'll clean up and go back downstairs."

"Sure, babe. Whatever you want to do."

She didn't make it five minutes before she was out cold.

TEN

GAVIN TOOK A DEEP BREATH AND COUNTED TO TEN.
Again.

It was Christmas Eve, and tomorrow, they'd have the whole
family over. Which meant for the past few days his wife had been
losing her goddamned mind.

He didn't see the big deal. The cleaning people had been here
yesterday, so the house looked great. They had all the food and
drink they could ever need, because Gavin had gone to the grocery
store at least twenty-five times in the past four days.

Okay, that might be an exaggeration, but it seemed like every
time he saw Liz, she handed him a grocery list. He had started to
hide from her.

Like now. He was currently in the basement TV room trying
to watch sports, and cringed when he heard her heels coming down
the wood stairs.

"Gavin? Are you down here?"

For a second, he actually thought about not saying anything. Maybe she'd think he'd left the house. But she'd eventually figure it out when she saw his truck in the garage.

"Yeah, babe. I'm here."

"Oh, good. I need you to go to the store for me."

Shit. He pushed off the chair and stood, then came around to the stairs to see her standing there.

"Seriously? We already own everything the grocery store has. What could you possibly need now?"

Throwing him a look, she waved a list back and forth. "You just have no idea the things I still need. Would you mind?"

If he said yes, he knew he'd be in for one hell of a lousy Christmas. "Sure. No problem. Just let me grab my coat and my keys."

"Great. Thanks."

He walked up the stairs, taking the list from her on his way. When he got to his truck, he looked at the list and mentally cursed.

Gruyère cheese? What the fuck was that?

Fresh cranberries. He was sure he'd just bought those yesterday. In fact, he was positive he had. He should go inside and double-check. He got out and went inside, and found Liz in the kitchen.

"I just bought cranberries yesterday."

She gave him a look like he was stupid. "Yes?"

"So . . . you need more?"

"Obviously."

"And what the hell is Gruyère cheese?"

"Just go to the deli. Melinda is working today. She'll help you."

"Fine."

"Oh. And stop at the liquor store and get one more bottle of that Australian Merlot Savannah and Cole like so much."

"We already have two bottles of that."

Again, she shot him one of those looks. "And your point?"

Count to ten. Count to ten. "Okay. I'll pick up another bottle."

He needed to get out of this house and away from Liz before one of them totally lost it. And by the looks she was giving him and his blood pressure, at this point he wasn't sure which one of them was going to explode first.

He was certain his mom didn't go to this much trouble when she had Christmas. Or maybe she did and he just wasn't aware of it.

He picked up his phone and dialed. His mom answered on the second ring.

"Hi, Gavin."

"Hi, Mom. How's it going?"

"It's going very well. I'm making a coconut cream pie. And how's it going over there?"

"Elizabeth is losing her ever-loving mind."

"Really? What's going on?"

He filled her in on Liz's craziness over the past few days, including his current trip to the grocery store to buy some crazy cheese and the repeat trips to buy things he'd already bought.

"Be patient with her, Gavin. This is her first time having the family over and she wants everything to be perfect."

"I don't remember you being stressed-out about having the family all these years."

"Well, not after doing it for thirty-some-odd years. But the first time I had Christmas for your father and his family? I broke out in hives and threw up the night before. Your poor father had to give me whiskey on Christmas Day just to calm me down."

He couldn't imagine his never-ruffled mother being afraid of anything. "You did not."

"I did. I imagine what's bothering Liz is just nervousness. She wants to satisfy everyone's tastes, and unfortunately, that's impossible to do. I'm going to finish up this pie and then drop by and see if there's anything I can do to help, providing you don't mind."

"I don't mind at all, and I think you can do a lot to ease her mind. Thanks, Mom."

"You're welcome."

After he hung up, he went to the store, got the cranberries and the damned cheese he couldn't pronounce. Then he stopped at the liquor store to buy yet another couple bottles of that wine that they'd undoubtedly have on hand until the end of time.

When he got home, Liz was bent over her laptop at the kitchen counter studying something in an online cookbook. He stored the wine and put the cheese and cranberries away. His first thought was to go hide in the basement again, but instead, he came up and kissed her on the cheek.

She lifted her face and frowned. "What's that for?"

"For having the family over tomorrow. I know this isn't easy for you and you're going to a lot of trouble to do it."

"Gavin, I love your family. They've been my family for even longer than you and I have been together. You know how much I've been wanting to do this."

"I know. But I don't want you to be stressed about it."

She laughed. "Not much you can do about that. It's a big deal to me and I want everything to be perfect."

He was about to tell her that perfection was overrated, though she likely wouldn't have listened to him anyway, when the doorbell rang.

Liz looked like she was about to have a panic attack. "Oh, shit. Who could possibly be here?"

"I have no idea, but relax. Whoever it is, I'll get rid of them."

"Thanks. I have to make this casserole."

He went to the front door and opened it.

"Hi, sweetie."

"Hi, Mom." He hugged and kissed his mother, and whispered to her, "I didn't tell Liz I called you."

She patted his shoulder. "Don't worry."

He followed his mother into the kitchen. When Liz looked up, she registered a combination of shock and dread. But then she managed a smile.

"Oh. Mom. Hi."

"Hi, Liz. I thought maybe you could use some help."

Liz's gaze flitted from his mother's to his. And he read the panic there.

"That sounds like a great idea, Mom," he said. "Though I think Liz is doing a fantastic job."

"Of course she is, but I'm always grateful for extra hands when I'm trying to do everything."

Thank God for his mother. "If you all don't need me, I'm going to get out of your way."

"That's a really good idea, son. We'll call you if we need you."

Liz didn't know whether she wanted to grab on to Gavin like a lifeline or kick his ass down the basement stairs. She'd wager anything he called his mother and told her she was losing her mind.

Which she was.

"How's it going here?"

"Oh . . . fine. I have the turkey cleaned and ready to go into the oven tomorrow morning. The side dishes are plotted out and well in hand. Some I'm prepping today, and others will be done tomorrow. I'm working on hors d'oeuvres right now."

"Hors d'ouevres?"

"Yes. I'm doing individual shrimp cocktails, stuffed figs, an olive and cheese spread, spinach and artichoke dip." She paused. "I know there's something else. Let me go grab my menu."

Mom nodded. "Uh-huh. You do realize it's just family, and that you're not serving Christmas dinner for the President of the United States, right?"

Liz laughed and waved her hand. "Of course. It's just that there're so many, and I want to make sure there's enough. Anyway, here's my list if you want to take a look and tell me if you think I'm missing anything."

Liz worried her bottom lip while Gavin's mom perused the list. When she looked up, Liz noted the look of concern on her face.

"Oh, crap. I've forgotten something, haven't I?"

"Yes. You've forgotten we're just the Rileys. We're very simple. Have you ever seen me serve anything like what's on this menu?"

"Well . . . no. But I thought I'd fancy it up a little."

"And there's nothing wrong with that, as long as you don't have a complete meltdown trying to do that. You know, once the family started to expand, I decided that holidays would be more like pot-luck, with everyone bringing a side dish. And I also enlisted help. Cara came over and started helping out with cooking the main dishes."

"Right. But I thought—"

"That you could manage doing it all yourself."

"Yes."

Kathleen took a seat at the island. "And how's that working out for you?"

Liz exhaled and leaned against the counter. "I feel like I'm about to drop. I'm so tired, Mom."

"So why are you doing all this?"

"I don't know. Because it's my first time, and I want everyone to be happy."

Her mother-in-law laughed. "Honey, no matter what you feed everyone, they'll be happy. It's Christmas, and we're all delighted to spend the day together with those we love. You could serve tur-key sandwiches and chips and we'd be content."

"I don't know about that, but maybe I have been overdoing it . . . a little."

Kathleen perused the epic disaster that was Liz's countertops and cocked her head to the side. "A little?"

"Okay . . . a lot. Gavin called you and said I was making him crazy, didn't he?"

"I refuse to answer that question on the grounds you might be angry with him."

Liz laughed. "I couldn't possibly be angry with him, since I'm so happy you're here."

"I've been offering to help you for weeks now, and you kept saying no."

"I know. I'm so sorry. I wanted to be the perfect daughter-in-law and do it all by myself."

Kathleen slid off the barstool, came around the island, and pulled

Liz into her arms. "You've always been the perfect daughter-in-law. You love my son and he loves you. It's all I will ever ask for."

Liz batted back tears. "I love you, Mom."

"I love you, too."

Liz took a look at her menu, then at her mother-in-law. "Okay, so help me out here and tell me how I can scale some of this back so I'm not hiding in a corner by tomorrow."

BY EARLY EVENING, GAVIN'S MOM HAD LEFT AND HE'D helped Liz finish up the last of the prep for tomorrow's meal. Then he'd done all the dishes and cleaned the kitchen. After that he'd gone out and picked up a pizza, because the last thing his wife needed was to cook dinner tonight or have anything else in the kitchen to have to clean up.

They had curled up in front of the television to watch a holiday movie. Liz was lying on the couch, her head in his lap. After the movie finished, she flipped over to look up at him.

"Have I mentioned today that you're my hero?"

"Uh, no, you haven't. What brought this on?"

"You got me a pizza. If I never see the kitchen again, it'll be too soon."

He rubbed his hand along her hip. "I told you I'd help you cook everything. You know I don't mind being in the kitchen, and I like to cook."

"I know you do, but this is my thing, and I volunteered to do it, so I'm going to suck it up and do it by myself."

"But you're not by yourself anymore. You have a partner to help. So you should let me be there for you. I can toss a turkey in the oven and peel and mash potatoes and do anything else you need me to do."

She finally nodded. "You're right. I guess I've bitten off more than I can chew, and I need some help."

"I'll be happy to be your bitch tomorrow."

She laughed. "I'm going to remember you said that."

They started another movie, and Gavin continued to move his hand along Liz's hip. She kneaded his leg, which made his dick hard. Hell, anytime she touched him, he got hard.

"Your erection is poking my head," she said, not turning away from the TV.

"Is it bothering you?"

"Immensely."

"I guess you could do something about that."

"I could, couldn't I?" She shifted, using her hand to lazily rub his shaft through his jeans.

Gavin spread his legs, in no hurry to get to the action. He enjoyed watching Liz touch him, even if it was through denim. He couldn't concentrate on the movie, though, because her head in his lap gave him definite ideas.

"If you unzipped me, you could put your mouth on me."

She didn't answer. In fact, she'd stopped touching him, too.

"Okay, how about if I do you first."

No reply.

"Liz?"

Her breaths had become deep and even, and when he leaned forward he realized she'd fallen asleep.

He smiled and shook his head. His poor, exhausted wife had finally given in and passed out.

He threaded his fingers through her hair. He'd always loved her hair. That beautiful natural red hair of hers had always been a turn-on for him, even when he'd been her client and she'd been his agent. She'd been a brilliant smart-ass with great legs and he'd admired the hell out of her, both for her talent and intelligence as well as her beauty.

They'd had one hell of a wild ride getting together. She'd pissed him off and challenged the hell out of him, doing everything in her power to drive him away. But he'd wanted her, and he'd been damned determined to have her.

Now he couldn't imagine a day of his life without her by his side. She was his rock of fortitude when things got rough for him, could always be counted on to calm the raging waters of his life.

He loved her like he never thought he could love a woman.

She sighed and curled her body up tighter, like she was cold. He dragged the blanket off the back of the sofa and covered her.

And while she might project a tough exterior, there was a vulnerability to her that never failed to bring out his protective instincts. He'd do anything to give her everything she wanted, including the baby she was convinced *he* wanted, when he knew damn well she was the one who wanted one with every part of her body.

He looked down at her and brushed a curl behind her ear. She looked pale, and he wondered if she was still secretly fighting that flu bug. Or maybe she was just tired.

She'd been working way too hard lately. And even though it wasn't even ten o'clock yet, there was no way in hell he was going to wake her. He settled in against the sofa and decided he'd finish watching the movie, and then he'd carry his wife up to bed.

She needed the rest, because tomorrow was going to be a long day.

ELEVEN

SOMETHING HARD POKED AGAINST LIZ'S BUTT. SHE blinked her eyes open, smiling as she recognized immediately what it was.

She vaguely remembered Gavin waking her up last night as he carried her to bed. She had practically sleep-walked through brushing her teeth and taking off her clothes before falling into bed and right back to sleep.

She did, however, remember that before she'd utterly passed out, she'd been rubbing his cock, making promises that her worn-out body had obviously been unable to keep.

This morning, however, was another matter entirely.

She wriggled against him. "Is this my early morning Christmas present?"

"Yes. How do you like it?"

"Mmm, I love it." Her breasts tingled and her pussy quivered as she anticipated him sliding his cock inside her.

And when he did, she was wet and ready for him, her body quaking as he entered her.

They made love slowly, Gavin easing in and partially withdrawing. It was a perfect way to wake up. And when he reached around to strum her clit with his fingers, she arched into his hand, letting him coax a delicious response from her. Tension coiled all too easily and she climaxed with an unabandoned cry, Gavin coming at the same time.

He held her, kissing her shoulder and stroking her hip as they settled.

"Merry Christmas, beautiful," he said.

"Merry Christmas." She got up and turned to brush a kiss on his lips. "I'm going to go take a shower."

"Okay." He grabbed the remote and turned on the TV. "I'll get in after you're done."

She went into the bathroom and closed the door, then turned on the shower. She was waiting for the water to heat up when a sudden, overwhelming burst of nausea hit her out of nowhere. She was shocked when she threw up, then held on to the counter when she stood, feeling weak, shaky, and utterly bewildered.

She brushed her teeth, rinsed her mouth, and climbed into the shower, ready to dash out just in case it happened again. But she managed to make it through her shower without incident.

When she got out, she wondered what the hell had just happened. Surely . . .

No. It couldn't be, could it? She counted back weeks. She'd had a period . . . sort of. Maybe a day, and it was light, which wasn't like her, but she'd figured it was stress. In a hurry, her fingers shaking, she dove into the cabinet for the store of pregnancy tests she kept on hand. She ripped open the package, wondering whether or not to even attempt it. If it wasn't what she thought, she'd end up with the worst Christmas ever.

But she'd drive herself crazy wondering, so she might as well get it over with. She peed on the stick and set the timer on her phone she'd left on the bathroom counter last night, hoping Gavin wouldn't walk in on her. To be on the safe side, she locked the door. This way, only she'd be disappointed, and he'd never know.

It was the longest few minutes of her life. She combed out her hair and tried to still her shaking limbs, no doubt an aftereffect of her recent illness.

She probably had the goddamn flu, and she was going to kick herself for even thinking otherwise.

The timer ran out. She looked over at the stick, not wanting to turn it over, a year's worth of disappointment a reminder of what was likely to happen.

Just do it, Liz. You're not a coward, and you'll deal with it, just like you've been dealing with it before.

She took a deep breath, and turned the stick over.

Pregnant.

Holy. Shit.

"Holy shit!"

"Liz? You okay in there?"

She looked at herself in the mirror, and grinned. The nausea and dizziness she'd felt the night of the wedding, her dress feeling too tight, and this morning's barf-o-rama. It all made sense now. She was pregnant. Thank you, God, she was pregnant.

She grabbed the stick and threw open the bathroom door and ran into the bedroom, then leaped on the bed.

"Gavin, we're pregnant!"

He shot up in bed. "What?"

"Look!" She handed him the stick.

He looked at it, then at her, his eyes wide. "Holy shit."

"That's what I said."

And then he grinned. "We're pregnant, babe."

And she grinned back. "I know."

He pulled her across his lap and kissed her—a long, glorious, we're-pregnant kiss that curled her toes and caused tears to prick her eyes. When he pulled back, he looked at her. "Our baby is going to look just like you."

"Or just like you."

"I love you, Elizabeth Riley."

"I love you, too, Gavin Riley."

"We have to get through Christmas now."

"Oh, shit. That's right. I don't even care anymore. This is the best day ever."

He laughed. "Yes, it is."

She leaped off the bed. "I have to get dressed. And you have to take a shower."

He got out of bed. "Okay." And then he stopped and turned to her. "How did you know to take a test this morning?"

"I threw up."

He grinned. "Awesome."

TRUE TO HIS WORD, GAVIN HELPED HER WITH THE food prep. Which was good, because oh, she was sick. After her initial euphoria faded, the nausea returned. And being surrounded by food didn't help.

Despite her protests, Gavin called in his mother and his aunt for help. He told them Liz was under the weather and the last thing she needed was to be surrounded by food. They both showed up within an hour and Gavin, his mom, and his aunt basically took over her kitchen. Under normal circumstances, she'd have vehemently objected, but after throwing up all morning, she was more than happy to surrender her kitchen to all of them while she headed upstairs to lie down.

After a two-hour nap she felt a lot better, and when she got up, the nausea was gone. She came downstairs and inhaled some wonderful scents emanating from her kitchen.

"It smells so good in here," she said.

Her mother-in-law smiled at her. "Oh, you're awake. And there's some color in your cheeks now. How are you feeling?"

"Much better, thank you. Where's Gavin?"

"He's over at my house picking up Dad. No sense in us having two cars."

"Thank you both for helping out. I'm so sorry I wasn't able to handle this."

"It's tough when you're in your first trimester. The smell of food is an awful trigger," Gavin's aunt said.

Liz didn't know what to say. "Did Gavin tell you?"

Kathleen laughed. "He didn't have to. You've been pale and nauseated for weeks."

"Plus, you just have a pregnant look about you," Cara said.

"I do?"

Kathleen nodded. "You definitely do. And congratulations, honey."

Liz took a seat at the bar. "Thank you. We just found out this morning. Apparently I wasn't as adept at recognizing the signals."

"Well, you've had a lot on your mind lately, so I'm not surprised. We women are the worst at reading our own bodies sometimes."

She nodded at her mother-in-law.

"So how far along are you?" Gavin's aunt asked.

"I'm not sure. I had a period last month, but it was only a little spotting at best. I thought I might be pregnant then, but the test was negative."

"Best you go see your doctor. He'll do an exam and tell you for sure."

"My dress at the wedding was tight. And when I looked at myself this morning, it's like there's this little belly that wasn't there before." She put her hand on her stomach. "I thought I was just putting on weight. How could I not have noticed that?"

"Like I said, we're not good at recognizing our own body's signals," Kathleen said.

Cara nodded. "But now you're going to notice everything. Like how fast your clothes are not going to fit."

"And how nauseated you'll get. And how your tastes in food will change."

Liz chatted with Kathleen and Cara while they cooked, and was so grateful for their help. When Gavin came back home with his dad, they settled in the living room to watch sports, but Gavin stepped in to see if he could help.

"How's that flu?" he asked, wrapping his arm around her to kiss her cheek.

"Cat's out of the bag. They know."

"Please," his mom said. "Give us some credit, Gavin. We've both been pregnant."

"Oh. Sorry. Liz and I didn't have a chance to talk about who we were going to tell and when."

"Understood." His mom came around the island and placed her hands on his cheeks. "Neither Cara nor I will say a word until you and Liz are ready to announce it. But congratulations. I'm so thrilled I'm going to be a grandma again."

He smiled. "Thanks, Mom."

After a while, everyone began spilling in. Liz didn't know why she'd worked herself into such a neurotic mess. Just as it was at Gavin's house, everyone was casual and relaxed, and of course, more than willing to pitch in and help with the cooking. While the guys worked on carving the turkey, the women set out all the side dishes.

The food was a veritable feast, and Liz could barely eat a bite of it.

"Tell me you're not dieting on Christmas Day," Jenna said, eyeing her barely touched plate.

"Hardly. You know I love food."

"All you did was push it from one side to the other."

Gavin speared one of the slices of turkey she hadn't eaten. "My guess is she stuffed herself prepping it all, and now she's too full to eat what's on her plate."

She could have kissed him. "You're not supposed to divulge my secrets."

"It's always a cook's prerogative to sample the food before it's served," his mother said with a wink.

"Well, it's all fabulous," Savannah said. "Thank you, Liz."

"You're welcome. Kathleen and Cara helped. So did Gavin."

"She lies. She did most of it herself," Gavin said. "The only thing I did was utilize my expert turkey-carving skills."

"He tried to slice his finger off with the electric knife," Mick said. "Thank God I was there to save him, or his career would have been over."

Gavin rolled his eyes. "In your dreams. My knifing skills are legendary."

"Yeah. In your own mind."

After dinner, Kathleen declared that the men were in charge of putting away the leftovers and loading the dishwasher. Despite much grumbling about missing the game, the guys headed into the kitchen to do their duties while the women settled into the family room.

"How have you been feeling since the wedding?" Tara asked her.

"Oh . . . fine."

"Really? No ill effects from that flu bug?"

"No. Not really."

Tara gave her a look. "Are you sure? Because you still look a little pale to me."

"Actually, you are a little pale, Liz," Alicia said. "There are a lot of people out sick on our therapy team with the flu. God, it's been awful. I've been hoping I don't get it."

"No, I don't have the flu."

"So, how far along are you?" Tara asked with a knowing smile.

"Excuse me?"

"You're pregnant? How did I not know this?" Jenna looked affronted.

And Liz knew she'd never be able to hide this from the women she held so dear. She gave them all a smile. "Actually, I just took a test this morning, and it said I was pregnant."

"Seriously? That's awesome," Alicia said. "Congratulations!"

Then she was surrounded by everyone and hugged. She couldn't help but smile and laugh and shed a few tears.

"Dammit, you're all making me weepy and emotional, and you know I hate that shit."

"Well, get used to it. It'll get worse before it gets better," Tara said. "I was a water faucet and an emotional basket case when I was pregnant with Sam."

"I'm going to get a grip here very soon. I don't intend to let hormones get the best of me."

Kathleen laughed. "Good luck with that, sweetheart. I don't think you get to control your hormones when you're pregnant."

She lifted her chin. "I refuse to let my body take over. It's bad enough I'm throwing up."

"It's only the first trimester," Alicia said. "After that, you'll be back to normal again."

She didn't think anything would ever be normal again. Her life—her and Gavin's lives—was about to change forever.

Surprisingly, and considering it was late December, the day had turned out beautifully. No snow, and it was in the fifties, so the guys went outside to shoot baskets. After that, everyone came inside for dessert.

Kathleen's coconut cream pie was a big hit. Liz had made pecan pie, which everyone loved, and Savannah had made a peach pie that was to die for. Though she wasn't hungry, Liz had to sample everything.

"And now I'm so full I think I'm going to explode," she said.

"Think how awesome it's going to be not to have to suck in your stomach anymore," Jenna said.

Liz laughed. "You're right. That's the most awesome thing ever." She rubbed her belly. "Thanks, baby. My diet is officially over for at least the next, I don't know, seven months or so."

They all opened gifts, and then everyone left early in the eve-ning, which suited her just fine. She loved Gavin's family—her family—but it had been one hell of a long day and she was utterly exhausted. Plus, after finding out she was pregnant, she wanted some time alone with her husband.

After they said good-bye to the last of the family, she and Gavin shut and locked the door. He slipped his arm around her waist and tugged her close, then brushed his lips against hers. She melted into him and took the moment to breathe in his scent, then laid her head against his chest.

"Thank you," she said, wrapping her arms around him.

"For what?"

"For loving me. For marrying me. For giving me a baby."

He tipped her chin up with his fingers, forcing her to meet his gaze. "How about I thank you? I was watching you when you fell asleep on my lap last night, thinking about how much my life has changed since I fell in love with you. And how much I want to make you happy."

Her eyes filled with tears. Gavin swiped them from her cheeks and kissed her again.

"You've already made all my dreams come true."

He laid his hand on her belly. "This is it, babe. You and me—parents. Think we can handle it?"

"I know you'll make a wonderful father. Now me as a mom? The poor kid."

"I don't know if I've ever known anyone with a deeper capacity to love than you. Our child is very lucky to have you as a mother."

All those years she'd fought so hard to become just as successful as her male counterparts in the sports world. She'd won that battle, but she'd never thought she'd have the man of her dreams.

She'd made so many mistakes along the way, and she'd almost lost Gavin. But he'd been there for her when she'd needed him the most, and he'd seen through all her bullshit and had wanted her anyway. She'd be forever grateful to him for busting through her walls and getting to her heart.

They spent some time sitting together around the Christmas tree, enjoying the quiet of the house and the twinkling lights.

"It's been a perfect day," Gavin said.

"A rough start to it, yet a happy one."

"You ready for bed?" he asked.

She nodded, and they turned off the lights and started up the stairs.

"You're off the hook now, you know," she said as they got into the bedroom.

He frowned. "Huh?"

"Well, now that I'm pregnant, I won't be after you to have sex with me every day."

"So now that you've used me for my baby-making abilities, you're casting me aside like a used condom?"

She laughed. "Yeah, it was good while it lasted, but we're through."

He picked her up and set her on the bed. "Nice try, Elizabeth." He loomed over her and tugged at her pants. "But I'm nowhere near through with you."

She reached for him to pull him against her. "And that's why I love you, Gavin."

Because she knew no matter how long they were together, every time would be as fresh, new, and exciting as the first time.

And the best was yet to come.

HOLIDAY ON ICE

ONE

PATRICK "TRICK" NIEMEYER WALKED INTO MCGILL'S, his favorite after-game bar hangout, with several of his fellow players.

It had been a grueling game tonight, and they'd eked out a win by only one goal over Winnipeg. Since it was Friday night and they were on home turf, they deserved to celebrate.

"I need a drink—or three," Drew Hogan said.

He and Drew were of like minds there, which didn't surprise him since they were friends and had been as long as they'd both played for the New York Travelers.

"Let's get this party started." Trick led the way to the bar.

"How many of us are having beer?" Avery Mangino, their goalie and the main reason they'd won tonight, turned and counted as all of them raised fingers.

"Okay, that's a half dozen." Avery turned to the bartender, who slid bottles across.

Trick took a long draw from the bottle, then sighed. Nice and cold, like the ice had been tonight. But the crowd had been hot, and so had the game. They'd had to work hard for this win, and it had been a nail-biter all the way to the buzzer at the end of the third period.

"We need to avoid these close ones," Avery said, leaning against the bar. "You all are going to have to score more goals next time."

"It's Trick's fault," Drew said. "He let that asshole steal the puck on a power play and slide one past you."

"I agree," Boyd Litman said. "Let's blame Trick."

"I don't know," Trick said. "You looked a little slow, Boyd. Stay up past your bedtime last night?"

"I say we blame the defense," Drew said.

Avery frowned. "Don't mess with my defense."

"Someone fucking with us?" Colin Kozlow slung an arm around Avery's shoulder. "If it wasn't for us, we'd have been down by several goals since you pansies could only sink two in the net tonight."

They spent at least a half hour giving each other shit, ordered up a few more beers, then set up at the pool table. Nothing like winding down after a particularly grueling game.

Trick had found a comfortable spot leaning against the wall, watching the guys take their shots, when the door opened and two women walked in. Not that women being in the bar was unusual, but these two caught his eye.

He noticed the blonde right away. Tall, with short hair and big blue eyes, she stood out even across the room. She was slender, and wore black leather boots over skintight jeans. She had on a long coat that hid the rest of her body, but Trick knew that body well, just like he knew the woman well.

Stella Slovinski.

He hadn't seen her in a while. They'd been hot and heavy on and off for several months late last year, and some earlier this year, and then they'd lost touch. She was a dancer, and about as busy as he was during his season. It had been a no-strings kind of thing, just the way he'd wanted it, and so had she.

He couldn't even remember why they'd stopped seeing each other.

Jobs, probably.

He sure liked seeing her right now. So did every other guy in the place. Stella was the kind of woman who commanded a man's attention without even trying. It was the way she moved, with a confidence and grace like she didn't give a shit if a man looked, but she had to know they were all looking.

She didn't make eye contact, in fact was laughing with her female friend as they grabbed a table at the opposite corner of the room. She shrugged out of her coat, and he saw she was wearing a body-hugging top.

She'd lost some weight since the last time he saw her, which was . . .

Hell . . . March, maybe? He'd been at the tail end of his season, and busy, trying to make the playoffs, working his ass off. He hadn't called her. She hadn't called him.

And then the Travelers had lost in the playoffs, and he'd taken time off, gone to visit his mom. He'd taken a vacation, done some endorsements, and he'd still never heard from Stella. It wasn't like they'd even dated. It had been more like a series of hookups.

Fun ones, too. His lips curved at the thought.

"You're up, Trick," Avery said.

He took his shot, and when he finished, he grabbed another beer and took up his spot against the wall, trying not to look at Stella, while still watching her.

Stella was deep in conversation with her friend and hadn't once looked his way.

He wanted to talk to her. It would be polite to go over and at least say hello, right? Otherwise, he'd be rude, and he wasn't an asshole. They knew each other, and he'd at least spotted her. If nothing else, they could put their relationship to bed.

So to speak.

He pushed off the wall and headed her way.

"SO THEN HE SAID— OH, SHIT."

Stella arched her brow at Greta's curse. "Oh, shit . . . what?"

"Oh, shit, you have *got* to check out the hot guy heading our way. And he's got eyes only for you."

She dragged her gaze away from Greta, and on . . .

"Oh. That's Trick."

"You know him?"

Her lips curved. "I most definitely know him."

She stood just as Trick got to their table. "Well, hi. I didn't know you'd be in here tonight."

He smiled back at her. "This is my favorite bar, remember?"

"I actually did remember that just now." She turned. "This is Trick. Trick, this is my sister, Greta."

Greta stood and shook Trick's hand.

"Nice to meet you, Greta."

"You, too, Trick."

Stella motioned for Trick to take a seat. He stretched out his long, oh-so-fine body next to hers.

It had been a long time. She normally never missed guys she'd slept with, but Trick? She'd missed having him in her bed.

"I didn't know you had a sister." He looked them over. Greta was pretty, blonde like her sister, with her hair worn longer and pulled back in a ponytail. Their facial features were similar, and they both had those striking blue eyes, though Greta's were a darker blue.

"She's visiting from out of town."

Trick made sure to give Greta some attention. "Is that right? And where is out of town, Greta?"

"Currently, I'm in D.C., but I'm in town for a job interview, so if it all goes well I might be moving here to New York City."

He grinned. "Great time of year for it, too. All the decorations are up for the Christmas holidays."

"I know. I've been gawking at everything and Stella has been showing me all the holiday sights. It's fantastic. The tree at Rockefeller Center is amazing. And the window displays are works of art. I love it!"

"I'm sure having you move up here would make Stella happy."

"It would make Stella *very* happy," Stella said with a grin. "Now we just have to hope she didn't bomb the interview."

"Hey," Greta said. "I totally aced it."

"Where are you interviewing?"

"A PR firm."

"And she's right. I'm sure she did ace it," Stella said.

"Did they say when they'd get back to you?"

"Surprisingly, by the end of the week," Greta said. "Usually these things take a while, but I'm the last candidate they interviewed. I talked to the head of the firm as well as the VP. I'm hopeful."

"She's very good at her job," Stella said.

Trick liked that Stella pumped up her sister. "So you're staying the weekend, Greta?"

"I am. And what do you do, Trick?"

"Hockey player."

Greta frowned for a few seconds, then her eyes widened. "Ohhh, of course. I should have known. You have the fierce, competitive look about you."

"Do you like hockey?"

"I love hockey. As a matter of fact—"

"Yes. She loves hockey," Stella said, interrupting her sister. "So maybe you can hook her up with some tickets if she gets the job and moves up here."

"I'd be happy to."

Greta shot a bemused look at Stella. "So . . . how do you and Trick know each other?"

Stella shrugged. "Oh, Trick and I go way back. We're old friends."

"Is that right? Knowing how much of a hockey fan you are, Stell, I don't doubt that. So you've been to his games?"

"A few." Stella gave him a knowing smile. "I'm kind of a fan."

Trick laughed. "We actually met through one of my teammates. Stella's a friend of Carolina Preston, and she was dating Drew Hogan."

Greta leaned back in her chair and picked up her drink, taking a sip through her straw. "Interesting. How come you never told me this?"

Stella shrugged. "Not much to tell."

It was obvious Stella didn't want her sister to know about what went down between them. He got that. Sometimes your sex life was your business, and he wasn't about to reveal anything.

He stood. "I won't take up any more of your time. Good to see you again, Stella."

"You, too, Trick."

"And great to meet you, Greta."

"Same here."

He walked away, wishing he could have had some alone time with Stella, but this wasn't the right time or place. She needed to spend time with her sister, and he needed to get back to his friends.

It was good to see her again, though, and it reminded him how much he liked being with her.

He wanted to see her again. The question was—did she feel the same way?

STELLA RESISTED THE URGE TO WATCH TRICK WALK away, knowing the view would be spectacular.

For some reason, when they chose this bar, she hadn't expected Trick and his friends to be here. How stupid of her. Maybe subconsciously . . .

Greta grasped her wrist. "You did not tell me you knew Trick.

And you could have introduced him as Patrick Niemeyer of the Travelers. I don't know how I missed that connection when he walked up. Probably because I've only ever seen him before in uniform."

She leveled a benign gaze on her sister. "Yes. I know Trick."

"Is that why you took me to the hockey game tonight?"

"No. I took you to the game because we both like hockey."

"Uh huh." Her sister tapped her nails on the table, studying her, then her eyes widened. "Oh, my God, Stella. Did you have a thing with him?"

"Define 'thing.'"

Greta rolled her eyes. "Now you're being coy, and you're never coy about men. Spill it."

Having a little sister had always been great. They were only a few months over a year apart, and it had been fabulous growing up together. But it also meant Stella had very few secrets. Though she had managed to keep a couple.

Trick had been one of them.

She waved her hand back and forth. "It was no big deal. We hooked up off and on for a while late last year. It ran its course."

Greta searched the bar, her attention settling on Trick and his friends. "I don't think it has run its course at all. Not for him and definitely not for you. I saw your eyes light up when he came to our table."

Stella tracked Greta's gaze, and found Trick leaning against the wall, pool cue in his hand. It just so happened right at that moment he looked over. His lips ticked up and she felt the shot of heat all the way across the room.

"See? See? I told you," Greta said. "God, I can almost feel that zap of chemistry between the two of you. So why aren't you still seeing each other?"

"I don't date. You know that. I'm too busy dancing."

Greta sighed. "Come on, Stell. It can't always be about work. You're entitled to have some fun."

"Believe me, I manage time for fun. I just don't do long-term fun with one guy."

"You have weird rules." Greta stirred her drink. "Why not do a long-term thing?"

She didn't want to think about how badly that had turned out the one and only time she had allowed a man into her heart. The way she did it now was much better. "Because I've been building my career, and men get in the way of that. They're fun for sex when I need it, and nothing more than that."

"That sounds cold and lonely."

Stella laughed. "Honey, I am rarely cold and lonely. I can get a man when I need one."

"So, random hookups? Bleh."

"Hey, I don't see you towing a man behind you right now, sis."

"And you won't. After that debacle with Richard, I need a break."

Stella wrinkled her nose. "Richard was an asshole who didn't appreciate you."

Greta raised her glass. "I'll drink to that, and enough on the topic of my dickhead ex-boyfriend. I'd much rather talk about all those hot hockey players over there. How many of them do you know?"

Stella took a sip of her beer, then smiled at her sister, who could probably use a really fun night. "Uh, all of them."

Greta slanted her a look of disbelief. "You are lying to me."

"I'm not."

Greta pushed her chair back and stood. "Come on. You're introducing me to them."

Stella laughed. It was a good thing she and Trick were still on great terms, because she was entering the fray once again.

Not that she minded. She wanted more time to talk to Trick, and this was her way to do it without strings.

And who knows? Maybe her subconscious did bring her to this bar tonight for a reason.

Maybe it was time to hook up with Trick again. She didn't know why they'd lost touch before, but he was the right kind of man for her—the kind who would enjoy playing, but didn't want attachments.

She was all for that.

TWO

TRICK SAW STELLA AND HER SISTER APPROACHING, so he put up his cue and headed their way.

"We saw you had a game going, and Greta wanted to meet the guys," Stella said.

Man, she looked good in her tight jeans and black leather boots, and the clingy top did nothing to hide that killer body of hers. He really wanted to gather her up in his arms and take a taste of her. Too bad they were in public.

"We were at the game tonight," Greta said, motioning to her sister. "Something Stella failed to mention."

Trick shifted his attention to Greta, before looking again at Stella. "You came to the game? You should have texted me. I would have gotten you tickets."

"I didn't want you to think I was going to hit you up again after all these months just for tickets."

"Why? We're friends, Stell. I'd be happy to give you tickets."

Greta elbowed her sister. "See? He'd be happy to give you tickets." Greta gave him a hopeful look. "I don't suppose there's a game tomorrow night."

"Sorry. I have the weekend off. But once you get that job, you can have tickets anytime you want."

Greta grinned. "Awesome. Now you can introduce me to all your friends."

"That I can definitely do." He swung an arm around Greta's waist and pulled her into the crowd. Stella hung back, waving at Drew, Avery, Boyd, and the rest of them. She and Trick would often go out after games and have a few drinks with the guys, before hitting up either her place or his for a wild romp of some amazing sex.

Just thinking about his hands and his mouth on her made her regret losing touch. But one of her rules was she never went back for seconds once a fling was over, because that might just mean emotional involvement, and that she just wouldn't do.

But Trick was fun and easy and sexy and hot and not at all demanding of her time. He understood her life as a dancer, how much of her days—and often nights—it commanded. He didn't whine or pout when she had to cancel on him. He traveled a lot, so he knew work took precedence over everything—including sex.

In a lot of ways, he'd been the perfect non-boyfriend.

So why had they stopped seeing each other earlier this year? She'd been slammed with performances for the show she'd been doing, and he'd been so busy with the end of hockey season, trying to make the playoffs. They hadn't had much time for each other and had to keep canceling. That much she remembered. They'd just drifted apart.

It happened.

After her show ended she'd taken some time off—but only a couple of weeks before she'd started auditioning again. There was no such thing as time off for a dancer. If you didn't work, you didn't eat or pay the rent. She really liked eating and enjoyed having a roof over her head.

She'd auditioned for a lead dance role in a new show on Broadway, and after a ridiculous amount of auditions, had gotten the part. Now she was even busier, but still . . . it had been a long time since she'd played with a hot guy.

Trick was definitely a hot guy. She watched him as he shot pool with his friends. He was tall, muscular, but not too much in that body-builder way. Just enough that he was strong. He wore jeans and a long-sleeve Henley, which showed off every one of those muscles, especially his biceps.

Plus, he had a fantastic back. Being a dancer, there was just something about a man's back that she found enticing. So much strength there, and in the arms and legs.

She'd seen Trick naked, knew everything about his body.

A flash of heat engulfed her, and after he took his shot, he turned and gave her a look that was pure sexual attraction.

Yes, it was still there between them. He grabbed his beer, laid his pool cue aside, and came over to her.

"Not playing?" he asked.

"I'm content to just watch."

"Your sister seems happy in the mix."

Stella's gaze drifted over to the pool table, where Avery was helping Greta line up a shot. "My sister knows how to play pool, but she's enjoying letting Avery put his hands on her."

"I'm sure Avery doesn't mind."

Stella nodded. "I'm sure he doesn't, either." She shifted her gaze back to Trick. "Greta broke up with her boyfriend recently. A real jerk. She could use some attention from a nice guy."

"Avery's a nice guy."

"I know."

Trick slid onto the barstool next to hers. "So am I."

She swiveled to face him, sliding her legs between his. "Oh, no, you're not. You can be very bad."

"You think so?"

"Definitely."

"You like me bad."

Stella laughed. "And this is a lot like verbal foreplay."

He slid his hands across her knees and down her legs. "I prefer the other kind of foreplay. Why don't you go home with me tonight?"

She drew in a breath. "As tempting as that sounds, I need to entertain my sister."

Trick looked over at the pool table. "Your sister looks like she's being entertained just fine by Avery."

"You know, if it was anyone else I'd say fine, they're on their own. But I haven't seen Greta for a few months and I promised her we'd spend the entire weekend together."

He nodded. "I understand. But I want to see you again, Stell."

This went against all her rules. But his touch seared through the denim of her jeans. "I want to see you, too. When's your next game?"

"Tuesday night. It's an away game, though. I'll be back in town on Thursday."

"Okay. I have rehearsal on Thursday until late."

His lips curved. "This is why we lost touch before. Those damn schedules of ours."

"True. But we'll figure it out."

"I'll text you when I get back in town."

"You do that." She slid off the barstool. "In the meantime, I intend to kick everyone's ass at the pool table."

He laced his hands with hers and drew her against him. "You can try. And until next week . . ."

Before she could object about being in a public bar and her sister being there, he'd cupped the nape of her neck and held her still while his mouth bore down on hers for a kiss that seared her feet to the floor.

It was everything she remembered about why she'd liked being with him—and so much more. A desperation, a hunger, a need that fed her desire as well. Before she knew what was happening, she was up on her toes, her body pressed to his, and his arm was around her waist, his fingers sliding down her back, nearly coming into contact with her butt.

"Holy shit," she heard her sister say, and that broke the spell.

But only barely. If there'd been anyone else but her sister there, she wouldn't have cared.

Trick looked down at her, and she was lost in the whiskey depths of his eyes. He smiled down at her.

"Next week, Stella."

She licked her lips. "Yeah. Next week."

THREE

STELLA STRETCHED AND WIPED SWEAT FROM HER brow. It had been a grueling dance practice today, worse than usual. The choreographer was kicking their asses. There were twelve dances in this show, and as one of the leads, she was front and center in all of them.

Not that she was going to complain. A career dancer never bitched about getting work. She'd deal with sore feet and screaming muscles every day as long as she had a job like this one. It wasn't all that often that she booked a show on Broadway, and the more exposure like this she could get, the better it was for her career.

Plus, she loved what she did. Dance wasn't just her job. It was part of her soul. She couldn't imagine not doing this. At the end of every rehearsal day, she felt equal parts brutalized and euphoric.

But right now, all she wanted was a long hot bath and a beer. Or a six-pack.

Okay, one beer, since Lawrence the bastard choreographer seemed to have a sixth sense and noticed every time she gained even an ounce of weight.

Prick.

She pulled on her jeans and sweater, slid on her tennis shoes and jacket, then found her bag and headed for the subway. It was late, and she was starving, so she grabbed a salad with grilled chicken at the corner restaurant on the way to her apartment in Chelsea.

She would have preferred a nice greasy pizza.

"After this show? You are totally a large pepperoni pizza," she said to her salad as she ate once she got to her apartment. "But I'm still having a beer."

She took a couple long swallows of beer, and sighed in contentment. She smiled at the bottle. "Mmmm. Screw you, Lawrence."

She looked around her apartment and at the tiny, one-foot-tall Christmas tree sitting on the pass-through between the kitchen and living area.

It was as holiday as this place got, but it was at least something.

She wanted a bigger place, but she'd gone the roommate route before and that had been a disaster. Her lease was up in January, so she'd have to decide whether to try the roommate thing again and opt for a bigger place, or maybe move. She could live with Greta, temporarily, but she and her sister had different temperaments, and while she loved her sister, they could not live together. They'd done that for too many years. Growing up together was one thing. Deliberately sharing living space together? No.

She didn't think she was cut out for roommates, so maybe she should just consider a move. Hopefully to someplace where the heat actually worked in the winter.

It was freezing in here.

After finishing dinner and her beer, she did dishes, then picked up her phone to check messages.

One from her best friend, Carolina Preston.

Dancing your ass off? Call me. Love you.

She smiled and typed a return text.

Wish ass had been danced off. Could have had the pizza I wanted for dinner. How about U? Saw your label in window when I passed by store on the way home. Want the B&W sweater! Off to take a bath. Call U later.

She sent the text, then headed into her oh-so-tiny bathroom. But at least there was a tub in here, something she'd insisted on before she'd rented the place. Dancers needed a bathtub. They couldn't survive without a hot soak after a grueling day of rehearsals or after a brutal performance night. And her quickly tightening muscles did not like this cold apartment. A warm bath would definitely help.

She put some lavender bath gel in the tub, set the water to ridiculously scalding, then stripped and settled in with a very loud, "Ahhhh."

She let the hot water do the trick of relaxing her muscles. When her phone buzzed, she picked it up, thinking it was Carolina replying to her text.

It wasn't. It was Trick.

Are U naked?

She laughed and shook her head. She hadn't heard from him since last week, and it was just like old times again.

She typed a return text.

As a matter of fact, I am. I'm in the tub.

It took him only a minute to respond to her text message with, *Rough day on the dance floor?*

Yeah. Current choreographer is an asshole.

She sent that back, and then her phone buzzed with a call. She punched the button and Trick's low, deep voice was on the other end.

"So, naked, huh?"

Her nipples hardened at the tone of his voice. "Yes. Unwinding after a tough day. And returning to a cold apartment."

"Poor baby. And I hate your apartment."

"I know. That's why we usually ended up at your fancy Upper West Side place."

"Yeah, because my heater works."

She laughed.

"Hey, did your sister get the job?"

She liked that he remembered to ask about Greta. "She did. She's really excited to be moving here. I can't wait."

"That's great. When is she making the move?"

"She has to give notice at her current job, and pack up her stuff, so not for about a month. But it'll be awesome to have her so close."

"I'm sure it will. Family's important."

He understood. She also liked that about him.

"So tell me about this new choreographer that has you soaking your sore muscles."

"He's a dick. I think he wants stick figures as dancers, so he watches all of us, especially the leads."

"You got a lead part, huh?"

She told him about the show she was in, and how she'd had to audition seven times for Lawrence before he announced her as one of the leads.

"I'm glad you got the lead, but this guy sounds like a class A douche, Stell."

"He is, but he's also a brilliant choreographer."

"I thought you looked thinner when I saw you last week. When was the last time you had a nice, greasy pizza?"

She groaned. "I don't want to talk about it."

"Too long, huh?"

"I was thinking about pizza on the way home, too. But ended up having a salad with grilled chicken."

"Your body is slammin', Stella. You can afford the pizza. You dance it all off, anyway."

She enjoyed the compliment. "See, now why aren't you my choreographer?"

"Because I can't dance for shit?"

"I wouldn't know about that, but you sure can dance on the ice."

"I'll have to take you dancing sometime."

She couldn't even imagine. "Now that I'd like to see."

"Anytime. Though I'm better on the ice."

"Ice dancing? Thinking of an Olympic career?"

"Ha. No. But speaking of ice—without the dancing, that is—are you coming to the game tomorrow night?"

"Wouldn't miss it. It's a Friday night and the start of my weekend, which means no rehearsals. At least right now."

"Great. I'll leave tickets at the window. Are you bringing anyone?"

"You mean like a date?"

"You're funny. You don't want me to have to hurt someone, do you?"

Her lips curved at the possessive tone. They'd never laid claim to each other. It had always been a very open relationship, with no strings. Exactly the way she wanted it. But just now? She couldn't help the little thrill of excitement that ran through her.

She didn't know how she felt about that.

"No, doofus. I'm not bringing a date. But maybe I'll bring a girlfriend."

"Oh, so you want a threesome."

She rolled her eyes. "Now you're being an ass."

He laughed. "Go enjoy your bath. I'll see you tomorrow night."

"Okay. Play good."

"Don't I always? See you, Stella."

She hung up and slid her phone onto the side of the tub, thinking about seeing Trick tomorrow. Her body tingled at the thought of getting her hands all over that man again.

She'd have thought she'd have lost interest. In the past years, she'd tired of men after only a few rolls in the sack. But seeing him again the other night sparked her up all over again.

That shouldn't surprise her. He was inventive, sexy, had a body that just didn't quit, and he'd learned her body fast. Every time with him had been like the first time, and she always eagerly anticipated seeing him.

There was something about him that completely frazzled every nerve ending, but at the same time, gave her a sense of calm in her whacked-out world. It was crazy. *She* was crazy for starting up this relationship—

Correction. She was not having a relationship with Trick. She did not have relationships. Not anymore. Not since that epic mistake she'd made. She'd vowed to never again give a man that much control over her heart, her soul, and her life. No one was going to hurt her so deeply again.

So far, it had worked. She was much happier controlling her own destiny. She'd worked her way up the dancing echelon in New York City, and now she was one of the lead dancers in a show that was going to premiere on Broadway next spring. She'd worked her ass off to get here, and it was because she'd let nothing and no one distract her.

Not even the incredibly hot man she was going to see tomorrow.

FOUR

"PULL YOUR HEAD OUT OF YOUR ASS AND FOCUS ON the puck, Niemeyer."

"My focus is on the puck, Hogan." Trick skated past his friend and teammate, Drew Hogan, and shot the puck toward the net, where the Travelers goalie, Avery Mangino, waited and easily used his stick to shove it out of the way.

"Shit," Trick muttered.

"Come on, Trick. You made that one too easy for me," Avery said. "How am I going to hone my goalie skills if you don't give me something to work with?"

It had been a long practice this morning, and Trick's head wasn't in the game. He'd even missed an easy shot on goal while Ray Sayers, the other Travelers forward, had distracted Mangino.

"I hope you don't play like that tonight, Trick," Drew told him. "Or we're screwed."

Leave it up to his teammates to call him on his shitty play.

"No problem. I'm working out all the kinks during practice."

It was a home game tonight, and he played best on home ice. They'd lost their last road game, and that sucked. It had been a close game, too.

He intended to play better tonight.

After sitting in the sauna for an hour to relax his tense muscles, he went home for a couple of hours, put his earbuds in, and listened to some music. After, he did an easy workout, trying to stay pumped up for the game tonight. Then he grabbed a small snack to eat and went back to the Garden to get ready.

Putting on his uniform always made him realize how damn lucky he was to be able to do what he loved the most. He'd been on skates from the time he was old enough to toddle. His father had loved hockey and had encouraged Trick to play, and he'd taken to it as if he'd been born to do it. He wished his dad were still alive to see him play now. He missed the enthusiasm and excitement his dad had shown at all his games. Trick always took a few seconds before the start of every game to focus on his father, to remember he wouldn't be here now without his dad's encouragement and the push he'd given him to stick with it when times hadn't been so good.

He still had his mom back in Milwaukee, and saw her as often as he could. She called and texted him all the time, and she was as big a hockey fan as his dad had been. She came out to New York a couple of times a year to see him play, and he always loved seeing her.

He smiled at that thought, and as he took the ice and heard the cheers of all the fans, wished he could see his mother's smiling face there. But he rounded the corner out of the box and saw Stella grinning down at him. His stomach tightened in a good way.

That woman did something to him.

He filed that thought away for later, because he had to concentrate on this game. The last thing he wanted to do was suck as bad as he had at practice today. So he shut out all the other minutiae clouding his brain and focused on his team and the opposition.

Tonight, it was Nashville, a really good team, and as Trick and the rest of the Travelers got into position, there was only one thing on his mind—the puck.

After the face-off, Drew had the puck and Trick followed Drew's lead on the other side of the ice. It was a lot of volleying back and forth at the beginning of the game as both teams warmed up, got a feel for each other. Trick took the pass and skated to the Nashville net, his teammates right on his skates. He passed it and the defenseman intercepted.

Shit. It went like this for a while, but they played a lot at the Nashville net, keeping the puck away from their defense, which was a good sign. It took patience and concentration, and Trick had plenty of that. He waited for another chance, which he got several minutes later, then passed the puck to Drew, who breezed past the defender.

Trick was waiting for the puck, fought the defender for it, and moved to the net.

Drew was there, and Trick shot it over. Drew slid it right in past the goalie.

The lamp lit.

They'd scored.

A minute and a half later, they scored again on a pass from Drew to Trick. The Travelers were the only ones to score in the first period, because Avery was on fire in the Travelers' net, fighting off multiple shots on goal.

In the second period, both Drew and Boyd scored, with one assist from Trick. They were up four nothing after the second period, but Nashville scored a minute and a half into the third period.

Trick went after the puck on the next face-off, relentless in his pursuit of another score. Drew and the others seemed to pick up on it, because they spent the majority of the third period at the Nashville net.

Offense was hot tonight, and it paid off with two more scores, one by Boyd Litman, the other by Trick. They ended with a victory in the Garden, and a well-satisfied, cheering crowd.

Even though they'd scored a lot, the game had been tough. Nashville was a really good team.

Sweat poured down his back, and every muscle in his body protested, but Trick didn't care. He celebrated by skating a victory lap around the ice, stick raised in the air as he virtually high-fived all the fans. After a miserable practice today, he'd been beginning to wonder if he'd be able to pull it together for the game tonight. He should have known he'd feed off the fans' energy. Between them and his teammates—and knowing Stella, his good luck charm, was in the stands—victory had been a foregone conclusion.

After doing post-game interviews, he took a shower and got dressed, then stepped outside the locker room.

Guys had wives and girlfriends waiting for them outside the locker room all the time. He never had. It had never bothered him before. Lately, it did.

He wondered where Stella was. He'd gotten her a pass so she knew she could come back here. She never had before, either, saying it would appear like she was his girlfriend, which she wasn't.

No big deal to him, but to her? Big deal, apparently. He texted her.

Where are you?

She texted back a minute later.

Out back. Figured you'd want to avoid your many fans.

He shook his head and headed to the back exit. Stella was out there, alone.

He stalked his way over to her.

"You shouldn't be out here."

She held up her pass. "You gave me this damn all-access pass. It got me through the gate."

He grabbed her arm and led her back inside. "Not what I meant. Jesus, Stell. Someone could mug you out here."

She rolled her eyes at him. "I'm perfectly capable of taking care of myself. Besides, there's a damn security guard at the exit. It's not like he's going to let muggers through to get to me."

While he appreciated her independent streak, sometimes it pissed him off.

"You're cranky," she said as he led her down an alternate hallway and out the side door to where he had a car waiting. "Shouldn't you be in a good mood since you seriously kicked some ass tonight?"

"I am in a good mood."

She leaned forward, gazing up at him, then shook her head. "Yeah. I can tell."

The driver opened the door for them, and Trick waited while Stella slid inside. He climbed in after her, trying to get his crazy emotions under control. He didn't know what the hell was wrong with him, but he needed to blow off this mood. Because Stella was right—the Travelers had won tonight, so he should be happy.

"Hungry?" he asked.

"Starving."

"We'll go eat somewhere."

She laid a hand on his arm. "Or . . . we could go to your place . . . then get takeout later."

She squeezed his upper arm, and he could tell she wanted the alone time.

So did he. He'd been waiting to be with her. "Sure."

He told the driver his address, then leaned back, drawing in a deep breath. Stella scooted next to him and pushed his hair out of his eyes.

"You worked hard for that win tonight," she said.

"Yeah. It was a tough game."

She reached over and laid her hand on his thigh, giving it a squeeze. "It was an exciting game. I was on my feet practically the entire time."

"Thanks."

"Now you just need a nice, relaxing night."

He looked over at her. God, she was a beautiful woman, with her short blonde hair framing her face, and those mesmerizing blue eyes that never failed to draw him in. "Is that right?"

"Indeed."

"I suppose you have a way to relax me."

Her lips curved, sensual promise glittering in her eyes like a sparkling sapphire. "You know it."

He leaned over and cupped her neck, holding her there so he could brush his lips over hers. She tasted of peppermint, her lips soft and yielding. He inhaled her scent and pulled her closer, wishing they weren't in the back of a car so he could slide his hand under her jacket and touch her. But, dammit, he couldn't, so he settled on just a kiss.

Just a kiss wasn't enough, especially when she leaned into him, making that sound in the back of her throat that always drove him crazy.

He pulled back, using his thumb to brush across her bottom lip. "Stop."

"Stop what?" she whispered, her eyes a little glassy.

"Moaning."

"I was not moaning."

"Yes, you were."

She drew back and pulled lip gloss from her purse, then a mirror. He liked watching her put her lipstick on. She had a great mouth and could do amazing things with it.

"I think that was your imagination. It was probably my stomach grumbling." She looked up at him. "I mentioned being hungry, right?"

"Because you don't eat enough."

She laughed. "I eat all the time. And burn it all off dancing. Which is why I'm hungry right now."

He shook his head. He loved that she was a dancer. She had strong muscles, just like him, only hers were a lot prettier. He moved his hand down her leg. Firm. Sexy. Tight. Just like all of her. But she was soft, too, in all the right places.

Unfortunately, that asshole she worked for was obviously a slave driver, demanding all his dancers starve themselves. When they'd met last year around this time, Stella had been curvier. Now, he was worried about her. She'd lost weight for this part. He wasn't sure he liked that.

Not that it was any of his business, since he had no rights to her. But still, he didn't like it.

He'd like to beat the shit out of her choreographer, and then feed Stella about four pizzas, her favorite food.

"Maybe we should stop for something to eat."

She climbed onto his lap. "Oh, we're going to eat, all right. I will, then you will, then we both will. After that, there'll be some other fun play."

He growled, squeezing her thighs. The woman did things to him no woman ever did. And he liked to do things right back to her, to elicit the responses that drove him crazy.

The one thing he'd had with Stella right from the first night they'd met was an easy slide into their sexual relationship. There was no performance between them at the beginning, no awkwardness, no sense of needing to show off sexual prowess, like he'd often had to do when he was with a woman at the beginning. With Stella, things had clicked between them right away. It was as if they'd known each other before, even though they hadn't.

He'd felt at ease with her, an immediate tumble of passion and a sense of rightness he'd never felt before. Maybe that's why he still wanted to be with her. She hit all his hot buttons, turned him on every time he was with her, but there was no sense of needing to prove who he was with her. With Stella, everything felt natural, like this was the woman he was supposed to be with.

Which didn't make any goddamn sense, but there it was.

Ignoring the driver, who probably usually saw way more in the back of his car than what Trick planned to do with Stella, he lifted into her and let out a soft groan. "You're making me hard."

She laid her hands on his shoulders and rocked against him. "That's the idea, right?"

Trick shot a glare at the driver, who was paying way more attention to his rearview mirror than he was to the road in front of him.

"Eyes in front, buddy," Trick said.

"Yes, sir," the driver said, but Trick caught the knowing smile on the driver's face.

Fortunately, the drive to Trick's place wasn't long. Good thing, too, because his dick was hard, and he couldn't wait much longer for Stella. They had some catching up to do.

"You're going to have to get off of me before we get to my place," he finally said. "Or I'm going to be walking to the door with a hard-on."

She laughed and slid to his side. "You need a long coat."

"I guess I do."

In a few minutes, they were at his building and he'd kept his hands to himself long enough to get his erection under control. He took care of paying the driver while Stella walked up the steps to the front door. He turned, watching her, wishing the tail of her coat didn't cover her very fine ass.

He liked the way she walked, liked the grace, the softness in her step. When she turned and slid a smoldering smile down at him, he shot one back at her.

Yeah, something was still there. It was as if no time had passed at all since the last time he'd seen her.

He walked up the steps and stopped in front of her.

"I've been thinking about this all week," she said.

She curved her hand around the nape of his neck and brought her lips to his for a blistering-hot kiss right on his front doorstep. People walked past to get inside, and this being New York, no one said anything. But he wanted to get her inside, needed to get his hands on her skin.

He pulled back and entered his code, then took her hand and led her to the elevator. When they stepped in, it was just the two of them. He pushed the button for his floor, and as soon as the door closed, he drew her against him. She came willingly, aligning her body with his to continue what they'd started outside.

It was always like this with Stella. From that first night they'd met at McGill's bar, when she'd asked him to take her home, it had been like sudden lightning between them. A hot passion that had ignited fast and hadn't burned itself out yet.

"They have cameras in this elevator," Stella said when Trick grabbed her butt.

"So? It's probably their best entertainment tonight."

She smiled, then flicked her tongue around his. "And you're hard. However will you explain that to property management?"

"I pay plenty for my apartment. They can suck my dick."

The elevator doors opened, and Stella grasped his hands, leading him out. "Oh, no. That's my job."

He followed, not even trying to hide his erection now. She had him, and she knew it. He let her have that power, because there was going to be a sweet payoff for him as soon as they got through his front door.

He pulled out his key and opened the door. She backed inside and he closed the door behind them, shrouding them in darkness. The moon cast enough light through the windows, though, and he could see her shrug out of her coat and drop her purse on the table next to the door. She pulled off her boots, then came toward him. He made sure to toe out of his shoes as well, because things were about to get interesting.

"I've been waiting for this, thinking about you," she said, stepping into him, backing him against the door.

One of the things he liked most about Stella was that she wasn't shy, didn't pretend to be coy about sex.

She liked sex, and she made no bones about showing it. Having her body pressed up against his made him ache, desperate to get her naked so he could touch her, taste her, and get inside her.

But he also knew she liked control. And when she slid her hands over his shoulders to take off his coat, rocking her pelvis against his hard-on, he was more than happy to let her have whatever she wanted as long as she kept touching him.

The thing was, though, he never gave up complete control, and she knew that about him as well. So when his coat dropped to the floor and his hands were free, he tangled his fingers in the thick softness of her hair, angling her head to the side.

He caught the slight curve of her lips before his mouth descended on hers. It was a hot, passionate kiss, one he'd been thinking a lot about since he'd seen her again. And now that they were finally alone, he could deepen the kiss, slide his tongue inside and taste her.

She moaned and reached for his shirt, clutching it in her hands, pulling it out of his pants, then palming his lower stomach.

"I like you touching me," he whispered against her lips before moving down to kiss and lick her neck. He breathed in the scent of her—she always smelled like something intoxicating to him.

"I need to touch you, Trick. I want you naked."

She snaked her hand down his abdomen and across the denim of his jeans. His breath rushed out when she palmed his erection and reached for his zipper.

And when she slid down his body, drawing his pants down his hips, all he could do was lean against the wall and let her have her way.

"Now," she said, lifting her head to look up at him as she wrapped her hand around his cock. "What were you saying about someone sucking your dick?"

She was on her knees, a blonde goddess with silver dangling earrings, her blue eyes seeming to glitter in the darkness.

"The only lips I want around my cock are yours."

Her lips tilted, her hand doing very distracting things to him. "That's what I wanted to hear."

He slid his hand over the silky softness of her hair. She tilted her head back, her sweet lips curving to smile up at him.

"I'm going to rock your world, Trick."

She always did, and the anticipation of it tightened him as she continued to stroke his cock with easy, lazy strokes. Her hand was so much smaller, softer than his, but he definitely liked the feel of her hand around him. She took her time teasing him, rolling her thumb across the head, then lifting his cock up, pressing it against his belly and dipping her head down. And when she took his balls into her mouth, he couldn't hold back the epic curse that spilled from his lips.

It was so goddamned good to feel his balls tucked into her hot, wet mouth, to feel her tongue rolling over his ball sac. He was steely hard and aching to explode, and she hadn't even put his cock between her lips yet.

When she slid his balls from her mouth, he groaned.

She cupped them in her hands. "Yeah, you like that."

He shuddered out a breath. "You know I do."

"You like this even more." She lifted on her knees, then took the tip of his cock and slid her tongue around the head, before engulfing him in her mouth, taking him deep.

He shuddered in a breath, mesmerized by her mouth. Watching her and feeling the way she took him in was magic. She knew him well, and she liked to take a long, slow journey when she sucked him. It was torture, but the best kind.

"Yeah, I like what you do, Stell." He cupped the back of her head, thrusting into her mouth. He could come, but he didn't want to spend what he had down her throat. Not when all he'd been thinking about was sinking into her and having those fantastic legs of hers wrap around him while he buried himself deep.

But this—this was so damn good he needed a few minutes of watching her. And goddamn it was hard not to lean back and let her go at it until he released. Because she could take him there so fast.

He finally pulled back, then lifted her, flipping her so her back was against the wall. He saw the challenge in her eyes.

"You take me right to the edge," he said, before kissing her, sliding his fingers into the softness of her hair. She moaned against his lips and his cock brushed her hips. He moved his hand down, unbuttoning her jeans.

Damn tight jeans women wore, making it hard for a man to get his hands inside. While he sure appreciated the effect when he looked at her, it wasn't making his job any easier. He tugged one side, then the other, finally sighing in frustration.

"Christ. Are these things glued on?"

She laughed. "I have every confidence you can get my pants off."

"Never failed before."

He struggled his way past the offending denim, finally dragging the jeans down her legs and off.

"The things you women go through," he said, happy to see red silk panties.

"But my ass looks great in these jeans."

"It does." He slid his hands up her legs. God, he loved her legs. So strong, so soft, and as he moved upward, he parted them, rewarded by the soft, hot, wet part of her. He slipped his fingers between, teasing her by rubbing over the silk of her panties.

"Those can go, too," she said.

"Can they?" He nuzzled her hip, then used his teeth to drag one side of her underwear down, kissing the area he'd bared. She smelled like cinnamon and hot, musky sexual desire, and he couldn't wait to put his mouth on her.

He pressed a kiss to her hip, then rolled his tongue along the soft juncture between her thigh and her sex. She moaned, her body wriggling against his mouth. And when he flicked his tongue against her clit, she arched backward, driving against his face.

She was soft here, giving her body to him in every way, telling him without words what she needed. This was where tough Stella melted into softness, and as he licked the length of her, she whimpered—the sweetest sound.

He wanted her to come, to give over to him completely. But he also wanted her teetering right on the edge, just like him. It had been a long time since he'd been with her, and he wanted both of them to orgasm when he was inside her.

So he took her there one lick at a time, feeling her body, remembering every taste, every scent, every way she moved until he knew she was close. Then he pulled back and stood.

She lifted her head, her eyes dazed with passion. He leaned over her, pulling off her shirt, unhooking her bra so he could slide it down her arms. He took a taste of her nipples, pulling one peak into his mouth for a long suck.

"Goddammit, Trick," she whispered, grasping his head to hold him to her breast. "Do that again."

He did, on the other side, drawing her nipple into his mouth, teasing her until she yanked his hair.

"Stop."

He withdrew.

"Too much?" he asked, hovering over her.

"God, no. Too good. I need you inside me."

Good to know they both wanted the same thing.

He took her hand and pulled her up, then walked with her into his bedroom. She fell onto her back on his bed and he reached into the nightstand for a condom.

"Always ready, aren't you?"

He shed his jeans and the rest of his clothes, then handed her the packet.

"For you? Yeah. Always."

FIVE

STELLA DREW IN A BREATH AT THE SIGHT OF TRICK standing over her. Naked, his erection prominent, his body a fucking work of art, all she could do was stare and appreciate that tonight he was hers again.

As he climbed onto the bed, she reached for his cock, wrapping her fingers around his length. She tore open the condom wrapper and applied it, then scooted down the bed.

There had never been any awkwardness between her and Trick. From the first night, it was as if they had known each other forever. Their chemistry had been hot and instantaneous, and it had continued like that until they'd lost touch. And now, months and months later, they picked up right where they had left off, knowing each other's bodies, their likes and dislikes. And as he parted her legs and slid inside her, she ached with the knowledge that this was a man she was connected to beyond just the physical.

No. She was not emotionally connected to Trick. She couldn't be, because she wouldn't allow it. He was fun and sexy and damn good in bed, and as she lifted and her body responded, she focused on that and that alone, because it was all she'd let herself have.

But oh, it was so good, the way he mastered her body, the way his hands glided over her hips and butt, clenching and arching her toward him so he could thrust deeper, giving her the ultimate in pleasure. Because the one thing she'd always loved—or rather liked—about Trick was that he made sure she got hers first.

He dropped his pelvis and ground against her. Every synapse in her brain exploded, sending pleasure right to her clit.

She lifted her gaze to his, arching against him, needing more. "Yes. That makes me come."

He gave her a supremely confident smile. "I know. I feel your pussy tighten around me when I do that, and it feels so goddamn good."

But he was still a man who liked to tease, to prolong the action to make sure that when she went off, she went wild. So he withdrew, easing out, then slowly inching back in.

"Trick," she warned, wanting to feel that deeper connection.

"Like this?" he asked.

And then he was there again, meeting her stroke for stroke, until she had no words left, because all she could do was hold on. Her world was rocking on its axis, then shattering all around her. She quaked with the force of it, dug her nails into his shoulders, and cried out with the power of her orgasm. Trick was right there with her, his mouth buried against her neck, causing chills to erupt all over her skin. And when he thrust over and over, groaning against her when he came, she held tight to him and closed her eyes, just *feeling* him as he rocked against her until he settled.

It was always like this with them. So fun at the beginning, and then so intense it shook her to her very core. But Trick was like a drug, and no matter how many times she left his place and she swore it was going to be the last time, she knew she'd want more.

He was very dangerous, but she was a strong woman. She'd walked away from him before, and she could do it again.

She *would* do it again.

Trick withdrew and left to dispose of the condom, then climbed onto the bed and pulled her against his chest. Unlike a lot of men, he didn't seem to have a problem with holding her after sex. Usually she was the one who was disconnected, needing that emotional distance. Tonight, though, she'd allow it. She enjoyed being back in his arms again.

"Hungry for that pizza now?" he asked as he smoothed his hands up and down her stomach.

"Stop. We are not having pizza."

"Look at your stomach. You look undernourished."

She laughed. "Trust me. I eat plenty. I have to or I'd pass out during rehearsals. I could use a little protein, though. You've depleted my reserves."

He rolled her over onto her back, then raised her arms above her head, pinning them with his hand. A rush of pleasure enveloped her.

"Is that right? If I depleted them a little more, can we order a pizza?"

He nibbled around her nipple, licked it, flicked it with his tongue, then devoured it with his mouth. Heated pleasure enveloped her.

"If you keep doing that, you can have anything you want."

He lifted his head. "Oh, I'm just getting started. By the time I'm done, we're going to have breadsticks, too."

"Give it your best shot."

He moved his hand between her legs, teasing her with his fingers. She wanted to touch him, but he still held her wrists with one hand, leaving her helpless. Not that she minded, especially with the way he stroked her with easy movements, coaxing her arousal. And when he dipped a finger inside her, she was already hot and ready to come again.

"You're wet, your pussy tightening around my finger," he said, whispering in her ear, his voice dark with promise. "I'm hard again, ready to fuck you. I think this time I want you on a pillow on your belly so I can enter you from behind. I love looking at your ass while I'm fucking you, Stella."

Her belly tumbled, a mix of desire and the visual of Trick pumping into her from behind. "Do it. Let's do it now."

He released her wrists, grabbed a couple of pillows, and plumped them up in the center of the bed.

"On your stomach on those," he said, helping her get into position by grasping her hips. He moved in between her legs. "That's it. Get your ass up in the air."

His words never failed to turn her on. He put on a condom, and she felt his legs brush against hers.

"I love your ass, Stella. So tight and beautiful." He ran his hands over her butt, gave her a light slap.

She shivered at the unexpected sting, but it only made her pussy quiver. "I liked that."

"Want more?"

"Yes."

He smacked the other butt cheek, and she arched upward.

This time, he slid his cock into her, grasping her butt cheeks as he withdrew and thrust. And when he smacked her again, she tightened around him.

"You're hot. Wet. And you like a little spanking, don't you?"

"Yes. Fuck me."

She was wild with the need for him. For what he did to her. For the things he made her feel. The sting of the swats only served to ratchet up her desire—a hot, coiling need of pleasured agony. She reached between her legs to rub her clit, to take her right where she needed to be.

"Are you going to make yourself come?" he asked, smacking her again. The red-hot sting almost tipped her over the edge, but she held back, wanting him to go with her.

"Yes. Oh, God, yes. Fuck me, Trick, make me come."

He dug his fingers into her hips and she knew from the hard

thrusts he wasn't far from going off himself. She hung on the barest edge, suspended, and when he gave her the last smack, she went over, this time with him, his groans and hard pumps into her sending her into a moaning orgasm that wracked her with wild shudders, leaving her spent and exhausted.

Trick smoothed his hand over her butt.

"You okay?"

She dredged up enough breath to nod and say, "Perfect."

He leaned over her and pressed a kiss to the back of her neck. "Perfect is right."

They ended up having pizza, salad, and breadsticks. She was going to have to dance her ass off next week to work it all off.

SIX

STELLA LAY ON THE FLOOR OF THE OLD THEATER where they rehearsed, her breaths sawing in and out.

"Get your ass up, Stella. We're not done yet."

At the moment she longed for something sharp so she could shove it in Lawrence's scrawny neck. Unfortunately, that would be homicide and she'd lose her job and her paycheck.

She stared up at the rigging and the lights, pondering whether that was a bad idea or not. As she lay in a pool of sweat, every muscle in her body screaming in agony, she weighed the options.

Nope. Not a bad idea at all at the moment. In prison, she'd probably get a lot more rest. And food.

"Come on, honey. I'll help you up."

She took the hand offered by Lisa Jeffries, her friend and co-dancer. Launching to her feet, Stella winced as she stretched.

"He's a dick," Lisa said as they stood side by side. "I think he gets off on seeing us suffer."

Stella watched Lawrence walk away. "I don't think. I know he does. What's with the extra rehearsal time this week? The show doesn't open until next spring. We haven't even moved into the theater where we'll be performing the show yet."

Lisa nodded, raising her arms above her head to extend the stretch. "If he keeps this up, we'll all be dead by then."

Stella was so damned excited to be one of the lead dancers in a Broadway musical. She had no problem with a grueling rehearsal schedule, or a choreographer who demanded perfection in his dancers. She had a high expectation of herself, and she'd work non-stop to make sure her performance was perfect.

But that didn't mean she wouldn't bitch, moan, and whine about how hard it was. They all did. It was a perk of the job.

They rehearsed the opening scene for seven hours that day, over and over again until Stella wanted to scream every time the music played.

"By the time this show debuts, I'm going to hate every note of music in it," Stella said after they were finally cut loose for the day and made their way back to the dressing-room areas.

Lisa nodded. "I wonder if the singers feel the same way. Can you imagine having to practice those songs over and over and over again for months?"

"I imagine they do." Stella paused in packing up her bag to look over at Lisa. "But then it's opening night and it's like the very first time you've ever heard the music or danced to those songs. And it's so exciting your heart wants to leap out of your chest, ya know?"

Lisa grinned. "I do know that feeling. And we're leads this time, Stella. You and I have danced together for five years. Remember starting out in the back of the chorus, where no one could even see us?"

"Yes." Stella took a seat. "Just another in a sea of dancers, indistinguishable. But we're dancing leads in this one. We'll be at the front of the stage."

She could hardly believe it was true. Years of hard work, of paying her dues, of taking shit jobs just so she could cover the rent, had finally paid off. She had worked nonstop in a lot of shows, and she was a damn good dancer. She never took time off, and as soon as one show closed, she hit the audition circuit for another.

Now, she was going to be at the front of that stage, dancing in every scene.

She glanced over at Lisa, who'd been just like her. A beautiful young woman with dark skin, a sea of tightly wound black curls, and a true dancer's body—all hard muscle and perfect lines. Working hard, perfecting her craft, and by Stella's side every step of the way. They'd often been competitors for the same part, but they'd always been friends.

"As much as I hate these rehearsals, Lisa, I also love what's going to happen on opening night. This is a big damn deal and we've worked our asses off for it."

"Amen, sister. Now I'm going to go home to my husband and beg him for a foot massage. Thank God for a man with big, strong hands."

The thought of someone giving her a foot massage made Stella groan. "Lucky woman."

Lisa pointed one slender finger at her. "You could have yourself a man. You push them all away."

Stella zipped up her bag and grabbed her coat, sliding her arms into it. "This is true. I have enough on my plate without dealing with a man in my life."

Lisa shrugged into her jacket. "Honey, you don't know what you're missing. Let me remind you. Foot. Massage. Did I mention Louis gives amazing back massages as well?"

Stella laughed. "You're a cruel woman, my friend."

Lisa waggled her brows. "Don't I know it. I'm just trying to remind you what you're missing by going the single route."

"I know what I'm missing. And what I'm not missing. You go enjoy your hot husband and his amazing hands. I'm going home to my bathtub."

Lisa left and Stella grabbed her bag, planning to go home and take a bath as well. Maybe soak for an hour. Or two. Or three.

But when she got off the subway in her neighborhood she changed her mind and ended up at her friend Carolina's design studio, since it was near her apartment. When Carolina debuted her line of clothes at New York's Fashion Week last year, her friend had been nonstop busy ever since, and they hadn't had a lot of time together. Plus, Carolina was in love—with Trick's best friend and teammate, Drew Hogan—which ate up the rest of Carolina's time.

Stella was thrilled for Carolina. Drew was a great guy. Funny, honest, and God, he really loved Carolina. It made her heart melt seeing how much that man loved her best friend. And he'd gone to great lengths to prove it to her.

Which didn't mean that Stella needed a man in her life. In fact, that was the last damn thing she needed. Sex? Definitely. True love? She'd tried that before, and it had laughed in her face. She didn't need to be mocked by love more than once in her life.

She rang the bell downstairs, and Carolina answered.

"It's me," Stella said.

"Shouldn't you be home soaking in a hot tub?"

"Of course I should. But I know you keep alcohol up there. And pretty clothes."

Carolina laughed and buzzed her up. When she opened the door, Carolina gave her a critical eye.

"You've lost weight. And you look exhausted. Do you ever sleep or eat?"

"Not right now. You know what rehearsals for a new show are like."

Carolina pulled her in for a hug. "God, I've missed you. It seems like it's been months since I've seen you."

"I know. Why are we both so busy?"

Carolina shut the door and Stella shrugged out of her coat. "Because we both have kick-ass careers?"

Stella laughed. "I guess. Though mine is currently kicking *my* ass."

"Come on. I'll open a bottle of wine. No beer here, sorry."

"Wine will do."

"Good. I needed a break anyway. Gearing up for fashion week again is killing me right now."

"It feels like you just premiered your line, and here you're ready to do it all over again. Do you ever feel like a hamster on a wheel?"

Carolina laughed as she grabbed a bottle out of the refrigerator in the break room of her studio and pulled a bottle opener out of the drawer. "Only all the time. It's one of those 'be careful what you wish for, you might just get it' type of things."

Stella took a seat at the bar. "But look at how far you've come in less than a year, honey. You've already moved into a bigger studio space, you've launched your design brand, your clothes are in stores, and Carolina Designs is a name people recognize. I couldn't be more proud of you."

Carolina poured the wine into two glasses and slid one over to her, then she took a deep breath. "Thank you, Stell. And the same goes for you. The lead in a new show. I'm proud of you, as well. We're both doing good."

"We are. Here's to us."

They touched glasses, and Stella took a sip. The wine tasted fantastic. She was normally a beer person, but the wine was flavorful and she knew it would help relax her so she could sleep tonight.

Carolina came around the bar and took a seat next to Stella. "Other than looking like you need to eat a few cheeseburgers, tell me what else is going on."

Stella took another few sips of wine, then set the glass down. "I hooked up with Trick again."

Carolina's eyes widened. "You did? When did this happen?"

"Very recently. Greta was in town and we went to the hockey

game, then hit up a bar afterward. Trick was there with some of the guys from the team, and we reconnected."

"As I recall, things had cooled between the two of you. But you didn't end it badly."

"No. It was more our work schedules. And you know how it is with me—I don't like to see a guy too much."

"Yes, I do know how it is with you. The love-'em-and-leave-'em type. Though I think having a man more or less permanently in your life might be good for you. Someone to be there for you, to remind you to eat . . ."

Sometimes having Carolina for a friend was like having another sister to watch over her. "Ha ha. I'm perfectly capable of taking care of myself and don't need a man to do that for me."

"Oh, but having a man around can be advantageous. Someone to take out the trash, replace batteries in the smoke detectors, sex on demand . . ."

"Speaking of sex on demand, how is Drew?"

"Oh, he's very good. At taking out the trash, of course."

Stella laughed. "Of course."

"I'm sure Trick is very good at taking out the trash as well."

"I can't say I've sampled his trash or battery replacing skills, but he's fantastic in bed." And just talking about sex revved her up when she should be trying to relax.

"So why are you here with me instead of with him?"

"Because I love you and haven't seen you in a while. And because it's not always about the men."

"This is true."

"So show me all your pretty clothes and what you've got going on, and tell me how crazy your life is right now so I won't feel like it's just me."

"Okay," Carolina said with a laugh, sliding off the barstool. "Let's go look at clothes."

Stella was amazed at Carolina's eye for clothing, at how she could spot upcoming trends and create something that she instinctively knew people would want. Or at least everything that hit Stella's hot buttons. Carolina had created lines for both men and women that were simple yet luxurious at the same time. As Carolina walked her through the sketches and some of her line that she'd already completed, Stella mentally ticked off items she wanted.

Mostly everything. And she could see Trick in so many of the men's clothes as well.

"This line is fantastic, Carolina. I love everything. And those leather pants with the ankle zippers, especially paired up with that sequined sweater? Those belong in my closet—now."

Carolina grinned. "Wait until you see the mohair ankle boots I'm putting the model in to walk with that outfit."

"I hate you."

"You won't hate me when I send you the outfit—plus the boots—after the show."

Stella threw her arms around Carolina and hugged her. "This is one of the many reasons why you're my best friend. But not for the clothes. Really. Not for the clothes."

Carolina laughed. "I know. Now, we need to get out of here. My brain is toast and I'm starving."

"If you're going to want to go out to eat, I need a shower."

"Okay, we'll stop at your place first."

Carolina closed up her studio and they grabbed a taxi to Stella's apartment, both of them complaining about how damn cold it was as they jumped in and out of the cab.

"Why is it so fucking cold already?" Stella asked.

"Because it's New York?" Carolina replied.

"Good point." Arm in arm, they hurried into the building. The wind was picking up. Stella could smell snow in the air. It was early December and she wasn't ready for snow yet.

Just the quick dash in the cold made Stella long for that nice warm bath, but it was going to have to wait. She thought the glass of wine might slow her down, but it was amazing what hanging out with a friend could do for her energy level. She stripped out of her clothes and took a quick shower, then chose a pair of skintight leggings, her favorite pair of combat boots, a dark tank, and a sheer silver top, topping it off with a leather studded jacket. She complemented the look with several necklaces.

"I love how you can take five minutes to put one hell of a kick-ass outfit together," Carolina said, studying her as she came out of her bedroom. "You should help me put clothes together for the show."

Stella laughed. "You don't need me. Your sense of fashion rocks. Look at you with your skinny jeans and those leather boots that, if you weren't my best friend, I'd kill you to take off of you. And I covet that black trench coat with all those zippers. You know I'm a sucker for zippers."

"I know. I designed this with you in mind. And you might be getting one for Christmas."

"I do love Santa. And you. Have I mentioned how much I love you?"

"Not more than three or four times in the past hour."

Stella grabbed her purse and looped her arm in Carolina's. "Be prepared to hear it a few more times. Let's go."

They both devoured huge chicken and cashew salads at a corner restaurant near Carolina's place, then headed up to her apartment.

"I have beer here, since Drew prefers it over wine," Carolina said after they hung up their coats.

"I'll just have water," Stella said. "I can only dance off so many calories."

Carolina gave her a sidelong look. "You could use a few more calories."

"So everyone tells me. Believe me, after the show I'm going to eat two pizzas and guzzle a six-pack."

They took seats on the sofa. Stella flexed her ankles, giving her legs a long stretch. She didn't want to tighten up after today's rehearsal, and since she'd missed her bath, she knew that was a possibility.

"Where is that hot boyfriend of yours, anyway?" Stella asked. "I know it's not a game night tonight."

"Some team meeting about something or other. I admit I was only half listening when he called me and told me about it because I was knee-deep in fabric selections."

"That's certainly understandable. Pretty fabric is much more important than hockey."

Carolina grinned. "To me it is. Probably not to Drew."

"And how are things going with the cohabitation?"

"It's actually pretty great for the most part. I thought we'd get in each other's way, but we don't. I mean, we have the usual getting used to each other stuff, but it's minor. For some reason he can't grasp the concept that dirty clothes go in the hamper, and it drives him crazy that I don't eat breakfast right when I get up in the morning. He wakes up starving and wants to cook a six-course meal when all I want is tea. We're learning all of each other's weird idiosyncrasies. But I like knowing he's here with me. I like sleeping with him when he's in town. The sex is outstanding, he makes me laugh, and I love him like crazy."

Carolina looked around the room. "He fills this space. I couldn't imagine him not in it."

Stella smiled at her best friend. "I love seeing you like this. You were always so driven, so focused only on work. Not that your work isn't as important to you now as it ever was, but sharing your life with Drew has changed you."

"It has. In ways even I can't explain. And I want the same thing for you, Stell, because you're just as driven and focused as I used to be—as I still am. But you don't have that someone to share your world with."

Stella felt a tug in the vicinity of her chest, but shrugged it off. "I don't need that. I don't want it. I told you, I'm a free agent, and I prefer it that way."

"It's a lonely way. I never realized how lonely I was until Drew came in and filled my world with all that love."

"Now you're starting to sound like one of those sappy greeting cards you buy at the store."

Carolina laughed. "I am, aren't I? Okay, enough love talk. I want to hear about this new show. Tell me all about it. What role you're dancing, who the cast is, and all the juicy gossip."

Stella spent the next hour filling Carolina in on the grueling rehearsals and the cast, and telling her all about the choreographer. She hadn't realized so much time had passed until she heard a click at the front door. She looked up to see Drew walk through.

With Trick walking in behind him.

"Well, hi, you two." Carolina got up and went to greet Drew, who wrapped his arms around her and gave her a warm kiss.

"Hey, babe," Drew said, his gaze lingering on Carolina. "We were talking strategy, so I thought we'd continue it here with a beer. Unless you two are talking strategy of your own."

Carolina laughed. "No, we had dinner, now we're gossiping." She moved to Trick and hugged him.

Stella got up and went over to give Drew a hug and peck on the cheek. "Hi, there, hot stuff. How's it goin'?"

"It's going great. And you?"

"Still dancing, as always."

"Good to hear."

She nodded at Trick after he hung up his coat. "Hey."

"Hey. Did you and Carolina have fun tonight?"

"We did. I stopped off to see her after rehearsal and we ended up spending the evening together."

"I'm glad to hear that."

"How did your meeting go?"

"It went fine. We're coming up on a game against Detroit and they're tough. We've got a couple of our key players injured, so we needed to talk strategy and replacements."

"You guys want a beer or wine?" Carolina asked from the bar.

"Beer for me, thanks," Trick said as he followed Stella toward the living room.

"Obviously it's a game you all really want to win."

"They've kicked our asses the last few meetings," Drew said, taking two beers from Carolina and handing one off to Trick. "Injuries or not, we intend to take them down this time."

Stella grabbed her water from the coffee table and took a long swallow. "When's the game?"

"Monday night."

"Home game, right?"

Trick nodded. "Yeah."

"I'll definitely be there to cheer you on."

"I can make it, too," Carolina said.

"Are you sure?" Drew had taken up a spot on the arm of the sofa, and smoothed his hand over her hair. "I know you're in crunch mode."

Carolina tilted her head back to look up at Drew and smiled. "This is an important game for you. I wouldn't miss it."

Drew leaned down and brushed his lips across hers. "Thanks, babe. That means a lot."

"You two should get a room."

"We have one. Or two. Right here, as a matter of fact," Drew said with a wide grin.

Stella stood. "That's my cue to leave."

Carolina laughed. "It was not."

"I've got to go anyway. I still need a hot bath or my muscles will cramp up on me."

"I'll go with you." Trick took a few deep swallows of his beer.

"You do not have to leave. Drew was just kidding, you know," Carolina said.

Drew slipped his arm around Carolina. "Was I?"

Carolina rolled her eyes. "You're a terrible host."

He laughed. "Hey, Lina's right. I was just joking."

"Oh, I know, but I'll head out with Stella anyway."

"And I really do need to be on my way." Stella got up and put her empty water glass in the dishwasher.

Trick tossed his beer bottle in the recycle bin while she went to get her coat.

"We can catch up on the strategy at the next practice," Trick said to Drew. "Give us both some time to digest it all."

"Agreed," Drew said, slapping Trick on the back. "See you an hour earlier, maybe?"

Trick nodded. "That's a plan."

Stella turned to Carolina and hugged her. "Thanks for spending time with me tonight. I'll see you at the game Monday night?"

"Of course."

Stella and Trick rode down the elevator together, Trick being surprisingly quiet. At least until they got outside.

"Share a cab with me?" he asked.

"Sure."

Trick hailed a taxi, which fortunately didn't take long since she really didn't want to stand at the curb and shiver in the cold. They climbed inside and Trick gave the cab his address.

"My apartment is closer," she said.

He turned to her. "But how can you take a nice hot bath at my place if I drop you off at yours?"

"You're assuming I want to take a bath at your place."

"I am. There's still time to give the driver your address."

She could say no, but she didn't want to. "Your place is fine."

"I knew you couldn't resist me."

She leaned against him. "You'd like to think that, wouldn't you? When in actuality, your tub is bigger and it has jets."

He put his arm around her. "Damn, Stell. I feel so used."

Her lips curved. She really, really liked this man.

And the warning bells clanged loudly in her head.

SEVEN

ONCE AT HIS APARTMENT, TRICK WASTED NO TIME IN heading to his bathroom. He wasn't joking about getting Stella relaxed. He'd seen her pointing her toes and wincing in just the short period of time he'd been at Drew and Carolina's place, and knew a hot bath was just the thing she needed.

"You should get naked," he said as she leaned against the doorway to his bathroom.

"Is that the line you use on all your women?"

"First, no. Second, I don't have *women*. I have you."

She gave him an unfathomable look. "You do have me—for tonight."

He looked up from his seat on the side of the tub. "That'll work. Now get naked. Tub's filling. Sorry I don't have bubble bath."

She laughed and turned to enter his bedroom, drawing her top over her head. "I don't need bubble bath."

She came back a minute or so later and she was beautifully bare. He couldn't help but take a minute to stare. Her body was a goddamned work of art. She was tall, with stunning long legs, her hair styled in short blonde spikes. She was a natural blonde, so the small tuft of hair at her sex was golden, making him go hard just thinking of touching her there, of licking her and relaxing her even more. Tonight she wore some kind of black sparkling earrings that only made the china-doll look of her face more prominent.

He could stare for hours at this amazing woman standing naked in his bathroom. But he wanted her warm and relaxed, so he held out his hand and guided her into the tub, grateful he'd selected a condo that had an oversize tub with the whirlpool jets. He often had his own sore muscles to deal with after a game, and while they had the whirlpools in the locker room, those aching muscles tended to stay that way, so he wanted his own tub. He was a pretty big guy, so a bathtub like this had been on his must list.

"This tub rocks, Trick," she said, settling into the water up to her neck. "And jets, too? I might never leave."

He turned on the jets and the water bubbled up all around her.

Stella leaned back and closed her eyes. "Oh, yeah. That's it, Trick. Never leaving. Go over to my apartment and move my stuff in here."

He laughed, but the thought of her staying here appealed. Seeing her makeup and things on his counter, her underwear and bras in some of his drawers? Yeah, he kind of liked the idea. He'd lived alone for a long time now, and had enjoyed his life as a bachelor. There had never been a woman who had ever tipped his radar in the way Stella had. She challenged him, wasn't a clinger, and he couldn't deny the chemistry they had.

But was that enough to want a long-term relationship? Hell, she didn't want any kind of relationship.

"Trick. *Trick.*"

He looked over to see her watching him. "Yeah?"

"Are you intending to be my bathtub bodyguard all night or are you going to get naked and get in here with me?"

He liked the sound of that. With a curve to his lips, he drew his shirt over his head and popped the button on his pants.

"Now this is bath-time entertainment." She leaned back in the tub and looked up at him.

Her nipples reacted to the cooler air by puckering, giving him his own version of bath-time entertainment.

She raised her knees and wrapped her arms around them, making room for him. It didn't take long for him to shed the rest of his clothes. Or to get hard.

"I like the looks of that," Stella said, eyeing his cock.

He slid into the tub, facing her, then drew her close. She wrapped her legs around his hips, sliding her sweet, hot pussy along his dick. He could so easily slip into her, fuck her like this in the warm tub. But that would be careless, and he wasn't a careless man.

But he could do something to relax her even more. He skimmed his fingers along her back, just rubbing her skin at first, then pressing in more, testing each muscle, using some strength to massage where she was tight.

She laid her head against his chest and he felt her entire body go lax.

"Mmm. That feels good."

Exactly where he wanted her, floating along on a cloud of boneless nirvana. He mapped her body inch by inch, dissolving her tension, enjoying the way she undulated against him, even if it cost him every ounce of his self-control.

"You keep touching me like that, we're going to have a problem," she murmured against his shoulder.

"Yeah?" He kissed the side of her neck and let his hands do a slow slide down her back. "What kind of problem?"

She rocked against his dick again. "That kind of problem."

He closed his eyes and let the sensation wash over him. It was torture and bliss coupled together, but he had patience and could wait. Right now this was about her.

He used his feet to push himself back against the tub, taking her with him, then turned her around so her back was against his chest. Steam rose off their bodies, enveloping them in a cocoon of heat. Desire sizzled around him as he cupped Stella's breasts under the water, the soft feel of her in his hands making his balls tighten. Her breath caught, her nipples hardening as he teased them with his fingers, knowing just how and where to touch her to evoke those moans he loved to hear.

She arched her back. "Trick. Where are you going with this?"

He slid one hand over her ribs and belly, then between her legs to cup her sex. "South."

She shifted, rising up to sling each of her legs over his, widening, giving him access. "Good spot. Touch me and make me come. I've had a hard day and I want you to make me scream."

She tilted her head back and he leaned in to kiss her, at the same time sliding his fingers inside her. Here she was hotter than the water surrounding them, her body welcoming his fingers by squeezing him, pulsing around him. He ached to be inside her, his dick arcing against her butt in search of her.

He could wait for his needs. Right now it was all about Stella's pleasure, coaxing her body to respond by sliding his hand over her plump lips, then tucking his fingers back inside, feeling her clench around him. He took his time, not wanting to rush things. He wanted to build this up slow and easy for her, making each second count.

Her skin was like silk under the water, her body rippling against his as he took his time, making gentle motions with his hands, his fingers gliding in and out of her. And each time he tucked back inside of her, she clenched, gripping him, sucking him in like a vortex, demanding more.

He knew when the time was right to increase the pressure of his hand, to slide his fingers over the tight knot of her clit. When she rose against him, when her moans grew louder, when he felt her entire body tense and shudder against him, he knew she was almost there.

He kissed her shoulder, took a little nibble of her flesh there.

"Trick. Dammit, Trick. I need . . ."

"Shhh," he said. "I know what you need. I'll get you there."

He shoved his fingers in her, no longer gentle. He knew her body now as well as he knew his own, felt the spasms and pressed down harder with the heel of his hand, rocking it with just the right tempo until she shattered.

"Oh, yes. Oh, God, yes."

He loved the sound of her coming, the feel of her body as she let go. He wrapped an arm around her and held tight to her, licking the side of her neck and lapping up those goose bumps with his tongue as she shivered against him while she came.

When she quieted against him, he held her, kissed her throat, and ached for her.

She finally turned to face him, tracing his jaw with her fingertip. "That was an epic orgasm. Thank you."

She kissed him and wrapped her legs around him, sliding her sex against his throbbing cock.

His fingers dove into her hair and he was lost in her taste, the scent of sex blooming around them.

She pulled back. "Stand up."

He arched a brow. "You ready to get out of the tub?"

"No. I'm ready to suck your cock and make you come."

He wasn't about to turn down an invitation like that.

She slid off of him and he stood, water dripping off his body. He looked down and Stella moved to the edge of the tub, finding a spot on the ledge to sit.

"Now, come closer and bring that fine cock of yours with you."

Seeing her naked, her body flushed from the hot bath and her even hotter orgasm, made his cock lurch upward.

She reached for him with her hands, circling his shaft with both of them.

She looked up at him. "The things you do to me make me hot, Trick. And wet. You make me come like no one else ever has."

He had to admit he liked hearing that. His lips curved. "Good. And I like your hands on me. Keep doing that."

She stroked him, starting at the base and curving her hands over him, all the way to the tip, where she teased her thumb over the crest. And when she leaned forward and flicked her tongue over the head, he could have exploded right then. Touching her and having his fingers inside her had primed him. He was ready right now, but he wanted to enjoy every second of Stella's hands and mouth on him, so he intended to delay his orgasm.

Until she took him in her mouth, swallowed him whole.

"Fuck," he said, leaning forward to palm the wall.

The heat of her mouth unraveled him, the way she wrapped her fingers around the base of his cock. Her mouth was wicked temptation, crushing him, making him want to erupt. He looked down at her, watching her cheeks hollow as she gave him pressure, her head tilted back so he could see her eyes while she blew his goddamned mind.

She was the most beautiful woman he'd ever seen, and she was ripping him apart with every flick of her tongue. And when she slid his cock from her lips, only to stroke him, lift his shaft, and take his ball sac in her mouth, he thought he'd fucking die from the pleasure.

He sifted his fingers through her hair. "You're killing me, Stella."

She rolled his balls around in her mouth, then let go, gave him a devilish smile, and took his cock again, this time relentless as she sucked him hard, giving him no mercy, her head bobbing back and forth over his shaft.

He'd held back long enough. "I'm going to come."

It was all the warning he could give because his orgasm rocketed through him. He felt the first spurt like a bolt of lightning, and then an explosion of hot pleasure as he emptied into her hot mouth, uncaring now for anything but his own needs.

Stella stayed with him the entire time, her nails digging into his ass as she held on to him while he shuddered through one hell of an orgasm that left his legs shaking.

She released him and he dropped down to kneel in front of her, taking her mouth in a deep kiss that told her how goddamn much he appreciated what she'd done for him. Then he pulled her back into the tub with him and she wrapped her legs around his hips again.

"This is where I like you," he said.

"Is that right? All wet and pruny from the bath?"

"No. Wrapped around me, my cock close to you."

She laughed. "It is a good position. We should try it sometime when we're having sex."

"Making a mental note."

"The water's getting a little cold, though, so we should probably get out."

"Okay." He stood and helped her out of the tub, reaching for a couple of bath towels. He pulled one around her, diving into it with her.

"Now this I like," she said. "You and me all cozy together in a warm bathroom. Thank you again for bringing me here."

"It was my pleasure."

She flashed a grin. "Yes. I definitely saw your pleasure. Felt it, too."

He took her hand and wrapped it around his cock. "Keep talking like that and you're going to feel it again."

She stroked him, hardening him.

"Promise?"

He dropped the towel and lifted her, her legs going around him as he moved them into the bedroom. Where he had condoms. And access to her body without water getting in the way.

He laid her on the bed and she shifted back along the headboard, her body a naked smorgasbord of everything he wanted.

But her gaze zeroed in on his cock. "Now, about that condom we didn't have access to earlier . . ."

Funny how their minds always seemed to be in tune. "I was just thinking the same thing."

"Good, because I'm aching to feel you inside me. And since you're hard, why don't you put one on?"

He didn't have to be told twice. He grabbed the condom box out of the nightstand and pulled a packet out, watching as Stella slid her hand between her legs. His gaze rocketed there and he was frozen to the spot. What was it about a woman touching herself that was such a turn-on to a man? He'd like to see her get herself off. He could take his dick in his own hand and jack off watching her make herself come. He wanted to know how she did it. Did she do it fast, or was it a slow and leisurely pace? He knew he could get her there, but a woman's body was always full of secrets. Sweet, hot, soft secrets just waiting to be uncovered.

"Sucking you made me hot."

"Watching you touch yourself is making me hard." He fisted his cock and squeezed, sliding it through his hand, using his thumb to curl over the head. "I want to see how you make yourself come."

"Do you? Well, aren't you the voyeur?"

"Yeah. So do it for me. Show me."

"Are you going to do the same?"

"Yes."

She slid her fingers over her sex, slick with her excitement. "Come closer. I want to see you."

He moved to the side of the bed, next to her. She snaked her fingers over her nipples, plucking them until they stood tight and erect. "I think about you sucking them when I do this," she said.

"And I think about your mouth on me when I do this." He stroked, slow and easy, his touch not feathery light like hers, but firm. Droplets formed at the head and he used his thumb to brush them over the crest.

She moaned, lifted her hips, and used her fingers to brush over her sex, her motions faster now, her fingers parting her sweet, plump lips. She knew her body so well, just like he knew his. She was delaying her gratification and he knew it. He could get himself off in a minute if he wanted to, but this was show-and-tell. They weren't alone and in a hurry to release tension.

He could watch her for hours, the moves of her body, the splay of her fingers across her sex. It made him ache, but she was perfection. The heady scent of her permeated his senses and he gripped his cock in a tight vise, his strokes intensifying in time to hers.

She squeezed her breast at the same time her fingers disappeared between her legs. "I'm going to come."

So was he. He lifted his cock, prepared to pepper his belly.

"Oh, no." She smoothed her hand over her breast. "I want to see your come spurt out of you. Right here on my chest."

He let out a groan and moved close to the bed, palming the mattress as his strokes increased, his attention focused on her hand between her legs. "Does it feel good, babe?"

She panted out her answer. "Yes. Oh, yes."

"Then come for me. And when you go, I'll go."

A fine sheen of perspiration coated her skin as she quickened her pace, the sounds she made a sweet agony as he held back, waiting for her.

And when her hips arched off the bed and she let out a wail of satisfaction with her orgasm, her gaze met his and he released, his come spurting over her breast, coating her. He rubbed the head of his dick over her, needing that connection, needing to feel her skin against him while he poured over her.

Stella looked up at him and smiled, then circled her fingers over her breast where his fluid had accumulated.

"Now I need a shower."

He laughed. "Yeah, me, too. You made me sweat."

He took her hand and hauled her off the bed, leading her into the bathroom. He turned on the shower and both of them hopped in for a quick wash and rinse. They dried off and climbed back into bed.

"Feeling a little more relaxed now?"

She yawned. "I can barely keep my eyes open."

She lay with her head on his shoulder, her hand resting on his chest.

"Good. Go to sleep."

"I really should go back to my own place."

He looked down at her. "Why?"

She shrugged, yawned again. "I don't know. Keep things light between us. If I stay over, it's too much like a relationship. And I don't do those."

He wanted to say something to her about wanting a relationship with her, but figured maybe now wasn't the right time. She was tired, and that was a conversation to have when she was more clear-headed.

Besides, her breathing grew deeper, and when he looked down at her again, she was asleep.

Okay, definitely not the time for that conversation. He pulled the covers over them both and reached to turn off the light.

He liked having her in his bed. In his life. He wanted to keep it that way, see where things went between them. But Stella always having one foot out the door didn't make for a relationship.

Taking up with her again had opened his eyes. He wanted this woman in his life, and not just on a casual basis. But he needed to know if he was the only one thinking this way. If Stella just wanted sex from him, he was going to have to take a step back.

Which meant they were going to have to figure things out.

And sooner rather than later.

EIGHT

STELLA HADN'T MEANT TO SPEND THE NIGHT. SHE usually didn't, preferring sex to just be sex and nothing more. It didn't set up expectations that way.

Though this was Trick, and he knew the way things were between them, so she supposed she could relax about that.

She'd just been wiped last night after a grueling day of rehearsals, a few drinks with her best friend, and the awesome addition of outstanding sex. She hadn't been able to muster up the energy to get dressed and go home.

Admittedly, having Trick's body to cuddle against hadn't been all that bad. In fact, it had been pretty damn good. Her apartment was notoriously freezing in the winter, and with the weather turning abruptly cold, she typically went to bed in sweatpants, socks, and a long-sleeved shirt. Her heating bills were expensive and she couldn't afford to crank the temp high enough to make it warm, so she had to rely on extra blankets and clothes to see her through a cold night.

Last night she had slept blissfully naked with Trick's hot body acting like a blast furnace to ward off the chill.

Not that there had been a chill. His place was cozy and comfortably warm, and when she'd slid out of bed early in the morning to go to the bathroom, her teeth hadn't been chattering.

A woman could get used to such luxuries. Plus the sight of a gorgeous, naked man when she came back to bed. She'd lain there for a while, but couldn't go back to sleep, so she figured she should get dressed and go back to her place. But a quick peek out of the window told her it had snowed last night.

Ugh. Maybe coffee first. Then she'd muster up the energy to leave.

She found her underwear and pulled on one of Trick's sweatshirts, which was utterly oversize and fell to her thighs. Awesome. She added her socks and went into the kitchen to brew a cup of coffee using his Keurig. The smell was glorious. She added cream and leaned against the breakfast bar, surveying his domain.

For a simple guy, he sure lived well. His apartment was gorgeous, with dark wood floors, a decent-sized kitchen with kick-ass appliances and modern furniture in the living room, plus a great view of the city. He had two bedrooms, two bathrooms, and, for a single guy—or even a couple with no kids—it was perfect.

Not that Stella was thinking of Trick being part of a couple, or of her being part of a couple with him. But if in her wildest fantasies she entertained the idea, she could definitely live here. It was close to the subway and she could be at the Theater District in no time at all.

Not that the thought had occurred to her or anything.

Okay, maybe the thought occurred to her. She took another couple sips of coffee and wandered over to the windows. Fresh snow coated the rooftops and down below, making everything look clean and giving the city a bright shine. From inside the warmth of Trick's apartment, it felt like Christmas. She turned around and slid into one of Trick's comfortable chairs.

The problem was, indoors it wasn't the holidays at all. He had no decorations. Nothing. Not even a wreath on the door, or a candle on any of the tables.

He at least needed a Christmas tree. Maybe one set off in the corner between the living room and entry area. There was plenty of space for one. Not a super huge tree, but a moderate-sized one would definitely fit there.

She was projecting and she knew it, but she had no room in her apartment for a real tree, so she had a tiny one-foot fake tree on her kitchen pass-through. It was the best she could do to bring the holiday into her place.

But here? Trick could do so much decorating, which had always been one of her favorite things about the holiday. She remembered all the Christmases she and Greta had shared with their parents.

She paused, drank her coffee, and thought about her mom and dad. Dad was always so busy with work that he never took the time to come out here to visit, had never once seen her dance. Work was always more important. Her mom had flown out a couple of times.

It wasn't the same.

"You look deep in thought."

She lifted her gaze to see Trick coming in, wearing a pair of low-slung workout pants and no shirt, his feet bare. His hair was sleep mussed and he looked absolutely gorgeous.

Yeah, she could get used to seeing him dressed like that every morning.

"I put a cup out for you."

"Thanks." He brewed a cup of coffee and came over to sit next to her. "So what were you thinking about?"

"My parents."

"Yeah? What about them?"

She shouldn't get into it with him, was surprised she'd even brought it up. "Oh, nothing."

He laid his cup down and grasped her hand. "Tell me."

She took a deep breath.

"I miss my parents. It's the holidays, you know."

"Yeah, I know. Where do they live?"

"Portland, Oregon."

"So why don't you fly back and see them over the holiday break? You get a rehearsal break, right?"

She nodded. "It's a really busy time of year, both for flying and for me. Such a hassle. Besides, Greta's going to come up here and look for a place."

"Okay. So have your parents come out here and spend Christmas with you."

She laughed. "My dad wouldn't take the time. He barely takes Christmas Day off work."

"He's come out for your performances before, hasn't he?"

"No."

He gave her an incredulous look. "Never?"

"Never. He owns a transportation company. He's always at work, always has been at work. I imagine he always will be at work until he dies. That's just what he does. Work is his life."

"I'm sorry."

She shrugged. "I'm used to it. He made his choices and we all live with it. My mom has seen me dance, when he allows her to get away. She works for his company, too, so it's hard for her to get the time off."

He looked offended. She liked that.

"Well, that sucks."

"Tell me about it." Tired of thinking about her parents, she shook off the melancholy and smiled at him. "Tell me about your family."

"My dad died five years ago. It's just my mom now, and she lives in Milwaukee."

She laid her hand over his. "I'm sorry, Trick."

"Me, too. He was a great guy. Loved hockey and always encouraged me. He put me on skates as soon as I was old enough to balance myself and I took to the ice like I'd been born there. He and I used to skate together, play hockey together, and he never missed one of my games. He either watched me on TV or he'd come to whatever games he could. I wouldn't be where I am today without him. I miss him a lot."

Hearing him talk about his dad made her sad, wistful, and just a wee bit jealous that he'd had that kind of relationship with a parent. "He sounds like he was a wonderful man. You should be thankful to have had a parent like him."

"I am. My mom is pretty awesome, too. You'd like her. She's funny and mouthy—like you."

Stella arched a brow. "You think I'm mouthy?"

"I know you are."

"Huh." She got up and brewed another cup of coffee, then made her way back over to sit beside him. "Is your mom coming out here for Christmas, or are you heading to Milwaukee?"

"She's actually going to my sister's in Cleveland."

"So . . . you have a sister, too. How did I not know this?"

"Because we never talked about our families before."

That was true. She'd never wanted to dig deep into family with Trick before. That was too personal. She wasn't sure why she was doing it now. "Younger or older?"

"Older. Brenna's married to a great guy, Paul, and I have a five-year-old niece named Arabella."

Stella grinned. "Cute name."

"Yeah, she's cute all right. She's the princess of the family. And you'll like this—she's taking ballet lessons."

"I do like that. I'll bet she's adorable."

"She might have her uncle Trick wrapped around her little finger."

Stella laughed. She could well imagine that. "So you like kids."

He cocked his head to the side. "I love kids. Do you?"

"Very much. Though I can't seem to convince Greta to settle

down and have any. And I can't see myself having any in the near future."

He sipped his coffee. "Is that right? Why?"

"Well, first, my career. And second, I don't see myself settling down any time soon."

"I see."

That had been a very cryptic *I see.* She wondered what he meant by that, though she shouldn't care. And they were teetering on some very precarious cliffs, topic-wise, discussing family and, good God, kids. She hadn't even thought about having kids since . . .

Well. Since that last disaster of a relationship, after which she'd decided she'd never have a relationship again.

Still, she was comfortable with Trick. And that wasn't necessarily a bad thing. Maybe . . . just maybe . . .

She got up and looked around. "You need a Christmas tree."

"I do?"

"Yes." She pointed. "Over there."

"Okay."

She'd expected more of an objection. Men typically didn't like women invading their space, making suggestions. "Seriously?"

"Yeah. I've never had one here and I figure it's about time, so let's go get one today. I don't have all the bells and whistles that go with a tree, so you'll have to help me pick all that out, too."

"Okay, now you're pushing all my happy decorating buttons. Are you sure you know what you're getting into?"

"Probably not, but let's do it anyway. We'll get something to eat and then do this tree thing."

"You're on."

Several hours later they'd made multiple stops—first to her apartment so she could change clothes, then to eat because they were hungry. After that they'd gone to the tree lot. She and Trick had chosen a perfect medium-sized tree that was to be delivered, giving them enough time to hit the store and pick out lights and tree decorations. She'd put Trick in charge of choosing a tree topper and he'd come back with a box that he refused to show her, saying it was a surprise.

She only hoped it wasn't a hockey player tree topper. Then again, it was his tree so she supposed he could have whatever he wanted. She was still surprised he'd gone along with the idea at all.

They got back to his place at just the right time. They'd barely put their bags down and set up the tree stand in between the entry and living room when the doorman announced the tree delivery. Two guys brought up the tree and placed it in the stand. Trick tipped them and they were off.

The tree looked great in the living room, and smelled so good. Like pine and Christmas. It was already an improvement to his apartment.

After placing some water in the stand, Stella turned to Trick. "Ready to decorate?"

"You're in charge. Let's do this."

Trick strung the lights and Stella supervised, telling him when they were off balance or where there was a gap. They worked well together, and, once the lights were up, they put the ornaments on, bumping into each other when they rounded the back of the tree.

"No, this one should go higher up," she said, eyeing his placement.

"You're crazy. There's already a bunch up here. I'm putting it lower."

She shook her head. "Too clustered. And you're putting too many in the front. We need balance."

"No one's going to see the ones in the back anyway."

She paused to look at him. "See, everyone thinks that, but it's not true. The back of the tree should never be sparse. Ornaments should be evenly distributed."

He took a step back. "I'm going to go grab something to drink and leave you in charge of finishing this up."

She gave him a side eye. "Is this your way of making me finish the decorating?"

"Yup," he said as he walked toward the kitchen. "Want some tea?"

"That sounds good."

There weren't that many ornaments left to be put on anyway, so she inspected the tree and decided where she wanted them to go and finished up, then walked back a few steps to inspect the tree from a distance, making sure there weren't any gaps she'd missed. Satisfied, she put the lids on all the boxes.

"Where do you want these?" she asked as Trick came back with two glasses of tea.

He set the cups down on the table. "Let me take those. I'll put them in the spare bedroom closet."

"I'll help."

They put all the boxes away, then came back into the living room. Stella picked up her tea and took a couple sips. Who knew tree decorating could make her so thirsty?

She sat on the sofa and admired the tree, then frowned. "Oh, the tree topper. We forgot that."

"That's right. Let me go get it."

He set his cup down and went into the other room and came back with a box. "I think you're going to like this."

"It's a hockey player, isn't it?"

He stilled, his hands on the lid. "There are hockey player tree toppers? How did I not know this?"

She laughed. "I don't know if there are or not. I just figured that would be appropriate for your tree."

"It's not really my tree, Stella. It's your tree."

Her heart squeezed. "What?"

"You wanted this tree. It's for you. So's the topper. Close your eyes."

"Trick."

He gave her a look. "Close your eyes."

"Fine."

She shut her eyes and waited. And thought. Her tree? This was his apartment, not hers. So it most definitely was not her Christmas tree.

"You can look now."

She opened her eyes, and lifted her gaze to the top of the tree.

And gasped. She set her tea down and got up, went over to the tree and tilted her head back.

There, on his tree top, was a beautiful blonde ballerina, dressed in pink tulle, her hands in artful grace, her toes en pointe. She was twirling around in circles, with the "Dance of the Sugar Plum Fairy" from *The Nutcracker* playing.

She was mesmerized. She'd danced to this music, back when she danced ballet. The memories it evoked were thick, reminded her why she loved to dance. And the dancing angel? Breathtaking.

"This? Really? So not a guy's tree topper."

He looked up at it, then at her. "She reminds me of you with her short blonde hair and her blue eyes and that froufrou dancing outfit, even though I know that's not what you wear. But still, I saw it and thought of you and thought she'd be perfect for the tree."

Her heart was crumbling at his feet. Goddamn him for doing this to her, for making her feel things she hadn't wanted to feel for a man. Not ever again.

Hell, she'd never felt this way about any man before.

She lifted her gaze to his. "It's beautiful. Thank you for thinking of me."

"You're welcome. Now, that wasn't too painful, was it?"

He had no idea. "I guess not. Are you sure your friends won't make fun of you when they see it?"

He laughed. "They probably will, but I think I can take the heat."

She stared up at the dancing angel again. "I love her."

He wasn't looking at the angel, but at her. "So do I."

Inhaling on a shaky breath, she said, "Well. What now?"

"Isn't it obvious?"

"Not to me."

"Now we go out and play in the snow."

"You are out of your ever-loving mind. It's nice and warm in here."

"I know. But we had some great snow yesterday. Where's your sense of adventure?"

"My sense of adventure is here. In your warm apartment. Besides, we already went out. We chose a tree. Outside. Isn't that enough?"

"No." He looked her over. "You're dressed warm enough and you have boots on. It'll do. Grab your coat and stuff."

She was not going to get out of this. "Okay, fine. But if you throw me in a snow pile, it's over between us."

"Jesus, Stella, I'm not twelve."

Maybe she was being too harsh. Or too suspicious. More likely she just didn't want to go out in the cold and the snow again. But Trick had been so sweet about the tree topper, she was going to be a sport about playing outside with him.

"Fine. We'll go."

"Good. And we'll have fun."

"Sure we will."

She thought they'd grab a taxi outside. Instead, he took her hand in his and they started walking. The streets and sidewalks had been cleared, and she had to admit, the snow was pretty. It was cold, but walking kept her warm. Plus, she had her hat, gloves, and a scarf on, so it wasn't like she was freezing or anything.

"Where are we going, exactly?" she asked after they entered Central Park.

He looked over at her and gave her a secretive smile. "I told you. To play."

With it being Saturday, the park was filled with kids as well as adults. The bare trees were a stark landscape against the as-of-yet undisturbed pure white snow that had piled up along the rocks and hills of the park. It was a gorgeous backdrop and she wished she had thought to bring her camera with her to grab some shots. She did have her phone, though, so she stopped to take a few pictures as they strolled along. Trick even asked one of the passersby to take a photo of the two of them on one of the bridges. He'd pulled her against him, her cheek resting against his shoulder. She looked at the shot and thanked the person for taking the picture.

It was a good photo of the two of them.

"We look good together, don't we?" he asked as he looked at it with her.

"Yes, we do." She'd left her knit cap on, but wisps of her hair peeked out and her cheeks were pink from the cold. Trick had a hat on, too, but he looked rugged and oh so handsome in his pea coat, and she looked like she belonged in his arms.

Whatever. Just a picture. She was making too much of it. It had just been a long time since she'd had a picture of her and a guy.

When he stopped at the ice rink, he turned to her. "Feel like a little skating?"

She wondered if he thought she'd balk. "Sure."

"Do you know how to skate?"

"Yes, I know how to skate." She grabbed his hand and tugged him toward the entrance. "Come on."

They rented skates, and without even waiting for Trick, Stella glided out onto the ice.

She twirled around, taking in the feeling of freedom she got on the rink. It had been a couple of years since she'd been skating, and as she took a lap, she'd forgotten how much she enjoyed it. It was so much like dancing, the movement of her legs, the sense of creation she felt as she directed her skates along the ice. As she made her way back to the rink entrance, Trick came out and joined her, slipping his arm around her waist. She lifted her gaze to his and smiled, and the two of them danced around the rink, their bodies close together. Here, he wasn't the tough hockey player. He was hers. And it wasn't a game, it was a dance on skates. Their bodies glided effortlessly together, in tune with one another.

"You're good at this," he said.

"You seem surprised."

He took her hands and, as he skated backward, because the ice was home to him, he swept her in a circle. "I am surprised."

"I skated all the time when I was a kid. When I took dancing lessons, I envisioned myself as a figure skater someday."

He skated around her, then came up behind her, sliding his arms alongside hers. "I could see you in those short skater outfits, doing flips in the air."

She leaned against him and let him lead her on the ice. "You could, huh? You're pretty awesome on the ice yourself. There's a lyrical way to your movement."

He stared at her. "Really? I thought I looked kind of tough."

"Trust me, you are tough. But there's also a beauty to the way you move on the ice."

"Thanks. Never saw myself as pretty on the ice, though."

"I didn't say pretty. I said there's a beauty to your movement. It's the dancer in me. Anyway, we're both good on the ice. Maybe we could do pairs. Or ice dancing."

He laughed, the sound of it rumbling against her back. "No dancing for me. I'm a klutz."

"Maybe on the dance floor, but on the ice? You know the ice." She swiveled in his arms, then assumed the dance position, taking his hand and sliding her other hand to his shoulder. "Come dance with me. You lead, I'll follow."

She thought he'd balk, but he pushed forward, and suddenly, they were dancing, her following his lead as they glided across the surface. There was music playing, and she lost herself in the song and the feel of the man beside her.

The man could dance. At least on the ice. He twirled her, pulling her tight against him, then pushing her out, the two of them in sync like nothing she'd ever felt before. She was giddy, laughing, and suddenly they had an audience as people stopped to watch.

It wasn't like they were Olympic-level ice dancers or anything. They weren't that good. It was likely that hockey fans recognized

Trick. She didn't care. She was having more fun than she could ever remember having while either dancing or skating.

It had to be the man, because Trick wasn't paying any attention to the gathering crowd. He was only looking at her, and it wasn't in a sexual way. It was a deeper connection, the kind of way a man looked at a woman when he . . .

She stumbled, and he caught her. She covered by laughing and falling against him.

"Okay, so maybe the Olympics won't be calling on us to join their ice-dancing team," she said, lifting her gaze to his.

Whatever spell had wound around them had broken. Their audience clapped, and it was as if Trick had noticed them for the first time. He looked around, smiled and nodded, then wrapped an arm around her and they resumed normal skating.

"Yeah, I don't think I'm cut out for dancing on the ice. My style is a little more aggressive, and I'm a lot more comfortable with a stick in my hand and a puck to chase after. But you're a great dancer on or off the ice."

She shifted, skating in front of him. "And how would you know that since you haven't seen me dance yet?"

"Call it intuition. And I have seen the way you move your body." He waggled his brows.

She rolled her eyes. "Not at all the same thing."

"Isn't it?" He gave her a very knowing look.

"Trust me. Sex and dancing aren't at all the same."

"I guess I'll have to watch you dance sometime. Then I'll draw my own conclusions."

"You do that."

They skated for another half hour or so, an exhilarating workout. Then they called it quits and left the ice.

"That was fun. Thanks for taking me," she said as they started their walk back to Trick's apartment.

"You're welcome. You need to get out and play more often."

They came across a group of kids playing in the snow pack on the sidewalk. One of them recognized Trick, so he stopped to talk with them.

Stella stood back and observed. Trick was a natural with kids. He wasn't condescending, didn't act like a superstar. He was just a regular guy around the boys. And when one of the kids hit his buddies with a snowball, Trick got into the middle of all of it, like he was one of them.

She laughed at it, until Trick bundled up a snowball and aimed it in her direction. She shrieked and tried to hide, but he ran her down and smacked her in the back with a soft snowball.

Then it was on, and they found themselves in the middle of a snowball war with the kids. Before long several more kids in the neighborhood joined in. Stella had never laughed so hard as she lofted one snowball after the other. These kids were good, obviously having gotten a lot more practice than either she or Trick. Trick was definitely a target—a rather large one—something he didn't seem to mind at all. Removing herself from the fray, she took pictures of the major battle, laughing at the same time as one of the kids hit Trick with a snowball to the back of the head.

They finally extricated themselves from the bombardment and said good-bye to the kids, making their way back to his apartment.

"I'm pretty sure one of those snowballs landed inside the back of my coat," she said as she hung it up, then pulled off her boots. "I'm all wet."

"But you had fun, didn't you?"

She still had a smile on her face. "I did. It reminded me of building snow forts with Greta when we were kids."

"Yeah, my sister and I used to do the same thing. Coffee?" he asked as they made their way into the kitchen.

"Definitely."

He brewed them each a cup, and took the cream out of the refrigerator for her.

"Thanks."

He laid his cup down, then went over and turned on the Christ-mas tree lights before taking a seat on the sofa next to her.

"Looks good there," he said.

She stared up at the dancing angel, still so surprised he'd thought of her when he'd bought it. She didn't know what to make of it—or of him. Or of their relationship.

Dammit. There was that word again, the one she so religiously avoided.

"Yeah, it looks good."

"You and I should spend Christmas together."

She nearly choked on her sip of coffee. She shifted to face him. "What?"

"You said you weren't going home, and your parents won't be coming here. We should spend Christmas together."

Christmas together? She waited for the panic to clutch her around the throat.

Nothing came. It always did when some guy asked her for any-thing that felt remotely like a commitment. And spending a holi-day together was a commitment. It was a relationship.

But Trick wasn't just some guy. He was becoming more than that.

She waited again for the terror, the need to end things, to run as far and as fast as she could.

Nothing. Still, she was going to have to handle this whole thing delicately.

"I told you Greta's coming for Christmas."

"Yeah. So we'll all hang out. I'll cook a turkey. She can adore this awesome tree."

He made it sound so simple. It wasn't. Not to her, anyway. "I'll give it some thought."

"You do that."

"Okay, well, I should go."

"You don't want to stay?" He moved over and slid his arms

around her waist. "I thought we'd have dinner and you might want to hang out. I could cook for you. Then rub your feet later."

He waggled his brows, the invitation quite clear.

He was almost the perfect man, which meant there had to be something lurking under the exterior. Some bomb he'd drop later to break her heart. She didn't trust her own instincts, not after the nightmare she'd endured the last time.

She laid her palms on his chest. "Tempting as that sounds, the only time I have to do laundry and grocery shopping and clean my apartment is on the weekend. So, sadly, duty calls."

He took a step back. "Gotcha. Some other time."

"Definitely."

He didn't even pout when he didn't get his way or she couldn't spend time with him.

See? Too perfect.

She gathered her things and put on her coat.

"I ordered a taxi for you," he said. "Should be outside waiting for you."

"Thanks."

He tugged on the lapels of her coat, drawing her toward him so he could kiss her. She fell into the kiss, against the heat of his body as he swept his hands inside her coat.

She could so easily get lost in him, in the way his lips moved over hers, and forget all her rules about not letting her heart get involved. But her steely resolve had protected her all these years, and for a good reason.

She pulled back. "I guess I'll see you after your game Monday?"

"Yup. Don't work too hard." He rubbed his thumb over her bottom lip, and that steely resolve melted a little. Inhaling a shaky breath, she moved away from him and grabbed her bag.

He walked her to the door. "Be careful out there."

"I will. Bye."

She went downstairs and, just as Trick said, there was a taxi waiting for her. She climbed in and gave the driver her address, then leaned back, already wishing she was still with Trick.

She'd had fun with him the past couple of days. He was sexy, romantic, and fun. A lethal combination. She didn't know what she was going to do. Normally when she started to feel things for a guy, she knew the next step—end things.

This time, though, it was different, because the thought of walking away from Trick and never seeing him again made her heart hurt.

She was in deep trouble.

NINE

STELLA GOT INTO POSITION AND WAITED FOR THE
music cue, her body tense, but her entire being focused. When the
music started, she felt it enter her soul, her limbs moving in time
to the strains of the recorded orchestra. Her body had memorized
every note, her soul embedded in this role.

This was what she loved the most about dance, the way she
could embody a role, letting the music carry her away. After months
of practice, she could dance this part with her eyes closed. She knew
where she needed to be. She knew every movement, every leap,
each turn, and where her partner was going to be so when she threw
herself into the air, he would be there to catch her. Because dance
was always about trust, especially when you were relying on someone else to be there for you. They had all been working so hard, and
it was finally coming together, especially this oh-so-important
opening scene. She felt this scene in her bones, dreamed about it at

night, made each step in her head when she stood in line at the grocery store.

The dance was fluid, each of them moving seamlessly around each other. It was a breathless feeling, and she wished she could be on the outside looking in. Even though they weren't in costume, she felt the perfection of it all, and when it ended, she lay on the floor in her partner's arms, the two of them looking up at each other and grinning.

"Good, huh?" Nevin said.

"Fucking perfect, if you ask me." Stella grinned back at him, then Nevin pulled her off the floor.

"Well, that was okay. You all can do better. Take ten, then we'll move on to the second scene," Lawrence said, then headed off the stage.

Lisa walked over. "He said it was okay."

Stella found her water in her bag and took several swallows. "I know, right? High praise coming from our esteemed choreographer."

"It's almost like he thought we were good," Nevin said.

Stella laughed. "Now don't go thinking that. You know he thinks we all suck."

Nevin nodded. "Alas, so true. Why he chose us, I'll never know."

They spent several minutes going over the next scene while also rehashing how very awesome the opening was. Stella didn't care what Lawrence said. She'd felt that dance deep inside. They'd nailed it. She'd nailed it.

"I need to make a call before he wants us up for round two," Nevin said. "Catch you all in a bit."

Nevin wandered off.

"I need to do the same," Lisa said.

"Okay." Stella just longed to sit down for a few minutes, so she went to the edge of the stage, figuring she'd let her legs dangle and rest.

She skidded to a halt on the stage when she saw Lawrence in deep conversation with a very tall, extremely good-looking man she recognized right off as Trick.

What the hell was he doing at the theater? And why was he talking to Lawrence?

"There's Stella now," Lawrence said. "I'll let you go. Nice talking to you, Trick. And thanks again."

"It was my pleasure, Lawrence. Say hi to Jonathan for me."

"I definitely will."

Trick and Lawrence shook hands—like they were old friends. For Christ's sake, Lawrence even smiled.

That man did not smile. Ever.

What the ever-loving fuck was going on? Had she fallen and bumped her head? Because this had to be some kind of dream.

She walked off the stage and met Trick.

"What are you doing here?"

"I sat in the back and watched your rehearsal."

"What—how? Rehearsals are closed. Lawrence is a monster about that. No one gets to watch. Hell, he wouldn't let his own grandmother watch a rehearsal."

His lips curved. "Well, I don't know about that, because I just did. You're incredible, by the way. The way you dance, Stella? I never knew you were that good. I'm really impressed. But I can see why you complain about Lawrence. He's really hard on you. On all of you."

Ignoring his compliment, her head spun at the information pouring into it. Not only had he watched the rehearsal, but—

"Oh, God, Trick. Please tell me you didn't say anything to Lawrence about him being hard on me." She'd die. She'd not only die, she'd get fired.

"Of course not. This is your job, Stella. I'd never interfere in that."

"And yet here you are. At my job. Don't you have your own job to go to? You have a game tonight."

He gave her a warm smile. He was obviously happy about being here, while she was not. It unnerved the hell out of her.

"Warm-ups aren't until later. I had some time, so I thought I'd drop by and see you dance. Is that a problem?"

"Yes, it's a problem. It's a big problem."

"I don't understand why."

She didn't know why, either, other than she knew he wasn't supposed to be here. Something just wasn't sitting right with her. "How did you even get in here?"

"Let's just say I know people who know people."

She laid her water bottle down on one of the seats and crossed her arms. "Explain that to me."

"I found out Lawrence's boyfriend Jonathan is a big hockey fan. So I might have pulled some strings and said I could get them season tickets if Lawrence would let me pop in this morning to watch some of your rehearsal."

Stella knew it was really damn hard—if not nearly impossible—to get Travelers season tickets. "It was that important to you to watch me sweat on stage during a rehearsal?"

"It wasn't that big a deal, honestly. You're blowing this way out of proportion. I wanted to watch how hard you were working—which is very hard, by the way. I saw an opening and I took it. Lawrence was happy to let me watch. It's not like I'm in here with some camera taking pictures that I'm going to sell to competitors or to the paparazzi, and he knows that. I wanted to see my girlfriend dance, and he gets to surprise his boyfriend with season tickets to the Travelers games. It's a win/win."

There were so many things wrong with what he'd just said, but she'd zeroed in on the one word that made her sweat more than all the grueling hours of rehearsal she went through.

"I'm not your girlfriend."

"Oh, I see. So I should have said 'that chick I'm fucking'?"

She rubbed the side of her head. "You're giving me a headache."

"And I don't get why this is a thing. What's wrong with me

watching you dance? I told you the other day I hadn't seen you dance yet, and I wanted to. I figured this was a great opportunity. I'm sorry it freaked you out."

It had freaked her out. For so many reasons it made her head spin.

He pulled out his phone. "Listen, I gotta go. You looked amazing up there—like you were born to be on the stage. See you at the game tonight?"

She nodded mutely, and he turned and left.

No good-bye. No kiss. No . . . anything.

Then again, she'd been the one to rain on his parade, hadn't she? So what did she expect? Flowers and him bending her over backwards with a swooning kiss? He'd tried to surprise her with something sweet, and she'd been a major bitch about it.

She was a moron.

A moron who didn't know what she wanted.

"I DON'T UNDERSTAND WOMEN."

Trick sat in the locker room after an intense late afternoon practice with his team.

Drew was sitting next to him and nudged him with his shoulder. "Dude. We're not supposed to. That whole mystery thing is what's so fun about them."

Trick shook his head and stared down at his skates. "I don't know. This whole thing with Stella is about as mysterious as waking up after an all-night bender with one hell of a hangover, cotton mouth, and no memory of the night before. Only you know you had a shitty night and not a good time."

Drew gave him a look. "That bad, huh?"

"Yeah."

"Wanna talk about it? Maybe I can help."

He gave Drew a look. "I don't know. Stella gives me mixed signals. She's with me, but it's like she doesn't really want to be."

"Carolina would likely say that maybe Stella's scared of commitment."

Trick snorted. "Wow, you've learned some things."

"I pick stuff up here and there. Living with a woman will do that to you. But seriously, have you talked to her about it?"

"She's not really into talking about the deep shit."

Drew's brows rose. "And you are? Since when?"

"I don't know. I guess since Stella."

"Huh. Big admission for you, since you were always such a player."

Trick shrugged. "Maybe I don't want to be a player anymore. Now I just have to convince Stella."

Drew laughed and slapped Trick on the back. "Try talking to her, and keep talking until she hears what you're saying."

"I guess."

"Now, enough about women. We have a big game tonight and you need your focus."

Drew was right about that. He had to shake off thoughts of Stella and put them where they belonged.

On the game, where they were supposed to be.

They needed this win tonight.

After they kicked Detroit's ass, he'd turn his attention back on the woman who was currently tying his stomach up in knots.

TEN

STELLA MET CAROLINA IN THE CLUB SUITE.

"You look hot, as always," Carolina said.

Stella looked down at her black skinny jeans, her knee-high boots, and her green sparkly top that she'd covered with a leather jacket. "I thought I was dressed kind of average tonight."

Carolina looped her arm through Stella's. "Honey, you are anything but average. You look gorgeous."

"So do you. I'm in love with that cream jacket. The strategic placement of those zippers is killing me."

Carolina laughed. "Of course. It's always about the zippers for you, isn't it?"

"All the time."

They wandered over to the buffet and found something to eat and drink, then grabbed a seat with a prime view of the guys during warm-ups.

"How's it going with the design stuff?"

"Actually, pretty good," Carolina said. "We're on schedule, I have amazing models to walk the runway for me, and we just finished a fitting for everyone this morning. Fingers crossed, because I don't want to jinx anything, but it looks like everything's going smoothly."

"I'm glad to hear it. Is Drew going to walk for you this year?"

Carolina laughed. "Unfortunately, no. He claimed that was a one-time thing last year, so he refuses to be a model for me again. Though the ad campaign he did on the ice was incredibly successful."

"Of course it was. Hot hockey player wearing Carolina Designs underwear? How could it not be?"

"He did look spectacular on those billboards, didn't he?"

"I'll say."

Carolina's gaze strayed to the ice, where Drew and Trick were passing the puck back and forth. "Maybe I could convince Trick to model my underwear this year."

"I'm sure you could convince Trick to model naked for you."

Carolina laughed and turned her attention back to Stella. "And you wouldn't mind that?"

She shrugged. "I don't own the man, or any part of his body. He's all yours."

"Hmm, that sounds a lot like you two might have had a fight."

"We didn't fight at all. To fight means we have a relationship, and you know I don't do that."

Carolina took a sip of water and leaned back in her chair. "Okay, spill. What's going on?"

"Nothing, really."

"Stell, I know you. You're always so free and easy about the men you see. There's clearly something more going on with you and Trick."

That was the problem with best friends—they knew everything about you. Or, almost everything, anyway. "Fine. We've been getting closer and it's unnerving me."

"Unnerving you in what way?"

She gave her friend a pointed look. "Mainly that I've allowed it to happen at all."

"Ah, I see. Because that goes against your standard MO of fuck 'em and leave 'em."

"Exactly. What's wrong with me? We hooked up last year, and that was fine and all. Okay, it was more than fine. It was great. But then we drifted apart, and here we are again. I never do this. I never see a guy twice."

"But, like you said, here you are. Why is that?"

"I don't know. I mean beyond the sex, we're going out and doing things. He took me to the park and we went ice-skating. We bought a tree for his place and decorated it together. And then he showed up at the theater today and watched me dance."

"Horrors."

Stella slanted her a look. "Seriously. Rehearsals are closed, and yet Lawrence welcomed Trick with open arms. I didn't even know he was there until we had a break."

"Maybe Lawrence is a big hockey fan."

"His partner is, and Trick snuck in there by promising Lawrence season tickets to the Travelers so he could surprise his partner."

"Awww, that's sweet. He cares enough about you that he wanted to see you dance, Stell."

Stella shrugged.

"And all the other things, like shopping for a tree, and going ice-skating together? That sounds like two people who enjoy each other going out and having fun."

"It sounds like a relationship," she shot back, then realized her voice had a little more force and venom than she would have liked.

"You're making it sound like a bad thing, when in fact, it sounds to me like the man is in love with you."

Stella took a long swallow of her water and sighed. "That's what I'm afraid of."

"So you don't return his feelings?"

"I do. That's the problem. The big, huge thing that keeps me up at night. I think I've fallen in love with him, Carolina. Do you know how awful that is?"

Carolina shook her head. "No, honey, I'm sorry, but I don't." She reached over and smoothed her hand over her hair. "What are you so afraid of?"

She'd never talked about it. Not to anyone. Greta knew about the breakup, but Stella hadn't even told her sister the real story. At least not what had kept her from committing to anyone all these years.

"I was dating this guy—Vernon—about eight years ago. I was eighteen when we met and we were together two years. It was so intense. We were in love. Living together. Planning a future together. We were both dancers. It was great, you know? He really understood me since we had the same career."

Carolina nodded. "Makes sense."

"I thought it was forever. Until he got a job offer to dance in Los Angeles. And he took it."

"Without talking to you about it?" Carolina asked.

Stella nodded.

"So he broke up with you?"

"No. He just assumed I'd give up my career here and move with him. He figured I'd get another job at some point out in L.A. Like my job at the time didn't even matter at all."

"That's insane."

"I agree. When I told him I wasn't moving, he got mad at me and complained about me not loving him. I did love him and I wanted to figure out a way to work things out, but with him there was no compromise. He'd made a unilateral decision without consulting me. I was heartbroken. I love New York, I had a great gig at the time, and I wanted to stay here. He said if I really loved him, I'd move with him. It was so black-and-white to him, when it was anything but to me."

Carolina shook her head. "Men can be so stupid and egotistical sometimes."

"Right? I told him I wasn't moving. I loved New York and intended to stay here. You would have thought from the way he looked at me that I'd cut off his right leg or something. He had the nerve to act like he was the one who'd been hurt."

Carolina rolled her eyes.

"The breakup was ugly. I thought I was going to marry him, and instead, he moved away. I lost trust in men after that."

"He hurt you. Badly. And no wonder you've been relationship-shy all these years. But all men aren't like Vernon, honey."

"Logic tells me that. My heart tells me something different. I just couldn't risk falling so deeply in love and letting someone hurt me like that again. Or maybe it's me. Maybe there's something broken inside of me."

"You're not broken, Stell. You were hurt, and when someone breaks your trust like that, it's hard to get over. I went through something similar with Drew, if you recall. It was hard for me to trust in him again."

Stella nodded. "I remember. And if I recall, my advice to you was to fuck him and dump him. Some sage advice that was. Drew's a great guy and he loves you. You love him. It all worked out for you, and clearly I had no idea what I was talking about. See? I don't think I can be trusted where men and my emotions are concerned."

Carolina laughed. "You were just trying to protect me. You were being a friend. And now I'm going to be one to you. Don't judge all men by how Vernon treated you. If you love Trick, maybe you should give him the benefit of the doubt. At least talk to him about your fears."

Maybe she should. She'd never told anyone about Vernon. And now she'd told Carolina, who hadn't made her feel stupid about it. "I guess. I'll try."

Carolina squeezed her hand. "See? Progress."

ELEVEN

THEY WERE TIED TWO TO TWO AFTER THE END OF THE second period. Trick's frustration level was high, but he was trying to keep his focus. They all were. It was intermission, so they sat in the locker room, attempting to figure out a strategy so they could win this goddamn game.

"They're killing off our power plays," their coach said. "We have to do better there."

Coach was right about that. They weren't taking advantage of the power plays. They'd had three so far and hadn't capitalized on any of them.

"Their goals have been lucky shots. We can beat these guys. Our strength and stamina are better, so let's go show them what we can do."

They stood, and raised their sticks in the air, touching them together.

"You guys are the best team I've ever coached," the coach said. "Now, let's kick their butts."

They took the ice to the cheer of the crowd, something that always fired up Trick. With the home crowd behind them, he knew they could win this. Now they just had to prove to their fans they were as good as the applause they were getting.

Drew took the face-off and Trick clutched his stick, ready for the puck. When it sailed away from him, he took off after it, only to skid to a halt when Drew scooped the puck up and shot it toward him. He was right by the net, so he took the shot.

It bounced off the right side of the goal and into the net, lighting up the lamp.

The crowd roared and Trick raised his stick in triumph, more shocked than anything because it had happened so damn fast. They did a quick celebration, then reset. It felt good to be up by a goal that quickly, but there was a lot of time left to play.

Detroit scored two minutes later, tying the game. Shit.

After fighting it out for another few minutes, they came off the ice for a break, and Litman and Sayers took over. It was hard not to be out there, but these guys were just as good. And when Detroit took the puck down to their end, the Travelers defenders kept them from scoring, even though Trick held his breath the entire time. Fortunately, Litman scored for the Travelers, and they could all breathe again. But going up one goal just wasn't enough.

When he and Drew made their way back onto the ice, he was determined they were going to score again. A little too determined, maybe, because he got called on a cross-checking penalty and had to sit in the box, giving Detroit a power play.

Goddammit. Stupid move on his part. He'd wanted to play clean, not give Detroit an advantage. He divided his time between watching the clock and his teammates, hoping like hell Detroit didn't score on his penalty.

He knew his guys, knew they could hold them, but Detroit played tough and they spent nearly the entire two minutes playing at the Travelers' end of the ice. When Kozlow shot the puck to the Detroit end with only fifteen seconds left in Trick's penalty, he hoped it was enough.

The last five seconds felt like an eternity, but he was out of the box and back on the ice, and Detroit hadn't scored. He didn't even have time to feel relieved about that, because they were in a battle with the clock. Time was running out on the game, and Detroit was relentless in their attack. But the Travelers' defense was solid, and by the time the puck came back to Trick and Drew, they felt they had this game. They were at the net, battling with Detroit's defenders, and Trick saw an opening. He slid the puck to Drew, who slotted it in behind the left post for another score.

This game was all but over. There was a minute left at the face-off, and Detroit fought hard for it, but time ticked off the clock, and when the buzzer rang, they celebrated hard. They'd fought for this win against a really tough opponent, and the victory was sweet.

In the locker room after the game, they were a few champagne bottles short of a massive celebration. And okay, maybe they were over-celebrating what was only a regular-season win. But they'd gotten a monkey off their backs, and it had meant a lot to them. Now they could move forward with the rest of the season, know-ing they were *that* good.

After media interviews, he showered and got dressed, and he and Drew met Carolina and Stella outside the locker room. That was a first for him, since getting Stella to come down here was like getting her to admit she might actually care about him, which he knew damn well was next to impossible.

Drew turned to him. "So, how about the four of us—"

"Actually, I have plans for you tonight," Carolina said, tugging on his arm. "Not to be rude, but I'm taking my man home for a private celebration."

Stella and Carolina exchanged knowing smiles.

"Can't turn down an invitation like that," Drew said. "Sorry, you two."

Trick's lips curved. "No problem. See you later."

Stella waved. "Bye. Love you both."

He took Stella's arm and guided her down the passageway toward the exit, then flagged down a waiting car. Once inside he turned to her. "Okay, what was that all about?"

"What was what about?"

"You and Carolina."

"I have no idea what you're talking about. Clearly she wanted to spend some alone time with her guy to celebrate tonight's victory." She scooted closer to him. "And I think we should do the same. Go to your place, order some takeout?"

He wasn't about to argue with her. Obviously she had something in mind for tonight, something she and Carolina had both cooked up. He was going to play along. "Sounds good to me."

They ended up eating takeout Thai food at his place, and Stella even opted for a beer, though she complained she'd have to work it off later. She'd taken off her boots and he'd kicked off his shoes, the two of them tangling their feet together as they lounged on his sofa.

He stared down at her feet, wondered if they hurt after all those hours she put in. They had to. He knew all the hits he endured took a toll on his body. Hers had to do the same. Different sport, but still, you didn't put that much energy into your job without suffering the consequences. "I don't know. I've seen how hard you work when you dance. Seems to me you burn off a lot of calories."

"Yeah, about that. I'm really sorry about this morning. I was an ass to you when you went to all that trouble to see me dance."

He shrugged and took a long pull of his beer. "No big deal. I freaked you out. I should have let you know in advance that I was going to be coming to the theater."

She leaned against him. "Then I would have been more freaked out knowing you were watching me. It was a nice surprise. Thank you again."

"You're welcome."

She climbed onto his lap, sliding her fingers into his hair. "No, really. Thank you."

He'd had the idea she'd orchestrated this move to be alone with him tonight so the two of them could talk. And he'd been fine with that, because there were things he wanted to say to her—important things he figured they needed to get clear with each other.

But right now it seemed she wanted to touch and be touched, and he sure as hell wasn't going to argue about that. Not when she was moving against his body in a way that made his dick sit up and take notice, her long graceful legs wrapping around his hips and her sex making contact with his quickly hardening cock.

"Got something on your mind?"

"Maybe. Definitely." She pressed in and rubbed her lips against his.

Her mouth was hot, her tongue darting in to flick at his, inflaming his senses, taking his cock to full mast. He lifted against her, needing to be inside her right goddamn now.

He stood, taking her with him, then turned around and deposited her on the sofa, reaching down to undo her jeans. Those tight barriers to what he wanted had to go first. She wriggled out of them as he pulled them over her hips and legs. He tossed them on the nearby chair, and then kneeled on the rug in front of the sofa and slipped his hand over the silk of her underwear. She was already damp. Ready.

So was he, but he pulled the silk aside and flicked her with his tongue.

"Trick."

The way she said his name heightened his arousal, made his cock press against the zipper of his jeans, demanding to be freed.

Ignoring those demands, he spread her legs and speared her with his tongue, flicking the soft bud until her hips rose.

"I could come right now," she said, more to herself than to him, he knew. She was lost and ready, and he intended to take her there.

He rose over her, spread her further, and laid his tongue flat over her clit, knowing that would get her off fast. He wanted fast. He wanted her to lose control, to give it all over to him.

And when she did, crying out his name with her climax, it was the sweetest reward. He licked her everywhere as she shuddered against his mouth with her release. He stayed with her until her trembles subsided.

Then he climbed up her body and took her mouth in a deep kiss meant to convey passion and need and everything he'd bottled up inside during the game today. While he'd shoved his feelings for Stella into the deep, dark recesses of his mind during the game, now they were fully present, and he intended to let her know exactly what he felt. Everything he felt whenever he was with her.

He wasn't going to hold anything back. He never had with her, and that had been the telling difference between her and every other woman he'd ever been with. He fished a condom out of his pocket and pulled away only long enough to undress, then helped Stella with her top and bra.

When she wrapped her fingers oh so delicately around his cock, he stood and watched her stroke him, steeling his resolve to climb on top of her and sink inside her until he was lost, until he couldn't think anymore. Because watching her small hand around his length, the way she looked at him when she held him in her hands, was a connection he never intended to lose.

And when she let go only long enough to slide off the sofa and get on her knees, giving him a wicked grin over her shoulder, he knew this was the woman for him. She always seemed to know what he wanted, and right now he needed deep, plunging passion, a hard connection with Stella, the kind that would cement her to him.

Maybe they hadn't shared the words yet, but he was in love with her, and he intended to tell her as soon as possible.

Now he'd show her.

He put on the condom and positioned himself behind her, sliding into her slow and easy, feeling every incredible inch until he was embedded deep. Her body surrounded him, squeezing him tight until there was nothing between them.

Then he began to move, easing out slowly, then thrusting deep again.

He didn't say anything, and neither did Stella. He focused on the way her breath caught whenever he plunged deep, and cupped her breasts so he could play with her nipples, feeling them harden under his fingertips. It was just the two of them in tune with each other's bodies, and the emotion swirling through him at the thought of this woman being part of his life.

He tried to push it aside, but Stella meant something to him, and he'd never made love to a woman that was part of his heart before.

He pulled out and drew her to the rug, then reentered her, this time making eye contact with her. She wrapped her legs tightly around him and as he cupped her butt and ground against her, her eyes widened. She reached up and skimmed her fingertips across his jaw.

"What are you doing to me?"

He wanted to say the words, but he was caught up in the emotion, didn't want to spoil the moment by saying something she might not be ready for yet, so he lifted her arm above her head and caught her hand in his, then drove into her, giving her what she needed—what they both needed.

Her breathing quickened, her sex gripping his cock in a stranglehold of spasms.

"Trick, I'm coming."

He bent and kissed her, absorbing her cries as she came. He let go, his orgasm like a lightning bolt of pure adrenaline as it burst from his body, pulse after pulse of pleasure that shattered him until he felt like he couldn't take his next breath.

He finally rolled over onto his back, not sure whose breathing was more ragged—his or Stella's.

"I think you might be trying to kill me," she finally said.

He turned his head to see her staring up at the ceiling.

"You okay?"

She looked over at him and grinned. "Definitely okay. But thirsty."

They cleaned up, then Trick fixed them tall glasses of ice water. Instead of getting dressed, Stella rummaged through his closet, found an old long-sleeved flannel shirt of his, and rolled up the sleeves.

He looked at her as she leaned against his kitchen counter. His shirt hung low on her thighs, showing off her long legs.

"I like you wearing my shirts. I was thinking about buying you some pajamas—the girl kind—to wear here, since we often end up naked, but I think I like this better."

She took a sip of water, then set the glass on the counter and came over to him, lifting up to press a kiss to the column of his throat. "Me, too. Your clothes smell like you."

A rush of possessiveness came over him, and he curled his arm around her waist and tugged her close for a long, deep kiss. When they came up for air, her cheeks were pink.

"Well, that was nice. Ready for round two, then?" she asked.

"Definitely, but first I think we need to talk."

She gave him a wary look. "Uh-oh. Does this mean we're breaking up? Though I suppose to break up we'd have to be a couple, and we're not really that, are we?"

"Aren't we? We've seen each other off and on for a year now, Stella. When I'm with you I don't see anyone else. And frankly . . . I don't want to see anyone else. So maybe it's time we call this what it is—a relationship."

Stella swallowed, hard. She'd meant to broach the subject with Trick tonight, but then she'd chickened out and they'd had sex instead.

Really great, phenomenal sex that had been emotional as well as physical. There had been something in Trick's eyes when he'd had her on the floor, looking at her as he'd moved inside her, something that had tugged at her heart and hit all her hot buttons. She'd tried to dismiss it as just their awesome physical connection, but she'd known deep down it had been more than that.

And now . . .

"You want a relationship."

"Yes. I'm in love with you."

Oh, shit. This she hadn't expected. "You are?"

His lips curved, and she lost herself in that sexy smile of his, the one that always mesmerized her and made her want to throw herself on top of him so he could have his way with her.

"Yeah. And I've never said that to any other woman before you, other than my mom and my sister. And that doesn't really count, does it?"

She laughed. "I guess not. Except to your mother and sister, of course."

Now was the time for her to confess her feelings. She opened her mouth to say the words, but hesitated.

"Trick, I . . ."

Come on, Stella. Man up and do this. You can trust him.

He rubbed her arm. "Hey, it's okay. You don't have to say anything."

"I love you." She'd blurted it, and made it sound rushed and empty. She was an awful person.

He laughed. "I said you didn't have to say it back."

She stepped into him and wrapped her arms around him, tilting her head back so he could see the truth in her eyes. "I love you. I really do. I'm just new at this. And a little bit afraid."

"You want to tell me why you're afraid?"

She did want to tell him, but not right now. "Let's just say love didn't work so well for me the first time I tried it."

"You want to tell me about it?"

She did. But for some reason, the words didn't come. "At some point, I will. But not now. That's the past, and it's unpleasant. Right now, I'm happy, so let's not go there."

"Fair enough. I'm going to want to hear that story sometime. But I can guarantee you I'm not going to hurt you. You're my future, Stella."

Her heart swelled with so much love and hope she didn't know what to do with all these feelings. For someone so used to cynicism about love, she wanted to burst with all the emotion welling up inside her.

"I'm going to warn you now that I'm not going to be good at this. But I'm willing to give it my best shot. Because I do love you, Trick."

He kissed the tip of her nose. "We're both new at this. It'll take some time to adjust to it. And I don't want to rush you. We'll take it slow."

"Okay."

"It's enough to know you don't have one foot out the door and you might be comfortable seeing me on a regular basis. The rest we'll handle one day at a time."

That she could live with. But she owed him an explanation for her skittishness about relationships and her trust issues. But tonight wasn't the best night for that. They'd had amazing sex and had declared their love. She could save the big talk for later, right?

Especially since he'd scooped her up into his arms and carried her down the hall toward his bedroom.

"Now, about round two . . ."

She laughed and shoved her nose in his neck, happy to breathe him in.

She was in a relationship. And in love.

She never thought she'd say those two words again. Or believe in them.

But this was Trick, and a whole new beginning.

TWELVE

SHE HAD STAYED THE NIGHT, AND SINCE SHE ACTU-
ally had a day off from rehearsal, and Trick didn't have a game,
they were going to spend the day together.

Trick was in the shower, and then they were going to go to her
place so she could shower and change clothes.

They hadn't talked much last night, but as she got dressed and
sipped coffee, she allowed herself to think about planning for the
future.

People in love tended to eventually cohabitate. As she stared at
the happy Christmas tree in his living room, she pondered the
thought of moving in here.

Would he want that? Was that the next step?

She sat on the chair and wondered what it would be like to live
with Trick. He traveled a lot during his season. And she worked a
lot, especially when she was in performances. If they wanted to see
each other at all, it would make sense to live together.

She drew her legs up on the chair, already envisioning a few of her things here. Gifts for each other under the Christmas tree. A few of her favorite knickknacks strewn around.

Not having to freeze to death in her apartment in the winter—a definite bonus.

Sleeping next to Trick at night—she found no flaws in that thought.

Maybe she'd bring it up and test the waters.

She went into the bathroom to grab her socks, and Trick's phone rang.

"Hey, can you get that?" he asked from the shower. "I'm expecting a call from my agent this morning."

"Sure." She pressed the button on his phone. "Hello?"

"Hello. I was calling for Trick."

"This is Trick's phone. This is Stella, his . . ." She fumbled for the word "girlfriend," in the end deciding on, "friend. He's in the shower and wanted me to answer for him. He said he was expecting your call."

"Oh, okay. This is Dave Mincus, his agent. Can you let him know I'm messengering over the paperwork for him to look at?"

"Sure."

"Great. Tell him this trade deal with Detroit is time sensitive, so I need to hear back from him right away."

Trade deal with Detroit? What trade deal with Detroit? Her heart sank. "Okay. Sure."

"Great, thanks."

They hung up and Stella sat on the edge of the bed.

He was working out a trade with Detroit? He'd just told her he loved her, and he wasn't going to tell her he was being traded to Detroit?

Feeling dizzy and just a little sick to her stomach, she gripped the edge of the mattress for support.

It was Vernon all over again. Telling her he loved her, then expecting her to drop everything and move with him, because his career was more important.

The same fear and devastation washed over her, but this time it was so much worse.

She loved him, loved him more than she'd ever loved another man. She'd fought it for so long, but she'd had such joy when she'd given in. She'd fallen heart first into this with Trick, given him her trust, and now he'd pulled the rug right out from under her.

How could she have been so stupid?

Tears pricked her eyes, one falling down her cheek. She brushed it away.

No. No.

She wasn't going to do this again, wasn't going to go through a "If you love me you'll go with me and give up everything that means the world to you" conversation.

It wasn't going to happen. This time, she was going to be the one to walk away first. She was stronger than the last time. She wasn't going to beg and plead for a man's love, for him to see reason.

She had a wonderful career, and stood on the precipice of something magical right now. This was where she belonged. And if he couldn't see that, if he didn't love her enough to see that her career mattered, too, then too bad for him.

She finished getting dressed, and paced the living room, letting anger take over the hurt. She had downed the last of her coffee by the time Trick came out of the bedroom.

"Coffee smells good," he said, and came over to press a kiss to the back of her neck while she was standing over the sink rinsing her cup.

She quickly pulled away, leaning down to put her coffee cup in the dishwasher. "I'll make you a cup of coffee."

"I can do that."

She moved some distance from him while he brewed his cup, her arms wrapped around herself as she watched him. His hair was still damp from his shower, the ends curling around his neck, making her want to touch him, to breathe in his scent.

No matter how angry she was with him, she still loved him. And that hurt most of all.

"So, I was thinking," he said as he leaned against the kitchen counter. "We should talk about you moving in here."

He had a sexy half-smile on his face that destroyed her.

"You know, since your apartment is so cold in the winter, and my place is actually convenient to you getting to work and all. What do you think?"

Last night and earlier this morning she would have thought it was a great idea. Now it just dug the knife in deeper.

"I've been thinking, too."

His smile broadened. "Have you?"

"Yes. I've been thinking that we rushed into this whole love-and-togetherness thing. Or at least I did. I'm not ready for it. I don't think I'll ever be ready for it."

His smile died. "What? What's wrong?" He set his cup down and started toward her. She put her hand out to stop him.

"I don't want this, Trick. You and I were fun, but I think it's time we end it."

"What are you talking about? Last night you loved me, and now it's over? Come on, babe. Talk to me."

She gave him a careless shrug, needing to hurt him like he'd hurt her. "It's just me. I tried, but I'm not a relationship type of woman. I like my freedom, and after thinking it over, any kind of commitment feels choking to me. Sorry."

"Sorry? That's it? That's all you're going to say? What the hell, Stella?" He dragged his fingers through his hair and she saw the hurt and confusion on his face as he paced back and forth. It killed her inside, knowing she put it there, but self-preservation was more important. Besides, had he been thinking of her when he'd made plans to move to Detroit? No. So she had to put herself first. She had to get away from him and move on.

"Yeah. That's all I'm going to say. I know this hurts for both of us, but trust me, you don't want to be with someone who doesn't want the same things you do."

He gave her a look like he didn't believe her. "Talk to me."

She shook her head, so afraid she was going to cry she couldn't say anything.

"I don't understand all this, Stella. I don't get this sudden turn-around. Are you sure something didn't happen to change your mind?"

"No. Nothing happened. I'm just being true to myself and who I am. And now I need to go before this gets more painful for both of us."

The hurt on his face was replaced by anger. "This is so much bullshit, Stella. I know it and you know it. You don't tell me you love me one minute and walk away the next."

She lifted her chin. "I said I was sorry."

"And that makes it okay? It doesn't. We need to talk this out. There's something you're not telling me."

"No, we don't need to talk, because there's nothing to say. I have nothing to tell you." Nothing he could say that could make her stay.

She grabbed her coat and her bag and went to the door. She turned to look at him, memorizing his face, knowing how much she was going to miss him. "Bye, Trick."

"Shit. I'm not coming after you. If you walk out, we're done."

"That's fine."

He stood in the living room, just staring at her, so many emotions on his face it took everything in her not to run to him and throw her arms around him.

But that would make her weak, and she wasn't weak. She had herself to think of, because he sure as hell hadn't.

She willed the tears back as she opened the door and walked out.

She'd never hurt so much in her life as she took the elevator downstairs and hailed a taxi outside. Fortunately, one came by quickly, because she was afraid Trick would run after her, despite what he'd said.

He hadn't. Of course he hadn't, because now he was free to move wherever he wanted to without having to deal with her.

This was better for both of them.

Definitely better for her.

She'd broken her golden rule of never getting involved, and it had cost her.

Because now her heart was broken, so much worse than the first time. The first time she'd been young and naïve. This time she'd gone into it with her eyes wide open—a woman, not a young girl. Trick was a man she could have spent forever with.

She should have known better, and now instead of loving him forever, she was going to hurt forever.

THIRTEEN

IT HAD BEEN A LOUSY WEEK. THEY'D WON ONE GAME and lost two shitty fucking games. Even the game where they'd managed to squeak by with a win, they'd played badly. Trick had played badly. And he had no one to blame but himself. Hell, the whole team had played like a bunch of amateurs the past few games. They'd been an embarrassment, and the only good thing—if there was a good thing—was they had been road games, so at least they hadn't sucked in front of the home fans.

At least now he was home. He sat in his apartment licking his wounds—in more ways than one.

He figured throwing himself into the games, into hockey, would be a way to get over Stella. That sure as hell hadn't worked out so well.

Now he sipped a beer in his apartment and stared at the stupid Christmas tree, which only reminded him of Stella. He should dismantle the damn thing and toss it in the Dumpster, because he sure as hell wasn't in the holiday spirit.

Except, for some twisted reason, the dancing angel on top gave him some sort of comfort.

"Aren't you a sorry, pathetic loser?" he said to himself as he stared at the angel twirling around the tree, listened to the music, then took another large guzzle of his beer.

He didn't understand it, didn't understand Stella. Why had she been in love with him that night and then made a complete turn-around the next morning?

He'd tried to call her and text her after she'd left, after he'd gotten over the shock of her abrupt announcement that they were over. She wouldn't answer, and after a few tries he'd decided he wasn't going to chase after a woman who clearly wanted nothing to do with him. He wasn't that kind of guy. If she didn't want him, then fine. He'd move on.

Except he loved her. And moving on wasn't working out so well.

He just needed more time. He'd be fine. Eventually he'd stop thinking about her, stop missing her, stop smelling her every-where, like on his pillow.

"Fuck." He got up and tossed the beer bottle into the recycle bin and grabbed another.

His phone rang. It was Carolina. "Hey, Carolina. What's up?"

"Trick? I don't normally interfere, but this is about Stella. She'd kill me if she knew I called you, but I know the two of you broke up."

He took a deep breath. "Yeah."

"I don't think she told you why."

"She said she changed her mind."

"Of course she did. But that's not the real reason. She's not talking to me about it, and that's unusual for her, because she and I share everything."

This wasn't helping. Obviously, Stella didn't feel it for him, which didn't make him feel any better.

"Look, Trick, I'm trying not to betray a confidence here, but I think what the two of you have is special, so I'm going to tell you something I probably shouldn't. She had a bad breakup in her past."

"Yeah, she told me about that. But didn't really elaborate."

"She's never elaborated to anyone that I know of, including me until very recently. But I think that's the key to what's going on. You need to talk to her, get her to open up to you. I know she loves you. And she's miserable without you."

At least that made him smile. "Yeah, the feeling's mutual. I love her, too."

"I was hoping you'd say that. Her sister, Greta, is in town and I'm going to take her Christmas shopping tomorrow. I told Stella we were shopping for her, which means Stella will be home alone. Please talk to her, Trick. I know the two of you belong together."

Carolina was right. He'd let Stella walk away without forcing her to talk to him. "I will. Thanks for this, Carolina."

"Hey, I believe in you two. You're welcome."

He hung up, feeling a lot more hopeful than he had the past week.

Now he just had to find out what was going on in Stella's head, and figure out a way to fix it.

She belonged with him, and he needed to make it happen.

FOURTEEN

STELLA SPENT THE MORNING WRAPPING CHRISTMAS gifts, not at all in the holiday spirit. But she refused to allow her current mood to affect her sister. Greta and Carolina were going Christmas shopping, and hopefully Greta would enjoy spending the time with Carolina, who was always excited about the holidays. Her sister needed to hang out with someone who was cheery and in a great mood, because that sure as hell wasn't her right now.

She loved having Greta here. She wouldn't have survived the past week without her. Despite her resolve to end things with Trick and move past it, she'd been a wreck.

What had she been thinking? She loved him. Did she think it would be easy to dump him and move on like it had been nothing? It hadn't been nothing. He hadn't been nothing. He'd become everything to her. The snow on the ground reminded her of him. When she turned on the TV and saw the hockey game on, her heart ached. When she walked past the ice-skating rink she thought of how much fun they'd had together. The big Christmas tree at Rockefeller Center reminded her of the tree they'd put up and decorated in his apartment. Even dancing reminded her of him.

Damn the man for infiltrating every part of her life. How was she supposed to get over him?

And why the hell had he decided to get himself traded to Detroit? Why couldn't he be different from other men?

When her buzzer sounded, she went to answer it.

"Yes?"

"It's me, Stella."

Her heart thumped, her eyes closed, and she leaned against the door. "Go away, Trick."

"I'm not leaving until you talk to me. And it's fucking cold out here. Let me in."

God, she wanted to see him, to touch him, to kiss him. But what was the point? Still, she was curious why he'd come over here. She hadn't answered his calls or texts. Maybe it was time for some closure, for her to tell him exactly why she'd walked out on him.

It was the only way she'd ever be free of him. "Come on up." She pressed the buzzer and ran into the bathroom.

Her hair was a wreck, and she had on yoga pants and a sweatshirt. She swished some mouthwash around, though she had no idea why. It wasn't like he was going to be kissing her.

Ever again.

The thought of it made her stomach clench.

He knocked on the door and she went to answer it. He looked tall, dark, and delicious in his navy blue pea coat and black jeans.

"Thanks," he said as he came inside.

"I'm only doing this so I can explain to you why I ended things between us."

He slid his coat off and laid it over the edge of her loveseat, then turned to her. "You walked out on me. We had something together and I think it's worth fighting for."

She crossed her arms. "Shouldn't you be spending your time worrying about your imminent trade to Detroit?"

He frowned. "My . . . what? I'm not being traded to Detroit."

"Aren't you? When your agent called that morning you were in the shower, he said he was messengering over paperwork, and that it was time sensitive and had something to do with the trade to Detroit."

He paused, and she knew then that she had him.

Then his face lit up with recognition. "Oh. That. It's part of contract renegotiations with the Travelers, Stella. It's all a ploy. My agent hits them up about a potential trade in order to get more money for me. Fuck no, I'm not going to Detroit. I love the Travelers."

Now she was the one who was confused. "You're not?"

"Of course not. I love New York. You thought I'd take a trade like that without talking to you?"

She looked down at the floor, then up at him. "Yes."

"Stella, I'd never do that. I had just told you I loved you. I wanted you to move in with me. Why in the hell would I do something like that?"

She breathed in a shaky sigh. "There's something you need to know about me. About that relationship I had in the past."

He took her hands and led her to her sofa, sitting them both down. "Okay. Why don't you tell me about it?"

She sat and told him about Vernon, about how much they loved each other, and what he'd done when he'd gotten the job offer in L.A. She told him how it crushed her when he'd expected her to leave her job and move with him.

"What a dick," he said when she finished. He picked up her hand. "Stell, I'd never do that to you. My job is no more important than yours. And I'd never accept an offer in another city unless I talked to you first. When I told you I loved you, when I asked you to move in with me, it was with the expectation that we were in this relationship together, you know? That means we'd make decisions about our lives together."

She was so stupid. She'd let her fear rule her, and she'd caused so much hurt. This time she didn't fight the tears when they came. "I'm sorry. I'm so sorry. I just expected the past to repeat itself."

He gathered her close and kissed her, absorbing her tears with the softness of his lips. When he pulled back, his face was only inches from hers. "Look at me and believe this. I will never hurt you that way, and I will always be honest with you. Do you believe that?"

She did now. "Yes."

"I'm sorry I didn't tell you about the contract negotiations. That's my fault. It won't happen again."

She waved her hand at him. "You didn't need to."

"Yeah, I do. And from now on, I will. Also, I can't guarantee that somewhere down the road the Travelers won't trade me somewhere. That's the nature of my career. Unfortunately, I won't have control over something like that. But as far as me asking for a trade, it's not going to happen. Not without you and I talking it over first. Your career is as important as mine, and I know how vital it is that you dance here."

Hearing those words was music to her very soul. "I know there are things you can't control, Trick. I don't expect you to. But knowing you value my career is all I needed to hear. Thank you." She threw her arms around him and held him close. "Thank you."

He pulled back and graced her with that sexy smile that rocked her right down to her dancer's toes. "You and me, babe. We're together in this."

She nodded and smiled back. "Yes. Together."

And for the first time in her life, she believed in the magic of love, and the power two people had to forge a future together built on trust.

"Now, how about you call your sister and we go out and celebrate?"

Stella shook her head. "She's out with Carolina today. They're Christmas shopping."

He grinned. "I know. Carolina called me and told me to talk to you. She's the one who made plans with Greta, so we could be alone and figure things out."

Stella cocked a brow. "She did, huh? I have half a mind to thank my best friend and my sister for that."

"Good. Let's do it over lunch. I'm hungry."

"You're on. Let me go change my clothes and I'll call Carolina."

She dashed into the bathroom after sending Carolina a text message, feeling lighter than she had since that day she'd walked out of Trick's apartment.

Now she had hope, and that was a new concept for her, a feeling she was going to have to get used to.

As she came out of the bedroom, Trick was eyeing her sparse mini Christmas tree that sat on her pass-through.

He turned to her. "I can see why you wanted the big tree in my place. This is kind of sad."

She laughed. "It is, isn't it?"

"So you and Greta will spend Christmas with me at my place?"

She went over to him and slid her arm around him, leaning against him, loving the warm feel of his body next to hers. "Yes, we will."

"And by that, I mean you're moving in with me."

She couldn't help the tiny thrill of excitement at his words. "Greta's staying with me until she finds a place to live."

He looked down at her. "I have an extra bedroom. She's welcome to stay there, too."

Her heart soared with so much love she didn't know what to do with it all. Tears filled her eyes. "I'm not sure I deserve you. I'm kind of bitchy and mean."

He shook his head. "You're a beautiful dancer with a kind soul. You're sexy and you've filled my world with laughter and love. I want you in my life, Stella."

She lifted up on her toes and grasped his face between her hands. "I love you, Trick."

He wrapped his arms around her and kissed her, a deep,

powerful kiss that cemented the bond they'd made together. "I love you, too, Stella."

As they left her apartment, she shut off the lights and stared at that tiny little Christmas tree. She couldn't help but feel like she was leaving the past behind and creating a new beginning.

This was going to be the best holiday ever.

EPILOGUE

STELLA WAS SO GRATEFUL TO HAVE THE CHRISTMAS break. And she'd needed every day of it so far. After giving notice to her apartment complex, she and Greta had packed up the place, put furniture into storage that Greta wanted to keep for her apartment, and moved the boxes and clothes into Trick's place.

For a guy, Trick was unreasonably easy about her taking over his apartment. Greta wasn't staying on a permanent basis, but Stella was.

It was a good thing his bedroom had large closets, because she had a lot of clothes.

And on top of trying to settle into living together, Stella had made the stupid suggestion to host a Christmas Eve party at the apartment. And even more foolishly, Trick had thought it was a great idea.

So now she was dressed in some slinky silver dress, her makeup done, high heels on, and she and Greta had already gone over the to-do list seemingly a hundred times. Since she sucked as a cook, they'd ordered food to be brought in, and they had ample alcohol, all of it set up in the kitchen.

The house was already perfectly decorated and the scent of cinnamon filled the air.

She dashed into the bedroom to take one last look at her hair, and she stopped to take in the sight of the man she loved finishing getting dressed.

He wore black slacks, his dark hair spilling over the collar of his white button-down shirt.

"I can't get these damn cuffs buttoned. You have to have little kid fingers to button these things."

She laughed and walked over. "Let me do it." Within a few seconds, she had the cuffs buttoned, then took a step back to admire him.

"You look incredible."

He slid an arm around her waist and pressed a kiss to her lips, the long, lingering kind that left her breathless. "No, you look incredible. I'm going to enjoy taking that dress off you later."

She laid her palm on his chest. "Now there's something for me to think about all night."

His fingers drifted down her back, teasing her bare skin. "Or, we could get a head start . . ."

The doorbell rang, and she slid him a look of regret. "Our guests are arriving, so you hold that thought."

Within the next hour the apartment was filled with their friends. Drew and Carolina came by, as well as several of the Travelers players who hadn't yet left town for the holidays. A few people from her dance company were there as well, including her friend Lisa and Lisa's husband, Louis. She was shocked as hell when her choreographer, Lawrence, and his boyfriend, Jonathan, showed up. She'd invited everyone who wasn't leaving town, including Lawrence, but never in her wildest imaginings did she expect Lawrence would show up. He never mingled with his cast.

Yet there he was, he and Jonathan deep in conversation with Drew and Trick about hockey, of all things. He was even laughing.

"We should take a picture of that," Lisa said.

Stella put her arm around Lisa. "I know. He almost looks human."

Lisa laughed.

The house was filled with the smell of Christmas, evergreen and eggnog and delicious food, and the warmth and laughter of new and old friends. For the first time in a very long time, Stella was relaxed.

And happy.

"I don't know when I've seen you smile so much," Carolina said later in the evening. The two of them sat on one of the corner sofas, staring out the window as snow flurries fell lightly from the sky.

Stella dragged her gaze away from the window to look at her friend. "I don't know when I've *been* so happy. My sister is here with me, and all my friends. I have this amazing new home, a career I adore, and most importantly, I've fallen in love with the man of my dreams. I don't know, Carolina. It almost seems . . ."

"Too good to be true?"

"Yes."

Carolina leaned over and squeezed her hand. "It's not. It's the happiness you deserve. The life you deserve, and the man you deserve."

Stella inhaled on a shaky breath. For so long she'd held the potential for happiness at arm's length, too afraid of hoping for it to believe it could ever come true.

But now, as she stared over the apartment, at all these people she lived with, worked with, and called friends, she was starting to believe that this happiness was real. That she did deserve it.

When Carolina wandered off to find Drew, she did her own wandering, stopping to talk to Lawrence. She was shocked to discover they had a lot in common. His parents had never wanted him to dance, and he'd struggled for years to find his footing and even longer to find success. When he finally achieved his goals, he swore he'd pay it forward, which was why he enjoyed being a choreographer now. For most of his life, dance had been the only thing that kept him going—until he'd fallen in love with Jonathan. She spent a good hour realizing that Lawrence worked his dancers hard not because he was an asshole, but because he wanted them all to be successful.

She had a new appreciation for her boss, who, it turned out, was a very kind man once you got him away from rehearsals. And Jonathan was adorable, and it was very clear the two of them were very much in love.

As she wound her way through the partygoers, she met up with her sister, and hugged her.

"Are you having a good time?"

Greta grinned and wrapped her arms around Stella. "This is going to be one of the best holidays ever. Thank you for letting me stay with you."

"I can't even imagine not having you here."

"You won't have me long."

Stella smiled. "Excited about your new apartment?"

"Ridiculously. It's like a whole new chapter of my life. New job, new apartment. New friends. I'm excited, Stell."

"I'm excited for you."

"And maybe a new guy." Greta smiled. "So if you don't mind, I think Avery is giving me that look."

Stella had noticed that her sister and Avery had been spending time together.

"Go ahead. And have some fun."

Greta gave her a wink. "I intend to."

A few hours later, the party wound down. They said their good-byes, and Greta informed her that she was going to go out with Avery for a while and may or may not be back later.

Which left her and Trick alone.

Trick was seeing the last of the guests out, so Stella stood at the window, marveling at how beautiful the city looked. The snow flurries had turned to actual snow now.

When she felt a warm set of arms surrounding her, she leaned against Trick's chest.

"It's going to be a white Christmas," she said.

"I guess that means we'll have to stay in tomorrow."

"I'm sure we'll figure out that whole 'cooking a turkey' thing."

He turned her around to face him, then tipped her chin up with his fingers. "Babe, I'm a master at that turkey thing."

"Yet something else I love about you."

"What? My cooking skills?"

She wound her arms around his neck. "No. The fact you don't panic about being snowbound on Christmas Day."

"Well, I think your sister might end up snowbound with Avery, which means we'll be snowbound alone together."

"I like the sound of that."

Trick kissed her, and it was as if the whole world fell away, and only she and Trick existed.

When he broke the kiss, he looked up at the clock on the wall. "Merry Christmas, Stella."

Her lips curved. "Merry Christmas, Trick."

"I have a gift for you."

She cocked a brow. "Is that right?"

"Yes. It'll require us to get naked."

She looped her arm in his as they headed to the bedroom. "Is this gift something I've seen before?"

"Well . . . maybe. But this gift can always be used in new and unique ways."

She tilted her head back and laughed. "Best. Gift. Ever."

HOT HOLIDAY NIGHTS

ONE

VICTORIA BALDWIN DETERMINED IT HAD BEEN SIX
months, three days, four hours, and—she looked at her phone and
calculated—approximately seventeen minutes since she'd last had
time off.

She was damned overdue. She normally took holidays more fre-
quently. Working in the sports industry for fifteen years should
have netted her vacation time whenever she wanted it, but being a
sports agent meant that sometimes you had to work your ass off,
and this had been one of those brutal kinds of years.

Not that she was complaining. Picking up a few new clients had
meant an uptick in her bank account, which allowed her to take
these getaways. So she'd suck it up and do the hard work when it
was necessary.

And now she had three weeks off. She could already feel the
stress melting away.

She'd vacationed all over the world, from Mexico to Fiji to

Europe to Asia to every island in the Caribbean, but she always loved coming back to Hawaii, and especially the island of Oahu. It was the flowers. She loved the smell of the flowers here, and the staff at her favorite hotel on the north shore were incomparable.

She'd been lucky to get in on such short notice. They were booked solid for the international surfing competitions that would start in a few days. Plus it was also the Christmas holiday. But they'd made a suite available for her, knowing she was a preferred customer and she tipped very well.

She threw on her swimsuit, then put on a pair of shorts and a tank top over it, laced up her shoes, lathered on the sunscreen, and grabbed her sunglasses. First item on the agenda was a run on the beach. It was the perfect way to release stress and unwind.

She'd landed late last night. When she'd arrived at the hotel she'd done nothing but strip naked, fall into bed, and pass out. The time change would play havoc with her for a day or so, but she was used to travel and changing time zones. She needed to acclimate.

She made her way to the lobby, noting the holiday décor. A giant tree stood in the corner, decorated in hues of glittering green and red. The twinkling lights definitely helped to wake her up and put her in a Christmas mood.

At home in New York, it had snowed before she left. Here, it was a balmy seventy-five degrees. Oh yes, she much preferred to spend her Christmas holiday in a warm climate.

She walked through the open-air lobby and onto the sandy beach.

It was a beautiful morning, warm and with a glorious sunrise that made her damn glad to be on vacation. Instead of gulping down caffeine and rushing off to an appointment or to catch a plane, she inhaled a long, solid breath of sweet-smelling air, stretched, and set off on a run. She started at a slow jog, adjusting to her surroundings, enjoying the sounds of the gulls as they flew overhead hoping for a seafood breakfast.

She ran every day, not only as a way to keep her body in shape, but also because she liked the way it made her feel. Drawing in oxygen, and the exhilaration she experienced when she dug in hard and pushed her body to its limits was something that never got old.

The waves were rolling higher than what she was used to. Then again, she wasn't typically here in December. She'd always come to Hawaii in the spring or summer, so the waves this time of year were new for her.

When she saw several surfers grab their boards and paddle out to tackle those waves, she was in awe to see humans battling Mother Nature. She wanted to stop and watch, but she needed to get her run in, so she pushed past, taking deep breaths and digging her feet into the sand.

When she'd gone a mile, she stopped, took a breather, grabbed the water bottle she'd strapped to her hip and drank, then walked for a few minutes, taking a couple of deep breaths, readying herself for the run back. By the time she made her way to the spot where she'd seen the surfers enter the water, there were at least five more. She saw two of them catch a wave at the top and drop down underneath a big wave that rolled over them.

She stopped, jogged in place, and watched them as they rode it out all the way to shore.

Amazing.

"Ready to catch a wave?"

She startled, so engrossed in the surfers she hadn't noticed the guy who'd walked up and was standing right next to her.

He looked like a surfer himself. He was young—younger than her, anyway, but not as young as the two she'd seen out on the water. Early thirties was her guess.

He was also very hot, with gorgeous, sun-streaked blond hair. Oh so sexy. He wore dark sunglasses and had a killer smile.

"No, I was out for a jog and happened to see them on my way down the beach and back up."

"You here on vacation?" he asked.

"I am. Just got in last night, so stretching out my stiff muscles. Are you here for the surfing competition?"

"Yes. Alex McConnell." He held out his hand.

She shook it. "Victoria Baldwin. You look a little old to be a surfer."

His lips curved upward. "Do I?"

Well, shit, Tori. Nothing like opening your mouth and insulting the guy.

"Sorry. I didn't mean that. I mean, you're not too old to surf. Or do anything, quite obviously. Just look at you. Your body is totally hot, and dear God, those abs and . . . I'm going to stop talking now."

That made him laugh. "All complimentary things. Do keep talking. Nice to meet you, Victoria."

He had an ease about him, a confident air, plus a sense of humor. She liked that. "Do you compete a lot?"

"I've been doing it since I was a kid."

She laughed. "You're still a kid."

He arched a brow. "Hardly. And we're about the same age."

He had no idea how old she was, but it was nice of him to say that.

She'd kept moving to keep her heart rate going. He'd started walking with her and she didn't mind. As eye candy he was gorgeous. And she did enjoy some good eye candy. She intended to have a good time this vacation.

So far—excellent start.

"What do you do when you're not on vacation, Victoria? Or do you go by Tori?"

She loved the way he said her name. "Either one is fine. I'm a sports agent."

He stopped. "Sports agent, huh? That sounds like a fun job."

"It is. It keeps me very busy, but I love it."

"How long have you been doing that?"

"Fifteen years."

He tipped his glasses down and she got a glimpse of beautiful sea-green eyes. "No shit."

"No shit."

"So you started when you were a kid?"

"And you're full of it, but thanks for the compliment."

"I'm not full of anything. I always mean what I say. You're gorgeous, Tori."

They arrived at the steps of her hotel. "This is where I'm staying."

"Nice."

"I was going to have breakfast. Would you like to join me?"

He shrugged. "Sure."

"Unless I'm keeping you from getting in the water?"

"No. I'll do a run again later. I was already in the water earlier."

They headed up to the outside restaurant. Tori ordered juice, yogurt, and fruit. Alex ordered bacon and eggs. And coffee. She definitely wanted coffee. Now that she'd had her run, she was hungry, and fortunately, the food arrived quickly.

She watched the waves as they ate.

"Would you like some bacon?"

She waved her hand. "No, thank you."

"Vegetarian?"

She laughed. "No. I like meat just fine. But I do like a light breakfast, and meat in moderation."

He popped a piece of bacon in his mouth. "Must be how you stay so slim."

"Thank you. I like to run."

"I like to run, too. When I'm not chasing a wave I'm usually on the beach taking a run."

They had things in common, despite the age difference. She liked that.

"So where do you live, Alex?"

He smiled. "I live wherever there's a wave, but I try to get back home now and then, usually just for the holidays."

When she gave him a long look, he said, "Home base is in San Diego. My parents still live there."

"Nice place."

"Thanks. But I don't get there as often as I'd like. I travel all over for work, as I imagine you do. I don't suppose you see your parents a lot either."

She laughed. "That's true. I do travel a lot. I have a sister in Virginia I visit when I can. Our parents are both gone now."

"I'm sorry."

"Thanks."

"And where do you live?"

"In New York."

"City girl, then."

"Very much so. Have you ever been?"

"To New York? Yeah. Great city. It has a killer energy."

She took a sip of her coffee and nodded. "That's what I love about it. Being there invigorates me."

"And what brings you to the islands?"

She leaned back in her chair, cup in hand. "Utter exhaustion. While I love my job and the travel and the fast pace, if I don't get away from it now and then I suffer burnout."

"So you come here to escape."

She nodded. "I take time off every December. I go to a lot of different places, but it's usually a tropical island. I like the ocean and the beach, someplace where I can turn my phone off and let my mind relax. Get away from the job, you know?"

Alex looked out over the water. "That is my job out there."

"I suppose that's true. To me, it's so calming. But to you I imagine it's very high energy."

"The best high there is."

She liked this guy. He was charming, intelligent, and extremely good-looking. It was obvious he was attracted to her. She always approached an island vacation fling slowly. One never knew who one was getting involved with, so she stepped in cautiously.

"You come out here before the competition starts so you can practice?"

"Yeah. Get a feel for the waves, see how they're climbing. The Pipeline is one of the most dangerous competitions."

"The Pipeline?"

He nodded. "The Banzai Pipeline is where the water and the coral bend the water to form what looks like a tubular wave. The swells can reach over twenty feet."

She arched a brow. "And you surf those."

"They're some of the best. But also the most dangerous because of the reef."

She shook her head. "You men and your extreme sports."

"Women surf them, too. And you represent athletes. You know how it goes. We have to do what drives us."

"Or you're simply driven by these insane competitive urges and nothing stops you."

He grabbed a few of her grapes and popped them into his mouth. "Maybe."

"Maybe I'll come watch you."

"I'd like that. And maybe you'll have dinner with me tonight."

She liked his confidence. "Maybe I will. Where are you staying?"

"Here, actually."

She arched a brow. "Really?"

"Yeah."

"This hotel is pricey."

He laughed. "Do I look poor?"

She laid her hand on his. "No. I'm sorry. I didn't mean . . ."

"Relax, Victoria. It takes a lot to insult me. Turns out I'm kind of an international superstud on the surfing circuit, so I've got enough coin to afford to stay in a nice shack like this."

She really had to learn to stop judging people on appearances. Just because he was more than a few years younger than her—and a surfer—didn't mean he wasn't successful and a moneymaker.

She obviously needed to do a little research into Alex McConnell. "I appreciate you giving me a break. I'm not usually such an uppity bitch."

"I think you're beautiful. And honest in your opinions. I like honest women. You're refreshing after some of the ones I've been with."

"It sounds like you have some stories to share."

"Honey, I've been with some beach bunnies that would make your eyes pop out of your head. Yeah, I've got a few stories."

"You'll have to share them with me."

He looked at his watch. "That's a conversation we'll have after dinner. I need to run." He stood and signaled for the waiter.

"I can take care of that."

He winked at her. "So can I." He signed for the bill, then leaned down and pressed a kiss to her cheek. His breath was warm, and she had to admit she liked the feel of his lips against her skin. "Come find me later, Tori. I'll be in the water."

"I will."

As he wandered off, Victoria smiled.

This was going to be interesting.

TWO

THE WAVES WERE ROLLING HIGH, WITH TIGHT TUBES just perfect for competition. Alex hoped it would stay this way for the week. He paddled out and waited, then got on top of a small wave for a practice run.

Not bad. He paddled out and waited for another, hopefully bigger one.

He wasn't alone out here. A lot of competitors came out early to ride the Pipeline, get a feel for how the waves were rolling.

He was always at peace on the water, had been since he was a kid. This was where he needed to be. Despite the dangers, when he rode the top of a wave, he felt a calm like nowhere else. When he dropped down on a particularly high wave, it was like he could see everything so clearly in his mind.

He smiled as he sat on his board and waited for the next wave to break.

Maybe it was a Zen thing, something nobody but other surfers understood. To outsiders, it looked like a dangerous sport. To be honest, it was. People got hurt or killed doing it. But Alex had always felt safe. He'd had a board in his hands since he was five years old, going on almost thirty years now. It was like another appendage. Going a day without surfing was like going a day without breathing. He didn't feel complete.

"This is going to be a good competition."

He turned to his left to see Zane Lee, one of his fiercest competitors. It figured Lee would be out here early testing the waters.

"Yeah. Waves are already coming in high."

"I'm going to kick your ass this year."

Alex grinned. "You can try."

"Catch you for a brew later?"

Alex nodded. "Definitely."

Lee paddled off. That was the one thing about his sport—they were all competitors, but they were also friends. Unless you were a total asshole. It was rough water out there, and they all knew they could wipe out, get hurt bad enough to end your career or even worse. You made friends with your competition, because you just never knew . . .

He hopped on a low-riding wave, dropped down into the tube, and rode it out. It was weak, but still good practice.

Before he turned to paddle back out, he caught a glimpse of Tori sitting on the shore watching him.

Now there was a sleek-looking woman. She had a certain spark, and he enjoyed an intelligent woman.

He wanted to spend more time with her, though he knew he should focus on the upcoming competition.

Then again, he always had time for some fun.

He grinned and paddled out onto the waves.

TORI HAD CAUGHT SIGHT OF ALEX. SHE WAS MESMER-ized as he rode the waves like a pro.

Of course he did. He was one. After she'd eaten, she'd gone up to her room, grabbed her laptop, and spent some time research- ing him.

Such interesting reading. He'd won several surfing champion- ships at the international level, and had started at the junior level when he was just fifteen. Since then he'd always placed in the top five, and he'd won a number of championships.

The guy was internationally famous and had been for nearly twenty years. He'd done multiple endorsements and commercials and was the highest-grossing surfer in terms of monetary prizes there was.

Alex McConnell was a winner.

Tori liked backing winners. She wondered who his agent was, and who did his PR. She'd looked into the endorsements he'd been doing, but it wasn't enough considering his appeal. Why wasn't he doing commercials for energy drinks or gracing the covers of sports magazines? She'd never even heard of him. Obviously his representation wasn't doing a good job for him. Granted, surfing wasn't a mainstream sport like football, basketball, or baseball, but she could turn that around.

She mulled that over while she watched the surfers master the incredible waves.

"Yeah, the waves kind of suck today."

She turned to look at a girl who'd plopped down on the sand next to her.

"Really? They look enormous to me."

The girl grinned. "They're okay. Kind of puny, actually. They'll need to roll higher for the competition."

Tori turned in her chair to face the girl, who had to be no more than in her early to mid-twenties. Absolutely beautiful, with long black hair, a sprinkling of freckles across her cheeks and nose, and the prettiest dark eyes Tori had ever seen.

She held out her hand. "I'm Victoria, or Tori."

The girl shook her hand. "I'm Whitney. Everyone calls me Whitney."

Tori laughed. "Are you a surfer, Whitney?"

"Yes. Been surfing my whole life."

"So you're here for the competition?"

She shook her head. "Oh, God no. I live here on the island."

"You do? That's great."

She nodded. "I think so. My dad manages one of the hotels."

"He does? Which one?"

She pointed a few hotels down the beach. "That one. My mom works there, too. So do I."

"That's convenient. So when you're not working, I assume you're surfing?"

Whitney grinned. "Yes. It's what I'd rather be doing, but you know, gotta pay the bills."

"I understand that. So you love surfing. Do you compete?"

"I'm not that good. I only wish I was. I surf for fun, and I love to watch the competitions every year." Her gaze drifted out over the water. "They're amazing."

"So I've noticed."

"Women compete, too, though not right now. They compete in a separate event from the guys. The one going on now is men only."

"I met one of them today."

"Yeah? Who?"

"Alex McConnell."

She nodded. "Alex is an unbelievable surfer. He comes here every year to compete, and he's won . . . so many times."

"Yes, he has."

Whitney frowned. "So you do know Alex?"

Tori was almost embarrassed to admit it. "No. I Googled him."

"Oh." She laughed. "Checking him out, were you?"

"I might have been. Though he's really too young for me."

Whitney leaned back and looked her over. "Too young? Please. You're hot."

Getting a compliment from a guy was one thing. Getting one from another woman—and a young, beautiful one? That was an entirely different matter. "Thank you. I'll live on that for the rest of my vacation."

"What are you, maybe thirty or something?"

"Now I'm in love with you."

Whitney laughed. "Come on. Age is only a number. The important thing is to live your life and enjoy the hell out of it. I know I'm young, but I live on the island, and while I might not have the job of my dreams, I get to surf every day. I have nothing to complain about."

She liked Whitney. "And what is the job of your dreams?"

Whitney shrugged. "Not sure I've figured that out yet. I'm twenty-four and I realize I can't hang out on the beach forever, but I can't think of any other life that suits me better. I work customer service at the hotel part-time, and I'm finishing up my degree in business at night. Once I graduate, I'd like to work for one of the sports management companies that oversee the women's surf teams. If there's one thing I do know about, it's surfing. If there's another thing I've learned a lot about, it's marketing and business."

"I think you're light-years ahead in terms of thinking like a grown-up."

Whitney gave her a smile. "Thank you. Could you tell my parents that? They think I'm wasting my life because I don't already have a master's degree at twenty-four."

"A little pushy, are they?"

"A little, but I know they want what's best for me, so I take it in stride."

"It sounds to me like you already know what you want for your future."

"Maybe. I want to get away from my parents. Not that I don't love them. I do. But I don't want to be part of the family business. I need to make my own life."

"I understand. You want to be independent. I was where you are once, needing to strike out on my own. It's tough, but doable."

Whitney shifted position to face Tori. "What do you do for a living?"

"I'm a sports agent."

Whitney's brows lifted. "Really? That must be an awesome career. Do you love it?"

"I do love it. It's been the hardest thing I've ever done, but also the most fun, most rewarding job."

"Not to mention all those hot and sexy sports players."

Tori's lips curved. "Those are the perks, honey."

Whitney laughed. "I can only imagine. See, that's the kind of thing I could see myself doing. I love every sport there is, and when I'm not working or studying or catching a wave, I'm glued to the television. The only drawback to living in Hawaii—and believe me, there aren't many—is no professional sports. So I have to get my fix by watching them on TV."

"I can't imagine many drawbacks to living here. I love the islands."

"Me, too, but I have a yen to go to the mainland every now and then. If for nothing more than to catch a football or baseball game. Or hockey. Oh, God, I love hockey."

"The grass-is-always-greener kind of thing."

"Exactly."

"I see you've found a friend."

Tori looked up to see Alex standing at the foot of her chaise. Dripping wet, droplets sliding down his magnificent body, she could already envision him in his wet suit, just like that, gracing the cover of a sports magazine.

"What's up, Alex?" Whitney said.

"Hey, Whitney. How's it goin'?"

"Good. Tori and I were chatting about our careers."

"Yeah?" Alex looked over at Tori, and she got lost in the sexy way he smiled at her. "You finding our girl here a new career?"

Tori laughed. "I think Whitney is doing fine on her own."

"She is," Whitney said, standing and brushing sand off her legs and butt. "And speaking of careers, I have an errand to run for the hotel, so I'll catch you both later."

Tori pulled her business card out of her bag and jotted down her personal cell number, then handed it to Whitney. "Call me when you have some free time and we'll have lunch. I'm here for a while."

Whitney beamed a smile. "Awesome."

Alex dropped down on the sand next to her. "Whitney's great. She's a champion for the surf crowd, and her parents rock. They put up a few of the new guys in their hotel when they couldn't afford a room last year."

Tori laughed. "I like her. She's very smart and fun to talk to."

"She is. She also likes surfing, so she's okay."

"Is that how you judge people? By whether they like surfing or not?"

"Totally."

He kept a straight face, but Tori knew he was joking. "So if I hated surfing, we wouldn't be having this conversation."

"No way. I don't waste my time with people who dismiss what I do for a living. Would you?"

He had a point. "Of course not. I've faced plenty of my own prejudices in my field."

"Yeah? What kind?"

"Men who think women shouldn't be managing the multimillion-dollar careers of top athletes, or people who, when they find out what I do, want to complain about overpaid, whiny athletes or agents who get paid too much money and think we do nothing to earn our pay. I get plenty, believe me."

"So what do you do?"

She shrugged. "I walk away. It's always best not to engage people like that, because you're never going to change their minds."

"Yeah, I get a lot of the 'surfing isn't a real sport' kind of people, and folks who ask me when I'm going to get an actual job."

"I imagine you make a decent enough living."

"Decent enough to be able to travel the world doing what I love. Of course sponsorship helps with that."

"I'm sure it does." She wanted to talk to him about that. She

had so many questions about his management team and his adver-
tising opportunities. But she didn't want to spoil the friendship
they'd started. She was attracted to him, plus she was on vacation,
and she'd long ago made a vow never to do business while she was
on vacation. Opportunities came and went. This was one of those
times where she'd just have to let it go.

"So, you want to surf today?"

"Me?" She took a look at those rolling waves that seemed to her
as tall and imposing as the high-rise she lived in. "No, thanks."

"Aww, come on. It's a challenge."

"It's a death trap. I like my waves a little more manageable."

"I can take you to another part of the island to surf. On the
south side the waves are much calmer."

She hadn't thought of that. "You need to concentrate on getting
ready for the competition. Some other time."

"Aw, come on. It can't be all about business. Now you sound
like Ben."

"Who's Ben?"

"Ben Reynolds. My business manager. And one of my sponsors.
Great guy. I can't wait for you to meet him."

"Is he here?"

"Not yet. He's flying in tomorrow. He's a former surfer. One of
the best."

"Did he teach you how to surf?"

"Babe, nobody teaches you how to surf. You're either born with
it or not."

"I see." She'd had lessons and certainly hadn't been born with surfing knowledge, but if that was his mantra, who was she to argue?

"Hey, I know I said I'd take you to dinner, but there's a party on
the beach tonight, kind of a precursor to the competition. Will
you come?"

"Is it open to the public?"

"No. But you can be my date."

She liked where this was going. "Sure."

"Awesome. I've got some interviews and stuff I need to do. How about I pick you up at your room at like . . . five thirty?"

"That sounds great."

He stood. "I'll see you then. Later, Tori."

She watched him walk away, admiring his great legs, his amazing strong back, and his very fine ass.

So . . . she had a date. With a hot surfer.

She got up and threw on her wrap, grabbed her bag and headed back to the hotel to take a shower, a smile creeping onto her face.

Apparently, she still had it going on.

ALEX SMILED AS HE WANDERED AWAY FROM TORI.

He liked this woman. She was smart, and kind of a smartass.

He liked smart women who thought of other things besides hooking up with a surfer. He'd met plenty of those—pretty women, sure, but after he got out of bed he wanted to be able to have a conversation. He already knew he could have an intelligent conversation with Tori. And he sure as hell wouldn't mind having her in his bed, either. Whether she was interested in that part or not remained to be seen.

Even though he was here for work, he could take some time for fun as well.

He walked along the shoreline, studying the swells and wind. Great timing for the event. Waves were solid and high, and should make for some stellar barrels.

He was itching to get out there and compete.

But in the meantime, he had a date tonight with a beautiful woman.

His smile widened.

THREE

VICTORIA HAD BEEN MORE THAN READY FOR TONIGHT.
She surprised herself by anticipating Alex's arrival with a bout of
nervousness. And she was never nervous.

Fortunately, Alex picked her up right on time. She'd dressed
casual, putting on a simple sundress and sandals, figuring this
wouldn't be a fancy event. Alex wore board shorts and a short-
sleeved shirt, so she'd guessed correctly.

He smiled and leaned an arm against the door. "You look
gorgeous."

She closed the door and slid her arm through his. "And you're
great for my ego. I might just stick you in my suitcase and take you
back to New York with me."

He shook his head. "Nah. The city would stifle me. Can't surf
in your Hudson River."

She laughed. "No, you definitely couldn't."

They walked outside and down the sidewalk leading toward where he'd surfed today.

"So tell me about this party tonight."

"Most of the surfers competing are already in, especially the newcomers. Sponsors and advertisers are throwing a party. Everyone will chill, unwind a little before the big events get started. It's a chance for some of the newer competitors to get to know everyone and do a meet-and-greet with the sponsors."

"That's nice for them."

"Yeah. Getting sponsorship is a big deal for the young guys. If they can hook up with someone, and do well in the competition, it'll keep them going for the next year."

"Is that how you did so well?"

"It helps to score high when you're first starting out. You don't have to work so hard to gain sponsorship. They'll come to you, then."

"So what you're saying is you didn't have to go to the sponsors."

He gave her a sexy, wide grin. "I won. A lot when I first started. After that, the sponsors started coming to me. I got lucky."

"Darling, I don't think luck had anything to do with it."

Tents had been set up on the beach with drinks and food. The sponsors each had a booth, too. Anything from surfboards and clothes to wax and tanning supplies was represented.

"Any of those your sponsors?" Tori asked as they walked by a tent to grab some food and a drink.

Alex leaned back to peruse the booths. "A couple."

"So when you're surfing, do you wear ball caps emblazoned with your sponsor logos?"

He laughed. "Uh, no."

There were a lot of people here—not just the guys competing, but apparently their families, too. Plus a lot of very young, very attractive women.

"Hey, Alex."

"Hey, yourself, Heather," Alex said to a girl who came up and hugged him.

The girl was wearing low-slung shorts and a skimpy bikini top that barely contained her ample breasts. She had a great tan and a model-type body, and she was definitely giving Tori the once-over.

"Heather, this is my friend, Tori. This is Heather."

Tori held out her hand. "Nice to meet you, Heather."

Heather smiled. She had perfect teeth, too. "Nice to meet you, Tori." She shifted her gaze back to Alex. "We're going to take a little dip tonight over at the cove. You up for it?"

Alex wound his arm around Tori's waist. "We'll see."

Again, Heather gave Tori a look. "Okay, then. Maybe I'll see you later. Nice to meet you, Tori."

"You, too, Heather."

After Heather left, she turned to Alex. "Ex-girlfriend?"

Alex cocked a brow. "How did you know?"

"I'm a woman. I know the vibe we give off when our ex is with a new woman."

"Oh. I don't get that vibe."

"That's because you have a penis. It blinds you to the signals."

He laughed. "Is that what it is? Come on, I'll introduce you to people."

They entered the fray. It was a wild party, but a lot of fun. Some surfers did, in fact, bring their entire families, so she not only met some of the competing surfers, she also met parents and brothers and sisters and in some cases, even grandparents. Wives and girl-friends were there, too. Of course, if she'd had a son who was a surfer, she'd have dragged her entire family to Hawaii to watch him compete. There was obviously a lot of family pride among the surfers, and as Victoria spoke to some of them she could tell they all supported their kids.

Some, like Alex, were there alone, and they formed their own family unit, hanging out together at a table, laughing and eating.

"Does it bother you to be here without your family?" she asked as they stood in line waiting to get something to eat.

"No. I mean, when I was younger and on the circuit my parents traveled a lot to these things. Now it's kind of old hat for them. They'll come to some of them, but they've got their own lives to live, ya know?"

"So they won't be coming to this event?"

"Nah. They're taking the RV up the coast for the holidays. They're kind of into camping and all that. But they have a satellite dish on the camper. They'll catch my event that way." He grinned.

She smiled. "I'm glad they'll be able to watch you. As far as the camping part? That sounds fun. In no way at all."

He gave her a feigned look of shock. "What? You're not a roughing-it kind of woman?"

"Not in the least."

He put his arm around her. "Anyway, everyone here is my family. Some of the other guys' families have adopted me. I'm never alone."

"It seems like you're all close."

"We are. We support each other and root for each other in the heats. Unless we're competing against each other. Out there it's every man for himself."

"I understand that. I have a couple agents I'm very friendly with, but we're very competitive with each other, too."

"Yeah, it's exactly like that. You can be friends with people you compete with. That's how it is here."

They got food and made their way to a long table where some of his friends were already gathered, including his ex, Heather, who was friendly enough, but her gaze continued to stray toward Alex. Obviously Heather had residual feelings for Alex.

Which wasn't Tori's problem, but she wasn't in the mood to deal with some young girl's jealousy issue. She was way past that at this stage in her life. If it was going to be a problem, she'd back away now. She was here to relax, not deal with tension.

"Hey, girl."

She turned around when Whitney slid in next to her at the table. "Hi, Whitney. I didn't expect to see you here tonight."

"Cade brought me." She motioned to her right, where a very attractive surfer grinned at her. "Cade, this is Tori."

"Nice to meet you, Cade."

"Likewise. You with Alex?"

"I am."

Cade shared a grin with Alex.

"No studying tonight?" Tori smiled at Whitney.

"I'm on break right now, which is perfect. I wouldn't miss a minute of the competition, including the partying."

Tori laughed. "This does seem like it's going to be a wild night."

"Well, it doesn't get too wild. The surfers have to keep their heads in the game. But everyone likes to have a good time. And there are a lot of hookups." Whitney kept her gaze on Cade, who'd moved over to talk with Alex.

"And Cade is someone you want to hook up with?"

Whitney laughed. "Maybe. I've had my eye on him since last season. He texts me all the time."

"He's very good-looking." Tall and well built, with a surfer's shaggy dark hair and amazing blue eyes, Tori could see why Whitney would find him attractive.

"I know nothing will come of it. He likely hooks up with a different girl in every place he competes. I'm a realist about that kind of thing. I've got my career and life plan in mind. In the meantime, I just want to have some fun."

Whitney reminded her of herself many years ago. And maybe today, too. Victoria had never been serious over a man, never wanted one to interfere with her career. Letting one get in the way of her number-one love—her job—had never been an option. Marriage and kids had never been part of her life plan, and she was perfectly content with that choice.

Which was why someone like Alex was perfect for her.

After dinner the music started up and everyone gathered in a circle near the bonfire to dance. She saw Whitney dancing with Cade. Heather was dancing with some guy, and for once wasn't watching them.

Alex took her by the hand and they danced together.

"You've got some rhythm," he said.

"Hey, I live in a city with the best nightclubs in the world."

He laughed. "So, you're telling me you get out a lot."

"I get out plenty."

"Boyfriends in every city?"

"Of course," she teased with a grin.

"I believe it. A woman as beautiful as you probably leaves them all crying when you dump them."

Now it was her turn to laugh. "You know it."

He slipped his arm around her waist and tugged her close. "I like a confident woman."

"Then you're really going to like me."

They swayed together as the music slowed. She liked the feel of his lean, muscled body next to hers, the easy way his hands glided over her. Her pulse picked up and her nipples tightened. And when his erection brushed against her hip, she shuddered in absolute delight.

This was one of the things she loved most about younger men—they got hard fast, they stayed hard, and they could rock her world.

It had been a while since she'd had sex. Work had preoccupied her for a spell, and she needed a release. Alex's eyes had gone dark, and the way he looked at her promised her she was going to have a very good night.

He pulled away from her. "How about we go up to my place?"

She liked Alex. He was direct, and apparently he didn't have any problem getting right to the action. And when the only thing on her mind was sex, game-playing could go straight to hell.

"Yes, let's do that."

He took her hand and they walked down the beach to the hotel.

She was surprised when they rode the elevator up to one of the penthouse suites, the same floor she was staying on.

"You must have really good sponsorships," she said as he slid his card key in and opened the door.

He smiled at her and shut the door. "I've been waiting all day for this."

He pushed her against the wall and put his mouth on hers.

In the dark, all she had were her senses. She focused on his lips against hers, his body aligned with hers.

Alex had a great mouth. Passion flared, and as he leaned into her, she swept her hands up his arms, memorizing the feel of his muscles, the softness of his skin surrounding the hardness of his body.

His cock nestled between her legs and a rush of dampness moistened her sex. She arched against him and he cupped her buttocks, drawing her closer. She moaned against his mouth and he rimmed her lips with his tongue, then sucked her bottom lip between his teeth, which only made her moan more.

"I need to come," she whispered.

"I can take care of that for you."

She loved how deep his voice had gotten, and how the room was cloaked in darkness. The drapes had been drawn, and even though her eyes had adjusted to the darkness, she still couldn't see a thing. It thrilled her as he reached behind her to draw the zipper down on her dress and pulled it from her. It fell to the floor and she kicked it aside, then stepped out of her sandals. In one deft move, he unsnapped her bra, freeing her breasts. He filled his hands with them, using his thumbs to tease the crests.

She put her hands over his. "Yes. Touch me. Lick me."

"Tell me where you want my mouth, Tori."

"Lick my nipples. Start there. Work your way down."

Her nipples tingled in anticipation as he kissed the mounds of her breasts, flicking his tongue over one bud, then the other, before capturing a nipple between his lips and taking it into his mouth to suck.

Her legs were trembling and she was glad she had the wall for support. His mouth was hot and wet as he sucked, hard, rolling the nipple with his tongue. He popped it out of his mouth, licked it, then went to the other, tormenting her in the same way before kissing a path down her belly, snaking his hands over her hips, dragging her panties down as he went.

And when he put his mouth on her sex she was nearly ready to explode right there. Getting herself off—which she did regularly—was one thing. Having a man's mouth on her pussy was something entirely different. There was nothing like a man giving her pleasure, and Alex knew exactly what to do with his mouth, sliding his tongue expertly over her clit, taking her there fast.

She laid her hand on top of his head, holding on to his hair while her pussy tightened. "Oh, God, you're going to make me come."

He murmured against her sex, licked her everywhere like he knew exactly what he was doing. And when he grabbed her clit and sucked, she cried out and came, thrusting her pelvis against his lips, and rode the wave of her orgasm.

ALEX ROSE, KISSING TORI'S HIPBONE AND STOMACH.

She was a beautiful woman. And she tasted as good as she looked.

But this night was just getting started, and he was hard. Achingly hard. He needed to be inside her soon.

He dropped his shorts, determined to get this party moving along.

Tori reached out to wrap her hand around his cock, and his shaft jerked. God, he liked her hands. He'd noticed them right away. Long, slender fingers, no fake fingernails like a lot of the younger girls seemed to like. Short, clipped nails painted some pale color. Really pretty. And right now she had a stranglehold on his dick, which he liked a lot more.

"I like your hand on me. Stroke it."

She moved her hand over him, sliding her thumb over the wide crest, then dropped to her knees.

This night just kept getting better and better. His balls tightened at the thought of her sweet mouth on his dick.

"Christ. Yes. Suck it."

He flipped the hall switch, bathing the hallway in muted light. He had to watch.

She lifted her head and smiled up at him. He crouched down and kissed her, a deep, powerful kiss that made his cock twitch.

"Damn, Tori, you are so beautiful."

"Stand up so I can get you in my mouth."

He stood, and she took his cock in her mouth, pressing her lips over the swollen head. He slid his cock partway into her mouth. She leaned forward, taking him fully inside, her tongue mapping every inch of him until he groaned and pulled back, then inched forward again.

She grabbed the base of his shaft and rolled her hand over him, squeezing him as she sucked him.

He laid his palm against the wall for support, then let her have the control. She took him deep, bobbing her head forward then back, taking him all the way into the back of her throat, constricting the head by swallowing.

"Fuck," he said, then lifted her, pushing her against the wall again. "You could make me come in your mouth."

She lifted her lips. "That's the idea, isn't it?"

"Yeah. But I want to fuck you right now."

He reached into the pocket of his shorts and grabbed a condom, put it on, then widened her legs. "I want you up against the wall like this."

"I want you inside me. I don't care where or how."

And that's why he liked her. She'd been direct since he'd first met her, and he'd had a feeling she'd be like that with sex, too. He wasn't wrong.

He paused at the entrance to her pussy, watching as she rested her head against the wall and met his gaze. When he eased inside her, her lips parted and her eyes widened.

Yeah, she was tight, her pussy grabbing on to him and quivering as he seated himself fully inside her. He shuddered as she grabbed onto his shoulders, wrapped one leg around his hip, then began to move as he pumped. And with each thrust, she tightened.

She was going to go off again. He loved a responsive woman.

"You going to come again for me?" he asked.

She met his gaze. "Yes. Fuck me like that and I'll come. Rub against me and I'll come."

He drove into her, then rubbed his body against hers. She dug her nails into his shoulders. She was so close he could feel the quivering inside her.

"Yeah," he said, taking her mouth in a deep kiss that sent her over the edge. She whimpered against his lips as she came, and he thrust hard, then groaned with her as his orgasm hit. He grabbed her ass and squeezed as he powered inside her and shuddered, the blast of his climax making him dizzy.

It took him a minute to catch his breath.

"Well, that was enjoyable," she said.

He smiled against her neck, then lifted his head and grinned. "It was, wasn't it?"

"I definitely had a good time, and I wasn't even invited."

Tori gasped.

Alex jerked his head at the familiar voice coming from the side of the room.

Oh, shit.

"Ben, what the hell are you doing here?"

FOUR

TORI LOOKED FROM ALEX TO THE DARK-HAIRED MAN
wearing shorts and a T-shirt and an awfully amused expression on
his face.

She looked back at Alex. "Who the hell is he?"

Alex turned his attention to Tori. "Ben. Remember, I told you
about him?"

"Right now I'm naked, you're still inside me, and we have an
audience. I don't remember much of anything."

She gave him a pointed look.

"Right. Ben. Piss off for a minute, will ya?"

Ben shrugged. "Sure."

He walked out of the room, giving Tori and Alex time to disen-
gage. Then Alex led her to his bedroom, complete with a bathroom where Tori could wash up and get dressed.

"Ben. That's your business manager or something?"

"Yeah. And one of my sponsors. A good friend, actually. I've known him since I was a teenager."

She turned her back to Alex, who helped her zip her dress. "I remember you mentioning him now. So you're rooming with him?"

"Yes." He kissed the back of her neck. "I'm really sorry. He wasn't supposed to be in until tomorrow. I would have never done that . . . in the living room . . . if I'd known he was here."

She turned to face him. "It's okay. It's just sex and I'm way too old to be embarrassed."

He took her hand. "You're making me like you more and more, you know that?"

She laughed. "Let's go out and officially meet your friend Ben."

Alex led her down the hall and back into the living room. Ben had grabbed a beer. He was sitting on one of the chairs at the island in the kitchen.

The suite was set up much like hers, with a living room and dining room area, and a kitchenette with sink and bar.

"Ben Reynolds, this is Victoria Baldwin."

Ben stood and held out his hand. "Nice to meet you, Victoria."

She gave him a wry smile. "You, too, Ben. I guess we'll all be very close friends now."

He laughed. "I guess so. Sorry about that."

"Not a problem."

"You could have told me you were coming in early," Alex said as he walked around the island and grabbed two beers from the refrigerator. He held them up to Victoria, who shook her head. "Water instead?"

"That would be great, thank you."

"I didn't think I'd need to. Sorry again," Ben said.

"Why the change in plans?" Alex handed the water to Victoria.

"I got a chance to hop on an earlier flight and took it. Figured I'd catch up on some sleep." Ben turned to Victoria. "I've been traveling a lot the past couple weeks and shifting through a lot of time zones, so jet lag has me screwed up. I had intended to be passed out."

"Obviously you weren't," she said. "Instead, you got a sex show."

He tipped the beer to his lips and smiled. "Yeah, thanks for that. It was quite an exhibition."

"My pleasure."

"Sure looked that way from where I was standing. I'm glad I got off the phone in time to leave my room and see it."

"You're a dick, Ben," Alex said, with a laugh and a shake of his head.

Ben tipped his beer to Alex. "So tell me what I've missed, besides you landing the most beautiful woman on the island."

Victoria couldn't help but be charmed by the compliment. As Alex filled Ben in on surfing competition stuff, she gave Ben a once-over.

Despite being sleep-deprived and jet-lagged, she definitely noticed Ben was an attractive man. In his mid-forties, she guessed, he had dark hair, slightly graying at the temples, but he was solidly built. About six-two, well tanned, he had stunning steel-gray eyes and full lips with a couple days' worth of stubble on his jaw that screamed rugged and utterly masculine. He looked like he belonged in a jungle somewhere, which Tori found utterly desirable in a man.

Not that she desired him. She'd just had amazing sex with Alex. Then again, she never put down roots on one man, so she could certainly admire another. And Alex and Ben were as different as night and day, both in age and looks. Which made her wonder at their friendship.

Business partnership she understood, but there was such an age gap between them. She was intrigued by their friendship. Had they bonded over surfing? Alex had said Ben was a close friend and they were rooming together. They interacted with an ease that Victoria found incredibly appealing.

In her business, men were often competitors. She enjoyed seeing a good male friendship.

"Are you here to watch the surf competition, Victoria?" Ben asked.

"No. I'm on vacation."

"So this is an added bonus for you."

She laughed. "I suppose it is."

"Are you a surfing fan?"

"I've surfed before, but never watched a competition."

Ben shifted his gaze to Alex. "You're going to enjoy this. Alex is a champion."

He was certainly a champion at sex. And they'd just gotten warmed up before they'd been interrupted. "I can't wait to watch him."

Alex grinned. "I'm ready to get started."

"You need some sleep. You know what the Pipeline can do to you. You don't want to be caught half-asleep in a wave."

Tori stood. "That's my cue to leave."

Alex stood, too. "I'll walk you to your room."

"Try to be back in less than an hour, my man," Ben said. "Nice to meet you, Victoria."

She laughed. "You, too, Ben."

They left the room and Alex linked his fingers with hers. Her room was just down the hall and around the corner, so it wasn't a long walk.

She slipped her card key in the door and turned to Alex. "You didn't have to walk me, you know."

He held the door open for her. "Now what kind of gentleman would I be if I let a lady walk herself home?"

"I'd invite you in, but Ben is right. If the competition starts tomorrow, you should probably rest."

"I probably should," he said, stepping inside and closing the door behind him. "But I feel like we barely got started before we were interrupted."

She pushed him against the door this time and fisted her hands in his shirt. "I don't want to wear you out."

He wrapped an arm around her and let his fingers trail down her back, giving her butt a gentle squeeze. "I'd like you to try your best."

His lips met hers in a kiss that stole her breath. She felt a moment of guilt, knowing she should have just said good night, but she still wanted him. His instant erection told her he reciprocated the need and desire that had welled up inside her.

Her clit throbbed and she knew she was going to get another orgasm before she went to sleep tonight.

"Come on. Let's go to the bedroom and try it in there," she said, taking him by the hand.

"Why? Do you have an unexpected roommate planning to show up?"

She laughed. "No. But I thought I might climb on your cock and fuck you."

"You have great ideas, Tori."

She turned and smiled at him as she led him into the bedroom. She'd left the sliding glass door to the balcony open. Moonlight streamed in, casting a silver glow onto the bed. Just the right amount of light.

"Why don't you get naked and climb on the bed?"

He gave her a sexy half smile. "Good plan." He drew his shirt off, dropped his shorts, and flopped onto the middle of her bed, propping the pillows up so he could lean against them. He waved a condom in his hand. She grinned.

"I love a man who's prepared."

She drew the zipper down on her dress, then pulled it off, leaving her in only her underwear.

"Did I mention earlier how sexy you are?" he asked.

"Yes. And thank you." She popped the clasp on her bra, pulled it off, and tossed it to the side, cupping her breasts and teasing her nipples before slowly drawing her panties down.

"And how hot and tight your pussy is?"

"You didn't mention that, but I also love your cock. You made me come so hard. Let's see if you can do it again."

His eyes gleamed with desire as she crawled onto the foot of the bed, making her way toward him.

"Why don't you take that condom out, slide it over your cock, and let me sit on you."

In record time, he was sheathed. She climbed up his legs, though honestly, she could have stood at the foot of the bed and just watched him. His legs wide, his cock erect, there was an air of confidence in his nudity that was so sexy. She rested on his thighs and splayed her fingers across his chest, enjoying the powerful feel of all that muscle.

At least until he dragged her forward, thrust his hand in her hair, and kissed her, stealing her breath. She moaned as his tongue slid between her lips, her body more than ready to take him on.

After he thoroughly kissed her, she pulled away, braced one hand on his chest, and lowered herself onto his cock.

"That's it," he said, caressing her thigh.

She raised her gaze to his, making eye contact as she seated herself on him.

"Oh, that's good." He fit her perfectly, her pussy clenching around him like a fist. She moved forward and his eyes went half-lidded as he reached for her breasts, cupping them and brushing her nipples with his thumbs. A rocket of pleasure shot to her clit.

She knew sex with Alex was going to be good, but she was already ridiculously close to another orgasm. She lifted, caught her breath, then eased back down on him again, needing to prolong the ecstasy as long as she possibly could.

She leaned forward, dangling her breasts near his mouth. He took one, slid a nipple between his lips while she braced her hands on the headboard.

She fucked him while he sucked the bud, the sensation maddening. She already knew he had a magical tongue, and he flicked it around one nipple, then let go and grabbed the other.

"That's going to make me come." She pulled back.

He grinned and grabbed her hips. "Isn't that the idea?"

"Not yet. I don't want to come yet. Fucking you feels so good."

He reached for her hips and dragged her forward. "But you feel so good when you come on my cock. Your pussy squeezes me."

He took her breath away. She raked her nails down his chest, then rocked forward, grinding herself against him as her climax rushed toward her. "Oh, I'm coming."

She arched back and he held her as she shuddered and let go. He thrust into her and she heard him groan with his own orgasm while she was wracked with spasms that sent her over the edge again and again.

Spent, she fell forward, resting on his chest, listening to the rapid thump of his heartbeat until it settled along with hers.

When she withdrew, he grinned up at her. She went into the bathroom and slipped on her robe while Alex got dressed.

"Preliminaries are tomorrow," he said as he put on his shirt. "Will you be there?"

"Sure. I'll come by."

"I'll leave a pass for you so you can get a good seat in the viewing area."

"Thanks." She walked him to the door and he wrapped his arm around her and kissed her. "Get some sleep."

After he left, she locked her door and went back into the bedroom, smiling as she took in her messed-up sheets. Her body fluttered in response.

It was going to be a great vacation.

FIVE

DESPITE BEING ON VACATION, TORI WAS UNABLE TO sleep in. Her body clock was always set to six a.m., and there was nothing she could do to change it. Years of conditioning had trained her body to wake at that time, and even a time zone change couldn't alter it. Her body just instinctively knew when it was six in the morning, no matter where in the world she happened to be.

Ugh. Damned traitorous piece-of-shit internal body clock.

She flopped around in bed for hours, determined to master her own universe. Just once she'd like to be decadent and sleep until eight or even nine—in her vacation time zone.

But no. She was wide-awake.

Admitting defeat, she grabbed her phone and looked at the time.

Ugh. She got up, threw on some clothes, and went for a run on the beach. She longed for the peace and quiet, the sounds of the ocean, the energy a run could provide. It centered her, giving her time to be alone with her thoughts. Maybe she could replay last night's events in her head. That should put a smile on her face and set the tone for the day.

But apparently not this morning, because it wasn't peaceful, wasn't quiet, and there would be no alone time. They were already setting up for the competition. She hadn't made it a mile before she ran into a brick wall of tents and announcers and people already setting up spots on the beach for viewing.

She stopped and caught her breath, surveying the setup, which was pretty impressive. Viewing stands had seemingly been erected overnight, there were tents for drinks and food, and a shaded, private area for both judges and announcers. She glanced over at the announcer's area, but didn't see Alex's roommate, Ben.

"Looking for me?"

She pivoted. Ben had come up behind her, obviously on a run of his own. Sweat dripped down his arms and neck and along his naked torso. For a guy in his forties, he was ripped as hell, with an impressive six-pack and lean muscle in all the right places.

"Actually, I was out on my run but was stopped by this wall of event mania."

He looked over her shoulder, then back at her, gracing her with a thousand-watt smile. "Yeah, it's great, isn't it?"

"It's formidable. Are the events always this spectacle-inducing?"

"Not all of them, but this is one of the bigger ones. It draws a huge crowd. The tubes are awe-inducing. Wait till you see them."

"I'm looking forward to it."

"Would you like something to drink?" he asked, leading her toward the vendor tents.

"A juice would be great."

He flashed the ID badge clipped to his shorts and security let them pass. The tent was cool and Tori breathed out a sigh of relief. It was going to be a warm day. She'd have to make sure to wear her hat if she was going to be sitting out in the sun watching the surfers.

Ben grabbed an orange juice for each of them, then directed her to a couple canvas chairs. She took a seat and a couple swallows of juice.

"Where's Alex?" she asked.

"In one of the competition booths, signing papers and listening to the jargon about all the rules. Standard stuff all the competitors have to go through."

She leaned back in the chair and gave Ben a quick glance. He was such a handsome man with his dark hair, his tan, and his incredible smile. He had a natural ease about him she found very attractive. Too bad she couldn't handle more than one man at a time. Besides, she typically never dated men her own age or older— they were too into commitment and that wasn't her style. Younger men were always more free-spirited and much easier to let go of.

"You competed before?" she asked.

"Yes, but it's been a while."

"Injury, or tired of the surfing lifestyle?"

He laughed. "Once a surfer, always a surfer. I hurt my back on a bad wave about ten years ago, resulting in the need for surgery. That was the end of my competitive surfing."

"I'm sorry. I can't imagine what it would be like to not be able to do what you love."

He shrugged. "I got over it."

"That's such a simplistic statement. It sucked, didn't it?"

He gave her a direct look that told her he was surprised she understood. "You're right. It did suck. For a long time."

"Like years?"

"Yeah."

She sipped her juice. "I'll bet you were a pain in the ass to live with for a while."

He let out a laugh. It was deep and filled with a dark, husky tone that made her tighten in places that had no business tightening considering her sex-a-thon with Alex last night.

"I was an unlikeable prick for about two years. Felt sorry for myself. Thought my life was over."

"I think you were due a pity party. If it were me, I might have taken another year or so."

"So what you're saying is I have another year coming?"

She laughed. "Sorry. No retro do-overs. You screwed up. Now that you've manned up and gotten over it, your complaining days are over."

"Too bad. I really enjoyed the drug and alcohol binges."

"That bad, huh?"

"The pain pills were fine for a while, but eventually the doctor put a stop to them. I used alcohol to dull the pain after that. It got pretty ugly."

"Did you have to go to rehab?"

"No. I never got that bad. I only drank at night so I could sleep, so at least I didn't become an all-day drunk. Couldn't stand myself after a while, and realized no one else could stand me either, so I cleaned myself up and rejoined the living."

She smiled at him. "You look pretty okay to me. Glad you found your way back from the dark side."

"Thanks. It was good for me, actually. Nothing like a long hard bout of feeling sorry for yourself to make you realize your life really isn't over."

"I deal with that with a lot of athletes, who often have very short careers."

"I imagine being an agent is more than just negotiating contracts and fielding offers for commercials. You also have to teach them about investing in their future, just in case an injury sidelines them, or even worse, kills their career sooner than they think."

She nodded, appreciating that he was so perceptive. So many people didn't "get" what she did for a living, and thought she sailed around the country romancing prospects, having them sign on the dotted line, then rushing off to snare a new conquest. Her job wasn't all big paychecks and sharing the spotlight with high-paid sports stars. It was a hell of a lot of work, and often a great deal of frustration.

"You're exactly right. A lot of these young kids think they're superheroes, that nothing bad will ever happen to them. One catastrophic injury and they're out of the game in an instant. I advise them to invest their money well, and to have a fallback plan for when their careers do end, because the large majority of them won't be in the game for as long as they think they will."

He tilted his head. "You're very smart."

She laughed. "And that surprises you?"

"Not at all. But it probably surprises many of your clients. I wish I'd had an agent like you when I was younger. You do realize a lot of them are out to make as much money as they can from their clients for as long as they can, and they don't give a shit about their clients' welfare."

"Sadly, I do know. There are many unscrupulous agents out there, but there are just as many who care about their clients' welfare. You obviously had one of the bad ones."

He finished his juice and made a perfect toss into the nearby recycling container. "Which is why I'm not retired and living on a beach somewhere, whiling away my days in a hammock."

"Awww, too bad. You have to work like the rest of us poor suckers."

"Yeah, my life is a living hell." He graced her with a wicked grin that made the female parts of her quiver.

She had no business quivering over Ben Reynolds. He wasn't at all her type. Which didn't mean she couldn't enjoy his company. He was smart and engaging, and after all, she was on vacation.

She broke a lot of rules while on vacation.

"Somehow I don't think your life is all that bad, Ben."

"I'm not complaining. I still get to travel, still get to attend all the surfing events, and I still don't have to pay for them, since my company foots the bill."

"That doesn't sound like such a bad life to me."

He stood, and she did, too. "It's a great life. Being as good a surfer as I was, I've learned to spot real talent. And when I do, I make sure I put my logo on their boards and their suits. They make me money. It's a pretty sweet deal."

"Sounds like your life is just where you want it to be."

He led her outside, and she was surprised by how many people had shown up in the short time they'd been inside the tent.

The smell of something cooking made her stomach growl. She laid her hand there.

"I think I'll go grab some breakfast. I rolled out of bed this morning for a run and haven't even had a cup of coffee yet."

"Me, either. Come have breakfast with me, and then I'll get you a prime seat for the morning practice runs."

She shook her head. "Thank you, but I need a shower first, and it's going to be hot as hell today. My hat is in my room. I'll need to gear up if I'm going to spend the day in the heat."

"You can sit in the tent area with me, out of the sun. Go take your shower. I'll still buy you breakfast. Stop at the registration desk. I'll leave you a pass for all the competition events and private areas."

She wanted to decline. No, that wasn't true. She should say no. She wanted to say yes. She liked spending time with Ben.

She also liked spending time with Alex, whose touch made her tingle in unexpected, delightful ways.

But Ben was Alex's friend, and he'd offered breakfast, not sex.

"Okay. Thank you. I'll be back in about forty-five minutes."

"Great. I'll be at the far end of the tented areas, the one with the Surf Hot logo."

He pointed, and she nodded. "I'll see you then."

BEN WATCHED VICTORIA JOG OFF, HIS LIPS CURVING as he admired her long legs and great ass.

It was really too bad Alex had met her first. She was beautiful and intelligent and the kind of woman he'd love to spend time with.

Plus, he couldn't help but focus on her mouth. He had a thing about a woman's mouth, and Victoria had a full bottom lip that begged to be tugged on.

His cock tightened. He finally tore his gaze away from her retreating form, searching the ocean for Alex.

He found him sitting beyond the waves and talking with a few of the other competitors. Even from a distance, Ben read the ease that Alex had with the board and the waves. The one thing Ben had always liked about Alex was his instincts. He knew when the right wave would come along, and when the wrong time was to drop in on one.

Ben would give anything to be out there, ready to catch one of the tubes. Dangerous to be riding the Pipeline, but he could still remember the adrenaline rush of dropping down into a wave of overpowering size and mastering it.

It might have been a lot of years since he'd ridden competitively, but the urge had never died. He clenched his fingers into his palm, sucked in a deep breath, then released it.

Give it up. It's over. It's been over and you're never going to ride the big waves again.

The dull, constant pain in his back reminded him why.

He pivoted and headed toward the promoter's tent.

VICTORIA SHOWERED AND CHANGED INTO HER SWIM-
suit, then tossed a pair of cotton capris and a T-shirt over it, slipped into her sandals, and grabbed her bag. She made the walk back to the competition area and went to the registration area first to pick up the badge Ben had said he'd leave for her. She flashed her badge to get in, and found Ben in the tent. He was talking to a few other people, so she turned to watch the surfers, some already in motion on the waves.

She searched for Alex, but couldn't find him in the sea of bodies undulating in the water.

"He's in the center, just to the right of the dude with the bright orange board."

Ben had come up behind her, and moved beside her. She followed where he pointed, then nodded as she spotted Alex, who had just popped up on his board to take the next wave.

Her breath caught as he slid down the curve of what she thought was a pretty big breaker. He dropped down, then disappeared under a crashing fall of water. She didn't exhale until she saw him come out from underneath it.

"Jesus, that's some scary shit."

Ben laughed and slipped his arm around her waist. "It's a thrill ride, that's for sure."

She was frozen to the spot, unable to move as she watched the other surfers do the same thing, certain at any moment one of them wouldn't come out the other side of those monstrous waves. But they all did. Only Ben's slight pressure on her hip convinced her to give up her spot.

"It's like a train wreck," she said as he led her down the beach walk to the street side. "It's awful, yet I don't want to look away."

"It's not awful. It's great."

"No, it's awful. They're taking their lives into their hands every time they slide into one of those gigantic waves."

"Those aren't even the biggest waves yet."

She stopped and her eyes widened. "They get bigger?"

He grinned. "Yeah."

"You all are insane."

"Nah. They know what they're doing."

He stopped at a little restaurant called Café Haleiwa that was super crowded. They had to wait for a few minutes for a table, but Ben assured her the wait was worth it. The smell of coffee and food made her stomach rumble. They took a seat and a waitress came by to take their drink orders. First item on the agenda was coffee. She looked over the menu, and they ordered when the waitress came back with their coffee.

She took a sip, closed her eyes, and sighed.

"You look like you're having an orgasm."

She opened her eyes and offered up a smirk. "Well, you would know since you've seen me have one."

His lips curved. "True. But it was from a distance. And I wasn't inside you at the time. Not at all the same thing."

Heat coiled low in her belly, swirling around her like a living thing. It shocked her, this instantaneous chemistry she felt with Ben. She'd never been interested in two men at one time. It wasn't in her nature to be multiflirtatious. Once she settled on a man, she was wholly focused on him and him alone until it was over. And she'd settled on Alex. He was going to be her vacation fling. So what was up with all this sexual friction between her and Ben?

"I guess you'll just have to use your imagination then."

The look he gave her melted her to the floor of the restaurant. "I have a pretty damn good imagination, Victoria."

His voice had gone low and deep. A whisper, a dare. Or was it an offer? She didn't know what to make of him. He was friendly, and nonthreatening, but also obviously attracted to her. And she'd be lying to herself if she said she wasn't attracted to him. But she was also very much attracted to his roommate, which put her in a deep quandary.

"You know, I really like Alex."

He leaned back, his coffee cupped between his hands. "So do I."

"Then what are we doing here, Ben?"

The waitress brought their food. Ben looked at Tori. "We're having breakfast, Victoria."

Somehow she didn't think it was that simple. But she was hungry and she didn't want to dissect something that was probably nothing more than a simple flirtation. She flirted a lot as part of her job. Anything to get a contract signed for one of her players, and being a woman sometimes had its advantages.

Ben obviously liked women, and she certainly liked men. It wasn't like they'd run off to have a quick fuck while Alex was busy in the water.

Ben was right. They were just having breakfast. And they had chemistry. Big deal. Nothing was going to come of it, so she should relax and enjoy his company.

The problem was this odd attraction she had to him. That was going to have to be tucked away and forgotten about.

Funny thing about attraction, though. It was there now, and she knew damn well it wasn't going away because she willed it to.

SIX

AFTER A FANTASTIC BREAKFAST, VICTORIA AND BEN made their way back to the beach. Alex was out of the water and talking to some of the other competitors. He wore his board shorts and a wet suit on top. And looked incredible.

He spied them and made his way over.

He pulled Tori into his arms and gave her a hard kiss that stole her breath and made her pulse race in all the right ways, reaffirming everything she'd thought about at breakfast.

"Where'd you two run off to?" he asked.

"Breakfast," Ben said. "I took Victoria to Café Haleiwa."

Alex grinned. "Awesome place." He looked at her. "Did you like it?"

"I did." She turned to Ben. "Thank you again for breakfast. I was about to drop on the beach, I was so hungry."

"You're welcome. I need to go do some promotional work, so I'll catch you two later."

He walked away as if what had passed between them earlier had been nothing. And maybe it was nothing. Maybe she'd been the one who was making more of it than it was. Ben might be one of those guys who flirted with every woman, single, married, or whatever. She decided to ignore it.

Alex put his arm around her. "Did you get a chance to watch me surf?"

She grinned. "I did. My heart was in my throat the entire time."

"Yeah? It's not that bad. Waves weren't charging this morning. Wait till they get big."

She laughed. "That's what Ben said. I think you surfers are crazy for taking those risks."

"We know what we're doing. Trust me. We might take risks, but we're not stupid. At least most of us."

"That's so comforting."

"Awww, you're worried about me. I like that."

She laid her hand on his stomach, still so awed by the rock-hard muscle she felt there. "So what's on your agenda the rest of the day?"

"I've got a break for a few hours while the rest of the group runs practice heats. I'll be up again later this afternoon. Then there's a get-together tonight on the beach for the official kickoff of the competition, which starts tomorrow. After that I'll be kind of busy."

She traced her finger over his wet suit. "Then we should take advantage of what little free time you have left."

"I like the way you think."

His eyes gleamed hot and desire shot through her. He took her hand and tugged her along the beach toward the hotel. Her mind was already awhirl in thoughts of what they would do once they got there.

When she was working, she was always knee-deep in deals and players and focusing on work. She rarely relaxed and she was always on, putting on the face of a hotshot sports agent. And while she made good money and lived a great life, she didn't get a lot of downtime. When she did, she liked to let go.

Alex was her let-go moment, and she was so glad they'd found each other, because he was young and hot, and a year's worth of tension and anxiety dissolved when she was with him.

And when they got to her room, she'd no more than slipped her key card in the lock when he pulled it from her hand and shut the door, then swept her into his arms to put his mouth on hers. Need skyrocketed to nearly unbearable levels in an instant. She slid her hands in his hair and breathed him in—salty, like the ocean.

He moved his hands over her body, sliding them behind her to cup her butt and draw her against his erection. Her clit quivered. She already felt swollen, tight—needy and near the brink of exploding. It wouldn't take much to make her come.

Alex backed her up, leading her toward the living room, his mouth still latched onto hers. She cupped his hard-on, and he groaned, pulling her down on top of him on the sofa.

Stretched out on top of all that lean muscle was a treat. She lifted and stared down at him, rewarded with his killer grin. He clutched her hips and dragged her against his shaft, causing sparks of pleasure to heat her from the inside out.

"I like you on top of me, Tori."

She pulled her top off, then stood, wriggling out of her pants before climbing on top of him again. She undid her bikini top and tossed that away. "Touch me," she said, desperate to feel Alex's hands on her.

He obliged her greedily, grasping her breasts and rolling the nipples until she was nothing more than a puddle of aching, aroused flesh. She surged against him, her bikini-clad bottom rolling over his erection. She reached between them and palmed him, teasing his flesh until he let out a curse.

He lifted her and carried her to the bedroom. "I need to fuck you."

"Yes," she said, her pussy quivering in anticipation.

He dropped her onto the bed and grabbed one of the condoms

she'd laid out on the nightstand. He dropped his board shorts and put on the condom while she shimmied out of her bikini bottoms. She started to scoot back, but Alex grabbed her ankle.

"Stay here," he said. "Just like this."

She planted her feet flat on the bed and widened her legs. Alex stepped to the edge of the bed and fit his cock at the entrance to her pussy, then leaned forward, bracing his hands on the bed as he eased inside her. He focused his gaze on her face and she held tight to his forearms as he pushed inside her, the look on his face telling her it felt as good to him as it did to her.

"Tell me what you feel," he said.

"I love the way you swell inside me, the way my pussy grabs on to your cock, like it never wants to let you go."

His lips curved. "Yeah. You have my cock in a stranglehold, squeezing me hard." He pulled partway out, then began a slow slide inside her again. "That feels so good, Tori."

She shuddered, lifting her hips to meet his thrusts. It didn't stay slow for long, and she didn't want it to. She could tell he was as pent up and eager as she was, and before long she had pulled him on top of her and he had fucked her halfway across the bed. He scooped his hand under her butt, raising her to meet every thrust. And when he rolled his hips, his body rubbing the sensitive tissue of her clit, she gritted her teeth.

"Come on me," he whispered, his words dark and promising as he moved inside her. "You know you want to come."

She dug her nails into his shoulders and wrapped her legs around him, her climax so close she felt suspended. It was right there. "Yes. Yes, make me come."

He levered his hips, and rocked sideways again, giving her exactly what she needed.

"Oh, yes." Her orgasm was intense, and when she came, Alex began to pump in earnest, intensifying the relentless waves of pleasure that rolled over her. And when he groaned and kissed her deeply as he came, she held tight to him and lifted while he buried himself deep inside her.

Spent and satisfied, she reached up to push away the hair that had fallen over his brow. Alex rolled to his side, taking her with him.

"Now I might be too wiped out to surf today."

She smacked his arm. "Don't even say that. I'd feel terrible."

He laughed and pressed a kiss to her shoulder. "I'm just kidding. Sex reenergizes me. I could fuck you six times and still handle a day's worth of waves."

The things he said made desire flame low in her belly. They were still connected, and the thought of doing it again sparked. "I have all the time in the world. You're the one on a schedule."

He pulled out, disposed of the condom, then reached for another one, tossing it next to them on the bed as he pulled Tori on top of him. "My schedule is embedded in my head like a clock lives in there, honey." He grasped her hips and she rolled against him, his cock hardening underneath her.

"So does that mean you want to do this again?"

She loved the way he looked at her, that surge of heat and desire and need that made her hot all over.

"Yeah. I want you to fuck me, Tori. Just like this."

That was one of the highlights of having sex with younger guys. They had a surplus of stamina, and they thought about sex a lot. A man like Alex was perfect for a vacation fling. She wanted sex and a lot of it, and he was ideal for her needs right now.

Alex's eyes were on her breasts, and as he grasped them and held them in his hands, she grabbed the condom and tore it open. He watched her as she slid down to apply the condom, unable to resist taking a quick swipe of the head of his cock with her tongue.

"Fuck, yeah. I like that, Tori."

She lifted her head and smiled at him, then took his cockhead between her lips, rolling her tongue over it. He shuddered, his lids dropping half-closed, his breathing labored as she took him deep between her lips, then all the way into her mouth. His deep breaths told her he liked what she was doing, and tasting him turned her on as much as it did him. Her nipples were aching points, tightening as he pushed his cock deeper into her mouth.

He withdrew and pulled her up. "You can suck me later. I want you to ride me."

Always happy to oblige, she rolled the condom on, then seated herself over his shaft, teasing him by sliding down ever so slowly onto his cock. He grabbed her hips and held her as she lowered herself on him, then clenched his fingers as she buried him in her.

"God, you feel good, Tori."

She smoothed her hands over his chest and leaned forward. The feel of Alex's cock swelling inside her took her breath away. "I can come hard when I'm on top like this."

"Yeah?" He dragged her forward. "Let's find out how hard."

ALEX SHIFTED HIS HIPS UPWARD, BURYING HIS COCK deeper. Watching Tori's face, seeing that flush spread over her body, made his balls tighten. He could shoot inside her right now, but damn if he didn't want to prolong this. She was beautiful and lush and he could spend all day fucking this woman, watching the ecstasy on her face as she tilted her head back and rode him.

Her breasts thrust forward as she rocked her hips up. Alex gritted his teeth and held on for the ride, giving her all the control.

He loved older women. They were into sex for their pleasure, and they knew exactly what they wanted and how to get off. Young girls often were so concerned about how they looked and whether they were pleasing the guy, worried about whether or not they'd get dumped. It seemed sometimes—at least to him—that they couldn't concentrate on their own pleasure. So many of them just damn well didn't know how to let go, relax, and have fun in the sack.

Tori knew. She took control of his cock and used him for her own pleasure, and watching her brought him right to the edge.

She was beautiful, her body flushed with sex, her nails digging into his arms as she dragged her sweet pussy over him. And when she reached between her legs to stroke her clit, and her pussy tightened around him, he knew she was ready to go off. He thrust into her and her eyes widened.

"Yes. I'm going to come."

He knew it, and he dug his fingers into her hips, lifting her, then impaling her onto his cock, pistoning into her with hard and fast strokes until she cried out and ground against him. Unable to hold back, he let go, the force of his orgasm making him shudder as he held tight to Tori, rolled her over onto her back, and thrust deeply into her for those last few strokes.

Parts of him tingled. Damn, that had been good. He loved the feel of Tori, inside and out, from the way she looked to the way she laughed and the way she smelled. He enjoyed talking to her and he sure as hell liked her sweet mouth. He kissed the side of her neck and lifted his head to find her grinning up at him.

"Ready for round three?" she asked with a wicked smile.

His cock twitched and she arched a brow.

"If I had a free day, babe, I'd wear you out."

"I don't doubt it. Now get off me and let's clean up so you can catch a few breaths before you have to get back in the water."

They took a quick shower, and Tori ordered room service so he could grab a bite to eat. One of the other things he liked about her was that she wasn't clingy, and didn't ask when she'd see him again, which was another reason he tended to avoid entanglements. There were a lot of women who wanted to latch on to him because of his connections in the surfing industry, or simply because of who he was.

Tori seemed to enjoy being with him just because of him. And he really liked that. He really liked her. She relaxed him, and he was always so hyped up around competition time that he needed to be around people who would help him take it down a notch, not someone who'd ratchet up his tension level.

As he finished his sandwich and polished off his glass of water, she picked up her phone again, obviously to check the time.

He smiled. "You trying to get rid of me? Got another date?"

She laughed. "No. I'm worried you're not going to make it back in time for your next heat."

He tapped his temple. "Like I told you. It's burned into my head." He pulled her phone across the table and noted the time. "I've got forty-five minutes. But yeah, I hate to eat and run."

She pushed her chair back. "Don't be ridiculous. You have a job to do. That has to be your primary focus."

She walked him to the door and he pulled her against him, burying his face in her vanilla-scented hair. "You make this way too easy on me."

"You don't need some woman holding you down. Concentrate on the waves."

He inhaled, sighed, then tipped her chin back to take a taste of her. Sweet, sensual, he could get lost in her. He could lose the whole day in her. But she was right. It was time to get in the water. "I had fun."

She smiled. "Me, too. I'll be on the beach cheering for you."

"Thanks."

After she shut the door, he made his way to the elevator, more relaxed than he'd been when he first hit the waves this morning.

Tori was exactly what he needed throughout this competition. A woman who knew what she wanted, who enjoyed sex, and who put no strings on him.

Damn, he was a lucky guy.

He hit the beach, watching the waves as he made the walk to the competition area. Adrenaline started flowing as he spotted the boards in the water. He stopped just as Matt rolled onto a wave and dropped down under it.

Whether it was him or someone else, watching someone shoot a tube never failed to spark him up and make him crave being out there. At thirty-five, he was a veteran rider. He wondered how many more years of competition he'd have before he'd have to yield to some of the younger boarders. He was already starting to feel the effects of years of surfing. You didn't do what he did without suffering some injuries, and the body started to notice after a while.

He was wavering between thinking about what the next step in his career would be to still feeling that longing to be out in the water every day. It still surged in his blood and gave him a reason to get up in the morning. He couldn't think of anything he loved more—or what the hell he was going to do when he didn't have surfing in his life anymore.

But he knew that time was winding down, and he had to be realistic about it. A smart surfer didn't push his limits forever.

And he'd always been smart about his career.

He saw Ben at the ropes to the competition tents, so he went over.

"Where've you been?" Ben asked.

"I had some free time between heats, so I took advantage of it."

Ben nodded. The one thing he liked about his friend, manager, and promoter was that he never asked questions.

"Okay. Time to get set, though. Your gear is stowed in my tent."

"Great. I'll get ready."

Ben clapped a hand on his shoulder. "You prepared for this? You feel good?"

Alex grinned at him. "It's in the bag. We're going to win."

"That's what I like to hear. I feel good about this one. These are your kind of waves."

Alex looked out over the water, the surge of excitement so strong he could barely contain the desire to dive headfirst into the water right now. "You're right. They are."

SEVEN

VICTORIA HUNG OUT ON THE BEACH WITH BEN AND
the rest of his team all afternoon to watch Alex and the others
during the practice rounds. She was learning a lot about surfing
competitions. It was fascinating. She'd always thought of surfing as
rather laid-back, except of course when she did it. Then it was
hard. The learning curve for her had been difficult, but she had
chalked it up to being a skill that had not come naturally to her.
After all, she was a city girl, not born and bred to the ocean.

She was realizing it was hard for everyone, and it took an awesome amount of skill, strength, and practice to perfect. The waves
she surfed were miniscule compared to the monsters these profes-
sionals rode.

After spending hours watching every one of the competitors, it
was obvious how good Alex was. No wonder he was a champion.
He caught the top of many of the waves, dropped down underneath them, which made her breath catch, and rode it out until the

wave disappeared. There was only one occasion when the wave seemed to swallow him up, and her heart lodged in her throat when that happened. She'd seen that with several of the surfers, and feared for their safety each time, though they all swam out from under it, seemingly good-natured and ready to catch the next wave that came their way.

Ben told her none of the rides they took today counted anyway, and semifinals were tomorrow, which was when official scoring would begin.

She was already getting nervous for Alex, who didn't seem anxious at all as he hung out and laughed with the other competitors. She really liked his body language, the way he carried himself with such a laid-back demeanor, leaning on his sand-jammed board while he casually chatted with the other surfers.

He occasionally caught her eye and glanced her way. Ben had invited her to spend the afternoon in the shaded promoter's tent with him, a blissful relief from the baking sand and sun. It also meant Alex knew where to find her, though he'd stayed with the crowd of other surfers. But he'd look over at her and smile, and she'd get these ridiculous butterflies in her stomach remembering the amazing sex they'd shared earlier in the day.

By the time the heats were over, she needed a nap.

"How about a drink?" Ben asked as he gathered up his paper-work.

He'd been an amazing host, explaining every part of the practice process to her.

"I'm exhausted. I need some rest."

His lips curved into a knowing smile. "Alex hard to keep up with?"

She lifted her chin. "I think I can manage, despite my advanced age."

He laughed. "I wasn't making a crack about you and Alex having sex. He's just pretty high energy and always on the go. He wears me the hell out. You should make a run for it now before he finds you and wants to drag you into the ocean for surfing. He could go all day. I'm thinking of disappearing myself before he wants to take me out to a bar, or surf with him."

Leave it to her to assume the wrong thing. "Yet you two room together."

He stuffed some papers into a backpack. "Yeah."

"Or is that more for business, so you can keep an eye on your investment?"

"Alex doesn't need a babysitter. He's an adult and can manage his life just fine without me. We travel all the time together, and we've grown close over the years. We're friends. We often share a suite during competition."

Well, hell. She'd heard her own voice snapping at him and she didn't like it. "I didn't mean anything by that."

He tilted his head her way, his smile genuine. "No offense taken, Victoria."

She really did need a nap. She was reading things into her conversation with Ben that obviously weren't there. "I think I'll head out. If you see Alex, tell him I'll be back tonight for the party."

"Will do."

Several hours later, she had rested, showered, and had even treated herself to a massage at the spa. Now she felt immensely better. And also much worse about being so defensive with Ben earlier. He'd been generous and kind and she'd done nothing but accuse him of age discrimination and running roughshod over Alex.

She owed him an apology.

She put on a sundress, slipped on her sandals, and walked down toward the beach. It was dark, so the tiki torches were lit and a bonfire was going strong. The competition area was crowded with people, some she recognized as the surfing competitors, some as the advertisers and promoters, and some she didn't know at all. There were a lot more people there tonight than had been around the day before.

Once she got past security with her badge, she wended her way through the crowd in search of either Alex or Ben.

She found Ben in the middle of a group of men. He smiled and waved her over, introduced her to several guys all in the business of promoting their own competitors in the contest.

He put his arm around her. "This is Victoria Baldwin."

One of them, a tall African American man wearing a white-and-red flowered shirt, narrowed his gaze. "Aren't you a sports agent?"

"I am. And you are . . ."

He held out his hand. "Sorry. Larry Banders."

The name sounded familiar. Why couldn't she place it? "Nice to meet you, Larry."

"You represent Malcolm King, the basketball player from San Antonio."

"Yes, I do."

"He's married to my sister, Cynthia."

Now she knew why the name had rung a bell. She smiled. "Of course. I love Cynthia. She's so supportive of Malcolm's career."

"Yeah, she loves basketball. Played some herself in high school and college."

"Yes. We've had several conversations about that. I tried to recruit her for the WNBA, but she refused to listen to my grand plans for her career."

Larry laughed. "Yeah, she wants to concentrate on my two nephews. I told her the same thing. I would have promoted the hell out of her if she'd let me. But she said babies first, career later. And now she wants to be a teacher."

Tori shrugged. "Not everyone wants the career of an athlete. What are you going to do?"

"Nothing. I love those kids, so if she's happy, then I'm happy. In the meantime, I put my label on everyone else. Like my kid here. In fact, I see him now, so excuse me. Nice meeting you, Victoria."

"You, too, Larry."

Ben led her away from the crowd. "Do you always run into people you know?"

"It happens sometimes. Indirectly or directly, I usually find someone in the business." As they headed through the crowd, she tilted her gaze up to his. The firelight highlighted the stunning features of his face and the utter sexiness of his eyes, something she tried not to notice. She was failing miserably. "Surely you have the same problem, since you're in the athlete business."

"True. I used to work with a lot of athletes, though I don't brand as many as I used to."

"Why not?"

He shrugged. "For one thing, I've made a lot of money over the years."

"There's always more money to make, you know."

"True. But I'm not looking to become richer than I need to be. I just want to live comfortably, and I do. Chasing money requires a lot of work and hustle and time, and I'm just not interested in putting that much time into it anymore. And second, I'm pretty selective about who wears my brand. Plus, I like surfing. It's still my passion, so limiting the chase for a higher income allows me to follow the waves. At least vicariously."

She smiled. "It's good that you still get to do what you love, even in this way."

"Having enough money has its benefits."

She wondered if she'd ever get to that point where it would be enough for her. She loved her career, adored her clients, and it was still an adrenaline rush for her. "I don't think I've reached the slow-down phase of my career yet."

"You'll know it when you get there."

She turned to face him. "Before Alex gets here, I want to apologize for earlier today."

He frowned. "What about earlier today?"

"I was tired and cranky and bit your head off about some things."

He stepped in closer and swept his hand over her hair. "I didn't even notice. Don't worry about it."

She shivered at his touch. "Well, thanks for being kind about it, but I'm pretty good at knowing when I'm being a bitch."

He laughed. "It's a good trait to have, but honestly, it takes a lot to piss me off."

"Also a good trait to have, Ben."

"I think you live longer that way. How about we find you a drink and you can really relax?"

"That sounds like a great idea. Is Alex here?"

"I saw him around earlier with some of the other surfers. I'm sure we'll run into him."

He led her to the drink station—an entire bar set up under one of the tents.

"What would you like?"

"Something hard. I'm in the mood to drink tonight."

He cocked his head to the side and gave her a grin. "My kind of woman. Two Jack Daniels—neat. And make them doubles."

He handed her the glass.

She looked down at the amber liquid, then back at him. "Are you trying to get me drunk?"

"Maybe." He clinked his glass against hers and downed his drink in one swallow.

She wouldn't dare do that, though she was good at holding her liquor. After countless years having cocktails with team owners and athletes who outweighed her by hundreds of pounds, she had learned to either pace herself or drink with them. She took a couple of sips, letting the liquid burn its way down her throat.

Mmm, smooth. She finished the rest in two swallows, then asked the bartender for water.

Ben motioned to the bartender, who handed over a bottle of water, and two more shots.

Victoria turned to Ben. "You *are* trying to get me drunk."

"Something tells me you can hold your own with a shot of whiskey."

She smiled over the rim of the shot glass. "Maybe."

She downed the drink. This one went down smoother than the first one. She handed the glass back to the bartender and opened her bottle of water to take a couple swallows, already feeling the warm mellowness of the whiskey making its way through her body.

It was getting crowded. The music had started up and everyone was headed toward the beach.

"Let's go find Alex," Ben said, sliding his hand into hers to guide her through the tight groups.

She liked his strong hand in hers, was still fascinated by the zing of attraction she felt for him. Her belly tumbled from the simple connection of their hands together. What was up with that? It certainly wasn't lack of sex, because Alex was taking good care of her in that department.

Maybe it was because they were closer in age, or maybe it was because they had similar types of careers. She'd felt a kindred spirit in Ben. But she had no idea what the reason was and wasn't about to take valuable vacation time dissecting it when this was her time to relax and enjoy herself.

He wound them through undulating bodies, where they found Alex talking to a couple girls. He turned to her and grinned.

"Hey, there you are." He waved off the girls, then swept her into his arms and planted a hot kiss on her lips. "I've been wondering when you'd show up."

"I'm starving," Ben said. "Are you two up for some food?"

"I know I am," Victoria said, looking at Alex.

"Sure. Let's grab some grub and a table before all the food's gone."

They went to the tent where a feast of food had been set out. Victoria filled her plate and sat between Alex and Ben.

"You looked great out there today. Are you ready for tomorrow?" she asked Alex.

"Thanks. I'm stoked. I can't wait for the competition to start. All this prep shit just makes me crazy. I want to get out there and score some points."

"He always gets like this," Ben said. "Nervous energy. A lot of the surfers hate the preliminaries. It's the real competition that gets their juices flowing."

Alex filled his mouth with a bite of chicken, and nodded, washing it down with a drink. "Fun is always in competition. You remember what it's like, Ben."

"Like it was yesterday."

She loved listening to the two of them talk about surfing. They launched into a discussion about tomorrow's event. She ate and listened while they went over the parameters of the competition. By the time she had emptied her plate, Ben had gotten up to talk to one of the judges, and Alex had finished off two plates.

"How do you stay so lean when you eat so much?" she asked as he tossed their plates in the trash.

"Surfing burns off a lot of calories." He leaned in close. "So does sex."

She shook her head, but smiled. "I would think you'd need to focus on the competition, not on sex."

"Honey, I'm never too busy to think about sex. It relaxes me, and when I'm relaxed, I compete better."

"Is that a line you give to all the women?"

He stopped, looked at her. "No. But is it working?"

She laughed. "Maybe."

They made their way back down the beach. Alex stopped and talked to . . . everyone. He was extremely popular. He signed several autographs, visited with a few people he knew, and was extremely gracious and friendly with everyone. She liked that about him. He didn't seem to have an ego and never brushed anyone off. By the time he extricated himself from the crowd, he took her hand.

"Sorry about that."

"Don't apologize for being nice to your fans. It's good that you take the opportunity to do that. I know a lot of professional athletes who don't. Once they have a little success, it goes to their heads and they forget the people who helped make them a success. They're total assholes."

"Hey, our sport struggles as it is. We have to give thanks to the people who love to watch us surf. That's the fans as well as the sponsors. Without them, we're just a bunch of penniless dicks sitting on surfboards."

"So true." She liked him more and more.

"Hey, the music's starting up," he said, grabbing her hand and leading her toward the crowd of people dancing.

After his busy day today, she thought he'd be exhausted. And yet here he was, ready to party it up with everyone. "You want to dance?"

"Hell, yeah." They found Ben along the way and Alex signaled to him. Ben came over and Alex gave him a report about one of the guys he'd spoken with in the crowd earlier who wanted to interview Alex.

"I'll take care of it later," Ben said.

"I knew you would," Alex said. "Come on, you two. Let's dance."

Victoria looked up at Ben, who shrugged, then grabbed her around the waist. Laughing, she joined in. The raucous beat was infectious, as was the crowd. And when Alex moved in behind her to grab her hips, she decided she was in heaven.

With Ben moving in front of her, and Alex behind her, it was the most delicious sandwich she'd ever been in, and gave her ridiculous, wickedly naughty ideas.

She locked gazes with Ben, who kept a respectable distance.

Until she held out her arms and pulled him in closer.

And the dance suddenly got a lot hotter.

Alex whispered into her ear. "You like Ben."

She flipped around to face Alex. "Of course I do."

Alex tugged her against him. "No, I mean you *like* Ben. You want him."

No reason not to be honest. "I find him attractive, yes."

He looked over her at Ben, then nodded. Ben came closer and wound his arms around her, the three of them swaying to a slow beat. "Tell us what you want."

Maybe it was the whiskey, or the heady, free environment. With men, she'd always taken exactly what she wanted, had always been free to explore her sexuality. "Let's get out of here," she said to Alex. "It's too crowded."

"Sure." Alex took her by the hand and started to lead her away from the people dancing.

She paused, and looked at Ben. "Aren't you coming with us?"

"Is that what you want?" Ben asked.

She had no hesitation when she answered. "Yes."

His lips curved. "Then, yeah. I'm coming with you."

EIGHT

ALEX AND BEN LED TORI BACK TO HER HOTEL SUITE. They'd asked if she wanted to go to her place or theirs. She had an oversize king bed and they had no objection, so she led them back to her room.

She fished into the pocket of her sundress for the key and handed it off to Ben. He unlocked the suite and she walked in, feeling more anticipation and excitement than she'd ever felt before.

She was a worldly woman, had experienced sexual delights with a lot of men.

But she'd never had two men at once.

As she turned and faced Ben and Alex, she couldn't think of anything she wanted more than these two men tonight.

Alex, with his sun-lightened blond hair and his amazing physique, and Ben, with his dark good looks and incredible eyes. They both pulled at her for different reasons.

Ben came over to her and skimmed his hands up and down her arms.

"You sure about this?"

She nodded. "Yes."

Alex came up behind her and pressed a kiss to the side of her neck. "Tori, we both know the meaning of the word *no*. You say it at any time tonight and this stops."

She turned to face Alex. "Thank you, but I know exactly what I'm getting into. I'm a grown woman and I know what I want. What I want is both of you."

She heard Ben's harsh intake of breath behind her, so she turned around.

Ben slid his hands around her waist and tugged her close.

"Been wanting to do this since that first night I saw you with Alex."

Ben's mouth fit to hers and where everything with Alex had been all about wild passion, with Ben it was a searingly slow exploration of lips and tongues, igniting her nonetheless like a wild bonfire. She moaned against his lips, and when he cupped her behind to draw her closer to his erection, she wanted everything she'd been fantasizing about with him.

Her breasts felt heavy, her nipples tingling with the need to have a hot, wet mouth sucking them.

And when Alex came up behind her, another hot, hard erection pressing against her, she felt like she had died and this must be what heaven was like—because all her dreams were coming true.

Alex kissed the back of her neck, and suddenly his hands were on her aching breasts, massaging them through the material of her dress.

She wanted to be naked, to feel all this delicious flesh pressed up against her.

With Ben's mouth on her and Alex's hands on her, she already knew how amazing this night was going to be. Her heart pounded and her sex throbbed, and when Alex unzipped her dress, she was more than ready to have it off.

So she could get off.

The dress puddled in a pool at her feet. Ben took her hands and led her forward. She stepped out of the dress, and Ben flicked the clasp at the front of her bra. She pulled the straps down and let the bra drop to the floor.

"You are damn beautiful," Ben said, cupping her breasts and leaning down to take a nipple in his mouth.

"Yes," she whispered. "Suck."

He did, his movements so gentle it made her ache with need.

Alex, still behind her, reached for her underwear, drawing them over her hips and down her legs. She held on to Ben while she stepped out of them. Alex smoothed his hands up her legs, then came around the front of her.

She gasped when he put his mouth on her sex.

She'd never had both her nipples and her clit sucked at the same time. The sensations were overwhelming in the most delicious way. She wrapped her arm around Ben's shoulders while he played with her breasts and nipples, her legs widening to give Alex access to her pussy. All she could do was hold on and watch as these two amazing men worshipped her body, making her quake with a hunger that took her to new heights of sensual pleasure.

It was heady and wicked and she wanted it to go on forever, but Alex had an expert mouth and before she knew what was happening she was coming, hard, crying out and shuddering while Ben held tight to her as the spasms of pleasure wracked her entire body.

She panted through the quivering orgasm. Ben's mouth was on hers, his grip on her chin light but oh so sexy as he took her mouth in a much more demanding kiss this time.

She felt a mouth on her breasts—Alex. It was going to take her some time to adjust to the idea that two men had access to her body.

"Don't think," she heard Alex say. "Just feel."

He was right. She had to surrender to the sensations, to enjoy every second of this night.

When Ben pulled his mouth from hers, she lost herself in the blue depths of his gaze. He smiled down at her.

"Good start?" he asked.

"Very good start."

"You came hard," Alex said, taking her from Ben's arms and into his. He kissed her thoroughly until her pussy quivered in anticipation. "Taste yourself on me?"

"Yes. And now it's time for both of you to shed some clothes."

Alex pulled off his shirt and dropped his shorts. "That's what I like about you," Victoria said. "You're always down with getting naked."

She turned to Ben and smiled. "Next."

"My pleasure." He unbuttoned his shirt and pulled it off, revealing the extremely well-toned arms and chest Victoria remembered from seeing him run on the beach. Once again she noted how in shape he was for a man in his mid-forties. He was tanned and muscled, with a dark sprinkling of hair at his chest. And when he slid out of his board shorts, her eyes widened.

"Uh, wow."

Ben grinned. "Thanks. Now how about we get you into the bedroom?"

"Yeah, let's get you spread-eagled," Alex said. "So we can really pay homage to that killer body of yours."

Victoria smiled. "I like that idea."

"I'm going to fix us all something to drink first," Ben said. "Victoria?"

"I'll have a tall glass of ice water. I have a feeling you're both going to make me thirsty."

"Same for me, Ben," Alex said.

Alex took her hand and led her to the bedroom.

When they reached the edge of her king-size bed—and oh, was

she ever happy to have a big bed at the moment—Alex pulled her
into his arms and kissed her. She lost herself in the passion of his
kiss, in the way his hands smoothed down her back to grab a handful of her butt cheeks to draw her closer to his hard cock.

He rubbed against her, then slowly moved his lips from hers.

By then, Ben was back, coming up behind her. He brushed her
hair to the side and pressed a soft kiss to her neck, the kind of kiss
that made her shiver.

"How many times do you think we can make you come tonight,
Victoria?" Ben asked.

She inhaled and sighed. "A lot." But then she pushed back from
Alex, and took his hand, leading him over to stand next to Ben.
"And how many times can I make the two of you come?"

When Victoria dropped to her knees in front of them, Ben
drew in a breath.

This night had been unexpected, sure as hell unplanned. He
liked Victoria—a lot. But he'd seen her as Alex's woman and he
would never get in the way of that.

Then somewhere along the way something had happened. Sure,
he'd felt a connection to Victoria from the moment he'd met her.
Hell, what man wouldn't? She was smart and funny and gorgeous
and she oozed sex appeal. But when a woman was taken, especially
by a good friend, a guy didn't step into that.

He and Alex had shared women in the past. Meaningless en-
counters that had been fun for all parties involved.

This didn't feel meaningless.

And now Victoria dropped to her knees in front of them,
grasped both their cocks in her hands, and tilted her head back,
her beautiful brown eyes filled with passion as she stroked both of
them from their root to the tips.

She had soft hands, her silky fingers sliding over his cock. He
was mesmerized watching the way she handled both him and Alex.

"That feels damn good," he said.

"I'm going to make it feel even better." She covered the tip of his cock with her lips, and he didn't even try to bite back the groan. Watching her suck him while she stroked Alex nearly destroyed him.

She had the best damn mouth. Hot and wet and those full lips made him want to pump hard and fast between them. But she was in control here, so he let her lead. And when she popped his cock out of her mouth and took Alex's between her lips, it was Alex's turn to let out a low groan.

"That's hot, babe," Alex said. "I love your mouth around my cock. Suck it hard."

She was stroking Ben and sucking Alex. Ben's balls tightened watching her. Hell, he could come with the way her soft, silky hands slid over his dick, watching the way she sucked his friend.

"Ah, you're gonna make me come, Tori," Alex said.

She let go of Ben and wound her hand around the base of Alex's cock. Ben watched as she gripped him tight, shoved Alex's cock into her mouth, and sucked hard.

Alex groaned and thrust and came, shuddering. Ben watched the way Victoria's throat worked, his balls tightening in reaction.

But Ben wanted to come inside of her, and he was going to use all the self-control he had to wait for that moment.

So when she pulled her mouth away from Alex, he lifted her up and took her mouth. He really liked her mouth. She had full lips and she tasted hot and needy. He liked the sounds she made when he slid his tongue alongside hers.

When he pulled back, she wrapped her hand around his cock, squeezing him.

"You didn't let me suck you until you came," she said.

He smiled at her. "I'll wait for it. I enjoy the buildup."

"Then I'll definitely have to make sure to build you up."

"You're doing that just fine. Now I want to taste you."

Alex had stepped out of the room, so Ben led Victoria to the bed and laid her down, sliding alongside her.

He swept his hands over her breasts, watching her nipples tighten. "You doing okay?" he asked.

"I'm doing . . . amazing. It's a little overwhelming, but in the best way."

Alex came into the bedroom and lay down on the other side of her. "Too much for you? Too fast? We can slow things down if you need us to."

Victoria loved the care these two men took of her. It made the experience so much more enjoyable. She felt safe with them, which made her want to explore and see just what would happen with them.

So far, she'd enjoyed every moment. And as Ben petted her, touching every part of her, Alex leaned over her, his eyes sparkling.

"You sucked me good, babe," he said, brushing his lips over hers. "I came hard."

"Mmm," she said, sweeping her fingertips over his delicious mouth. "So I noticed."

Alex kissed her, a deep, passionate kiss that made her lose herself. He teased her nipples, rolling them between his fingers.

Her legs were spread and she knew it was Ben there, his hair tickling her thighs as he shouldered between them. When he put his mouth on her, she gasped, the tickle of his beard scruff a delicious shock to her senses.

He took a long, slow swipe of her sex and, as he'd kissed her, seemed in no hurry to give her a climax, instead teasing her with slow licks and sucks guaranteed to drive her absolutely crazy, while Alex kissed her and played with her nipples.

A woman could get used to being worshipped by two men. Especially when pleasure was like this—unhurried, with Alex leaning over to tease her nipples, sucking and rolling his tongue around them, and Ben lapping her pussy and making her arch against his oh so talented mouth.

It didn't seem fair that she should feel this way, that they concentrated so much on her—on her body and on her orgasm. But she wasn't about to complain, not when she hovered on the brink of a climax. Moans and whimpers fell from her lips and she lifted her hips to feed her pussy to Ben, who slid his fingers into her, pumping them while he lapped at her with his magical tongue.

Alex lifted his head and looked down at her. "That's it, babe. Let Ben take you there."

She cried out as the pulses exploded into an orgasm that made her shake in an all-consuming rush of pleasure. Alex kissed her while Ben continued to slide his fingers in and out of her, prolonging the wild tide of her climax.

When she finally settled, Alex was above her, smiling down at her. "I love the look on your face when you come. You put your whole heart and body into it."

She inhaled, then sighed. "There's no point in doing it if you're not going to do it fully."

Ben pulled up beside her and Alex moved away. He brushed his lips across hers. "You taste sweet, Victoria."

She ran her fingertips across his chin. "And you know how to make a woman come. But you haven't come yet."

"Plenty of time for that."

"How about now?"

He lifted her up and held her glass of water near her lips. "Take a drink of water first. All that screaming you're doing must be drying out your throat."

She laughed, leaned up against the pillows, and took several swallows of water. "You're right about that. I was thirsty. Thanks."

"Hungry?" Alex asked.

"No, I'm good."

He smoothed his hands up and down her leg. "Yeah, you are."

She grinned, ended up finishing the entire glass of water, then excused herself to head into the bathroom. Once in there, she took a look at herself in the mirror. Her hair was a wild mess, her lips swollen from their kisses, and her body bore red marks from their mouths and their hands.

She felt . . . glorious. Worshipped. She'd used that word more than once already tonight.

She smiled at herself in the mirror.

She was looking forward to what was going to come next.

NINE

ALEX WATCHED TORI COME OUT OF THE BATHROOM. Damn, she was beautiful naked. He liked the way she walked, the confidence in the way she held herself as she made her way back to the bed, climbed on, and nestled herself against him.

"I ordered some champagne and some other stuff in case we get hungry," Ben said. "I'm going to go get dressed so I can answer the door."

"Okay," Alex said, turning his attention to Tori.

"You two are treating me like a queen."

He propped the pillows up against the headboard, leaned against it, and pulled her next to him. "That's because you're the center of attention tonight."

She lifted her gaze to his. "Somehow I always envisioned this type of scenario as the other way around. That it would be the woman giving the guys all the attention."

"Yeah? Maybe in some cases that's how it goes down. But that's not how I see it. We're here to make sure you have a good time."

She slid her foot alongside his calf. "My kind of night."

She rolled on top of him and he wrapped his arms around her.

"You know," she said, using the tip of her finger to brush across his bottom lip. "I can be all about your pleasure, too. Yours and Ben's."

"I like the sound of that, but let's have some champagne first."

Ben had come into the room pushing a cart. He pulled a bottle of champagne out of the ice bucket and popped it open.

Alex got off the bed and looked over at the cart. "What else have you got in there?"

"I ordered some sparkling water, figuring you'd want to lay off the champagne since you compete tomorrow."

"You're right about that." Alex opened a sparkling water and took several swallows. "Oh, and strawberries, too." He held one in his fingers, turning to Tori. "This could be fun."

Tori laughed. "I love strawberries. And champagne."

Ben had poured two glasses, and handed one to her while he kept the other. He took a seat at the edge of the bed.

She sipped the champagne. "Mmm. This is very good."

"I thought you might like it," Ben said.

Alex brought the bowl of strawberries over, picked one up, and slid it between her lips. She took a bite. "These are sweet."

"So are you," he said, brushing his lips over hers.

Ben took a strawberry in his hand and teased around one of Tori's nipples with it. Alex watched as Tori's breathing deepened, as her nipples tightened to tight points.

Her reactions made his cock twitch, made him ache to be inside her. But he wanted Ben to experience her. He took the strawberry from Ben and popped it into his mouth.

Tori laughed.

After he swallowed, Alex said, "Hey, I can't have champagne. So I'm stealing all the strawberries."

Ben grinned. "Not all of them." He picked up another and trailed it down Tori's stomach. When he got to her sex, Ben ate the strawberry, then put his mouth on her pussy.

Tori moaned.

Alex really liked the sounds she made. He loved a woman who was vocal during sex, and Tori had that part down. She was unashamed about her sexuality. She knew what she wanted and she went after it with her whole body.

What man wouldn't appreciate a woman like that?

"Come here, Alex," she said, twining her fingers around the back of his neck to draw him closer.

He kissed her, and her lips tasted as good as the strawberry had. She was like a drug, her tongue winding around his, sucking him in and making him lose himself in her.

She whimpered against his lips, and when he pulled back her beautiful eyes were pools of half-lidded desire.

He brushed his mouth against hers. "Anything you want."

Victoria was awash in sensation, her pussy throbbing from Ben's tongue and lips. She hovered on the brink of orgasm, only this time she wanted to come with a hot cock inside of her. Two hot cocks inside of her.

"I need to suck your cock, Alex. And then I want you to fuck my ass. Ben, I want you to fuck my pussy. Condoms are in the nightstand and there's a bottle of lube in my bag on the bathroom counter."

"I'll go get the lube," Alex said.

Ben got up and grabbed a condom from her nightstand. But first, he came over and kissed her, a hot, dizzying kiss that left her wanting more.

"You're sure that's what you want," Ben said.

"Yes. Oh, yes."

Ben nodded. "We'll make this good for you."

She swept her fingertips across his jaw. "It's already good for me."

His lips curved. "Then we'll make it even better."

He moved away and Alex's mouth replaced Ben's. She never

expected it to feel this way, to be so overcome by emotion. She'd prepared herself for the amazing sex, but not this whirlwind of warmth and feeling of protection.

They'd been so gentle with her. Passionate, definitely, but also so sweet. They'd taken their time with her, hadn't rushed anything. It hadn't been shoving cocks at her expecting her to do anything. Instead, it had been all about her pleasure. She'd already come so many times. And now, she wanted them both inside of her. In her mouth and in her pussy. And then in her ass, all of them fully joined until they all exploded together.

She'd fantasized about this for years, wondering if she'd ever experience it. And now, she would.

Alex leaned forward and slid his cock between her lips. She sucked it greedily, taking him fully into her mouth.

"That's it, babe. Suck it hard. You know how I like it."

Sucking his cock made her pussy quiver, made her nipples tingle and her breasts feel heavy. She grabbed the shaft and stroked it while she fed his cock into her mouth.

"Oh, yeah," Alex said. "That's what I need."

She loved that he was so vocal with her, that he told her what he liked.

And when he pulled away, he grasped her face and kissed her, a gentle, sweet kiss that made her tremble.

Ben positioned himself on the bed and she straddled him.

"I've been waiting to slide inside of you," he said as he grasped her hips and helped her get into position. "I've been thinking of this since that first night I saw you and Alex together."

"Have you?"

"Yeah. You were beautiful with the moonlight streaming in. Like a goddess demanding to be pleasured. That's what we're going to do for you tonight, Victoria. We're going to give you everything you've ever wanted."

She slid down on top of Ben's cock, moaning at the thickness of him, her pussy quivering as she fit herself around him.

"Mmm," she said, closing her eyes and letting herself feel the utter wicked pleasure of filling herself with Ben's cock.

"You feel so good, Victoria," Ben said, arching upward as she began to rock against him.

Tingles of pleasure arced throughout her body, making her gasp.

Alex came behind her, planting a kiss on that tender spot between her neck and shoulder. "You have a beautiful ass, Tori. And I'm going to fuck it good."

She reached up to curve her fingers behind his neck. "I know you will."

"Lean forward on Ben."

She did, bracing herself on Ben's shoulders.

"I'm going to spread your ass cheeks so I can lube you up nice and good," Alex said.

She felt him spread the cheeks of her butt, then the lube was there, followed by Alex's fingers.

"It feels good."

"Yeah, it does, doesn't it?" Alex said. He teased the entrance with his fingers, and her pussy clenched.

"Oh, yeah," Ben said, driving into her and making her spasm with sensation.

"Now you're going to feel the head of my cock. Nice and easy and we're all lubed up back here. You call all the shots, okay?"

She was so ready, her pussy clenching as Ben stilled. "Yes. Let's do this. I want to feel both of you."

"Look at me, Victoria," Ben said.

She met Ben's gaze. He swept her hair behind her ears.

"We're all going to do this together. Then we're all going to come hard together."

She smiled down at him.

"Now get that pretty mouth down here and kiss me."

She leaned down and met his lips. Ben held on to her head and his kiss was fierce passion, their tongues meeting as his cock lifted into her.

Alex's first penetration into her ass was like fire. It hurt, and yet it felt so good she felt tremors of pleasure arc out toward her sex. She gasped, but Ben rimmed her lips with his tongue, holding on to her and making her focus on his mouth as Alex pushed farther into her. She moaned, cried out, and then Alex forced himself fully into her. She reared up and reached behind her.

Alex's hand was right there to grasp onto her.

"Yeah, babe, I'm in your ass."

Her pussy clenched around Ben's cock.

"And I'm in your pussy," Ben said.

"Both of you, hold for a second," she said.

Neither of them moved. She felt like she was burning from the inside out, and yet it was the most glorious sensation. Ben in front of her, Alex behind her, both of them embedded within her. Her body throbbed.

"Now move."

Alex pulled back, then drove in, and Ben did the same, grinding up and into her.

"Oh, God, yes," she said, resting her hands on Ben as Alex pumped into her ass.

She felt so full, so gloriously, deliciously full.

"We're going to make you come," Ben said. "And when you do, Alex and I are going to come hard in you."

"Yes," was all she could manage because she was bombarded by strikes of pleasure from both sides. It was more than she could process, so she let her body take over and just . . . felt.

And what she felt was magnificent. Throbbing, arcing sensation after sensation pummeled her. Bursts of pleasure all centered in her pussy.

"I can't . . ."

They both stopped.

"What's wrong?" Ben asked.

She dug her nails into his chest. "Nothing. Nothing is wrong. It's all so right. Don't stop. Keep fucking me. I'm going to come."

She pushed back against Alex, then rocked against Ben. And when she heard them both groan, she knew they were all going to go off.

When the bursts exploded into an all-consuming orgasm, she screamed. A hard, wild cry that made her shake all over. It continued and Alex leaned against her, shuddering as he shoved into her and came. And Ben locked gazes with her, lifting up and holding on to her as he thrust into her as his orgasm hit.

It was the wildest, most exponential orgasm she'd ever had, because it kept coming and coming as they came and she came again.

She was torn apart, shattered, and thoroughly exhausted. Alex withdrew slowly. Ben rose up and scooted to the side of the bed with her in his arms. Alex was there to lift her off and the two of them led her into the bathroom.

She leaned against Ben while Alex turned on the shower.

"A little tired?" he asked.

She gave him a half smile. "A little."

"Come on. Let's clean up."

They all stepped into the shower. Alex and Ben dipped her under the hot water and they both washed her body.

"I have to admit it feels pretty good to be pampered like this."

"You deserve it," Alex said as he used a washcloth to clean her.

After, they used two fluffy towels to dry her off.

"Drink?" Ben asked.

"Water. Definitely."

Alex was right there with a glass of water.

She climbed into bed with her glass of water and took a couple of swallows. "You two spoil me."

Ben climbed into bed next to her. "As you should be."

She handed the glass to Ben, who put it on the nightstand, then wondered if one or both of them would want to take off now.

She got her answer when Alex climbed into bed on the other side of her.

Ben turned off the light, then they all got comfortable together.

She laid her head on Alex's shoulder and Ben moved in behind her, his chest against her back.

She hadn't expected this. And she had to admit, sleeping with two men in her bed tonight was . . .

Amazing.

"Rest now, babe," Alex said.

Within a minute she was asleep.

TEN

VICTORIA WOKE ALONE IN HER BED THE FOLLOWING morning.

Well, not exactly alone. There was a large pot of coffee on the table with a note from Ben.

Alex had an early practice. I've gone down to see to a few things.
Enjoy the coffee. Back soon.

Ben

She got up and stretched, her body aching in some very interesting places. She went into the bathroom, brushed her teeth, then grabbed one of the robes from the hook and slid into it. After pouring a cup of coffee, she went outside on the lanai and took a seat on the chaise.

The view of the ocean was spectacular, so she sipped her coffee and let her mind wander over the events from last night.

She'd often fantasized about a threesome over the years, especially when she masturbated. In her mind, it had been wild and crazy and she'd been overpowered by two lust-crazy men. She'd come over and over again in her fantasies.

The reality of it had been so much different from her imagination. Of course she had come—a lot. But Ben and Alex had hardly been lust-crazy or overpowering. Instead, they'd cared for her with such sweetness, had asked her more than once if she was certain about the situation. They'd put the power entirely in her hands, and she'd appreciated it so much. She'd felt safe with them, safer than she'd felt on a lot of dates with just one man.

That said a lot about the character of the two men she'd spent the night with.

Not to mention their rock-hard bodies, their amazing cocks, and their mouths.

Her body heated, which surprised the hell out of her. She would have thought that after last night, her body might need a break. Judging from her throbbing breasts, tingling nipples, and quivering pussy, apparently not.

She stared out over the water and imagined Ben stepping outside, parting her robe, and putting his hands—

"I see you're up."

Speak of the sexy devil.

She tilted her head back and smiled. "Good morning."

"Morning." He leaned over the chaise and kissed her. "Sleep well?"

"Like the satiated and sex-satisfied dead. How about you?"

"Great."

"How's Alex?"

He had a cup of coffee in his hand, so he took a seat on one of the chairs. "Already on the board and in the water."

She sat up and swiveled her legs around. "I'm not missing competition, am I?"

"No. Just practice. Competition's in a little while."

"Good. And what will you be doing today?"

"Keeping an eye on Alex. I have some business to attend to later this afternoon, but otherwise, I'm free."

She reached out to lay her hand on his knee. "That's good to know."

He picked up her hand. "Why? Do you have something in mind?"

"I might. While I was having coffee out here I was . . . thinking. Fantasizing, actually."

"Yeah? About what?"

"About how I used to masturbate imagining a threesome. And how my reality was nothing like my fantasies. And then I got hot just thinking about it."

He laid his cup on the table. "You're making me hard telling me about it."

She zeroed in on his board shorts, on the oh so impressive erection pressing against them. "I like you hard. I mean, I like you all the time, but hard? Oh, most definitely."

He stood. "Lay back against the chaise and touch yourself. Show me how you do it."

"Only if you show me how you do it."

He started to untie his shorts. "I plan to."

Since they were on the top floor penthouse suite, and she had no neighbors on either side, they had plenty of privacy. There was a roof and a balcony wall and they were high enough no one could see them. And she had every intention of enjoying this moment with Ben. She lay back and spread her robe open, exposing herself to Ben.

Her pussy quivered as she splayed her fingers over her breasts, teasing her nipples.

Ben dropped his shorts and pulled out his cock. It was hard already and she swallowed, licking her lips.

"Yeah, I liked your mouth on me last night. Tell me what you imagined in that scenario."

"Two men, ripping my clothes off."

He fisted his cock in his hands, drawing the shaft through. "Do you like it rough?"

"Sometimes. Last night, though? You and Alex handled it perfectly. Just the way I needed it."

"And this morning?"

She snaked her fingers down, over her abdomen, tapping at her sex. "This morning I need to come again."

He stroked his cock, using slow, rhythmic movements. "I want to watch you get yourself off, Victoria."

She used one hand to play with her nipples, the other dipped lower, over her pussy to tease at her clit.

"Tell me how that feels," Ben said.

"My clit tingles. My nipples are tight. I feel warm all over. It feels so good, Ben."

"Yeah, I know that feeling. My cock is swelling hard in my hand, making me want to be inside you."

As she rubbed her clit she watched Ben's movements. He'd go slow, threading his cock through his closed fist, then jack his cock faster. It made her breathing quicken watching the features on his face tighten, knowing he was giving himself pleasure.

She quivered all over, and when she tucked two fingers into her pussy, using the heel of her hand to rub her clit, she heard his breathing deepen.

"Yeah, that's it," Ben said, speeding up his movements. "Fuck yourself."

She felt the stirrings of orgasm and lifted her hips as if she was offering her pussy to Ben.

Heat penetrated her body, and pleasure swelled her sex. Her clit throbbed. She slowed her movements, watching Ben as he stroked faster.

It was the most delicious thing she'd ever seen.

"I'm going to come," she said.

"Oh yeah," he said. "I am, too."

He drew closer, the movements of his hand over his cock swift. His cockhead spilled pearly drops of liquid and he used them to lubricate the shaft.

She spread her robe as he moved in even closer. Now she was ready—ready for him, ready for herself to go off.

"Oh, fuck," Ben said. "I'm coming."

Ben let out a strangled groan as come spurted from his cock, the glorious white stream jettisoning into a perfect arc onto her belly and breasts. Watching him set her off and over and she cried out as she came, her hips undulating toward him as waves of orgasm catapulted her in a frenzy of wild pleasure. Her pussy squeezed her fingers in a tight vise of rhythmic contractions, sweet sensations that she reveled in while she watched Ben in the throes of his orgasm.

When she finally dropped her hips back to the chaise, she smiled up at Ben and swept her fingers over the ropes of come on her breasts.

"Now I need a shower."

He leaned down and brushed his lips over hers. "And now we both need breakfast. How about I clean up a little, then order something for us while you shower?"

She cupped his chin, drawing in the kiss, letting it linger before letting go. "That sounds good. I'll be right back."

She went in and showered, then towel-dried her hair and slid into a sundress. When she came back out on the lanai, breakfast had just arrived.

"My timing is good, I see," she said.

"Perfect." He held the chair out for her and she sat.

She took a sip of the orange juice in front of her, then took her fork and stabbed a slice of cantaloupe.

They ate and she asked Ben questions about the surfing competition.

"There are three heats, which start this afternoon," Ben said.

As she enjoyed her oatmeal, she asked, "And what do you think Alex's chances are?"

"Good. Better than good."

She looked out over the water, saw several surfers riding the tops of the waves. "Some of those guys are much younger than Alex."

Ben took a swallow of juice and nodded. "Younger, yes. Not as experienced. Not as good as he is. Trust me, he's got several years of competition left in him, providing he stays healthy."

She wondered if Ben thought about still being out there, if he hadn't gotten hurt. "Do you still surf?"

"Of course. Not the bigger waves, but I surf for fun. I can take you out there or Alex and I can both take you."

She laughed. "I don't think I can hang in there with the two of you."

"Sure you can. We'll take care of you."

She pushed her plate to the side and poured another cup of coffee. "So tell me about yourself, Ben. Where are you from?"

"San Diego. That's where I fell in love with surfing. Been doing it since I was a kid. Started competing when I was young."

"And obviously you were amazing at it."

He leaned back in his chair. "I was great at it. Won a lot of competitions, picked up some incredible sponsors, and learned a lot about the business side of surfing, which helped after I got hurt and transitioned into the management and promotion aspect."

She loved talking business with Ben. "You've obviously done well for Alex. He seems to have thrived."

"Thanks. I manage a couple of other younger surfers as well. And it doesn't hurt that these popular surfers promote my products. So we work well for each other."

"But you're not just using them. You actually like them. It shows."

"I'm glad you see that. There are some unscrupulous promoters and business managers out there who take advantage of young surfers, especially the ones just starting out. I try to advise the kids to steer clear of them, but some of them don't listen."

She shrugged. "It's the same way in my business. Agents just trying to make a quick buck off young and upcoming athletes, but they don't care about their futures. There's not much you can do about it. There's always going to be sharks in any sport."

"True. Fortunately there are good people like you to steer them in the right direction."

"And people like you."

He laughed. "Okay, now that we've mutually admired each other, how about we hit the beach?"

"Sounds great."

She changed and put her swimsuit on under her sundress, slipped on her sandals and sunglasses, and grabbed her beach bag. Ben took her hand and they rode the elevator down and walked out onto the sand.

"We can sit under the tented area," he said. "It'll be cooler in there."

"I like that idea." It was already shaping up to be a warm day. The sun shone bright and though it was still early in the day, she was sweating in the heat.

Ben found her a chair with a great view of the competition. Alex came over and gave her a kiss, his body dripping water on her.

"You look beautiful today. Did you rest well?"

"I did. How's it going?"

"Great," he said. "I'm ready to get this thing started."

She pressed her palm to his chest, wishing she could touch his bare skin instead of the wet suit. But she'd take what she could get. "Best of luck out there."

"Thanks, but luck has nothing to do with it, babe."

She loved his confidence. "Then go kick everyone's ass."

"I intend to." He grinned, then went over to have a conversation with Ben before wandering off to the competition area. He gave her a wave before he disappeared.

Ben left the tent for a while, standing outside to have a conversation with some of the other promoters.

"Hey, Victoria."

Whitney leaned into the tent.

"Hi, Whitney." Victoria stepped outside the tent and stood on the sand next to Whitney. "Are you here to watch the competition today?"

"I am. Got the day off and everything. How have you been? I haven't seen you around."

"Oh, yes. I've been hanging out with Alex."

Whitney cocked her head to the side. "And with Ben?"

"Well . . . yes. With him, too."

Whitney shoved a shoulder into her. "Lucky you. You've really scored two winners there. Ben's a little old for me, but oh is he ever hot."

"I think so. And how about you and . . . Cade, is it?"

Whitney sported a sly smile. "Things are going well. He seems into me. I'm definitely into him."

"I'm glad. You should be having some fun."

"Oh, we're doing that. I think I'm going to pull up a spot near the water with a few of my friends. Catch you later?"

"Absolutely. Nice to see you."

"Aloha." Whitney jogged off with a wave, and Victoria headed back into the tent.

The competition began, so she settled in to watch. The waves looked big—overwhelmingly large compared to the guys aiming to master them.

Ben finally came back and took a seat next to her as Alex paddled his board out.

"Tell me how the scoring system works," she said.

"The guys go out based on a priority system based on previous scores from other competitions. Alex has top priority so he can choose what wave to go after. Other guys can choose the same wave as well, as long as they don't impede his run. Scoring-wise, each surfer will try to lock in their three highest scoring waves. The max they can score is ten points per wave."

"So the highest they can score in each round—or heat, as you call it—is thirty points."

Ben nodded. "Thirty points max per heat. Then those scores are added into the competition total. It's all about a championship total. Whoever wins today will be on the leaderboard. It's not like this is a final event. That won't take place for a while. The competition continues in other countries."

She nodded. "Got it. So what are the judges looking for?"

"Degree of difficulty, innovation, and the different variety of moves they make."

"What are the types of moves the judges look for?"

"Speed, power, control of his board, where he is in the tube, and how long he rides it. There are varying factors that go into scoring a ride and it takes years of expertise to become a judge. They know what they're looking for, and they know, from varying degrees of difficulty, who's mastered a wave and who's blown it. So it's critical for the surfers to not just get up on any wave and ride it."

She blinked. "Wow. That's a lot of work."

He nodded. "It is. It's more than just riding the wave. There's so much finesse that goes into it."

She leaned forward in her chair as Alex approached a wave, her heart in her throat.

Ben took her hand and squeezed.

"Relax. He's got this."

So it appeared, as he dropped down on what she thought was a huge wave, slid down over the top of it, then underneath that massive, rolling tube of water, much to the enthusiasm of the crowd. It was as if he owned that wave, riding it for what seemed like an eternity.

While Victoria was terrified, she could see Alex's comfort level, the ease with which he mastered what she thought was a treacherous wave all the way through and out of it. He flipped his board out from under the wave, then back over the top of another, making her hold her breath. When he coasted to calm waters and wild applause and cheers from the crowd with a grin on his face, she knew he'd done well.

"He should score high on that ride," Ben said, his gaze fixed on the scoreboard.

So was Alex's as he sat on his board and grinned when he popped a ten for that ride.

"Perfect," Ben said, nodding and smiling. "It doesn't get any better than that."

Victoria had never seen anything like it. It had been death defying and the most amazing ride she had ever seen.

She watched other surfers, trying to gauge what the judges would see, but she was no expert. Unless the wave collapsed over them or they crashed, they all looked amazing. But she had Ben telling her where some of them went wrong, or how they did well, so eventually she could see the subtle differences.

Alex went out for two other waves. One pinned him down and crimped over him.

"He's okay. He'll pull up on another," Ben said.

Alex dropped down on top of another huge wave for a long ride in the tube, scoring a seven point nine.

"Great score for his second ride," Ben said.

Victoria had no idea, so she'd take Ben's word for it.

"It seems like many of them wait for just the right wave," she said to Ben.

He nodded. "The right wave is everything."

She watched the other surfers. Some did equally as well on their rides, some couldn't seem to catch a decent wave.

When Alex took another, it seemed as high as the first one he'd ridden, though he wasn't in the tube for as long a period of time. But he flipped an aerial on top of the wave to polish things off, which, to Victoria, had looked spectacular.

"That's the way it's done," Ben said with a wide grin.

Victoria leaped from her chair and cheered.

"That was . . . fantastic," she said.

Ben smiled and nodded. "It was a stellar wave and he rode it for all it was worth."

She wanted to go to Alex and hug him, to tell him how magnificent he'd looked out there. But she knew he was in competition mode, and since she dealt with athletes in her business, she knew he didn't need the distraction. Right now he needed to focus on the waves.

Alex had moved from the quarterfinals to the semifinals. And Victoria was in awe. It was as if he was one with both his board and the monstrous waves.

She'd never seen anything like it.

By the end of the day Alex was tied at the top of the leaderboard with two other surfers.

Ben gathered up some paperwork. "There's a party and bonfire on the beach again tonight for the surfers and other attendees, sponsored by the promoters. With food and drink. Alex and I want you there with us."

She linked her arm with his, feeling warm and cared for again and happy that Ben had told her he wanted her there with them. "I wouldn't miss it."

"Good. Alex is going to spend some time in post-competition meetings. How about you and I go surf for a bit?"

She cocked a brow. "Seriously?"

"Yeah. You know you want to get out in that water."

She pointed to the high-rolling waves. "I do not want to go out in *that* water."

He laughed. "I'll take you to another beach. One that has smaller waves."

She had to admit that watching the guys surf made her itch to try it. It had been years since her last attempt. "Okay."

He took her hand and led her through the hotel and out front. "Wait here and I'll get the boards."

He stopped to talk to the valet, then disappeared. By the time Ben returned with two surfboards, the valet had pulled up an SUV. They strapped the boards to the top of the vehicle, climbed in, and they were off.

She hadn't left the hotel area since she'd gotten here, but now she was eager to see more of the island.

She'd almost forgotten it was the holiday season. Sure, the hotel was decorated thematically with trees and garland and seasonal wreaths, but the lack of cold weather—and snow—made it feel a lot more tropical and much less like the holidays. Just the way she wanted it.

But now as they drove past decorated homes and buildings, she started to feel the holiday spirit. Green and red décor abounded.

"Christmas is coming," she said.

"Yeah. Alex and I will hang out here until after the holidays. What about you?"

"I'll be here."

He gave her a quick look. "We should spend Christmas together."

She smiled, again a warm feeling suffusing her. "I'd like that."

He pulled down a narrow street and parked in front of a beach.

"The waves here aren't as high," she observed when they got out of the SUV.

"Yup. It'll make it easier for you to catch a wave."

She pulled off her sundress and kicked off her sandals, leaving both in the car. Ben drew off his shirt and tossed it inside as well.

"I can carry one of those boards if you'd like."

He gave her a look. "Why? You've got me."

She leaned into him and brushed her lips across his. "Okay."

He wrapped his arm around her and tugged her close, kissing her back, letting that kiss simmer, turning it into one that made her boil.

When he pulled back, she was breathing hard. "Now I need to cool off."

He looked around. They were alone, so he took her hand and placed it on his erection.

"So do I."

"Too bad we're not in the hotel room. I could take care of that for you."

He backed her against the car and kissed her with a hard, driving passion, his body pressed against hers, his erection rubbing her clit. Passion exploded and she suddenly wanted him inside of her.

The beach was deserted and there were no other cars around.

"I need you to make me come, Ben."

Without a moment's hesitation, he said, "Hang on."

He reached inside the front of the SUV, grabbed something, and then shut the door, locked it, and said, "Come on. I know a private place where no one can see us."

He left the boards stowed and took her hand, leading her down the walkway a short distance to what looked like a lifeguard shack. There was another one a ways down the beach, manned by a lifeguard. This one was older, bleached out, and seemingly abandoned.

He shoved a shoulder into it and the door gave with a creak and a groan.

"Are you sure about this?"

"No one uses it," he said. "And trust me, I'm going to get you off fast."

"I like the sound of that because I need to come."

He shoved the door closed and there was a hook to lock it, which he used. Then he turned to her and kneeled, drew her swimsuit bottom down, and put his mouth on her pussy.

Shocks of pleasure ignited her like a fast-moving wildfire, taking her from a frenzied passion to out of control in seconds. She tethered her fingers in Ben's hair and held on while he licked and sucked her sensitized flesh, making her gasp and writhe against him, pushing her sex against his face as her orgasm hit.

"Yes. Oh, Ben, yes, I'm coming."

Her climax was wild and made her legs tremble. Ben wrapped his arm around her and held her close to him while she bucked against him, still quivering from that epic orgasm.

He stood, grabbed a condom out of his pocket, and dropped his board shorts. She wrapped her fingers around his cock and stroked the hot, heavy shaft in her hand.

"That's it," he said. "I like your hands on me, Victoria."

She stepped back so she could wriggle out of her swimsuit bottom while he applied the condom.

He backed her against the wall, lifted her hands above her head, and slid into her, then took her mouth in a blistering kiss while he thrusted and grinded against her, rubbing her clit in a perfect way that made her temperature rise in the hot shack.

His tongue warred with hers, a perfect thrust and parry, matching the movements of his cock, which seemed to swell even larger inside of her.

He pulled his mouth away and laid his forehead against hers.

She was panting, hot and sweaty, fired up and filled with Ben. And the way he moved against her made her tighten around him, her pussy quivering.

"Are you gonna come for me again?" he asked as he drove deeply into her.

"Yes. Oh, yes."

"I'm so ready to shoot hard into you, Victoria. Make us both come."

She moaned at his words, and when he pulled the cups of her bathing suit top aside and sucked her nipple, she orgasmed, her pussy gripping his cock in a tight vise as contractions rippled through her.

With a loud groan, Ben drove hard into her. She held tight to him as he came, giving her everything she could possibly want at that moment. And when he kissed her, it was fierce and passionate as he rode out his orgasm.

His lips gentled on hers, his hands stroking down her slick, sweat-soaked back.

She pressed a kiss to his chest. "That was . . . everything."

His tipped her chin so she met his gaze. "Jesus, Victoria. I lose myself when I'm inside of you. And all I can feel is you and me—like we're one."

She shivered at his words. Powerful words that she wanted to contemplate, but not here. And not now.

"Come on," he said, his lips curving in a teasing smile to break that suddenly serious mood he'd created. "Let's head out before someone finds us in here fucking like teenagers."

She laughed.

They righted their clothing and Ben unlocked the door, took a quick look outside, then they exited the shack. He disposed of the condom in a nearby trashcan, then they made their way back to the SUV.

"I'm really looking forward to the water now," she said.

He grinned. "Me, too. You made me sweat."

He carried both boards down to the edge of the water, then handed her one of them. She attached the surfboard leash to her ankle.

"Need any instructions?"

"It's been a while. The last thing I remember is to stay balanced and don't fall."

"Okay. We'll go through a few things to remind you. Which foot do you put forward if you were on slippery ice and you were going to fall?"

She thought about it for a minute and put her left foot forward.

"Okay, so you'll want to use your right foot to steer, so when you pop up on the board, slide your left foot forward and your right foot back."

He worked with her on the sand, making sure she had an understanding about how to pop up—first crouching, then standing—once she caught a wave.

Once she had enough confidence, she was ready for the water.

"Remember to use your back foot to steer," he said.

"Got it. Let's do this. I'm hot."

"Yeah, you are."

She shook her head, but smiled at him. Ben took the lead and she paddled out behind him. He was the expert and she intended to let him show her the right waves.

They finally got to where Ben wanted them, water-wise, and she turned her board around and sat up next to Ben, the waves undulating underneath them.

He passed up a few, explained that some were too rough, some too high, some too puny.

"Good wave coming up," he said, pouncing onto his feet in a crouched position. "Get ready."

She did the same, and when the wave hit, she tried to balance herself and ride it.

This was not like riding a bicycle. She had forgotten how to surf, so while Ben rode the wave easily, she only made it a few feet before she tumbled off the board and had to pull herself up and try again.

And again.

And again.

It was exhausting, but Ben came back out each time and rode with her, giving her encouraging words and telling her she could definitely get up.

When she fell again, she was pissed.

"You can do this," Ben said. "Balance is the hardest thing. Try just going up on one knee first. Once you grab your balance that way, you'll be able to stand."

"I'll try."

She was determined to succeed, so next time she did the one knee thing, and got up that way. She didn't make it all the way into the wave, falling off halfway, but it was something.

Ben caught up to her and smiled. "See? Progress. You'll get there."

"Yes, I will."

She was nothing if not determined. She'd stand on this damn board. Sometime today. Maybe.

After several more attempts, she finally stood, on a very small wave that she rode all the way onto shore. It was the most exhilarating ride she'd ever taken.

She raised her arms in triumph. Ben was there to swoop her off the board and plant a hot kiss on her lips.

"I did it."

He grinned. "Yeah, you did. I told you that you could."

She swept her hair off her face, staring out at the water. "It was work." She blew out a breath.

"It always is."

She patted his chest. "You looked magnificent out there."

"Thanks. I'm hardly competitive, but I can still surf."

"You sure as hell can. And I really had forgotten how damn hard surfing is. I have a new appreciation for the sport."

Now that she'd managed to master a wave, she wanted to do it again. They surfed awhile longer, then called it a day. Ben packed the boards up on the SUV and they drove back to the hotel.

"I need a shower and a change of clothes before tonight. And quite possibly a nap."

He laughed. "Okay. I'll see you tonight."

She kissed him good-bye, then went up to her room and stripped out of her sundress and swimsuit.

She thought about taking a shower, then yawned.

Surfing was exhausting. She should consider doing it more often. Holy crap, what a workout.

She yawned again and stared longingly at her bed.

Okay, nap first. Shower later.

She shut the drapes, climbed into bed, and closed her eyes.

ELEVEN

IT HAD BEEN A DAMN GOOD DAY. ALEX RODE THE ELE-vator up to the hotel suite with a grin on his face.

He'd scored high today. He was primed and ready for tomorrow's competition.

Tonight, though, he was ready to kick back and relax.

He slid his key in the door, breathing in a sigh of relief at the cold air-conditioning. Leave it to Ben to know he'd be hot and tired after a long day and he'd need the A/C cranked to arctic.

Now all he needed was a cold beer and a hot shower. He stripped out of his board shorts and headed straight for the shower, letting the hot water rain down on him for a few seconds before grabbing the soap and scrubbing the salt water from his body. After his shower, he put on a pair of shorts and a T-shirt and grabbed a beer from the wet bar.

The door opened and Ben walked in, giving him a smile.

"You did great today."

"Thanks. The waves were killer. Not too hard to command, but high enough to give me a challenging ride, which gave me a scoring advantage."

Ben went to the wet bar and pulled out a beer, then sat across from him on one of the leather sofas.

"I didn't see much of you today after the competition," Alex said. "Did you hang out with Tori?"

"I took her down to one of the other beaches where the waves were smaller so she could surf."

Alex nodded. "What a good idea. I'm sure she wanted to get in the water and try out her skills. How'd she do?"

"She did well. Fell the first several times, but she didn't give up."

Alex grinned. "That's our girl. I knew she wasn't a quitter."

"She's going to meet up with us tonight at the bonfire and dinner. I know she's anxious to see you."

"Good. I want to see her, too."

"Then finish your beer and let's go get her."

Alex downed the contents of his beer then tossed it in the trash. He and Ben headed over to Tori's suite and knocked on her door.

She answered, wearing a red sundress that outlined her killer curves. And her smile always kicked him in the gut.

"Hi, guys."

"Hey, yourself," Alex said. "You look beautiful."

"Love that red on you," Ben said.

"Not even in the door yet and you both have me blushing," Tori said. "Come on in."

He and Ben stepped inside. Alex pulled her into his arms and kissed her. A nice, deep, long kiss that told her how much he'd hated being apart from her today. When he stepped back, Ben did the same.

"Whew," she said, fanning her face with her hands. "Any more of that and we won't make it out of the suite tonight."

"And that's a bad thing?" Alex asked.

She laughed. "Normally I'd say no, but I'm hungry and I know you have to put in an appearance at tonight's event, right?"

Alex shrugged. "Maybe."

"Maybe yes?" she asked.

"Okay, fine. I do. But I'm not letting you out of my sight tonight."

"Deal."

Ben laughed. "Come on. Let's go. I'm hungry, too."

They headed downstairs and outside. Tables were set up with plenty of food and Alex was hungry, so he guided Tori to the plates so they could get started. He loaded his with chicken and fish and plenty of vegetables, then grabbed a bottle of water and they found seats at one of the nearby tables.

Whitney and one of the other surfers, Cade, sat at their table, along with some of his surfer friends, Matt, Silas, and Zane.

"This your girl?" Zane asked him.

"Yeah."

Victoria shook his hand. "I'm Victoria Baldwin."

Alex introduced Tori to all the guys at the table. "She's a sports agent."

"Is that right?" Matt asked. "Who do you rep?"

She told them about some of her clients.

"No kidding," Silas said. "Garrett Scott is one great pitcher. I'm from Saint Louis originally. Well, I was born there anyway. So the Rivers are my home team."

Alex listened while Silas and Tori talked baseball. He was fascinated by her knowledge of the sport. And when she got into a football discussion with Matt, she knew more players than Matt did. She knew more football *plays* than Matt did. And Matt knew a lot about football.

His woman was impressive.

His woman. Huh. He'd never once thought of a woman as his. But he couldn't deny Tori had gotten into his blood. He thought about her all the time. Other than when he was competing, when his focus was entirely on the waves, on his board and the skill it took to do his maneuvers, his thoughts had been on Tori.

Just a holiday fling, right? Nothing more than that. It was just hot sex. Amazing hot sex.

But as he watched her laughing and talking with his friends, their gazes met.

Heat and sexual chemistry, definitely. But something else, for sure.

He had to admit right from the start there had been something special about Tori, an instantaneous connection he'd never had with any other woman.

His gaze drifted to Ben. Ben watched her the same way, took every opportunity he could to run his hand up and down her back. Ben liked touching her, liked being with her. Ben was more animated with Tori than any other woman he'd been with before. He'd never known Ben to take such an active interest in a woman.

Interesting.

Alex's entire career had been spent analyzing everything. The height and velocity of the waves, the water temperature, the wind, the way his body moved on the board. His success or failure depended on his ability to step back from emotion and let his analytical ability come into play.

But with Tori, he felt a fierce rush of emotion whenever he was with her, and that was something new. The thought of walking away from her when this was all over seemed . . . unsettling. And that had never happened before. He'd enjoyed women his entire life. He'd treated them right, had always been up-front and honest with them, and had never led them on. But when it was over, he walked away without a backward glance.

He'd also shared women with Ben before, and that had never been an issue.

As he watched Ben slide his fingers into Tori's hair, he waited for any jealousy to creep in.

No. Not there. He liked Ben. Though there was the age

difference, they were and had been best friends for years. Ben touching Tori made him feel closer to both of them, so that wasn't an issue.

The only issue right now was with how he felt about Tori. That was something he might have to analyze further. Only this time, he'd leave the emotion *in* the mix and see what came of it.

IT HAD BEEN A FUN NIGHT. THE FOOD HAD BEEN amazing, the company even more so. Victoria liked all these people. Some were a lot younger than her, but they were smart and savvy and their entire lives weren't focused only on surfing.

She and Whitney had sat next to each other and caught up. Whitney was having a hot fling with Cade, but Whitney was also smart. She knew it wasn't going anywhere beyond the time Cade was going to spend on the island.

"I know not to get emotionally invested in him," Whitney said as the guys had temporarily left to help build the bonfire. "I'm smarter than that. He's leaving, and I'm staying put. We have no future together. But right now? We sure are having fun."

Victoria laughed. "You're young. Plenty of time to find your forever love. This is the time in your life to explore and have new adventures."

Whitney's gaze tracked over to the bonfire, where Cade stood next to Alex. "He certainly is sexually adventurous."

"As long as you want the same things he wants, then it's all good."

Whitney pulled her gaze away from Cade and smiled at her. "I'm very open to what he wants. And the best part is he's definitely open to what I want. The sex is fantastic."

Victoria laughed. "Then it's definitely all good."

"How about you? Where do you see yourself with Alex and Ben?"

She looked over at the two men standing side by side, both so utterly different. "I . . . don't know. I imagine it'll run its course and then I'll head back East."

"You don't sound so certain about that."

Was she? When on vacation, she was always firmly planted in the right now, enjoying every second. And when it was over, it was over. She flew back home with great memories and not a second thought.

But as she looked over at Ben laughing with Alex, her heart clenched.

What was *that* all about?

She did not get emotionally attached to men. She never had.

Before now. And now? She had . . . feelings. Not just sexual feelings, but emotional ones.

What the hell was she going to do about these feelings?

Nothing. She was going to do nothing about them, that's what she was going to do. Because they were ridiculous and she had a life and a perfect career in New York, and Ben and Alex traveled all over the world for surf competitions. Their lives would never mesh.

She chewed her bottom lip and stared at them some more.

Yes. Ridiculous.

And yet when they turned and they both smiled at her at once, her heart clenched again.

Goddammit.

"Hey, they're waving us over. Let's join the guys," Whitney said.

What she really wanted to do was run like hell. Away from these strange emotions that stirred in her heart.

Instead, she gave Whitney a smile. "Sure. Let's do that."

Whitney moved over to Cade and gave her a wave.

When Victoria stepped in between Alex and Ben, Ben put his arm around her.

"Are you all right?" he asked.

She tilted her head back to meet his gaze. "Of course I am. Why would you ask that?"

"You looked . . . uncomfortable when you were sitting over there with Whitney."

He'd read her mood, her confusion. It was as if he knew her already, even after such a short time. She laid her palm on his chest. "I'm fine. But thank you for asking."

Alex leaned in. "If you want to cut this short tonight, we can leave. You're way more important than a party."

If either of them got any more solicitous of her feelings, she might just cry.

"And miss all this fun? Not a chance. What I would like, though, is a Bloody Mary."

"I'll take care of that," Ben said. "Be right back."

He wandered off. So had Whitney and Cade, leaving her alone with Alex, who took her hand.

"Seriously, babe. We'd be happy to take you back to the suite if you're tired or just not up for a party."

She nudged him with her shoulder. "And I'm seriously fine. So stop asking."

He gave her a grin. "In that case, let's dance. This song is slow and sexy."

He pulled her into the middle of the dancers, planted his hands on her hips, and the two of them swayed together to one seriously hot song. Alex drew her in and wrapped his arms around her, then buried his face in her neck.

"You smell good, Tori."

It felt so perfect when he held her like this, his body aligned with hers. He was tall and lean and his muscles—all hard, pressed to her. She closed her eyes and breathed in his scent—something crisp and clean. She wound her hand around the nape of his neck and lost herself in him.

And when the dance ended and they walked back to the side-lines, there was Ben, holding her Bloody Mary for her, smiling at her as if she hadn't just had her hands all over another man.

"Thanks," she said, and rose up to press a kiss to Ben's lips.

"You're welcome. You looked hot as hell dancing out there with Alex."

Ben put his arm around her, his fingertips resting against her hip.

How was it that these two men weren't jealous? Were Ben and Alex unique, or were there relationships like this and she'd spent her entire life living in a bubble?

When Alex came up to her other side and they led her away from the crowd, walking her down toward the beach, she decided to ask.

"Is this familiar to the two of you?"

"Is what familiar?" Alex asked.

"Sharing a woman. Without jealousy."

"We've shared women before," Ben said. "But if you're asking if we've had the kind of relationships with women like the one we're currently having with you, then the answer is no."

"You both seem to handle it so well. When I'm off alone with one of you, neither of you seems to be jealous or asks me probing questions about what we did when the other was away."

Alex took her hand, squeezed it. "Probably because it's you, Tori. I don't know, it seems to be a pretty unique situation for all of us."

"Alex is right. We both want you to be happy. I'm not jealous of Alex giving you pleasure. I doubt he's upset when I'm with you."

Alex shrugged. "Why would I be? Ben's making you happy."

Her heart filled with so many emotions she didn't know what to think. "You both make me happy. I'm having such a wonderful time with you—with both of you."

They'd reached a cove where the waves crashed against the shore. It was private—no other people around.

Ben led them toward a hill of tall rocks, their view obscured, so they climbed, Alex leading the way and Ben next to her, holding her hand.

"Check this out," Alex said, his voice dropping to a whisper.

High along the shore was a couple. She didn't recognize them, but it must have been one of the surfers and a beautiful young woman with shoulder-length brown hair. She was on her knees and he was naked, his cock thick and hard, and the woman was sucking him.

Her pussy quivered as they watched.

She tugged Alex's hand. "We should go."

Alex laughed. "Why?"

"So they can have privacy."

Alex looked down at her. "Babe. I know Rob and Belinda. Trust me, if they wanted privacy they'd be doing this in the hotel."

"Okay. You might have a point."

Ben came up behind her, smoothing his hands down her arms. "They probably don't care who sees them. So . . . let's watch."

She had to admit the sight of the man's cock sliding between the woman's full lips was an absolute turn-on. And when the woman pulled the straps of her dress down to fondle her own breasts, Victoria's breath caught. It made her want to do the same thing.

She was on fire.

"Is it turning you on watching them?" Ben asked.

"Yes." She could barely get the word out. Her gaze was fixed on Belinda sucking Rob, on the way she drew her lips slowly along his shaft. And when Rob pulled his cock out and raised Belinda up to stand, their mouths fused in furious passion, Victoria wanted that, so she turned to Ben and kissed him, feeling that same feverish need she'd witnessed in Belinda.

After she'd thoroughly kissed Ben, she turned to Alex, who was waiting behind her. She put her mouth on his, and felt the explosive desire in his kiss.

Knowing they both felt the same passion and need she felt inflamed her. She pulled away from Alex to watch more of the action.

Rob had Belinda on her knees and had put on a condom. He pushed his cock inside of her and despite the crashing waves, she could hear Belinda cry out in pleasure.

"We're going to make you come," Ben said, pulling her against him. He pulled the straps of her sundress down, revealing her breasts. "Just watch them while we make you come."

"Yes." She was hot and her sex throbbed. They could both make her come.

Right here and right now.

Alex moved in next to her, raising her dress. "Is your pussy hot and wet, Tori?"

"Yes."

He slid his hand into her underwear, cupping her sex. "I'll bet you come fast watching him slide his cock in and out of her pussy."

"I love watching. Look how hard he's fucking her."

"I see it," Ben said. "Do you want us to fuck you like that after we make you come?"

Just the thought of it made her clench, made her dampen with desire. "Oh, yes. Just like that."

Alex slipped his fingers into her pussy.

"You are so wet, Tori. I can already imagine my cock inside of you, pumping hard into you. Do you want to suck Ben while I fuck you?"

Between watching Rob and Belinda and imagining herself on her knees with Alex pumping into her from behind while she sucked Ben's cock, it was too much.

"Make me come, Alex."

Ben rolled her nipples between his fingers, lightly pinching them.

She bit down on her lip to keep from crying out as she came. Alex pumped his fingers into her and she pushed her hips against him as the waves of her orgasm overcame her.

She panted, out of breath from that magnificent climax.

Alex leaned over and kissed her, then smiled. "That was good, babe."

"It was."

"Down on your knees, Victoria," Ben said after she pulled away from Alex's kiss. "I need your mouth on my cock."

Alex pulled out a condom, and she was so glad he'd thought to be prepared.

He raised her sundress over her back. She wasn't even paying attention to Rob and Belinda now. All she knew were these two men she was with and their pleasure—and hers.

Alex fit his cock into her pussy while Ben slid his between her lips.

"Oh yeah," Alex said. "Just like I imagined. Tight and hot and wet, Tori."

"Suck me, Victoria," Ben said. "Suck my cock and make me come."

Her pussy tightened around Alex's cock, making her quiver with undeniable pleasure. And as she wrapped her lips around Ben's shaft and drew it into her mouth, she couldn't think of any place she wanted to be other than right here. Or any men she wanted to be with other than Alex and Ben. They had given her such pleasure, and now it was her turn to pleasure them.

She drank in the sounds of their groans as she pushed back against Alex while she drew Ben's cock from her lips, only to slowly take Ben's shaft inch by inch deeply into the cavern of her mouth, withdrawing her pussy from Alex, making him thrust hard into her.

It was the sweetest, hottest sex play, and she enjoyed every second of it. The fact they were outside where anyone could see them only heightened her own pleasure. And when she met Ben's gaze and saw his features tighten, when he thrust more deeply and Alex pushed harder and faster into her, she knew they were both going to come.

She took Ben's shaft deep, then pulled back, accepting the first spurts of his come along her tongue. She gave him more suction during his climax, sucking him in deeper and harder as he groaned and shuddered.

Alex called her name as he ground against her with his orgasm, his body pressed to hers, his fingers gripped tightly to her hips.

It was perfect.

Ben withdrew, and so did Alex. Ben pulled her to a standing

position and helped her right her clothing before grabbing his board shorts from where he'd flung them on top of the rock.

Then Ben kissed her and so did Alex.

"Good for you?" Ben asked.

She inhaled, let it out, and smiled. "Perfect for me."

"Good," Ben said. "Let's go back and join the party. I'm thirsty."

"Me, too," Alex said.

She fit herself in the middle of them and they walked back to the main beach, staying close to the water. Victoria settled into the silence, lost in her thoughts.

She was equal parts deliriously happy and at the same time utterly conflicted. In such a short period of time she'd become attached to both Alex and Ben.

She didn't like attachments. They made everything so complicated.

Sex was fun. It was easy and uncomplicated and typically at the end of her vacation flings, she found it easy to say good-bye.

But when it came time to return home, she didn't think it was going to be so easy to say good-bye to these two amazing men.

TWELVE

ALEX HAD SLEPT LIKE THE DEAD LAST NIGHT, SNUG-
gled against Tori's perfect backside. Unfortunately he'd had to get
up early again to prep for the second day of the tournament.

Waves were cranking today. He was ready to score at the top of
the leaderboard.

His practice runs had been good, though he'd been raked over
by the waves each time he'd paddled out.

The runs were going to be gnarly today, no doubt about it. But
with waves this impressive, all the guys should have notable
showings.

He was just going to have to be the best.

He ran over to Ben's tent while he had a few minutes before the
first heat started. Victoria was there in a white sundress, taking his
breath away as usual. He leaned over to kiss her.

"Best of luck today, though I doubt you'll need it."

He loved her confidence in him. "Thanks, babe."

He grabbed a sports drink from Ben.

"Those waves are killer today. And by killer . . ."

They didn't have to say the words to each other. Alex knew what Ben meant.

The waves could make for some spectacular rides. But they were also dangerous.

"I know. I'll be careful."

Ben grabbed his shoulder. "Go kick the Pipeline's ass."

Alex grinned and made his way to the water.

He paddled out along with three other surfers. Priority indicated he or Matt could drop in first. Not seeing a wave he liked, he let Matt take the drop.

Matt rode the wave like the pro he was. Scored high, too.

Shit.

That was okay. Alex thrived on pressure.

He sat out there and waited through two other waves. Then a big one came and he dropped in, sliding into the barrel.

Now it was just him and the wave, alone in the tube. This was his sweet spot. He'd surfed his entire life and when he was on the water riding a wave he felt an adrenaline rush like nothing else. He could reach out and touch the monster, so he leaned in and ran his hand along the underside of the wave, then flipped out the end of the tube and did an aerial.

He could hear applause, the sound of clapping carrying across the water, and he knew he'd mastered it.

His second and third heats were good, too, though not as stellar as the first one had been.

Good enough to land him solidly in the top three at the end of the day. He'd move on in the championships. And at his age, with all these young and hungry surfers coming up and nipping at his board, he'd take it.

He made his way to the tent where Tori came over and threw her arms around him.

"You did it. You were amazing."

Having her confident in him made a difference. "Thanks." He brushed his lips across hers, then shook Ben's hand.

"Took some chances out there on that monster wave," Ben said.

Alex shrugged. "You know me."

Ben smiled. "Yeah, I do."

"I was so afraid during that first heat," Victoria said. "But oh, my God, Alex, the way you rode inside the wave—you were beneath it for so long before you came out the other side. I know I need to learn the lingo—but it was amazing."

He slung his arm around her. "Trust me. I know what you're talking about. It felt amazing, too. I had a good run."

"It sure seems that way. So now that the competition is over, what happens?"

"It's an accumulation of points," Ben said. "He'll move on to the next competition, and do it all over again."

"Where's the next one?"

"Australia."

As they made their way back to the hotel, Tori shook her head. "It must be an incredible life to be able to travel the world like you do."

Alex nodded. "It has its benefits. Then again, you do the same thing, don't you?"

"Well, not for work. But yes, my work has its perks, definitely. It has allowed me to do a lot of traveling."

They stood in the lobby, waiting for the elevator.

"You could meet us in Australia," he said to Tori.

She laughed. "Unfortunately, after the holidays I have to go back to work."

"Yeah, we all know about work," Ben said with a wry grin.

"I'm going to head upstairs to shower," Alex said as they stepped into the elevator.

"I'm going to do the same," Victoria said. "Catch up with both of you later?"

Ben nodded. "We'll call you."

They got out and went to their separate rooms.

Once back in the suite, Alex told Ben he was going into his room to shower. Ben waved him off, saying he had a call to make.

Alex went into the bathroom and turned on the shower, then stepped in under the hot spray.

It had been a really good day. Until they'd started talking about what came after this.

He didn't want to leave Tori. He knew she had a successful career. So did he. So did Ben.

So what the hell were they going to do about that?

When he got out of the shower, Ben was in his room.

"Need something?" Alex asked.

"Yeah. I want to talk to you. About Victoria."

"Okay." He grabbed a clean pair of board shorts and slipped them on. "What about her?"

"I need to know if what I'm feeling for her is just me. Or if it's both of us."

They went out into the living room. Alex grabbed a beer for himself and one for Ben and handed it to him. They both sat on the sofa. Alex knew how he felt. This was as good a time as any to talk it out with Ben.

Ben had been holding this all inside for a while now. But he trusted Alex, his best friend, and knew that before he said anything to Victoria, he had to talk to Alex first.

"Tell me how you feel about Victoria, Alex."

"I think I'm in love with her."

"You're not the only one who feels this way. I'm in love with her, too, Alex."

Saying the words out loud was like a gut punch. First a little bit of fear, followed by overwhelming relief.

Ben blew out a breath. "Okay. This is both good and bad, Alex."

"I know."

"I don't even know how to approach this," Ben said. "It's not something that's ever happened with us before."

"Yeah. In love with the same woman. I never saw that coming."

"Neither did I. It happened so fast. I never thought I'd ever fall in love. But Victoria. She's—"

"Unique. Smart. Fun. Sexy. Beautiful."

Ben smiled. "All those things and more. She's warm. Generous. Everything I've ever wanted. Maybe everything I never even knew I wanted."

Alex nodded. "Exactly."

"And the worst part is, we have no idea how Victoria feels. She might see us as just a vacation fling."

Alex sighed. "Yeah, that's a possibility. But the only way to find out is to tell her how we feel."

"Scary thought." Ben stood and walked to the doors leading out to the terrace. He stared out over the water, then turned to face Alex. "I'm going to be honest with you, Alex. I've never been more scared of anything in my life. I've faced monster waves, the end of my career, and nothing was more daunting than that. But laying my heart at a woman's feet and asking her to love me back—that is something that scares the shit out of me."

Alex stood, too, and walked over to Ben. "I've never told a woman I loved her before. Hell, I've never had these feelings before. She could shoot us both down, you know."

Ben took a long swallow of beer, staring at the can before lifting his gaze to Alex. "There would be a lot of good reasons for her thinking we were both crazy. I mean, we both travel nearly all year long. And she has a career where she travels as well. This could never work."

Alex went back to the sofa and sat. "It's a pretty fucked-up situation. But you know what? We don't even know yet how she feels. Maybe she feels the same."

Ben raked his fingers through his hair. "God, I really hope she does feel the same."

"So maybe we should talk to her about it first, and figure it out from there?"

"Yeah. You're right about that. Let's give it a few more days. She wants to spend Christmas with us. We'll do Christmas, then talk."

Alex nodded. "Sounds like a plan."

"And whatever happens when we tell her," Ben said, "we'll deal with it. Either way, we know how we feel. And we'll accept whatever her decision is."

"Agreed."

At least Ben knew he and Alex were on the same wavelength as far as their feelings for Victoria.

The bigger question was—how did Victoria feel? And how would she react when they told her how they felt about her?

THIRTEEN

AFTER THE COMPETITION ENDED, EVERYONE PACKED up and left.

Everyone except Victoria, Ben, and Alex.

She was glad they had decided to stay through the holidays. To her, the holidays always meant vacation. Though she normally didn't mind spending Christmas alone, this year she would have felt something was missing.

Which got her to thinking about Ben and Alex again.

Soon they'd be off to their next surfing competition, and she'd head back to New York.

And they'd never see each other again.

The thought of it made her rub her stomach. She'd been doing that a lot lately, and she knew why.

She was in love with them. With two men. It was the most ridiculous thing ever.

Or was it? And how was she ever going to tell them? Would

they laugh at her and tell her it had been fun sex, but that was all? And would they run like hell to get away from the crazy woman who thought she'd fallen in love with her hot island flings?

She might be insane for even thinking she was in love. What the hell did she know about love, anyway? Sure, she'd had friends who had fallen in love. But it had never happened for her and she'd been more than satisfied with how her life had turned out. She had a great career that made her happy.

She didn't need all this . . . turmoil.

But she'd never run from anything in her life, and she didn't intend to start now.

She planned to tell them today. And if they laughed at her, or abruptly left her, then she'd deal with it.

It wouldn't be the first Christmas she'd spent alone.

She'd gotten small gifts for Ben and Alex and they were going to a holiday luau today to celebrate Christmas.

She'd stayed with them last night in their suite. Actually, she hadn't spent a night alone since the first night they'd all slept together. Normally she liked sleeping alone, sprawled out on her big bed, but she was growing accustomed to sleeping with one of them on either side of her. She'd occasionally wake up in the middle of the night, knowing she could reach out and touch both of them.

And if one—or both of them—woke her to make love . . .

Well, a woman couldn't complain about being wanted like that, could she?

This morning she told them she had a few things to do before the luau, so she'd headed back to her suite to shower and get ready. She'd put on her makeup, chosen a red sundress—appropriate for Christmas—and was slipping on her sandals just as they knocked on the door.

When she opened the door, her breath caught.

Sure, they wore shorts and button-down short-sleeved shirts, but they still took her breath away. Alex wore a white shirt and Ben wore black.

"Aloha and Merry Christmas." She kissed them both and invited them inside.

"Merry Christmas," Ben said. "You look beautiful."

"Gorgeous as always, Tori," Alex said. "We'll be proud to have you by our side today."

"Thank you. Both of you." She was going to miss being with them.

Blinking back the stupid tears that for some reason decided to well in her eyes, she smiled at them. "I have gifts for you."

Ben arched a brow. "Gifts, huh?"

"Yes. Hang on a second."

She went into her bedroom and brought out the gift bags. "They're silly little things, really. Nothing much."

They sat on the sofa with their bags. Inside each of the bags was a New York T-shirt, something one would get in the tourist section of her city.

Thank God for her assistant and express shipping.

They both laughed.

"Hey, you have to have something to remind you of me."

"Thanks," Ben said. "This is perfect."

"I love it," Alex said.

Then they both pulled out watches. Separate and distinct, Alex's had a leather band and Ben's was chrome.

"They're world-time watches, so you can set them for whatever time zone you're in, and also for New York. So you'll always know my time. A small way to remember me."

Alex came over and kneeled in front of her, pressing a kiss to both her knees. "It's perfect. Like you. Thank you."

Ben had already put his on. He came over and brushed her hair away from her face and kissed her. "I love this. I . . . thank you."

"You're welcome. If it hasn't become apparent, I'm having a difficult time thinking about leaving both of you."

Ben looked over at Alex, who nodded. "Alex and I are having the same problem. Actually, there's something we both want to say to you. We wanted to wait until after Christmas, but maybe now is the right time."

"Okay." Her heart started pumping fast. She had no idea what was coming, but she took a deep breath.

Alex got up and sat next to her. He picked up her hand. "I've never met anyone like you, Tori. You're the first person I want to see when I wake up in the morning."

"And I want you in my bed every night," Ben said. "You're smart, beautiful, and I love making love to you. More importantly, you make me feel things I haven't felt in a very long time. I'm in love with you, Victoria."

Alex squeezed her hand. "I'm in love with you, too. When I get out of the water, you're the face I look for in the crowd. You're the one I want cheering me on."

She couldn't breathe. She hadn't expected this. "You both love me?"

Alex smiled at her. "Yes. We do."

"Are you sure?" she asked. She needed them to be sure.

"Of course we're sure," Alex said. "I'm sure. I don't take this lightly, babe. Love is a big goddamn deal."

"I was in love once," Ben said. "A long time ago. It kicked my ass, so trust me, I know what it feels like. It's painful as hell and the best damn thing in the world, both at the same time."

Ben had nailed it. That's exactly what it felt like.

Her heart was racing so fast she felt dizzy. "I'm in love with both of you. At first I thought it was ridiculous. I mean, how could I love two men? How could I love both of you? It happened so fast and I've been overanalyzing it to death over the past few days. But it's there and it won't go away and I don't want it to. So here's the fact. I love you both and there's no explaining it. I don't want to analyze it."

She turned to Alex. "I love you, Alex."

"I love you, Tori." He kissed her, and she felt passion and love in his kiss.

Then she turned to Ben. "I love you, Ben."

Ben cupped her face. "I love you, too, Victoria."

He brushed his lips across hers, and her heart ached with the tenderness of his kiss.

This time, she didn't try to hold back the tears that welled in her eyes. She let them fall down her cheeks.

"I'm sorry. I'm not normally the emotional type."

"Be as emotional as you need to be," Ben said. "This kind of thing doesn't happen to us every day, either."

She leaned back on the sofa and squeezed their hands. "The question is, now that we're all in love, what the hell do we do about it? You two travel all the time. So do I. And we'll never see each other."

"We'll make it work, Tori," Alex said. "We get time off. We're not constantly at surf events. And when we're not, no matter where you are, we'll come find you so we can all be together. Or if Ben's busy and I'm available, I'll see you. And if I'm not available but Ben is, he can see you."

"Like Alex said, we'll figure it out. If we want something badly enough, we'll move mountains—or oceans—to make it work. And we want this. We all want this."

She heaved a sigh. "Oh, God. Could we really? Would you really do that for me?"

Alex picked up her hand and kissed the back of it. "Hell yes we would."

Now that the emotions had settled, it was time to think logically. It couldn't be just them moving mountains and oceans to get to her. "I've worked my ass off all these years to build my agency, to gain this measure of success. It's time to start enjoying the fruits of my labor. I've thought about hiring another agent or two to help me handle the workload. Which would mean I could take a step back, let them handle the day-to-day and I could see the two of you more often."

"I know we'd both love that, but it can't just be on you to come to us," Alex said. "I've been doing some thinking as well. I'm thirty-five and I can't ride those monster tubes like the young guys forever. I'd like to go out while I'm on top. I haven't even discussed this with Ben yet, but after this year's competition I want to start transitioning more into managing and promotion and less into active surfing."

Victoria looked to Ben, who nodded. "You know I'd love to have you partner with me in that aspect of the business. But you have to be ready to walk away from the waves."

Alex nodded. "I know. And I'll be sure before I do it."

Ben picked up Victoria's hand. "We'll make it work. We have to, because we love each other."

"Speaking of that," Alex said. "We got a gift for you."

Victoria cocked her head to the side. "You did?"

"We did." Ben pulled it out of his pocket and handed it to her.

She cradled the velvet box in her hand, then carefully opened it. Inside was a delicate silver chain necklace with three diamonds. Inscribed in the middle was the word *Ours*.

Victoria took the necklace out of the box and dangled it in front of her. "Oh. This is beautiful."

"It means we're all one, and you are part of both of us," Alex said.

The tears fell again. "I love this. Thank you both."

She kissed them both, then pulled her hair to the side so Ben could put the necklace on her while she looked at Alex beaming a smile at her.

She stood, then held her hand out for both of them. "I need you to make love to me right now."

They went into the bedroom and undressed. Victoria lay on the bed and Ben put his mouth on her sex while Alex slid his fingers into her.

"Yes," she said, lifting her hips, watching as they pleasured her. "Make me come like that."

They worked in tandem, switching off so it was Alex sucking

her and Ben pumping his fingers into her. They both drove her crazy, and when she orgasmed, she cried out, knowing this was what she wanted to spend the rest of her life experiencing.

They both put on condoms, taking turns sliding their cocks inside of her. Their patience and the way they watched when the other was thrusting into her was such an incredible turn-on. And the sensation of feeling two different cocks inside of her pussy was amazing. Alex would fuck her for a few minutes, then withdraw and move away so Ben could take his place.

She came—then came again—and again.

And they both came inside of her, Ben watching her and stroking her breasts while Alex came, then taking his place and taking her mouth in a deep, passionate kiss, groaning against her mouth when he came.

After, all three of them lay sprawled on the bed.

"We still have time to make the holiday luau," Alex said.

Victoria smiled, turned over onto her belly to face her two men. "Or, we could order room service and have holiday sex the rest of the day."

Ben grinned over at Alex. "There's a reason we love this woman."

"Because she's so smart and has such phenomenal ideas."

It was the best Christmas she'd ever had. Spent with the two men she loved.

TURN THE PAGE TO READ AN EXCERPT
FROM THE NEW PLAY-BY-PLAY NOVEL

RULES OF CONTACT

COMING SOON FROM BERKLEY!

FLYNN CASSIDY SAT AT ONE OF THE CORNER TABLES at Ninety-Two, his new restaurant in San Francisco.

They'd opened just two weeks ago and so far, things were going well. Right now one of the major entertainment media outlets was doing a feature on the restaurant, so he had to be present for it. Which meant a camera crew and bright lights and a lot of damn people in the way of regular business. He had already wandered around and apologized to his patrons, who seemed to take it all in stride. Hopefully the crew would get all the film and sound bites they wanted and would get the hell out shortly.

"This is so thrilling, Flynn."

He dragged his gaze away from the camera crew and focused on Natalie, the woman he'd been dating the past two weeks. She was a looker, for sure, with beautiful auburn brown hair that touched her shoulders and the most incredible green eyes he'd ever seen.

"Yeah, 'thrilling' isn't the first thing that popped into my head when the crew showed up today."

Natalie grabbed his hand. "Oh, come on. Who doesn't want to be on TV?"

Him, for one. As a defensive end for the San Francisco Sabers football team, he'd had plenty of cameras and microphones shoved in his face over the years. But since the restaurant was new, he wouldn't turn down some publicity for it. So he'd done the interview and now he just wanted to stay out of the way while the film crew got their overview shots of the restaurant.

"Do you think they'll want to get some film of the two of us together?" Natalie asked. "You know, kind of get some background on your personal life, like what you do on your off time away from football and the restaurant, who you're seeing, stuff like that?"

Warning bells clanged loud and hard in Flynn's head. He'd gone down this road with more than one woman and had ended relationships because of girlfriends who were way more interested in the limelight than in him.

So lately he'd made sure to steer clear of any woman who had an entertainment background. No models, no actresses, no one he could suspect of chasing face time in front of a camera. He figured since Natalie was a financial analyst, he was safe.

But seeing her gaze track those cameras like a vampire craved blood, he wasn't sure career choice had much to do with someone needing popularity and limelight in their life.

"Maybe we should move to one of the more prominent tables, Flynn," Natalie said. "You know, that way we might be in one of the camera shots."

He bit back a sigh. "I don't think so."

She pushed back her chair and stood. "I'm going to go to the bar and get a drink. You know, all casual like, and see if maybe they notice me."

He leaned back in his chair. "You do that."

This relationship was doomed. Just one of the many Flynn had seen go down in flames in the past couple of years.

Maybe there wasn't a woman out there who was interested in him. Just him. Not Flynn the football player. Just Flynn the guy.

He shook his head, mentally notched up another failure, and took a long swallow of his beer.

SINCE ORDERS HAD SLOWED DOWN AND SHE HAD THE kitchen under control, Amelia Lawrence washed her hands in the sink and tried her best to hide, avoiding the cameras. The last thing she wanted was to be on television. She was head chef at Ninety-Two. This whole publicity thing was on Flynn, and she didn't need to be interviewed, filmed, or in any way noticed.

But as she did her best game of hide-and-not-be-sought, she also spotted Flynn's new girlfriend doing her best job to try to be seen by any of the camera crew.

Oh, no. Not another one of *those* kind of women.

Amelia had worked with Flynn the past couple of months, even before Ninety-Two had opened. And in that time period she'd seen him go through no fewer than three women, all of whom seemed to be way more interested in his prowess as camera candy than anything else.

She felt bad for him, and nothing but disdain for the women who couldn't appreciate what a fine man Flynn Cassidy was.

He was supremely tall and ridiculously well-built, with a thick mane of black hair and amazing blue eyes. She could spend at least a full day doing nothing but appreciating his tattoos. And who didn't love football? Plus, the man had fine culinary taste. When he'd hired her, they'd spent several weeks arguing about the menu for the restaurant. She had to admit he had good ideas.

So did she, and she appreciated that he listened to hers. But the bottom line was that it was his restaurant and his call on the menu.

But in the end they'd blended both their ideas and she loved the way it had turned out.

So why couldn't the man find a decent girlfriend? He kind of sucked at it, actually. If she'd been a native to San Francisco, maybe she could have helped him out, but she'd just moved here recently from Portland and she knew only a handful of people. Her only ties here were a friend from college and her friend's husband. Otherwise, she was pretty much alone.

Just the way she wanted it.

She still thought she could find better women for Flynn to date than the ones he'd been parading in and out of the restaurant lately. She could spot posers a mile away. Maybe she could offer her service to Flynn.

"Orders up."

She focused her attention on the incoming orders, on directing her staff, on minding her own business, and not on Flynn's idiot girlfriend, who was currently preening for the cameras.

With an eye roll, she dismissed the woman and set about making scallops.

Because Flynn Cassidy was decidedly not her problem. And no matter how much she felt sorry for him, she wasn't going to get involved in his personal life.

Jaci Burton is the *USA Today* and *New York Times* bestselling author of the Play-by-Play series, including *Unexpected Rush*, *All Wound Up*, *Quarterback Draw*, *Straddling the Line*, *Melting the Ice*, and *One Sweet Ride*, and the Hope series, including *Don't Let Go*, *Make Me Stay*, *Love After All*, *Hope Burns*, *Hope Ignites*, and *Hope Flames*. Visit Jaci online at jaciburton.com, facebook.com/ AuthorJaciBurton, and twitter.com/JaciBurton.